# The Sorrow Stone

## J. A. MCLACHLAN

The Sorrow Stone
Copyright © 2017 by Jane Ann McLachlan
All rights reserved.

ISBN: 978-0-9936306-7-5

Cover Design by Marija Vilotijevic at Expert Subjects
Editing by Ian Darling
Formatting by Chris Morgan from Dragon Realm Press
www.dragonrealmpress.com

*For my brother Richard*

*"Because home was home and family was family,*
*and everywhere and everyone else was not.*
*If that was no longer true, then Jean was no longer Jean."*
*~p. 149*

# Chapter 1

At first he did not know it was a human being. She lay crumpled on the ground like a bundle of dirty rags tossed aside by some trader. Even when Jean was close enough to see the tangled black hair, the small, bare hand, his inclination was to hurry by. A corpse could pass on the terrible fever that had razed this village.

He had wasted his time stopping at Sainte-Blandine-de-Lugdunum. The few villagers who came to market were silent and glum, barely talking to one another let alone to a spice peddler from some distant town. He had sold one pair of woollen hose and two denier's worth of salt all morning—barely enough to pay for his dinner and lodgings, let alone feed his family through the winter. The plague had run its course by now, otherwise Jean would have sold some of his side items: pilgrims' badges and handkerchiefs blessed at the holy shrines of Santiago and Jerusalem. People will give up their last denier when death grins at their windows. Now, if he had been here a few weeks earlier…

He shook his head, glancing at the inert form lying beside the road just ahead. He had known a priest who took his holy pardons, with the Pope's sin-erasing signature, into towns where illness raged. The traders called him 'Reaper', but it was the last of their coins he went in for, not their souls. And what good did it do him? He handed all the profits to the church. The man was a fool. His body was found lying beside the road like this woman's, his money pouch as heavy as a drunk's bladder and the agony of his final convulsions frozen on his face.

Jean would not tempt such a death. He survived by his wits, never forgetting that Death, with his sickle sharpened, followed impatiently in a man's shadow, waiting for a momentary slip. He did not want to die on the road. It was Mathilde's secret fear, he knew: that she would never know what had happened to him. And what if he did not die? What if he carried the fever home with him…?

He pulled roughly on the halter of his donkey, as though the creature were to blame for his turn of mind. The animal accommodated its owner's mood sullenly, ears angled backward, rolling its eyes at each jerk of the halter.

Two heavy wooden barrels hung behind the bulging woven panniers strapped across its back. Several large, rough wadmal bags were tied in front of them. Despite being tightly sealed, the barrels emitted tantalizing scents. The pleasant aromas did not mollify Jean. If his donkey's load were lighter and the money pouch at his waist heavier, he would be in better humor now. He quickened his step, leading the donkey as far from the dead woman as the narrow dirt track allowed.

He was nearly past her when she looked up.

The donkey snorted and stopped. Jean gaped at the woman, too startled to urge the animal forward.

She stared straight ahead as though unaware of his presence and his stunned regard. She was barely out of girlhood, with raven hair and high cheekbones in a delicate, oval-shaped face which showed no sign of rash or fever. Not ill, then, but yet too pale, too thin. The way she lay, the way she held herself, revealed a vulnerability that repelled him. Nevertheless, he moved closer, taking in her beauty and her youth and the intensity of her need. How might he turn that need to his advantage?

She turned her face toward him. He looked into her eyes and sucked in his breath sharply. They were so black Jean could not tell the iris from the pupil, so raw with suffering he felt the ache of it himself.

"Solange!" he whispered, crossing himself. Sorrow. She was not merely grieving; she was grief itself.

She raised one arm several inches, holding it out before her. Her hand was small, her fingers long and slender and tightly closed around some object. She cried out a single word. The hair on the back of Jean's neck rose, as though she had heard the name he had given her: "Sorrow!"

He shivered and stepped backward. Was she possessed?

"Buy my sorrow!" she cried, with a shrill, unearthly keening that did not seem to be directed at him.

She held out her closed left hand. "Buy it! For the love of God, buy my sorrow before I go insane!" Slowly she opened her fingers. A long black nail, slightly bent near the flattened head, lay across her small white palm.

"Damnation!" The word burst from him.

Another woman had tried this on him a year ago. She was so poor she had not gone to market, just run out from her tiny mud hovel while he was passing by. She was dirty and scrawny with an ugly, puckered scar across her left cheek that stretched up to her eyebrow and she was missing several teeth. The nail that woman offered him was old and rusted, thin to the point of breaking. It had been pounded back into shape many times and she had not risked trying to do so again.

"Buy my sorrow," she had cried, just like this girl lying beside the road, and she had held out her worthless little nail. As if he ought to give a flea's cuss about their suffering. Everyone suffered. Only a fool would take on someone else's as well as his own. And only a fool would believe she could escape her grief by selling a nail from her child's coffin to a peddler!

The world was full of fools and he had run into more than his share, peddling his wares from Saint-Gilles to Cluny and back again, year after year.

"Take my sorrow from me!" the girl cried again.

Did she think his hesitation showed weakness? In two strides he could step full weight on her hand, maybe break the wrist and a couple of fingers. Show her who was weak.

But this nail was well-made and new, though bent a little at the end from the extraction. He could straighten it and it would be worth something... He caught the glint of gold on her finger and leaned forward to look more closely at her hand. The palm and pads of her fingers were soft, well-cared for: evidence of an easy life.

"Turn your hand over."

He had to hold his breath when she did, to keep from shouting. A ruby nearly the size of his fingernail glittered blood-red against the white skin of her fingers.

"I can end your suffering," he said softly, bending nearer to her. "I will buy your sorrow." He looked around. There was no one on the road. The shrubs and brush on either side might conceal any number of observers, but the carefree twitter of birds among the branches reassured him. He squinted against the noonday sun, looking back the way he had come.

The Abbey of Sainte Blandine was several hundred yards behind them, enclosed in a high stone wall with an iron arch reaching over the wooden front gates. One of the gates hung half open.

He was about to turn back to the girl when a nun hurried through the open gate toward them, the folds of her habit flapping around her portly frame. Jean gritted his teeth against the expletive that rose in his throat. He looked back down at the girl.

She had raised herself to a sitting position. A streak of dirt across her wet cheek enhanced its youthful curve. A light flush had brightened her face and her wide, dark eyes focused on him. The firm swell of her breasts was visible beneath her black kirtle. By god, she was beautiful!

If only the nun were not coming. A little time with her and his day would be perfect.

He held out a coin in his left hand, stretching the other toward her, too, palm up. "I want the ring as well."

She stared at him.

"The ring." Jean gave a small jerk of his head. "Hurry, someone is coming!"

She twisted around to look at the abbey. When she turned back she looked frightened. So the nun was indeed coming for her, as Jean had feared.

He stepped closer and crouched down in front of her. "We can do this," he whispered, "if we do it quickly. She will never know." A thought struck him. "And if she does, she is under a vow of silence, heh?"

Her expression told him he was right again. He extended his left hand toward her until the coin almost touched her empty hand. "Give me your sorrow."

With a groan she thrust the nail into his hand. He watched her twist the ring, trying not to smile in anticipation. It stuck at her knuckle. She twisted it harder, her face tense with the effort.

Jean glanced up. The scarlet-faced nun was running now, holding the skirts of her habit up to her ankles. Jean grabbed the girl's wrist, pushed her other hand aside, and ripped the ring from her finger.

She gasped and held the bruised finger to her lips, like a child.

Jean dropped the nail and the ring into the pouch on his belt.

"Guard this coin." He pressed it into her hand. "It has bought your sorrow." As though he believed such nonsense. But lucky for him that she did.

"Let me help you to your feet," he said, more loudly than necessary. He cupped his left hand under her elbow. The other he closed over the little hand that clutched his coin. "Are you feeling better now?" He raised her to her feet just as the good sister panted to a stop before them.

The nun placed her arm firmly around the grieving young woman. She slumped against the nun, shrinking away from him, but her fist stayed closed around his coin.

"Can I help you with her, Sister?" Jean asked. It made him appear weak to help a woman with her tasks, even a bride of God; but considering the fortune that had come his way, some show of humility was called for. Perhaps it would appease Sainte Blandine, if she were watching over her abbey.

The nun shook her head and started back toward the abbey. Jean watched them go, grinning to himself.

A girl burst through the open gate and raced toward the others, holding her black shift halfway up to her knees. Her face was plump and rounded with youth, her figure small and wiry. The dress she held so high was a simpler cut, less wasteful of material than either of the others. She was clearly a servant but very young, not yet out of childhood.

She did not notice Jean. Her frightened gaze was on the nun and her charge. As soon as she reached them, she slipped her arm around the young woman's waist and assisted the silent nun in drawing her back inside the walls of the abbey.

When they were almost at the gate, the young woman looked back over her shoulder: a searing, inhuman gaze. Her lips parted.

Jean was seized by a sudden urge to return the ring. He took a step toward her. His left hand hovered uneasily over his money pouch. Why had she given it up so easily?

Demons bribe men with gifts!

Jean shivered. He took another step toward her.

The nun's arm tightened around the young woman's shoulders, pulling her forward again.

And what would he have said, anyway? He had already accepted the ring; it was too late to alter his destiny now.

# Chapter 2

**C**eleste staggered in the nun's arms. Her stomach heaved. She held her breath, horrified, until the nausea eased. What was happening to her?

The ground swayed beneath her. The nun's arms held her, barely keeping her from falling. She gulped for air and the sensation passed, leaving a dark stillness.

Celeste had never known a silence like this. It was nearly palpable, a heavy weight within her, like an overfull belly after a long fast. She clung to the nun, but was numb to her touch. Only the silence was real to her, the turmoil of emotion stilled at last.

She had contemplated another type of silence, the silence that was a mortal sin. She had longed to succumb to it; and she might have, had it not been for the demons. She had seen them lurking in every corner, red-eyed and red-fanged, enticing her and repelling her simultaneously. Only the silver cross the nuns had given her, which burned at her neck whenever the demons appeared, had prevented her from throwing herself, with some violent act, into their eager embrace. With her free hand she touched her chest, feeling the little cross under her shift.

This silence was better. She focused on it, yearning into its oblivion. Whatever its source, she welcomed it. But how long would it last? That worry, a tiny irritation at the edge of the silence, was the sole mar upon her blessed numbness.

Not the sole mar. Something else. A prickling sensation at her back. She twisted in the nun's arms, looking back.

A peddler stood by the road watching her. She looked at him, surprised then alarmed by the intensity of his stare. Something had happened between them, something unthinkable. Her lips parted but she had no breath to scream. He took a step toward her. She felt herself wavering on the edge of chaos. She swayed backward, her knees beginning to give.

The nun's arm tightened around her, strong and merciful. She stumbled, but the nun caught her, supported her, turned her once again toward the quiet abbey. She clutched the nun's arm, and felt something in her hand, small, round, and hard. She tightened her fist around it.

Another figure appeared, running through the abbey gates toward them: a peasant girl. She skidded into an awkward curtsy then threw her skinny arm around Celeste.

The young arm was warm across her back, just below the nun's firmer support. Celeste let them hold her. The girl murmured something, to which Celeste was deaf. She focused only on the silence, holding on to it. She was safe within this shroud of silence. She must not even think about losing it. If she did, the thought would gnaw at her like a splinter until it ruptured her newfound tranquility. She stumbled between the two people supporting her, giving herself up to them.

They led her through the iron gates of the abbey, which hung open. Once inside, the child supported her while the nun shut and bolted the gates behind them. The haste with which she did so impressed upon Celeste how disturbed she must have been over going outside the convent to fetch her back.

What was she doing here? Celeste opened her hand and stared at the coin in her palm. The peddler's face came back to her—who was he? Why had he given her his coin? Everything that had happened before he pressed his sweaty denier into her palm and helped her up from the side of the road was a blur. She looked about the abbey, seeking something she could recognize.

A stone pathway led from the gate to the abbey church. Weeds swayed defiantly between the wide, flat stones, and the grounds beyond had a weary and unkempt look. Palmiers lined either side of the path, their huge fronds sweeping the ground as the late summer breeze moved through them.

The nun and the young girl helped her along the pathway toward the church. They passed two nuns returning from the low building to the main cloister, carrying platters with scraps from the midday meal and half-empty jugs of mead. Several others crossed their path, leading a line of small children toward the vegetable garden. They all looked exhausted, shoulders drooping, eyes cast down in pale faces. Why were they doing the work of servants with only children to help them? None of them glanced at Celeste or the nun and the servant girl supporting her. The feeling of being invisible pleased her.

As they approached the church, the late afternoon sun directly behind Celeste lit up the large front doors. They were made of thick oak, adorned with life-sized carvings of Sainte Blandine, who shone as though alive in the ray of light. On the left door the saint offered a basket of food to a beggar; on the right she knelt in prayer before a shrine.

The nun and the little maid led Celeste to the right, where a long stone building ran perpendicular to the church nave. They entered at a small wooden door and passed through to a large inner courtyard, surrounded on three sides by cloisters. The high stone vault of the cloisters arched out from the stone walls of the abbatial buildings, with the church serving as the fourth side of the quadrangle. Beyond the tall columns supporting the cloisters was a well-tended garden of herbs and flowers. Their sweet fragrance enticed Celeste as the nun and the girl led her along the cloister to the open door of a small guest room.

The room was narrow and dark. Celeste stumbled, hesitating at the doorway, searching for demons in the corners. She dared not break the silence that protected her to voice her concerns, but squinted anxiously into the shadows. The room appeared empty. She let them assist her inside.

It was furnished with a wooden bed along one wall, a plain table and stool, and a low bench on which lay a white linen undershift, a silver comb, a little blue linen bag, a basin of water and a hand cloth. A heavy black robe with fur at its neck and hood hung from a wooden spike in the wall.

Why would she need a furred robe in summer? Celeste stared at the cloak. Had she been here since last winter? Did she live here? No! It was not possible! Why could she not remember?

The peasant girl patted her shoulder in a display of familiarity which struck Celeste like a blow. How dare she presume such impertinence? Was Celeste not a Lady?

Yes, but not a Lady born, she remembered. She was Lady Celeste, married to Lord Bernard de La Roche. Lady: her title was as precarious as the internal silence that made her so forgetful. She herself was only Celeste, the fortunate youngest daughter of an ambitious landowner.

Had she been set aside, abandoned here? Was she no longer a Lady? The thought stopped her breath. She closed her eyes, concentrating, but nothing more came to her. Her memory was sparse and fragmented, like a length of cloth after the dress pieces have been cut away from it. The reason for the peasant's familiarity was lost along with the rest of her past.

"My Lady," the child murmured. With a rush of relief Celeste let herself be guided to the bed.

It was firm and solid underneath her, cushioned by a thick feather mattress. She sat, swaying with fatigue as the girl undressed her. Silence was better than answers, and she was so very tired. When she lay down, she felt her body release, every muscle giving into the mattress, as though she were a bowstring unloosed. A sigh of relief came from so deep within her it emerged as a groan.

Tomorrow she would remember. Tomorrow she would insist on more respect. Tomorrow… She turned her face to the wall.

The soft sweep of the girl's kirtle receded across the stone floor. The door closed quietly behind her.

The reverent silence of the faithful shrouded the abbey.

The deep, empty silence within her kept her awake although she ached for sleep. Why was she so weary? What had tired her so? She curled onto her side on the feather mattress, letting her body relax completely into the bed's softness…

The abbey bell wakened her. She rolled onto her back in the dark room, listening to it. Despite having just awakened from sleep, she was groggy with exhaustion. The bell tolled again. A small, gray rectangle, barely discernable against the black stone wall, indicated a narrow window high above her bed. Lauds, then. The nuns would be going to chapel to pray through the last hour before dawn.

She peered around her room. A dark, still form lay in the corner by the door. She caught her breath until she realized it must be her maid, asleep on the straw pallet provided for her. No rising at Lauds to pray for her mistress's soul from that one.

Celeste felt the urge to relieve herself and sat up. She swung her legs out from under the linen sheet to the side of the bed. Sparks of light appeared behind her eyes as the room lurched around her. She grabbed the wooden plank of the bed and sat still, hunched over with her eyes shut until the vertigo passed. She had been very ill. She felt it in her body: a ragged slackness in her muscles, an ache deep in her bones.

When she felt safe letting go of the bed she touched her hand to her head. The palm first and then the back of the hand.

*As she had done so often to Etienne. Chubby, rosy Etienne, with his mother's dark hair and eyes, every feature hers, a miniature, masculine Celeste.*

Her forehead was clammy but not hot. *Not like Etienne's, which burned her hand when she touched him.*

14

The memory was clear but dispassionate, as though it had happened to someone else. Did she have a son? Where was he now?

Nothing else came to her.

Her own need returned with more urgency. She bent to feel under the bed for the chamber pot. There were no clean, dried rushes on the floor to catch up spills and dirt—just the cold, hard stone beneath her feet. What a disgusting place!

When she was finished squatting over the chamber pot she called out, "You!"

Was that her voice—the husky croak of an old hag, barely audible?

"Get up!" she croaked, but she was too spent to put any force behind the words. How long had she been ill?

The bundled body in the corner did not respond.

No wonder she was ill in such a place. Why would her husband not have had her better cared for? She tried to picture him but could not recall his image clearly. Even worse, she had no sense of him, no understanding. Had it always been like this, or had the sickness made her forget? And not only her husband: there was something else, something important. So important that even trying to remember disturbed her. Panic rose up inside her. She pushed it down, forced herself outside the fear. She was sitting on a chamber pot in an abbey. There was nothing alarming about that. She waited until her heartbeat slowed, then tried to rise. Her legs were too weak to elevate her.

What was the girl's name? She must know her own maid's name. It would be something common—Lise, Jeanne, Marie—that was it. "Marie!"

Marie tumbled to her feet. Her mouth opened in a little "O" of surprise as she rubbed the sleep from her eyes.

"M-m-My Lady," she stammered.

Celeste regarded her through narrowed eyes. It was the peasant girl from the day before. Had she only a child to attend her? She reached out her arm impatiently. Marie rushed over to help her rise, then stood gawking until Celeste gestured sharply toward the chamber pot.

15

Her left hand, as she moved it, felt too light. She brought it closer to her face, squinting in the darkness. Her ring finger was bare. What had happened to her husband's ring? She stared at her finger. The missing ring was clearer in her mind than her husband's face. What did its absence mean? Her head began to throb.

Marie returned with the emptied chamber pot. "Is that all, My Lady?"

Celeste dropped her hand behind her back. Had she left the ring at the castle when she came here? She could not remember coming. Had she been so ill they brought her without her knowledge? In that case she may well have been stripped of her jewels for safekeeping. Her other jewels, perhaps, but not her ring.

"Is there something else you need, My Lady?" Marie's eyebrows puckered into a small frown.

Had her husband reclaimed it? Had he set her aside, cast her off like worn clothing? Oh Saints, how her head ached!

"My Lady?" Marie stepped closer.

Perhaps she had lost the ring. She recalled wandering outside the convent, being guided back by a nun. Something had happened before the nun found her. It was there, nagging at the edge of her thoughts.

"I cannot remember," she said. She had had this problem yesterday, but she had been certain a night of sleep would resolve it.

"You are not well," the girl's voice trembled. "Do not fret. You will recover." She patted Celeste's arm.

Celeste's cheeks burned. This peasant treated her as a simpleton, and likely everyone else here did as well. Yet how could she object? The strange confusion in her mind rendered her utterly helpless. The thought brought a flutter of panic. Helpless against what?

She drew in a breath and held it until she was calm. Until she knew what had happened to her, it would be better to keep quiet. She had been ill and was still weary, but the fever had broken. Her memory would return soon enough. Meanwhile, no one need know. She took a step toward the bed and teetered. Marie leapt forward to help her.

Embarrassed by the weakness in her legs, she slumped on the edge of the bed, breathing heavily.

"There, there." Marie stroked her hair.

Celeste gritted her teeth.

"Are you thirsty?" The child finally asked.

Celeste nodded. Would she think to offer food? Celeste was famished. How long had she gone without eating? Too long, judging by the thinness of her arms visible through the lace sleeves of her nightdress. She had always been slender, but now she was as scrawny as a peasant in time of famine. Marie, on the other hand, looked plump and fit, so there must be food here somewhere. Celeste's stomach growled. She stopped herself from placing a hand over it, pretending instead not to notice her grumbling stomach.

"Something to eat?" Marie sounded doubtful.

"Perhaps," Celeste murmured.

Marie grinned. She curtsied awkwardly and ran out, as though afraid Celeste would change her mind.

Celeste lay back on the bed and stared at the window, watching the little square of light get brighter. No more memories came to her. When the light had turned a soft rose, she sat up again. Where was that girl?

Was she taking advantage of her mistress's forgetfulness? No. Even if she had noticed it, she would never dare let on. Her situation was tied to Celeste's. If she displeased her mistress, she would be sent home in disgrace. She would be lucky to get work as a field labourer after that. Marie would agree with whatever Celeste told her, and keep quiet about it.

The door to her room squeaked open. Marie entered with a mug of ale in her hand. A novice from the kitchen stepped in behind her, carrying a wooden platter of bread and cheese and olives. She placed it on the table beside Celeste and stepped back. Celeste waited. Instead of leaving, the novice handed her a knife. Her knife. Celeste stared down at it. Something about the knife repelled her, some lost memory associated with it. She did not want to touch it. Instead, she lifted the entire chunk of bread and bit off a small piece, forcing herself to chew it slowly before washing it down with a trickle of ale. The novice shrugged and placed the knife on the table. Celeste nibbled at a corner of the cheese and put a single olive into her mouth.

Marie and the novice watched her. Celeste set the wooden platter aside and took another sip of ale. Then she sat still, slouched over, holding the mug in her hand and ignoring the platter of food on the bed beside her. It required all the will-power she had.

"Will you eat more?" Marie asked anxiously. At the same time the novice said, "Are you finished, Lady?" She reached for the platter.

Celeste waved vaguely without looking up. "I will try to eat more later," she mumbled. Would the novice never leave? Celeste fumed silently, hiding her eyes behind drooping lids.

At last the novice asked, "Will that be all, then, Lady?"

Celeste nodded.

The moment the door closed behind her, Celeste grabbed the cheese in one hand, the bread in the other and stuffed them alternately into her mouth, tearing off great chunks and swallowing them barely chewed, washing them down with deep chugs of ale when they threatened to choke her. The wooden platter was empty within minutes. She was tempted to lick it even after she had picked up every crumb. How soon could she ask to eat again?

She looked up.

Marie stood staring at her, her mouth agape.

How had such a silly, awkward child come to be her maid? "Lower your eyes," Celeste said. "Do not stare so at your mistress."

Marie bobbed her head, and kept it bowed. She was too young to have been in service long. Nevertheless, there was something between them, Celeste could feel it. She saw Marie as a little girl, playing in a corner… No, the memory was unclear, if it was a memory at all.

Celeste stood up. Her stomach heaved. She was nauseous again, violently so, and grabbed up the chamber pot just in time. Marie was at her side before she finished, wiping her forehead with a cloth. She leaned over the stinking pot of vomit, letting Marie wipe her face, until her stomach calmed. When she was sure she was finished, she put the chamber pot down and straightened. She should have made herself eat more slowly.

The empty platter was still on the bed. She placed it on the table, meaning to lie down again. As she did, she noticed a dirty coin lying there. At once she recalled the peddler pressing it into her hand. She slid the platter over to cover it, but Marie had already seen.

"You sold it," Marie said, tearing her gaze from the grimy coin to stare at Celeste. "To that peddler." Her voice was hushed, her eyes wide in her round face.

Sold it? Celeste's heart pounded. Then she remembered the feel of the cold, hard nail in her hand and the silly fable Marie had told her about peasant women relieving their grief by selling a nail from their child's coffin.

*She saw the peddler's face—*

Marie broke into a delighted shout of laughter. "And it worked! You are better!"

"Do not talk foolishly," Celeste snapped. Was the girl really so simple as to think that a person could sell her sorrow and be rid of it? Had she made Celeste believe her? Her cheeks flushed hot. "I had a fever." At least it was only a nail.

*—The peddler's sharp face, leering over her—*

Marie's grin wavered. "Yes—" She rallied. "Your forehead was hot. But it was because of—"

"Because I was ill. My fever has broken, that is all. That is why I am better."

*—Leering over her as he seized her ring! Her husband's ring!*

"But you did do it." Marie pointed to the coin.

She had sold her husband's ring! She put her hand to her head, which now pounded unbearably. She had been mad, mad! But she had still worn the ring. Lord Bernard had not set her aside when he sent her here. She was still Lady Celeste.

The peddler's grinning face mocked her. He had stolen her ring with the nail!

"Where did I get that nail?"

"From the coffin." Marie took a step toward her.

Celeste held out her arm, warning her back. What coffin? Who had died? Someone close to her if she had been grieving. She could not ask Marie, the girl would be convinced she had lost her wits.

"You helped me pull it out?" Something about the nail frightened her. If only she could remember. She frowned, trying to concentrate despite the pain.

"N-n-no," Marie stammered, her eyes wide, anxious.

"Speak," Celeste commanded.

"You were not in your right mind, My Lady. You insisted the coffin be placed beside your bed until the funeral. Your husband—" She stopped.

Her husband? Had he died? Was that why she was living in an abbey? A vague face, masculine and powerful, came into her mind. She grasped at the memory. Something else was there. Some emotion, struggling against the cocoon of silence that held her. A stab of pain made her gasp. She closed her eyes.

And saw a coffin. She had lain in bed staring at the small wooden coffin. A child's coffin. Not her husband, then. Perhaps the infant—Etienne? But she had not touched the coffin. Surely she would remember extracting a nail from it. She had a brief vision of blood on her fingers, of someone else's hands on hers—it was gone. She swayed. The pain in her head was making her dizzy; she was seized by an inexplicable terror. She swallowed, breathing deeply. Silence was better. Silence was safer. Silence would not push her toward the darkness she had so recently emerged from.

She must not think any more about the past. It would come back to her when she was stronger. Already she was remembering a few things. Things she might prefer to leave forgotten.

"You sold it." Marie pointed to the coin, her mouth set in a stubborn line. "And you are better now."

Celeste glared at the girl, but she would not argue with a servant. "You may have the denier."

Marie shrank back from the table. "Oh no! That is yours, in place of your sorrow. Who knows what you would open yourself to if you do not keep it?" She spoke with such horror that the back of Celeste's neck tingled.

"What foolishness," Celeste said, shaking her head to throw off the sensation. "It is only a peasant's fable."

"It is true," Marie cried. "My mother's cousin sold a nail from her babe's coffin and she was much better. Then she gave the denier to my uncle, to buy a piece of rope for the cow, and afterwards she hanged herself with that very rope! My mother told me."

Celeste stared at Marie. After a moment she forced out a sceptical laugh. Nevertheless, she picked up the coin.

Marie gasped. "My Lady, your ring!"

Celeste's hand froze over the denier. They stood in a silent tableau staring at Celeste's bare finger.

"I have lost weight. It must have fallen off." Celeste snatched the denier from the table and buried her hand in her skirts. "It will turn up somewhere." She tried to lock eyes with Marie, to stare her down.

Marie did not look at her. She ran to the bed, skimming her hand over the blanket, then yanked the blanket off and shook it vigorously. When nothing fell out of it, she threw it to the floor and grabbed the bottom of the mattress, lifting it high to peer underneath. "Help me, Lady," she cried, sounding so shaken Celeste overlooked the impertinence.

Celeste put the coin in her purse and took hold of the side of the mattress. She bent and gave a perfunctory look underneath.

Marie ran her finger quickly along the stitching at the edge of the linen, seeking a hole through which the ring might have fallen inside the mattress.

"My Lord will be displeased if we cannot find it, but he will soon forget it. He has other concerns to think about." Celeste spoke casually, trying to reassure herself as much as Marie.

"Forget it?" Marie turned to stare at Celeste. "He wed you with that ring. Do you not remember, My Lady?" Her voice rose, taking on a desperate edge. "He said as long as you had that ring, the marriage would hold!"

Celeste's eyes widened. She covered her mouth with her hand to prevent herself crying out. Was it true? She remembered the ring, the physical weight of it on her finger, knew it to be her husband's marriage token. But she could not remember receiving it. She knew her husband's name but could not visualize his face. He was like a silvered image in her mind, flat and cold, without any distinguishing features.

"Lord Bernard de La Roche," she murmured to herself. She felt no response, neither attraction nor repulsion, only a kind of dizziness, like a moth beating against the numbing silence that bound her. What was wrong with her, that she should have no feeling for her Lord husband?

"What does he look like?" she whispered.

"My Lady!" Marie wailed.

Was there a reason she could not remember, something about *him* that caused this emptiness inside her? Celeste swallowed, her mouth dry. The mattress dropped from her hands.

Marie's face loomed before her, pale and twisted with fear.

Celeste backed away from her. "He could not have meant..." Her legs trembled. Why could she not recall his image? She looked around and saw the black cloak hanging on the wall. Last winter, or next?

*If you tell him, he will put you aside.* Someone had said that to her, a man's voice. Whose? Was it real, or only a fevered dream? She put her hand to her throat. She was going to be ill. She felt the stool behind her and dropped onto it.

"And with the heir you gave him now dead, and you so wild with grief he had to send you away," Marie's voice rose to a frightened shriek, "and now the ring gone missing!"

22

"Quiet," Celeste whispered. "Be quiet." She could barely force the words past the tightness in her throat.

"It must be here!" Marie ran back to the mattress. Grabbing the linen on either side of the stitching she ripped it open, scattering feathers everywhere. She hoisted the other end high above her and shook it fiercely. Feathers flew wildly around the room.

"Stop," Celeste whispered.

Marie shook the mattress again, and then again.

"Stop. It is not there."

Marie shook the mattress once more. Celeste heard her sobbing from inside a cloud of feathers.

"Tell no-one," Celeste said. She wrapped her ringless finger into the folds of her kirtle.

The empty linen casing fell slowly to the floor, feathers rising and dipping in the air around it. Marie stepped through them and fell at Celeste's feet.

"We will say I had a—a fevered nightmare, and that I did this." She did not look at the mattress casing or at Marie. She stared up at the narrow little window. A thin shaft of sunlight came through it. It did not reach Celeste, but shimmered in the air above her.

Marie lay on the floor before her, weeping.

Celeste did not move.

"I will think of something," she whispered, staring at the beam of sunlight high above her.

# Chapter 3

What had he done? Had he bartered with a demon?

Jean stared into the girl's black eyes until the nun pulled her around again, toward the abbey. He watched, sweating, as the young woman, half-carried between the nun and the child, passed directly under the tall, black cross in the center of the iron arch above the abbey gate.

No demon could pass under a priest-blessed cross set to guard an abbey.

Jean wiped his damp forehead. He gripped the pouch, feeling the shape of the ring through the leather: a fat band of gold with a large ruby winking from its center. A beautiful stone, well-cut to enhance its natural brilliance. Of course he would not give it back. But he would break it down and sell it as soon as possible.

Jean grinned. It would be worth a small fortune. He pulled the donkey's head up by its worn halter and began walking. It was still early enough to reach Cluny before nightfall. He walked briskly without looking back. The gates to the abbey clanged shut behind him. The bell in the tower began to ring the end of Sext.

He was already well into his route, trading and selling in the towns and villages from Saint-Gilles to Marseilles, where he picked up his spices, then north to Cluny in time for the Festival of the Assumption.

After Cluny, he would retrace his journey back down to Lyon and then home to Saint-Gilles for Yuletide. He had little to show for his trek so far but sore feet and enough deniers to eat for the next few days. The ring was an unexpected kiss of fortune.

Far ahead, the distant bells of Cluny chimed their summons to midday mass. The bells of Lyon peeled behind him. Birds on either side of the road joined in the medley, the leaves of the trees rustling softly with their movements.

*"Buy my sorrow,"* the birds sang.

*"Sorrow, sorrow,"* the leaves whispered in response.

Jean blinked. The whispering stopped. No, there was never any whispering; he was becoming as foolish as an old woman. He clucked to the donkey and picked up his pace. But the face of the girl lying in the dirt and the soulless, desperate look in her eyes filled his mind, no matter how he sought to dispel her image.

"No looking back," he muttered to himself. He had made a life out of not turning back and he would not change now. Why should he? Every day on his trade route he passed people as broken and even more destitute than she. What could he do for them? Nothing good came of charity; he had learned that as a child. Only tears, salty tears. That was what happened to Lot's wife. She looked back and became a pillar of salt tears. Served her right.

Still, the girl's wretched face haunted him. The sun beat down, radiating heat like fire, so hot the air shimmered with it. *He could almost hear the crackle of hungry flames, and the smell—*

Jean shivered, pushing away his thoughts. Not real. None of that was real. It was only a mirage caused by the heat and the image of the girl. It had nothing to do with that other fire, the one he used to dream of...

"Enough," he said out loud, shaking his head clear of such thoughts. The donkey snorted and shook its head as well.

At least his pouch had some weight to it, now. He reached between the folds of cloth and grasped the pouch tied to his belt, feeling again the hard shape of the ring with its blood-red ruby.

Why did she wear a ruby? Rubies were the symbol of martyrs, who shed their blood for God while sending up ardent prayers for the souls of their tormentors. Had he taken the ring of a martyr? Had he taken the sorrow stone of one of God's chosen?

Was that why he remembered the fire? Martyrs often died by fire.

No, the fire was not a memory, only a nightmare from his childhood. He had not actually seen that fire, and he had stopped dreaming of it years ago.

Besides, he had bought the ring, not taken it. Bought it from a madwoman, not a martyr. Why should a madwoman wear such wealth on her finger while others went hungry? She did not appreciate what she had, or she would never have parted with it. At the least she should have bargained for a higher price. Well, what you do not treasure, you deserve to lose. That was the truth he lived by, and he was content to pass that lesson on to her.

He squeezed the pouch. The gem was larger than any he had seen. He was tempted to take it out and look at it again, to see the sun sparkle against its hard crimson brilliance. His fingers played with the drawstring of his pouch...

"Way!" A rider cantered up, brushing against him on the narrow track. He dropped the pouch back into the folds of his tunic and leapt aside, cursing himself for a fool. His hand shook as he grabbed the donkey's halter, resting the other hand on the hilt of his knife. How had he failed to hear the thud of horse's hooves approaching?

*A momentary slip, Death whispered, grinning.*

The rider sped past him. Jean let his breath out slowly. No more woolgathering! He had been doing too much of that today.

The narrow track that wound past the abbey soon met with the main road. He was farther south than he had expected. Even at a brisk pace, he would be lucky to reach Cluny before dusk. At least there were others on this road, also heading for Cluny to celebrate the Festival of the Assumption.

Jean walked without stopping. When he was thirsty he drank from the wineskin at his waist and when he had to relieve himself he paused at the side of the road. Only a fool would leave a full-laden donkey to go into the bushes. He was content with the firm Roman road under his boots, the warm summer sun listing toward the trees to his right and the knowledge that his donkey carried full packs of profitable goods that would soon become coins in his purse.

With luck, half of his spices would go to Cluny, another half when he reached Lyon, and the rest at Vienne on the way home. The wine merchants at Lyon were rich, but Cluny Monastery was richer and they would want to put on a fine feast for the Assumption. He could make them pay a good price and they would buy large quantities. But they were shrewd, too. No tampering with his scales or dampening the dried stalks to add weight, as he did at the small town markets. Well, he would make a profit at Cluny without that.

Behind him he heard the excited chatter of a woman's voice and the low murmur of her husband's responses. He nodded to them as they overtook him.

"God be with you, peddler."

"And with you," Jean addressed the man who had spoken. He was an ordinary-looking fellow, shoulder-length brown hair, large, rough hands and a friendly smile. He wore a thigh-length tunic over well-worn breeches, both made of coarsely-woven russet, but his boots were made of leather, not felt. He was not as tall as Jean, few people were, and he looked older, entering his fourth decade, Jean guessed. He was breathing deeply with the exertion of walking so quickly.

"Guillaume," he introduced himself. "And this is Liselle." He pointed to the woman beside him. The woman smiled and dipped her head politely. She wore a loose kirtle, also of russet, but she had embroidered yellow flowers at the neck of her shift, where they would show above the kirtle. Her hair was braided about her head with blue and yellow ribbons woven through it. The ribbons were dyed unevenly and frayed at the edges, but in her dark hair they looked festive. She had been good-looking in her youth, and the sense of it lingered, taunting her, most likely. Good soil for a peddler to till.

"Jean le Peddler." He inclined his head toward her in a slight bow. "You must be going to Cluny for the Feast of the Assumption?"

"And the market an' all," she nodded enthusiastically. "Oh, there it is!" she cried out, as they crested a small rise in the road. "I see it already." The straight line of the road and the woods on either side dipped below the hill where they stood, giving them a clear view of Cluny, several miles ahead. Even in the distance its size was breathtaking, the largest church in the world.

Jean shaded his eyes. The town that sprang up around the monastery had grown in the past year. At least fifty or more new huts nestled against the high stone walls of the monastery. Behind its walls, the twin chapels of the church and the pointed arches and barrel vaulting over the nave rose one hundred feet into the sky; almost as high as the four soaring bell towers. Even from here it was an awe-inspiring sight. More important, the town looked well-kept and prosperous, a result of the increasing number of pilgrims who stopped at Cluny on their route to Santiago de Compostella, or to Saint-Gilles or Marseilles to board a ship for Jerusalem. The hub of every major pilgrimage route, Cluny was, and the church had enough holy relics to justify a pilgrimage itself. Good for everyone's business, including his.

The woman, Liselle, turned excitedly and waved her handkerchief to those behind, to let them know Cluny was in sight. It was an old kerchief, and threadbare. She would be wanting a new one soon.

Jean's wife, Mathilde, had sewed a dozen silk handkerchiefs and embroidered crosses on them. They could sell profitably in their own right, but Jean tripled their value by claiming that they had been blessed at the Saint's shrine in Santiago. The wealthier merchants, too busy to go themselves, and ailing pilgrims who feared they might not reach the end of their pilgrimage, would buy them eagerly. Mathilde made a dozen linen ones, too, for those who could not afford the silk. People like Guillaume and Liselle. Jean glanced surreptitiously at the pouch hanging from Guillaume's belt. Yes, it appeared to have a little weight to it.

"Perhaps I will see you at market. I have some wares that might interest you." He smiled directly at Liselle. "Something pretty for a pretty woman. I see you like ribbons, and you wear them well." He reached into one of the bags tied across his donkey's back and pulled out a scarlet ribbon which he had placed there for just such an opportunity.

Liselle's cheeks reddened with pleasure. She patted her hair.

"Or something holy, for a pious woman." He showed her a linen handkerchief. "Blessed at the Apostle's shrine in Santiago," he murmured, as though awe-struck himself.

Liselle's eyes widened.

"Now wait, Liselle—"

"Oh, I am not selling anything just now," Jean interrupted the nervous husband before he could put his misgivings into words and make them that much stronger. "Come and see me at the market." He smiled at Liselle.

"Oh, I will," she said.

"What we need comes first," Guillaume explained. "Our rooster died and the hens are off laying until we get a new."

"A rooster and laying hens," said Jean. "I can see you are a man of some substance."

Guillaume straightened. "Better than some others, I suppose," he said, smiling around the words as though they tasted good coming out of his mouth.

"D'you know about the stoning?" Liselle asked.

Jean raised his eyebrows politely.

"An adulteress," Liselle nodded solemnly. "She goes to the square on Saturday, at noon, right after the morning's market. They caught her undressed—"

"Liselle!" Guillaume objected.

Liselle blushed, but she could not resist telling the rest. "—Right after he left her. She confessed to everything, enticing the poor man against his will, bewitching him with her wanton ways."

"That will add to the festivities," Jean said dryly.

"It will, that." Guillaume said, earning a nod of approval from his wife.

"I never saw a stoning. Will it last very long, d'you think?" She shivered in anticipation. "Will a demon come up and snatch her down to hell?"

"Probably not." Jean struggled to keep his expression neutral. What had come over him, to evoke such disgust at the thought of a stoning? He had seen many punishments during festivals. Anyone caught wrong-doing for months before would be held in chains until the event. Their castigation added to the general attractions and served as a warning to anyone considering using the crowded festival as a cover for similar crimes. Thieves, especially, served the purpose well. Jean had never felt sympathy for those who were stupid enough to be caught, and shrugged away the useless sentiment now. Their deaths were completely avoidable. This adulteress should have been more careful if she valued her life. What you did not treasure, you deserved to lose.

Mathilde's shrine-blessed handkerchiefs always sold well after a public execution. The thought did not cheer him as much as it should. He was over-heated and was tempted to feel his forehead to see if he was ill—a financially fatal gesture for a peddler to make in public.

"Fare well." Liselle looked at him strangely before hurrying down the road. Guillaume nodded, hastening after her.

Jean cursed under his breath. If he had lost a sale, he had only himself to blame. He could ill afford such moody thoughts stilling his tongue when he should be sociable. And why was he suddenly so weary of witnessing just punishments? He looked around and quickly felt his forehead. Cool and healthy. Nevertheless, he slowed his pace. No need to push himself or the donkey now that the monastery was within sight.

It would still be there when he reached it. The monks knew him; they would find a place to lodge him and his wares.

Should he have the ring broken down here? There would be metal smiths in the town who would pay well for gold and a jewel like this one.

No, Cluny was too close to the Abbey of Sainte Blandine. The girl might have kinfolk here. The metal smith himself might recognize the ring, might even have made it! Not here, certainly. And the same was true for Lyon. He would be safer selling it in Avignon on his way home to Saint-Gilles.

He need not keep the nail that long, though. In fact, he would be glad to be rid of it. He reached into his pouch and drew it out. How long it was, and thick. He had not remembered it being so large. But then, once he saw the ring he had stopped looking at the nail. He passed it from one hand to the other while he examined it.

Who would use such a nail to make a coffin? A coffin only had to hold together until it went into the ground. No coffin maker would use this much iron when half would do the job; no, less than half, for it would have been a child's coffin. This was no nail from a child's coffin.

What had he bought? He looked at the nail, passing it from hand to hand.

Why was he doing that? He felt sweat on his forehead.

The nail was cold in his moist hands. Suddenly, he wanted to be rid of it. It was a cursed thing! He closed his fingers around it and raised his hand to hurl it from him.

And stopped.

What was he thinking? It was only a nail. And he was a peddler, after all. Iron is iron. He laughed shakily under his breath and lowered his arm. He raised the other hand to his brow and wiped his sleeve across his forehead. Idiocy, sheer idiocy. He opened his pouch to return the nail.

But then he did not want it in his pouch or anywhere on his person. Instead, he reached back and loosened the top of one of the wadmal bags across the donkey's back, and pushed the nail deep inside.

The donkey slewed sideways, braying and rolling its eyes. Startled, Jean yanked his hand away.

He was reluctant to touch the sack again and left it slightly loosened.

# Chapter 4

*L*ady Celeste." The Abbess glanced up from her writing table as Celeste was ushered in. She inclined her head slightly. "Please sit."

Celeste sat stiffly on the high-backed wooden chair in front of the Abbess' table, folding her hands in her lap, right over left, to hide her ring finger.

The Abbess finished writing and pushed her papers aside before looking up again. "I have been told you had a fit. That you tore apart your mattress and ripped your clothing."

Celeste met her gaze. *I am a Lady,* she thought. *I am a guest here, and need not answer to the Abbess.*

"We do not care for the ill here, as I told Lord Bernard. We made an exception in your case, of course."

*Of course?* She pressed her hands into the folds of her kirtle, feeling them tremble against her thighs. Why could she still not remember her past? She dared not speak for fear of betraying herself.

The Abbess frowned. "We are not ungrateful for your husband's gift, nor insensitive to your loss. But we cannot have such displays of intemperance here. It distracts the Sisters from their prayers, which is their holy duty and the true purpose of this abbey. It sets a bad example for my novices. And it is not in your own interest that I permit you to so indulge yourself."

"Indulge myself?" Celeste's hands clenched within the folds of cloth. She would like to slap the woman, but it would risk exposing her finger.

Slap an Abbess? She blinked, shocked at the thought. Where had such an impulse come from?

"The servants believe you are possessed. They are only peasants, but the novitiates have heard them talking. They do not admit their suspicions to me, but I see it in their eyes."

Celeste sat very still. "There is no demon inside me," she said. Her voice was faint, the words sticking in her mouth. Had someone else seen the eyes glowing in the shadows of her room? How could she prove that none of those demons had slipped inside her? Had one? Was that why she could not remember her life before? If the Abbess learned of her memory loss, would she take it as proof? Would they put her to the test?

The Abbess made a dismissive gesture. "I have known you since you were a child. You have ever had a sweet and loving nature, and a devout faith."

The Abbess knew her as a child? Or did she mean she had known Celeste since she married Lord Bernard? To this gray-haired Abbess, a fourteen- or fifteen-year-old woman might seem like a child.

Celeste pressed her lips together, afraid to speak.

"Your maid tells me you sold a nail from your baby's coffin to a peddler."

She looked up before she could stop herself.

"So it is true. I hoped your maid was wrong. You must know that is only a superstition."

Celeste flushed.

"Even if it were possible to sell our sorrow for another to bear, it would be a wicked thing to do." The Abbess' voice warmed to her topic. "Imagine what you might become if you could feel no sorrow.

And the poor man who bore a double load, what would become of him? It is neither possible nor desirous to do such a thing: God gives and takes for reasons he alone knows, and it is our duty to submit with grace. Pray for forgiveness and the fortitude to bear your troubles more stoically."

A hot rage swept over Celeste. How dare the woman speak to her thus, Abbess or not? She was a guest here, not a novitiate. Her hands curled into fists beneath the folds of her kirtle. How dare Marie speak of her to others, even the Abbess? When they were back in her room, she would beat her.

"Courage, child," the Abbess said sharply. "Where is that boldness that worried your mother and irritated your father so? Do not let your courage fail you when it is most needed."

"I am not your child! I am a Lady!"

"Good." The Abbess smiled briefly. "Anger is better than despair. Now you must conquer it also. I will keep you here as long as I can, but you must practice temperance and self-control. Remember that you *are* a Lady. There must be no more fits, no more tearing sheets and running out through the abbey gates, dabbling in superstition: a very dangerous thing for you right now."

Celeste endured the reprimand in silence. It was the Abbess, not she, who needed to remember Celeste was a Lady.

As soon as Marie closed the door to the cell behind them, Celeste rounded on her, boxing her ear with a satisfying *clap!*

"Do not talk to the Abbess about me," she hissed. "Or to anyone else."

Marie cringed, holding her ear and snivelling.

"Quiet," Celeste ordered. "If you complain I will slap you again, much harder."

It was Marie's fault the ring was lost: Celeste would not have wandered out and met the peddler if Marie had not left her alone. She paced the room until her anger eased. Marie sat on her floor mat, her cheeks damp with tears.

She had never struck Marie before. She had seen that in the child's face, the moment she slapped her. She felt a strange impulse to apologize—it passed quickly. Marie deserved her chastisement; a Lady's maid must learn to be discreet. She did not regret punishing her, but she had not done so before.

She had changed. She was not "sweet and loving" now. She did not even want to be, but she did want to know why she had changed. This helpless feeling that everyone knew more than she did, that something terrible had happened to her and she had no control over how it had changed her, this was unbearable. Unbearable!

She covered her face with her hands.

The room was quiet. She felt a shift in the air and looked up. Marie stood beside her. "I am here," she said softly. "I love you, Lady Celeste."

Celeste slapped her hard across the cheek.

Marie gasped, wide-eyed with shock, then whirled and ran from the room.

Celeste stared, outraged, at the door swinging shut. Her maid had left without even asking her leave! She stamped her foot. A peasant declaring love as though she was an equal? And then to leave without permission? She stamped her foot again. The world was mad, not she.

Marie did not reappear.

Outside the window an owl hooted; a derisive sound.

She was no Lady; they all saw it and mocked her: the Abbess, her maid, even a foolish bird. She crossed to close the shutters, pausing to stare out the little window. Had she cared for Marie? For a peasant child?

Far away, a sparrow cried. The thin, high trill drifted through her window. She had seen one once, crying like that as it struggled to escape the talons of the hunting falcon. She had refused to go falconing after that. How foolish of her. What had made her decide that? And why was she trembling now, at hearing the distant cry?

Celeste stepped back from the window. She closed the shutters and stood with her arms wrapped tightly about herself.

The room was full of shadows and ominously quiet.

She had to get out of this room. It closed in around her, tiny and dark and cramped, like the room at the bottom of the tower stairwell where Lord Bernard kept condemned men waiting for execution.

She had heard one once, weeping in the small, dark cell. She remembered the sound he made, a low, animal noise, reverberating off the stones of the stairwell. She had begged her husband to be lenient—until he told her what the man had done.

The memory came to her stripped of all emotion now, but she had felt a torrent of emotions at the time—horror, pity, fear, anguish, compassion—over a stranger, a man she had never seen, simply because she heard him weeping. He had done an evil, traitorous thing and would be duly punished. Why had it upset her so? She had lain awake wondering if he had repented, and in the morning had insisted a priest be sent to him. Why? What was his immortal soul to her? She had never used the tower stairwell again, even when the prisoner's cell was unoccupied.

All that intense caring. What an exhausting person she must have been.

And now here she was, trapped in this little room as though she, too, were a criminal, unable to reclaim her position as mistress of Lord Bernard's castle because of a lost ring.

Was Marie right in thinking Lord Bernard would set aside their marriage? Marie was only a girl of eleven or twelve years. She had barely begun to show a woman's figure.

But Marie had not been ill. She must know what Lord Bernard was like; she had lived at the castle as Celeste's maid. And Marie was terrified. Celeste shivered, remembering the pitch of her voice as she wailed, "and now the ring gone missing!" She could still hear Marie sobbing within the cloud of feathers. Was Lord Bernard truly so fearsome?

Courage, the Abbess said. Had she shown courage in coming here? Or had she been running away from something, like a coward? She had not taken her life; she had resisted the demons tempting her. Perhaps there was still some boldness in her, then. So she had not entirely changed.

A vicious stab of pain lanced her temples. She pressed her hand to her forehead. If she thought too hard, would she go mad again?

"You are unwell, My Lady." Marie's timid voice startled her.

She should reprimand the girl for leaving her. "Undress me," she said, wearily raising her arms for Marie to remove her kirtle. She was unwell indeed, but she would recover. Leaving Marie to tidy the fallen robe, she walked to the bed.

"How can I help you, My Lady?" Marie asked, her voice small and sad.

"Tell me—" *Tell me what I have forgotten.* No, she could not confess to losing her memory. The child was impertinent enough without learning that. She must find a less direct way to coax information from the girl.

"Tell me a story."

Marie looked up, wide-eyed. "A story?"

"I am tired, Marie. The sound of your voice would soothe me. Talk about whatever you wish. Something you remember, perhaps."

"It is you who used to tell the stories," Marie muttered, frowning.

"I did?" Celeste managed to keep the horror from her voice.

A smile tugged at the child's face. "Wonderful stories. We could listen for hours, Lise and I—" She stopped abruptly.

Celeste waited in frustration, trying not to picture herself spinning tales to amuse a crowd of peasant children.

"I did not want to hear stories after Lise died," Marie said in a low voice. "They reminded me of Lise. That is why I cried. I am sorry."

"That was long ago," Celeste said, hoping she was correct.

Marie nodded. "I was but a baby then."

"Do you remember when Lord Bernard gave the abbey his gift?" she asked, as though the question was of little importance.

"Lord Bernard," Marie cried. "*You* had the orphanage built here. You always give others the credit for what you do. But I know."

Celeste observed Marie thoughtfully. *I know.* And what else did Marie know? Had she made a peasant child her confidante? No wonder the girl forgot her place. She must change that. For now, however, she would learn more if she let Marie talk. "How could I build an orphanage?" she asked with a coaxing smile.

"You are trying to fool me, but I saw you. You sold your jewels to pay the labourers. Lord Bernard was angry when he got home."

She sold her jewellery? To build an orphanage? Was the child lying, trying to trick her?

"Then you told him why you did it. You told him—" Marie broke off abruptly.

"Go on. You may say it." It must be important for her to hesitate.

"That you were carrying his child. Etienne," she finished in a low voice.

Celeste closed her eyes. She felt his weight against her breast, his warm, downy head tucked into her neck, his little body shedding heat…

She swayed and sat down suddenly on the side of the bed. What use was a memory like that? But it was gone already; only the memory of a memory remained.

She glanced at Marie. The girl looked so downcast it was impossible not to believe her.

"You may leave me."

"Forgive me, My Lady. I did not—"

Celeste waved her out wearily. She lay on her bed and tried to summon again the peaceful silence she had felt when she returned to the abbey. But it was a wilful companion, dependent entirely on her loss of memory. The minute she tried to recall her life before the peddler took the nail and her ring, or consider what she should do next, the silence was replaced by pounding headaches. Was there a demon inside her? She put her hand to her head, wincing, and closed her eyes, and thought of nothing.

*It is night time, all the rush lights in the castle keep have been extinguished. She is standing in the great hall, blind in the darkness. Where is the door, or the stone steps leading up to their private rooms? She looks around for something to orient herself, but even the huge central hearth is invisible, its embers as cold and dark as the night. The snores and sighs of sleeping people are all around her, mingling with the quiet yip of dogs dreaming of the hunt and the rustle of the floor rushes when someone turns over. The night-noises echo around her, hemming her in, trapping her.*

*She must not waken anyone. Something terrible will happen if she is found here. She must get out, but it is so dark; surely she will stumble over someone. She crouches low and stretches her right arm out before her. The dark to her left seems more intense: a wall? If she can reach a wall, she can feel along it until she touches something that will orient her.*

*Cautiously, she steps to her left. The floor rushes crackle, loud in her ears, but it is such a common sound no one is wakened by it. Another step, and a third and fourth. Her outstretched fingers brush against a woollen cloak. Hardly daring to breathe she traces the form with her fingertips until she knows where she can walk around it. At last she reaches a wall. It is easier walking along the wall; no one wants to sleep against cold stone and she can move more quickly, while taking care to disturb the rushes as little as possible.*

*Her hand sweeps up and down the wall ahead of her as she walks, up and down and into empty air. She stops, confused. In the dark she feels the stone wall beside her and the place where it abruptly ends. If she has reached a corner, there should be an adjoining wall; if it is a window she should feel the night air through it. But there is only an empty space as high as she can reach. She kneels. The end of the wall reaches all the way to the ground. The stone floor turns at the end of the wall and heads away from the great hall.*

*Impossible. She rises, resting her right hand against the corner of the wall, and steps ahead. Her toes bump something hard. She yanks her foot back and stumbles, falling forward.*

*Instead of landing on a sleeping body, her outstretched hand hits a waist-high stone block. The corner of a higher stone strikes her chest, driving the air from her body. She clings to the stones to keep from falling sideways as she tries to breathe; nothing, then a gasp and she is finally sucking air into her throbbing chest.*

*Someone snorts in the darkness behind her. She freezes, listening to the sound of rushes scratching against the floor as he turns over. She waits, breathless, for his snoring to resume. When it does, she feels along the blocks protruding from the indent in the wall, then grimaces at her own obtuseness. It is the stone stairway that leads to the upper rooms.*

*Not that way! But there is no other escape. The great door is at the other end of the hall; she will not reach it without waking someone. She has failed.*

*As she climbs the stairs, a terrible foreboding fills her. Stop! She must stop! Yet step by step she advances against her will, fighting the urge to scream—*

Celeste sat up in her bed gasping for breath. Where was she? She listened intently. Marie's even breathing was the only sound in the darkness.

The abbey. She let her breath out and breathed again, slowly, to calm the uneasiness that remained. It was only a nightmare. But when she closed her eyes, she saw that stairway in Lord Bernard's castle. It was real. Something had happened there. Her heart began to pound again.

Had Marie witnessed it? Was that why she was so frightened of Lord Bernard?

Celeste put her hand to her chest. Underneath her thin nightdress she felt the silver cross. She traced it with her finger in the darkness to calm herself, listening to Marie's soft breathing until both dream and memory faded.

She got out of bed. Bending down, she fetched the chamber pot from under the bed and used it. Deciding not to waken Marie, she opened the door and placed the pot against the wall outside.

The moon was full in the deep night sky. Beyond the cloister, the garden shimmered in its unreal light, a mixture of black silhouettes and eerie, silvery leaves and blossoms, as beautiful and haunting as a dream. She watched the play of black and silver, breathing in the cool scent of night simmered in moonlight. Standing at the open doorway within the dark shadow of the cloister, she imagined ghosts flitting through such a landscape, and finding death peaceful there. She took a step toward the garden, and another…

The snide "Whoooot, whooot!" of an owl disturbed the night.

Celeste blinked. She leaped backward into her room and closed the door, leaning against it a moment. Awake and asleep she was drawn to… What? What terrible secret hid in the darkness, calling to her? She shook her head. Let it stay forgotten.

Returning to her bed, she lay on her back with her eyes open, shivering in the silvered darkness until she fell asleep. Behind her dreams, a land of silver and black where nothing was real mingled with the memory of sleeping bodies, breathing and shifting around her in the night.

Marie entered with her mid-day platter. She placed it on the table and backed away before Celeste approached.

Celeste began to eat, reminding herself to chew and swallow slowly. She was always hungry, then nauseous afterward if she ate too quickly.

Marie watched her silently. "What is the matter?" Celeste demanded, looking up.

Marie looked away and did not answer.

"Marie? What is it?" The child had barely spoken all morning, helping her dress and combing and plaiting her hair in a welcome silence which only now seemed unnatural.

"N-nothing."

"Look at me." When the girl at last met her eyes, she said: "Tell me."

"T-they say you are possessed by a demon. That you caused the fever that killed so many in the village."

Celeste swallowed the food in her mouth. With deliberate slowness, she took a drink of small ale. "The kitchen servants," she said scornfully, when she could command her voice. She forced herself to take another bite of bread.

Marie shook her head. "The nuns say so." Her voice quavered.

Celeste coughed out the bread. The Abbess had warned her, had said she did not believe it. Had she changed her mind? What if she declared Celeste possessed? "Aieii," she moaned, hugging herself.

Marie backed away from her, poised to flee.

"It is not true." How could Marie believe it? Marie knew the fit was an invention to cover their search for the missing ring. She knew about selling the nail and—

*Not both, she did not know Celeste had sold the ring, too—*

—and through it all she had not been afraid of her mistress.

*—sold her marriage ring for a single denier. That was the act of a crazy woman, one possessed with the urge to destroy herself—*

*Could it be true? Was she possessed?*

She had wanted to strike the Abbess: that was the desire of a demon. She still wanted to, when she thought of the woman's presumption. She bit her lip against such unholy thoughts. Did anyone ever know if they were possessed?

Celeste stared around the room. Shadows and stone surrounded her. She felt a scream rising in her throat, and stifled it with difficulty.

She must be calm, must reassure Marie. Marie was her only ally here. The nuns—

"The nuns are under a vow of silence," she said.

"The novices," Marie said. "The novices said it."

"The novices? But they are only children. And you believed them?"

Marie flushed. "You are not yourself." Her lower lip protruded stubbornly.

Ah, the slap. Celeste was tempted to slap her again. To believe servants and children over her mistress! But what if the rumour spread? How would she defend herself? Everywhere she looked, the room closed in on her.

"I have to get out of here," she cried.

"Where would you go, My Lady?" Marie asked. Her voice was thin and nervous, as though she had been ill, not Celeste. As though she had been confined in this room day and night for weeks. Ah, no, Marie had gone on any number of errands, to the kitchen, the gardens, the hen house. Even the hen house sounded like an excursion! Celeste laughed shakily. No wonder she seemed mad.

Marie clutched her hands together, twisting them into the folds of her kirtle. What a child she was. A silly, ignorant child, no help at all. "To the courtyard!" Celeste snapped, leaping to her feet. "To walk among the flowers and shrubbery. To the guesthouse to eat with others for a change. To hear the travelers' stories and drink a mug of ale with them—"

Marie leapt backward, arms wide open, as though to prevent her from striding through the door. "What will we say? How will we explain?"

"Say I am better!"

"And then Lord Bernard will come for you, or send his men to escort you home." Marie looked pointedly at Celeste's left hand.

"I will return to him when I am ready. Why should he come for me?" Her heart pounded at the thought of returning to him, a strange, quick stutter in her chest.

"My Lady!" Marie gasped. "We could not travel without an escort!"

Celeste frowned. "No, of course not." Even outside this room she was fettered. Had she been so well-tamed she had never noticed it, or had she been so indulged she had never had to?

She put her hand to her head. She could not continue to let others care for her. She had succumbed to their influence long enough—Lord Bernard, the nuns, Marie, the peddler—and this was what it had brought her to. Had she ever thought for herself? No matter, she would learn to now.

"How far is my husband's castle?" She had to remember at least the most basic things.

"Near Le Puy," Marie stammered.

The name meant nothing. She shook her head, frustrated.

"Two days' ride from here. Can you not remember?" Marie took another step backward.

Celeste ignored her. At least Lord Bernard was a good distance away. She could be able to think of something before he came to fetch her. But first she must get out of this cramped, dark room. She was so weary of it she could not think.

She pushed aside the half-eaten platter of food. When Marie did not retrieve it, she looked at her sharply. The child stood at a distance, refusing to meet her eyes. Did she fear her mistress' glance would ensorcel her?

"Tomorrow I will go to Mass." That should dispel this rumour of a demon.

"Yes, Lady." Marie's lips trembled. She blinked rapidly against the tears brimming in her eyes.

"Marie, look at me."

Marie's glanced up, her eyes quick and frightened as a rabbit's. She looked down again before Celeste could speak.

Celeste sighed. "Take my platter away."

If she could not convince Marie, how would she prove her innocence to anyone else?

# Chapter 5

Jean woke to the patter of rain against stone walls. The patch of sky visible through the window shutters was iron-grey, until a bolt of lightning briefly illuminated it. The other two merchants sharing this small room at the end of the Cluny guesthouse were already gone.

Loud scraping noises came from the outer hall as tables and benches were pulled into place for the guests' meal. Jean dressed and washed his hands and face in the basin of water provided. After breaking his fast with porridge, fruit, and ale, he asked a novice where the kitchener could be found.

"In the undercroft of the grainery, meeting with the cellarer," the novice replied, barely looking at him as he supervised the peasants hired by the monks to serve their guests.

Jean remembered the cellarer: a suspicious man who kept a tight hand on the monastery's expenses. He would do better if he saw the kitchener alone. However, he must meet with him today, while the roads were thick with visitors pouring through the gates, seeking food and accommodation. Those with money would follow their noses to lodgings that promised to feed them well. The kitchener understood this, but the cellarer… He had a bulbous, red nose that wept constantly and could not tell him the difference between an onion and a rose petal.

"I will need your help later to carry a barrel of spices over for the kitchener's inspection," Jean told the novice.

He waited, sipping the last of his mug of ale. A number of the wealthier merchants would want to see him before he offered his wares at the general market, which opened tomorrow. But he could not sell to them ahead of the monastery. He tapped his fingers against the table, drank the last of his ale. Surely the kitchener was free now. Had the novice forgotten?

At length the fellow returned and together they carried one of the large, sealed barrels through the gardens and across to the grainery. The kitchen was separate from the other buildings, being prone to fires despite all the kitchener's precautions. The spacious undercroft below it had a good flagstone floor and a curved vault ceiling supported by thick stone pillars, all designed to resist fire. They stood the barrel just inside the door, and the novice hurried off.

Jean breathed in the aroma of stored food—salted fish and smoked meats, apples and pears and onions and garlic cloves. The expensive foreign spices were in a locked room at the back, but he could smell them faintly nonetheless.

Two monks were talking together in the center of the room. Jean was annoyed to recognize the cellarer as one of them. What was he doing lingering here after his meeting with the kitchener? The kitchener himself was nowhere to be seen. He was quite old, Jean remembered, possibly entering his sixth decade. Had he gone to rest before preparing the mid-day dinner, leaving the cellarer to meet with Jean? Jean nearly groaned aloud at the thought.

The young monk talking with the cellarer glanced up and saw Jean standing by the door. Jean nodded with an affable smile. The monk signalled to a novice barely out of boyhood, who approached Jean and asked his business.

"I will inform the kitchener," the novice said, handing him a cloth to wipe the rainwater from the barrel before it was opened. He crossed the room and whispered to the young monk.

Jean bent to wipe the barrel dry. A new, young kitchener and a stingy cellarer. With any luck the cellarer would leave, but Jean did not feel lucky. Would this new kitchener want to impress the cellarer with his thrift, or the prior and the monastery guests with the flavour of the food that came from his kitchen?

He wiped his hands on the cloth. Cluny was his biggest purchaser. His heart thumped loudly in concert with the monks' murmured conversation. Where would he sell his excess spices if this new kitchener did not buy?

He leaned against the stone wall, feeling its cold firmness at his back, and forced himself to breathe slowly. Cluny would buy. They had guests to feed, and they must feed them well in order to guarantee their return year after year. Surely they could afford to, with money pouring into the monastery from visitors and pilgrims come to celebrate the Feast of the Assumption.

He scrutinized the cellarer. Was the fellow's face more dour than usual? One never knew if a prosperous-looking establishment had just suffered a set-back. He would not find that out here—the monks were a close-mouthed lot, even those not under a vow of silence.

The young kitchener beckoned him over. Apparently the cellarer was staying.

"What spices have you?" the kitchener asked.

"Let me show them to you," Jean said, "so you may judge their quality as well." He gestured back at his barrel. Let the spices talk to him with their rich, sensual aromas. Let him smell them here in his own storeroom and he would have to buy.

The kitchener glanced at the cellarer.

He wanted to buy; Jean could see it in his face. But would the cellarer let him? The cellarer was his senior in years and until recently had been his senior in position, also.

Jean bowed his head briefly to the cellarer. The cellarer smiled: a tight clenching of the lips that did not reach his eyes. He could not eat spiced foods, Jean remembered, because of a sensitive stomach. He was not willing to let others enjoy what he could not.

With the help of the novice, Jean carried his barrel over to the long table beside the two monks. He could have hefted it onto his shoulder himself; he was accustomed to carrying heavy loads and the spices were packed carefully. But he lifted it upright here, letting his care emphasize the value of the contents.

He should have introduced himself to the kitchener the night before. He would have, had he known there was a new one. Now he must bargain with a man he knew nothing about, in front of the resentful cellarer. He could not chatter as he did at fairs, or smile familiarly or pay overripe compliments such as the merchants' wives loved. He must appear relaxed and confident, but not overly so, and watch them carefully, letting their eyes and gestures guide him. If he undersold his goods he would set a standard that he would have to live with for many years, but if he demanded too much, he could lose Cluny. He and Mathilde and the children would be hungry this winter. And if he did not sell well at Lyon, either, they would be ruined.

No. Never think of home when he was peddling his wares. He could not barter shrewdly while thinking of them. What had made him do so now? He wiped his hands again.

Removing his knife from its sheath at his waist, he pried open the barrel lid, taking slightly longer than was necessary to impress the two monks with its tight seal. "This barrel has not been opened since I left Marseilles," he said, glancing at the kitchener.

The kitchener nodded.

A tantalizing mixture of fragrances greeted them when Jean lifted off the lid. He reached in and began to place his goods on the long wooden table. The fragile loafs of sugar were on top, wrapped tightly in waxed cloth. He placed all seven on the table, carefully unwrapping one to show the dark-brown, cone-shaped loaf. The cellarer blew his nose loudly into a handkerchief which had already seen too many uses. He was fond of sweets, Jean remembered. He broke off two small pieces and handed them to the monks, who popped them into their mouths and sucked on them like noblemen's children.

While they were enjoying the sugar he took a large, tightly-woven linen bag from the open barrel. He unfastened the drawstring ties and poured a small pile of dark yellow mustard seeds onto the table. The cellarer frowned, but the kitchener took a pinch of the seeds and lifted them to his nose, as though their sharp scent had not filled his nostrils as soon as the bag was opened.

The cellarer swallowed the last of his sugar and cleared his throat noisily.

The kitchener dropped the mustard seeds into their bag.

Jean placed a half-dozen smaller bags on the table. He opened one and pulled back the neck to display a small bundle of cinnamon sticks, still encased in their smooth, yellow-brown outer bark.

The cellarer leaned over to take in their aroma. His nose dripped threateningly. Just in time he pulled his grubby handkerchief out and blew into it.

"Cinnamon is referred to in the Holy Book. In Proverbs, I am told," Jean murmured, looking down at the open bag with a feigned reverence.

The cellarer, his nostrils temporarily clear, breathed in and licked his lips.

To complement the cinnamon Jean opened a bag of cloves, pouring a few into his hand and holding them up for the kitchener to inspect.

The kitchener's lips twitched, not quite a smile, at being deferred to in this way. The cellarer frowned.

Jean tipped the cloves back into the bag and pushed everything further down. He lifted three clay vessels out of the barrel and placed them on the table. Their tops were sealed with wax.

"Yes, we need salt," the kitchener said, glancing at a similar container standing beside the door to his spice room, which Jean had brought the year before. Salt was a prudent purchase which showed thrift as well as culinary skill: it not only enhanced food but also preserved it. Jean let his breath out gently. The kitchener had committed to buying from him. Now it was only a matter of quantity and price.

Beside the vessels of salt Jean placed a large bag of dried black peppercorns, their sharp scent temporarily gaining ascendancy as he opened the bag and sifted his fingers slowly through them before half-closing it again.

"We do not need pepper," the cellarer said, watching his movements suspiciously. "Pepper is not easy on the digestion."

"Important people are coming to celebrate Saint Mary's Assumption," the kitchener murmured, staring like a greedy child at the spices laid out upon his table.

Jean leaned back, giving him time. The longer he stood intoxicated by the rich scents, the more he would want to buy.

"Piety is the spice that honors the Virgin's Assumption," the cellarer sniffed.

"Of course," the kitchener agreed, folding his hands together obediently.

"And good wine," Jean said, hoping to flatter the cellarer.

"Which we can make without expensive spices. We do not need to see the rest of your wares."

Jean waited. The kitchener said nothing.

"No matter," Jean said, as though his heart were not pounding in his ears so that he could barely hear himself. "Your guests will be grateful for lodging even without the well-seasoned food they have been served in past years."

The kitchen was silent. Had he overstepped? Jean dared not look at either of the monks.

"I will look at the rest of your spices," the kitchener said.

Jean bent into the half-empty barrel. He was not ruined. Not yet. Should he set a lower price? He would have to if the cellarer stayed. But he must live through the winter, and have enough money for next year's spices, as well.

He placed a long, flat wooden box on the table and lifted the top off. A pungent aroma floated up from it. The wood was thin—just enough to protect the fragile threads of saffron, tied into bundles with string, inside it. The kitchener's eyes gleamed, but the cellarer, well aware of the price of saffron, scowled down at it.

"You might as well put that back at once," he said.

The kitchener sighed.

"No, no. The saffron is already spoken for," Jean said. "I have just taken it out to reach the goods underneath. Monsieur Robert is entertaining Lord Imbert de Lyon and wants to make sure his guest is satisfied. Lord Imbert is a generous friend, although I understand he can be fickle. I hear Monsieur Robert seduced him with a meal no man could resist."

While he was talking, Jean drew out more spices, as though he did not know Lord Imbert used to stay at the monastery. He reached the root spices, and placed them on the table: the thick, fleshy white gingerroots first and then, after the kitchener had examined one and returned it to the pile, the narrow, twisted yellow tumeric roots. Finally he placed the last bag on the table and opened it to show large, light beige cardamon pods. By now the rich aromas of the fresh spices so permeated the room that even the novice had stopped his work to stare at the laden table, breathing in deeply. The cellarer, looking more dour than ever, shifted his weight and blew his nose loudly into his sodden cloth.

"Shall we use your scales?" Jean asked, as though the kitchener had already agreed to buy. As though it were only a matter of weight and price. He held his breath.

The kitchener nodded to the novice, who promptly brought a set of scales over to the table. He handed the novice the key to the spice room and bade him take stock of what they needed.

As though he does not already know, Jean thought. He would be a poor kitchener if that were the case. But he must show the scowling cellarer his prudence.

The novice returned and murmured into the kitchener's ear. He nodded solemnly.

"Sugar cones," he said. The novice placed the one Jean had opened on the scale. The kitchener weighed it carefully. He weighed each of the others in turn, although the variance between them was too slight to make much difference in price. He marked down their weights on the waxed cloths they were wrapped in.

"Salt."

The cellarer nodded his approval.

When the kitchener had weighed each of the vessels of salt, he directed the novice to retrieve the empty vessel lying outside his spice room, and marked down its weight as well. He sent the novice for last year's books and leafed through them slowly, adding up the amount of pork and venison and fish the monastery had salt-dried, and calculating the amount of salt it had taken.

The cellarer shifted his hefty weight from one leg to the other.

When the kitchener began to tally the increase in monks and novices over the winter and the number of visitors in their guesthouse during the past year, the cellarer frowned and cleared his throat.

"I leave you to your calculations," he said. "I do not have time to watch you weigh and tally everything. Buy only what we need."

As soon as the cellarer left, the kitchener closed the books and signalled to the novice to return them to their shelf. He weighed the rest of the spices carefully but without undue deliberation.

Jean watched, not daring to comment. The monastery scales appeared accurate, but there had been no mention of price.

"I am sorry you have promised this to Monsieur Robert," the kitchener said, when there was nothing left but the saffron.

Jean hesitated. Was he hinting for a gift? "Saffron is an expensive spice," he said, trying to steady the nervousness in his voice.

"The cellarer has left us."

Jean looked up. The young kitchener smiled at him. "Does Monsieur Robert want it all?"

"One sprig should be enough to flavour his meat," Jean replied, smiling back.

The kitchener's smile widened.

He bought the entire barrelful of spices, settling on a fair price with little haggling. Jean left the kitchen undercroft, rolling the empty barrel ahead of him and carrying the box with a single sprig of saffron under his arm. His step was as light as his barrel.

Jean was content on the last day of the market as he wrapped up his herbs and whole spices and placed them in the open barrel. During the four-day-long market, he had sold nearly a third of his second barrel of spices to innkeepers and wealthy merchants, as well as twelve pair of woolen hose, most of his squares of shoe leather, several pieces of heavy felt for poor man's shoes, four of Mathilde's linen handkerchiefs and three of her fine silk ones: he reviewed his sales, smiling to himself as he packed up his wares.

Most visitors had gone off to their dinner. The town merchants had left with them; only a few peddlers like Jean, too poor to buy proper stalls and therefore stationed off to the edge of the fairgrounds, were still packing up. The sharp scent of sweat, both human and animal, and the earthy smells of trampled dirt and spoiled farm produce lingered in the field. After four days of raucous noise—the rough voices of traders haggling over prices, the cooing of doves and pigeons, the scuffling of caged rabbits and squealing of pigs and crowing of roosters, the constant noise of people calling and chattering to one another—the sudden quiet made Jean's ears ring.

He packed his scales into one of the panniers and began strapping them onto the donkey. Tomorrow, after the Feast of Holy Mary's Assumption, he had arranged to see the Abbot of Cluny, in order to sell him the nail. He had thought up a fine story to sell it, along with a pilgrim's badge which he carried in his pouch.

He would tell the Abbot he came across an ailing pilgrim just off a ship from the holy land when he was in Marseilles buying his spices. He brought the pilgrim to the inn where he was staying and paid the pilgrim's board, and nursed him. But his care was in vain; the poor man was mortally ill. Just before he died, the grateful pilgrim embraced Jean, called him his Good Samaritan, and pressed his pilgrim's badge into Jean's hands. Then he asked Jean to lift the hem of his robe, his holy pilgrim's robe, the hem of which had brushed the ground Christ walked on. He instructed Jean to tear the hem, and when Jean did, he beheld a nail.

"From the Cross of Christ," the pilgrim whispered.

The nail shone as bright as the halo around our blessed Lord's head, miraculously preserved through the centuries. Jean dared not touch it, but the pilgrim urged him to take it, and his pilgrim's badge as well, and sell them and keep the money in return for the care Jean had given him. Only he must sell them to a monastery, where pilgrims would be drawn to see them, and pray before them, and have their faith strengthened, to the eternal glory of God.

It was an excellent story. Jean would enjoy telling it, and the Abbot would want to believe him, in order to entice even more pilgrims to visit Cluny and fill its coffers. He would pay well for a nail from Christ's cross. To think Jean had almost thrown it away!

The Abbot had agreed to spare him a few minutes just before Vespers the next day, when most of the monastery guests would be gone. Jean assured him that it would be worth his time. He must remember to clean the badge and polish the nail well before he went.

Jean folded the last sprigs of dried rosemary into their parchment wrapping and placed them in the barrel. No one would ever find out, this far from Marseilles, that the pilgrim died before the ship docked, that Jean had paid two deniers to claim the body as kin (for two deniers he could be kin to any pilgrim who died shipboard) and one more denier to have him dumped into a mass grave. He thought he had wasted his money when he saw that someone had already stolen the pilgrim's scrip, but the gamble paid off when he found the pilgrim's badge from Jerusalem sewn into the hem of his long gray tunic. Jean sold the pilgrim's cloak and tunic, which only just covered his costs, but he held on to the badge: a fine silver token, stamped with the sign of the cross and a fish, symbol of the early Christians. A stroke of luck that he kept it—it would give authenticity to his story of the nail. Too bad he had sold the tunic, but he could say he had given it to a poor pilgrim bound for Jerusalem, who had promised to bring it back to Jean, twice blessed, when he returned. It would be easy enough to secure another gray pilgrim's tunic, dusty with wear, and bring it to Cluny next year.

Jean placed the lid on the barrel and pounded it down with a stone. Yes, this trip was turning out exceedingly profitable. He might even be able to set aside some money, above the amount he needed to buy next year's spices and feed Matilde and the children. A little extra to guard them against the dangers and misfortunes that kept him awake worrying. That would be fine, indeed.

He looked up to see Liselle and Guillaume standing before him. Guillaume held a squawking, struggling rooster under his arm. A narrow string was tied to the rooster's leg and the other end to Guillaume's wrist in case the rooster gained the upper hand, which it looked imminently about to do. Jean greeted them with a smile. He had not yet packed away the handkerchiefs. Liselle fingered a pretty yellow silk one.

"How much?" she asked wistfully.

"It has been blessed at the tomb of the Apostle James in Santiago de Compostella." He didn't need to tell her it was fine, imported silk, or that she could never afford it. She knew.

"Seven deniers," he said, watching Guillaume.

Liselle touched it reverently. She glanced across at her husband.

Guillaume shook his head. "I told you, Liselle," he said softly. "I knew they would be too much." He looked at the handkerchief regretfully.

"These linen ones have also been blessed at the Apostle's tomb," Jean said. He held up the top one, a pretty light blue. "The same blessing, for only four deniers."

Liselle's eyes brightened, but Guillaume shook his head again. "Four deniers is all we have left." The rooster squawked and struggled. He tucked it further under his arm. "Come, Liselle."

Jean shrugged. He began folding the pretty cloths to pack into his sack, but he did not hurry about it.

Liselle stood watching him, even when Guillaume touched her arm, and took a couple of steps, and paused, waiting for her to follow.

Jean looked up and caught the sadness in her eyes. He looked away, frowning.

Liselle blinked, still gazing at the handkerchiefs.

Was that a tear on her cheek?

What did he care if it was? Let her husband mind her tears, he thought fiercely.

But he did mind them. He could not help himself. He stopped folding the linen squares and reached into his sack to pull out a bundle of ribbons.

"One denier each," he said, noting with irritation that the scarlet one was among them. He could easily get two deniers for it, if he offered it to a wealthier woman.

Liselle shook her head. "I wanted something blessed," she whispered. "I never owned a blessing." She bent her head.

Jean felt it in his gut. He pushed the feeling aside. It was bad for business, going soft like this. Guillaume had four deniers; he had admitted it. He could please his wife if he wished. It was not up to Jean to care about her. He had his own wife to feed.

Liselle straightened her shoulders and looked over at her husband. "I never thought I would, neither," she said, smiling at Guillaume through her tears.

Mathilde would say something like that. Why did they always give in? The look on Guillaume's face made Jean's stomach turn. It was like that, between men and women. Their quiet endurance unmanned you.

He was ready to tell Liselle the ribbons were blessed, too, but she would be sure to talk that around, and someone would wonder why he had not said so before. Then they would begin to wonder about the handkerchiefs.

Never change your story; that was the first rule. He wound one of the ribbons around the others, twisting the end inside.

Never get greedy and push it too far; that was the second. No one would believe that everything he had to sell had been blessed.

Never let the customer know he is a fool. That was third. Even Liselle, however much she might want to, would not really believe that he had forgotten to mention until now that the ribbons had been blessed. He tossed the bundle of unblessed ribbons into his sack.

And never forget that the customer is only a fool with some money. That was the final rule. He folded the silk kerchiefs quickly and threw them in the sack. He would not look at Liselle. She was just another fool with a little money.

She did not look at him, either, nor at Guillaume. She could not take her eyes from the linen squares. She reached out her finger slowly, as though unaware of doing so, to touch the pale blue one on top.

Jean had to stop himself from snatching it away. Why was she torturing herself?

And why should it bother him, her longing? It never had before. He gritted his teeth and let her linger over them. Let her husband see her wanting one so badly. He glanced over at Guillaume.

Guillaume stood still, watching his wife.

Jean found he was holding his breath. No, that was Liselle. She was holding her breath as he lifted the linen handkerchiefs. It was suffocating him, the way she held her breath and watched him fold away the blue linen square with its embroidered cross and its claim to a holy blessing, folding it inside the others, almost out of sight now.

"All right!" Guillaume cried. "We will buy it, Liselle, if you want it so much."

Jean breathed in deeply.

"I want it for us," Liselle said, wiping at her eyes. "For our home. And for the boys when they come round with their families. To touch it, like. And be blessed." She whispered the last words.

Jean looked away, angry. It held no blessing for them. He did not want to sell it, after all. And he had been so desperate for her to have it earlier, as desperate as she was. But Guillaume already had his money out; there was nothing Jean could do but take the coins and hand over the false blue cloth.

He watched them walk away together, Liselle holding the handkerchief to her breast, her face shining, and Guillaume grinning that he could so please his wife, and worrying a little over the money gone and struggling to hold on to the furious rooster, which scratched at his tunic and pecked his hand and left a ridiculous scattering of feathers behind them.

# Chapter 6

The little window in her room was bright with sunshine when Celeste awoke. A moment later the door opened, dispelling the last of the shadows. Marie entered carrying a mug of small ale. She handed it to Celeste without meeting her eyes.

Celeste drank slowly, watching Marie. She had made a great show of praying aloud the previous evening, hoping to disperse the girl's doubts. Apparently in vain.

"Dress me and braid up my hair for Mass," she said, standing and placing the empty mug on the table. She felt Marie staring at her finger. "And find me some gloves. To prevent my hands from darkening in the sun."

"Yes, My Lady."

Marie's anxious voice reminded her of the girl's warning: Lord Bernard would come for her if he learned she was well. She would be glad to leave the abbey, but she was not ready to face him yet. Especially with the suspicion of possession lying over her. Why tempt him with a reason to set her aside if he had not already done so? Her cheeks burned at the thought of the shame such an action would incur. Better anything, better to die, than to be publicly humiliated by her husband's rejection.

"If anyone approaches us at Mass, you must speak for me, Marie. I have been ill and will be tired." Let everyone think she was still recovering. People would speak more freely around her if she did not seem fully alert. She might learn something that would help her regain her ring.

"What shall I say?" Marie's hand, combing her hair, faltered.

"Tell them you heard me praying last night. That attending Mass might help me shake off my melancholy." She turned to smile at Marie over her shoulder. "That is true, is it not?"

She had never been deceitful. The taste in her mouth as she made up these lies would have proven that to her, even without the look on Marie's face. No wonder the novices' talk had convinced Marie she was possessed. But what was she to do without any memory to advise her whom to trust? She must rely on her wits. She raised her chin. "Is it not true, Marie?"

"Y-yes," Marie stammered, looking away quickly.

Ridiculous. The girl could not avoid looking at or speaking to her forever. She turned around sharply, ignoring the tug of the comb in her hair. "Marie, I am not possessed. At first I was ill and feverish. And then I was distracted while I thought what to do."

Marie looked unconvinced.

"You know I did not really have a fit—it was you who tore the mattress."

Marie bit her bottom lip. Her face was easier to read than a parchment.

"Here." Celeste pulled the chain at her neck, exposing the silver cross beneath her kirtle. She kissed it.

Marie sighed with relief. "And you truly want to attend Mass?"

"Of course I do," Celeste said, pressing the little cross to her forehead, chest and shoulders. *Demons lie,* she thought. *So do people, when need be,* she answered herself.

Celeste stepped through the door of her room and stood blinking in the daylight. How different the courtyard garden looked this morning! The arbour was a profusion of colors and scents: sunlight on rosemary bushes and neat, aromatic plots of herbs intermingled with lilies, iris, daffodils, roses and gourdon flowers, all carefully planned to glorify God and inspire meditation. A stone pathway, accented by a low wall of shrubbery on either side, wound in concentric circles toward an open central garden where a long wooden bench invited contemplation. So bright and welcoming now, how had she imagined it spellbound and sinister in the moonlight? Her dream, which had so alarmed her in the night, was similar to this garden; threatening then but harmless now. She was tempted to believe last night's silvery vision had also been a dream.

"Please, My Lady, it would not do to be late," Marie whispered urgently beside her.

Celeste allowed Marie to lead her along the cloister to a tall wooden door which opened directly into the church. She stepped through it into the transept parallel to the nave. Narrow arched windows cut into the exterior walls let in fresh air and sunlight, which fell across the nave in stipples of light and shadow created by the twin rows of stone columns between the side aisles and the centre of the nave. Celeste leaned against one of the pillars, playing the part of someone beginning to recover from illness.

The priest climbed slowly into his pulpit to the side of the elaborately carved wooden altar. His solemn voice echoed in the nearly empty church.

The church did not have a flagstone floor and the hard earth was dusty under Celeste's feet. The north and south transepts on either side of the altar were still unfinished, waiting for the sacristy and the vestry to be built into them. The spire directly over the nave and the chancel, where the sanctuary should be, were not finished, either, and had simply been thatched over to keep out the weather. Celeste stared at the unadorned walls and the thatching. Had her husband sent her to the poorest and meanest nunnery he could find? No wonder the Abbess was willing to put up with her behaviour.

Celeste endured the Latin service. If she had once been pious, she was no longer. The thought was alarming. It was one thing not to care for people; quite another not to care for God. Whatever else had changed in her nature pertained to her heart and mind; this was in her soul. She thought of her dream, bodies lying in the dark castle as still as death. Where had such a dream come from? She shivered in the cool stone shadows.

The nuns began to sing. Their pure, clear voices soared above the altar, carrying her with them. It will all come right, they seemed to be saying, and Celeste's fear slowly subsided. She glanced at the priest, an old man leaning against the railing of the pulpit, then across the front where the nuns who were not in the choir stood, behind them a dozen or so visitors from the guest house and the village.

At the end of the front row, as if feeling her gaze, the Abbess turned and looked straight at her. Too late to turn aside, Celeste was caught in the older woman's piercing grey stare. Startled, she returned the unblinking stare, raising her head proudly, and was further surprised when the Abbess' mouth twitched slightly upward before a movement among the young novices forced her to return her vigilance to her flock.

After the service, Celeste bid Marie lead her along the circular path to the bench at the centre of the garden. Delighted by the morning breeze on her face and the spacious garden, Celeste ignored Marie's presumption in sitting beside her. She closed her eyes, enjoying the warmth of the sun, the heady fragrance of the flowers, the lilting song of birds among the shrubs. Opening her eyes, she was once again struck by the beauty of the garden, with its brilliant colors and wash of golden sunlight. Despite the neglected state of the exterior vegetable gardens, the nuns had maintained this colorful labyrinth cloistered against their church: a single respite of beauty in their silent, colorless lives. Yet how often did they get to enjoy it? Celeste glanced around: she and

Marie were alone in the garden. The lives of these nuns were meaner than those of the poorest peasant, for they must work as hard in the daylight, and rise from what rest they might take in the night to pray.

Surely her husband could not intend to leave her here?

Marie shifted on the bench beside her. Celeste turned. A peasant woman she recognized from the morning Mass had entered the narrow path of the labyrinth, swaggering toward them with some purpose that made her bold beyond her station. She stopped directly in front of Celeste. Her feet were bare and dirty below her plain brown kirtle. She smelled of sweat and fresh baked bread. Her hands, which Celeste could see without raising her head, were chapped and red, but clean. Someone working in the kitchen would have such hands.

Someone from the kitchen would know what went onto a platter for a guest of the abbey, would notice when the amount of food increased.

"I saw you at Mass."

Celeste gazed ahead at the garden as though unaware of the woman's presence. She need not fear a kitchen wench, and yet her heart was pounding. No peasant should speak thus to a Lady.

Would Marie be able to maintain the charade they had agreed upon? Celeste dared not look at her, but she could see the child's hands clasped tightly in her lap, her knuckles turning white. She should have coached the girl on how to respond.

But she had not really believed her husband had a spy. Even now she could not think so. Perhaps the Abbess had sent her. No, that was even less likely. She felt the tightening in her forehead that threatened another headache.

Why did Marie not say something?

"Is not the garden beautiful, My Lady?" The woman spoke more loudly, bending a little toward Celeste.

"M-My Lady is not well," Marie stammered.

"She went to Mass, and she is eating more, and she is sitting here in the garden." The woman crossed her arms as though she had made a clever argument.

Marie's mouth gaped open. Celeste vowed to box her ears as soon as they were alone in her room.

The woman bent down to peer into Celeste's face. "You are looking better, My Lady," she yelled.

Celeste shrank back. "I am tired," she said, trying to sound ill and confused rather than furious.

"It was my idea!" Marie cried, jumping to her feet. "I thought it might help her regain her health if I took her to Mass. It was my idea to sit in the garden! She is not better yet!"

Marie was babbling like a fool. Even this simple peasant would recognize that she was lying. Celeste staggered to her feet. She swayed a moment to alert them, then let herself fall. As they rushed to catch her she threw up her arms, managing to smack them both, though not nearly as hard as she would have liked.

"Please, help me get her to her room," Marie said, rubbing her cheek and winding her arm under Celeste's.

Celeste let them support her back to her room and help her onto the bed. "That man—the one who was kind to me—is he here?" she murmured.

"Who is she speaking about?" the woman asked in a carrying whisper.

"I think... I think the one who found her when she ran outside the abbey." Marie sounded puzzled.

"The spice peddler! I saw him at the market. He is long gone now, up north to sell his spices. Why is she talking of him?"

"She is ill. Her mind wanders."

A good answer, though spoken a little too hesitantly. Celeste closed her eyes; it was not necessary to feign exhaustion.

"She is gone," Marie said unnecessarily, closing the door behind the peasant woman. Her voice shook.

Celeste opened her eyes. That foolish, interfering woman. How could she go to the guesthouse for dinner now? She must stay here and pretend to rest. The room seemed even more confining after she had been outside. She sat up, glaring. And he was gone. Up north somewhere. How could she retrieve her ring now? She stood up and went over to the window. Its little square of sunlight taunted her.

Why should she care about her husband's ring? He had been faithless when she needed him, that much she did know: he sent her away. What attachment did the ring hold, then? Little enough for him, and therefore, none for her. But she should not suffer for losing it, and she would not. Lord Bernard wanted to keep her in this abbey, but she would find a way to leave.

She would have to. The kitchen servant had already noticed her increased appetite. Her body had begun filling out beneath the drab black kirtle that covered her from neck to foot. Already her stomach was slightly rounded. Her arms and face must be filling out also. She could not continue to feign illness for long.

He had put her in this position; he had sent her here, ill and helpless. She felt a rush of heat, thinking of him. That spark again, like a fall of fire landing on one's skin, blinking out as quickly as it lands, leaving only its heat. And an emotion she could not identify because it disappeared as soon as it touched her. Anger? Fear? He was her husband. What else was he?

Behind her, Marie's straw pallet rustled as she stood up. Celeste turned. Marie stood there, grinning.

"What are you smirking about?"

"Now we know who is watching you for Lord Bernard."

Just that quickly the morning's disaster was reversed. Yes, indeed, they knew, and the knowledge was useful, if bitter. She could no longer deny that her husband had someone watching her. Was he hoping to find a reason to denounce their marriage?

"I have seen her scrubbing the pots after mid-day dinner," Marie continued eagerly, "but she is never there when I fetch your evening platter."

Celeste smiled. She had misjudged Marie. The child was as superstitious as any peasant, but not dull-witted, and she was more observant than Celeste had expected. She wished she had not slapped the girl quite so hard.

What was wrong with her, one moment insensitive to others, the next regretful? *Was* she possessed? She shrugged the thought away uneasily. "How is a kitchen servant to get a message to my husband?"

"Her son is a stable boy. I have seen her talking to him. He exercises the horse Lord Bernard left in the stables." She hesitated. "I saw Lord Bernard give him a denier and heard him say there would be another if the boy did as he was bid. I remember because I was—I was angry that Lord Bernard gave me naught and you required more care than a horse!" She said the last indignantly, then slapped her hand over her mouth. Not only had she compared her Lady to a horse, but the comparison had favoured the horse.

Celeste frowned.

Marie's other hand crept up to cover her cheek.

Celeste ignored the gesture. Something else bothered her, something Marie had said. She reviewed Marie's earlier comments until she came to it: Lord Bernard's horse. One horse? What had happened to her dun gelding? ...Honey, that was what she had called it. She cringed inwardly at the thought of having named a horse. What a sentimental girl she had been. Nevertheless, her horse should have been in the stable, and Marie's pony, also. Had her husband taken them back with him in order to imprison her here?

'I will keep you here as long as I can,' the Abbess had said. Celeste glanced at her winter cape on its hook and shuddered. Had they reached some agreement, Lord Bernard and the Abbess? She turned toward Marie.

"Let us play a game, Marie. I will think of something, and you must guess what it is."

Marie looked up. "A game?" The expression in her eyes was hopeful, childishly eager. Celeste felt an inexplicable sense of remorse. She should strive to be more patient with the girl.

"How can I know what you are thinking?" Marie's face wrinkled into a worried frown.

"I will tell you when you are right. And I will give you a hint. It is about someone we both know."

Marie grinned. "Ahh…about the Abbess? Oh, I am wrong!"

"You are not wrong," Celeste lied quickly. "I am surprised you guessed so soon." She sat down on the bed. She had hoped for information about Lord Bernard, but now she wondered what Marie knew about the Abbess. "You must tell me more than that in order to win the game." She gestured for Marie to sit as well.

Marie pulled the little stool beside the bed and perched on it. "When your mother was ill, the Abbess came to visit, to take care of your mother and the household. I was little, but I remember. She was only a nun then, not an Abbess. I asked her why she could talk, and she told me she was excused from her vow of silence while she was at her sister's house."

"Her—" Celeste stopped herself. "Her hair was long then, was it not?" she amended. *Her sister's house? The Abbess was her aunt?*

"I do not know, My Lady. She always wore a veil. Perhaps you saw her brushing it, in private. You followed her around and would not play with Lise and me. You told us you were going to be a nun and could not play anymore."

Celeste leaped up, on the verge of accusing Marie of lying when she recalled that Marie was recounting the words of a child, play-acting adult roles as children do. Of course she had not meant it—she had married Lord Bernard.

And lost his ring. Celeste rubbed her thumb against her bare finger, momentarily distracted. What if that was all the excuse he needed to shut her away here forever? Who would speak on her behalf?

"My mother—"

"Your mother died," Marie said solemnly. "Why were you thinking of that, Lady? Are you sad again?" She clutched her hands together, an anxious expression in her eyes.

"No, no." Celeste forced herself to smile. "I am thinking of her and my father—"

"You mean your step-mother," Marie said matter-of-factly. "Your step-mother and your father."

Celeste drew her breath in. This was unfortunate news. A mother might have prevailed upon her husband to grant their daughter asylum, but she could not reveal her loss of memory to a stranger who had taken her mother's place. A second wife would not want the first one's grown daughter in her home.

"You did not say to guess your father." Marie looked at her accusingly.

"I did not mean to think of him. You are right, I was thinking of the Abbess first. Tell me about her if you would win." Her aunt. That would explain why she was here, in this drab little abbey. Her husband had sent her to her aunt in her illness. He had not meant to cast her aside.

The woman had not acted as an aunt. Of course, an Abbess would not; she had a higher calling. Celeste must not trust her too far, aunt or not.

"The Abbess went back to the abbey and you played with us again. That is all." Marie frowned, twining her hands in her skirt. Her face brightened. "She visited again two years ago, when you were married. Is that it?"

Celeste nodded. "That is what I was thinking all along. The second visit."

"That is not about the Abbess. That is about your wedding." Marie looked at her reproachfully. "Your hint was false."

"I was remembering the Abbess at my wedding." Celeste spoke sharply, frustrated at having to rely on foolish tricks to prompt her memory.

"I do not like this game," Marie said, pouting.

Celeste gritted her teeth behind her smile. "But you have almost won. Just tell me about the Abbess and my wedding."

"You already know. It was but two summers ago. Are you well, My Lady?" Marie looked at her warily.

Celeste's hand trembled with the desire to slap Marie again. She opened her mouth to rebuke her for her insolence when someone knocked at the door.

Marie turned quickly.

"Wait," Celeste whispered.

The knocking sounded again, harder.

Celeste hurried to the bed, thankful now that there were no rushes on the floor to betray her. "Open the door. Say I am asleep," she whispered, lying down with her back to the door.

The door squeaked open.

"I have brought Lady Celeste's dinner."

Celeste recognized the voice of the woman who had spoken to them in the arbour. She lay still, hardly breathing.

"It is not yet dinnertime," Marie said. "My mistress is asleep." She spoke too loudly in her nervousness. It would sound as though she were not concerned about waking Celeste. Celeste clenched her hands beneath her, struck with the indignity of her position. Here she lay, pretending sleep, afraid a kitchen servant would find her out. She had to depend on a child to rescue her from a servant!

"I thought she would be hungry," the woman persisted. "She seems to be getting better?"

Despite her annoyance, Celeste almost laughed at the woman's anxious tone. She must be desperate to send her message—she had probably been promised a reward, which she would never see if the Abbess contacted Lord Bernard first. At the same time she would be terrified of what would happen if Lord Bernard arrived and found the report to be false.

"Thank you for bringing her dinner," Marie said. "I will try to get her to eat some of it when she awakes."

When the door closed, Celeste sat up. She examined with disgust the platter of bread and cheese and salted fish. She had looked forward to eating at the guesthouse.

She picked up the bread and bit into it. It was dark and flavourful and still warm from the oven. She chewed it slowly, washing it down with ale. Tomorrow she would sit in the garden again, then afterward take her dinner in the guesthouse. It was better after all not to do everything on the first day, if she wanted appear to improve gradually.

She reached resolutely for her knife, quelling her strange antipathy toward it—the past was the past; she would master it, not fear it—and speared a piece of the fish on its blade. So the Abbess was her aunt. Perhaps Lord Bernard did not have everyone on his side.

The sun had already brightened the sky, erasing the flush of dawn, when Marie rushed into the room sloshing water onto the floor from the washbasin she was carrying.

"What is the matter with you?" Celeste demanded, sitting up and frowning at Marie's carelessness.

"The stable boy has gone," Marie gasped as soon as she closed the door. "One of the garden men has taken his place."

"He may be ill…" Celeste did not believe her own words. A sense of dread had come over her as soon as Marie had spoken. "The horse is gone," she whispered.

"—And Lord Bernard's horse is—How did you know?"

"I did not know. I only feared it was so."

How much time did she have before he arrived? Two days for a messenger to reach her husband, Marie had said. The boy would be there in two days. And two more for Lord Bernard to ride here. Four days, if he left at once.

"We must be gone before he arrives."

# Chapter 7

The Latin chants sung by the Cluniac monks reverberated off the walls and high, vaulted ceilings of the huge cathedral, which leant their voices an unearthly majesty. Beneath the soaring choir peasants and pilgrims, landowners and nobility maintained a busy hum of conversation and movement in the impossibly long and wide nave.

Jean stood near the back, masking his bad humour with a smile whenever someone addressed him. He had been in a foul temper since the market ended yesterday. There was no reason for it: his sales at Cluny and at the market ensured his survival for another year, even without the ring. His rumbling belly would soon be satisfied at the Feast of the Assumption, and his story of the nail and the pilgrim's badge was sure to convince the Abbot to pay good money for them. Nevertheless, he was tense and irritable, and the pious choir only increased his irritation.

Liselle's brimming eyes and Guillaume's proud smile lingered in his thoughts, taunting him. He did not want any part of their emotions, which seeped into his awareness with unaccountable persistence. They had chosen to buy the handkerchief. They had willingly participated in the deception. They were pleased with their purchase and that should be the end of it. But then what, when they needed the blessing they had paid for, and none came? The thought sickened him, a reaction so absurd he could scarcely believe it. Had not his parents' deaths wiped such softness out of him? Something else must be the cause of his present discomfort. Indigestion, perhaps.

The monks' chanting died away, and the buzz of conversation with it. The Bishop, from his elevated podium, addressed the nobility in ringing Latin. Jean recognized the term for the Assumption and the Virgin's holy name, but little else. He would not even be listening, like most of the congregation, except for the need to still his own thoughts. Finally, the Bishop spoke briefly in French, extolling his restless audience to confess their sins and to seek the intercession of the church to save them from the eternal torments of the afterlife. Prayers and pardons, candles and confessions, and certainly tithing. It was a simple, financial message, and it improved Jean's mood considerably.

Back at the guesthouse, servants and novices hurried about, taking the long, wooden tables down from the walls and setting benches alongside them in preparation for the Feast. Jean passed them on the way to the room where he had slept.

His wares were packed, ready to be strapped onto the donkey, exactly as he had left them. He untied his purse and checked that the pilgrim's badge was near the top, then opened one of the panniers to fetch a small flask of oil. He reached into the wadmal bag.

The nail must have slid down inside. He dug down deeper but could not find it, even when his fingers felt the bottom. Had it fallen out? He should have left it in his purse with the ring and the badge! What if it were lost? He wiped his brow with his sleeve and reached in again.

Aha. There. He pulled it out.

Its size still puzzled him. His earlier unease returned, but he shrugged it off. Perhaps someone had given it to the woman and told her it was from the child's coffin. He remembered her soft little hands. She had never helped her husband build a home, or cobbled together a hen coop, like his Mathilde. Someone had given her the nail, and played her for a fool. The thought angered him.

He laughed at himself. Had he not done the same?

It was better for him that it was not a coffin nail. Christ's cross would not be held together with a flimsy little bit of iron. Should he straighten the end? No, let it look as though it had been extracted from the wooden cross. He poured a fat drop of oil onto a cloth. A nail that had touched Christ would shine for all eternity.

He polished the nail until it gleamed in his hand. It lay against his skin, black and glistening. As black as her eyes. He opened his money pouch and took out the ring. The large ruby was brilliant against his palm. As red as her trembling lips when she cried, "Take my sorrow!"

They lay together in his hands, hard and bright. Neither one was a child's coffin nail, but they were her sorrow, nevertheless. They should not be separated.

A strange thought, but he was convinced of it.

An absurd thought! What made him think such things?

He closed his hands. They may be her sorrow, but they were his wealth.

He tightened his fists around them until they dug into his palms, the iron nail in his left, the ruby ring in his right. He clenched his hands tighter, until the iron and the gem bit into his flesh.

It was wrong to separate them.

He gripped them even more tightly, ignoring the pain. They were his, now. He would control them, not they, him. His breathing grew ragged as he squeezed his fists tighter and tighter.

A loud thud made the door shudder.

He gasped and opened his eyes.

Outside his room a low voice grunted, "Watch yourself." A heavy table scraped across the stone floor.

Jean opened his hands slowly, panting for breath. His palms were marked with deep red bruises. The nail had drawn blood from his left palm.

What madness had come over him? Thank the Saints, it had passed quickly. His hands shook as he returned the ring and the nail to his pouch. He sucked the wound like a bewildered child, until it stopped bleeding.

The guest house was full and every bench occupied by the time Jean left his room. The noise of their talking and laughter echoed against the close stone walls. Some benches had so many squeezed along them that those at the ends had to angle their outside legs to the side to prevent themselves tumbling onto the floor. The servers would have to look sharp to avoid tripping on them.

Through the far door he saw more tables set up outside, where villagers and townspeople would be eating. The tables were already filled, and people stood in the field holding their mugs and their knives, waiting for the feast to begin as they watched the jugglers and dwarves and other entertainers in their midst.

Dried rushes crackled under his feet as Jean crossed the room, looking for a place to squeeze himself in. The tables were bare, except for the knives and cups each traveler brought to his place, waiting for servers to carry in trenchers and platters of food. Someone moved aside, exposing a narrow space on the bench, and Jean placed his knife and cup on the table in front of him, taking care not to expose his palms.

A hearty meal was what he needed to banish whatever had come over him in his room. He exchanged greetings with the man who had made room for him, a fellow he had seen at the fair selling pots and metal implements. Trade had gone well for the metal smith, as everyone in earshot already knew. He boasted about his good fortune, a foolish thing to do before starting his journey home. Jean congratulated him, implying he had not done as well himself, which not only assured his own safety should scoundrels be listening, but endeared him so much to the metal smith that the man offered to buy his meal. Jean was sorry to say his meal and lodgings had already been paid.

"Then we will share a meal on the road." the metal smith declared. "You are headed for the market at Lyon, heh?" Lyon timed its market to follow Cluny's, taking advantage of all the pilgrims heading south.

Jean nodded politely. There was no point denying it, the metal smith would see him there; but he had no intention of walking anywhere near a man with money and a loose tongue.

The fellow across the table held up his hand. Jean turned. A portly, middle-aged monk had entered the room, followed by several servants carrying jugs of wine. The monk waited until the hall was quiet and then announced that as soon as everyone had had a mug of wine to quench their thirst, they must proceed to the square where the adulteress was to be stoned. The Feast of the Assumption would be served afterwards.

A cheer went up. The postponement of the stoning had not been received favourably on the first day of Market.

Jean did not cheer. He drank his wine sullenly but without comment and slapped his mug down on the table.

"'Twas the Bishop who delayed the stoning."

Jean stiffened, half-way to his feet.

"I hear he blanched when he heard the name of the adulteress. And now he has been called away, on church business. Called away from the Cluny Feast of the Assumption?" The metal smith shook his head, smirking.

"The Bishop is a busy man," Jean said. He did not smile back. This man was dangerous company. Jean left quickly, walking toward the square with everyone else. He bent down on his way, collecting good-sized stones, whether he wanted to or not. When he reached the crowded square he pushed his way near the front, where his righteous indignation at the sight of a sinful woman would be noticed by the monks and the bailiff, and be good for future business.

A wooden stake had been pounded into the ground in the centre of the square. An iron circlet was attached to its top, about a foot above the ground. Jean had seen such things before. The woman's hands would be bound behind her to the circlet, forcing her to her knees. She would not be able to shield herself. There was something pathetic about a woman hiding her face, and something brazen about one who did not. Justice was generally more palatable when the condemned were brazen—or at least appeared so.

At the edge of the crowd across the square from Jean people began moving, parting and surging back as two strong men pushed their way between them. Jean made out a dark head between the guards, bobbing sideways and backwards as though the person was fighting their hold. Then they were through the crowd.

The adulteress was small and slender, with long, dark hair that swung across her face as she struggled between the guards. She barely slowed them down as they crossed the open ground toward the wooden stake. When she saw the stake she stopped struggling abruptly and slumped forward, so that they had to carry her between them the last few feet.

The crowd quieted as the men reached the stake. They stood there, holding the woman up exposed for all to see. She wore only a thin undershift and shivered despite the heat, her arms crossed over her breasts to hide her shame.

The guards shoved her down onto the dirt. A ragged cheer broke out across the crowded square.

The woman raised her head defiantly and stared out at those who had come to watch her die, turning a scornful and accusing glare upon them. For a moment she stared straight at Jean, her face no longer hidden by the guards.

It was Sorrow! The same unearthly pale face, the same black hair, black gown, the same dark eyes, burning into his soul! He gaped at her, caught in her knowing eyes, exposed in all his petty lies and cruelties. She saw him as he was, as he let no one else see him.

The stones fell from his hands.

Then the guards pushed her against the low stake, forcing her sideways, and bound her hands to the iron circlet.

Jean stepped back into the crowd, ducking his head. She could denounce him, even now, and he would be lost. The ring would be discovered in his pouch; no one would believe she had given it to him. He must get away!

Yet he stood frozen as the crowd surged around him, unable to look away from the woman. She closed her eyes and bent her head when the stones began to hit her, but made no sound, even when they cut into her. Seeing blood, the crowd became more excited, yelling insults and curses as they pelted stones at her.

Jean stood still among them, willing himself to leave but unable to move. When she was dead, he would be safe. But when she was dead, she would take the truth of him with her, and she was dying in sin…

The thud of stones meeting flesh filled his ears. He felt, in his own body, the hot, burning pain as each one hit, tearing the thin fabric of her shift, digging into her bruised and bleeding flesh. It should be him there, not her. He could not move, speak, breathe…

Something shoved up against his leg. His breath emerged in a gasp. "Mama!"

A girl of five or six squeezed past him. She pushed her way through the crowd till she reached the front, crying all the while, "Mama! Mama!"

The woman's face was hidden, covered by her hair. The air was thick with stones. Again and again they struck her, but still she did not cry out.

"Mama!" the child screamed again.

The woman looked up.

"Mama!" She sprinted across the open ground. A stone whizzed past her ear. A second hit her back, flinging her to the ground.

The woman cried out then, a wild, animal shriek. It echoed, hideous and compelling, across the square.

She would be killed! The horror of it swept over Jean as he stared at the fallen child. No! He could not bear that! He shoved his way through the crowd, unable to look away from the woman, unable to escape the terror in her eyes as she strained against her bonds, struggling to reach the child sprawled on the ground. She shrieked again, a high, keening noise. Jean gritted his teeth to keep from screaming with her.

At the edge of the crowd he stopped. What was he doing? What in the name of Heaven had come over him?

Then the child moaned and the woman screamed again and Jean ran forward, unable to stop himself. The little girl tried to roll over as Jean reached her. He was no longer looking at the woman, but he felt her strain toward him as he bent down and scooped up the child.

A stone struck the side of his head as he straightened. He staggered, almost dropping the child. He regained his footing and turned to race back to the safety of the crowd.

"The adulterer!" a man cried.

Other voices took up the cry. He stepped forward, but the gap in the crowd where he had pushed through to get to the child had closed against him. A second stone hit his arm. There could be no mistaking that this one was meant for him. He saw the metal smith among the crowd, his arm drawn back, aiming. As Jean watched, he flung his stone.

It hit Jean's shoulder with a stinging blow that took his breath away. He crouched over the child, holding her tightly to him, more aware of the woman's anguished cries behind him and the child's terror than his own pain. Two more stones came flying at him; one missed its mark but the other hit the child's leg. She screamed and twisted, trying to burrow into him. A third stone hit her cheek, drawing blood. He wrapped both arms around her, leaving his own head exposed as he searched for an opening in the crowd.

To the left, several people turned, looking behind them. Jean ran toward them, taking advantage of their distraction. He was about to plunge among them when a large, burly man stepped forward and pushed him roughly back into the square. He looked up.

The cellarer stood, arms crossed, before him. "Set her down. There is sin in her, too. You saw how she is drawn to her false mother."

Jean blinked at the monk. He began to bend down, opening his arms. Feeling his hold loosen the child whimpered and grasped at his tunic.

He could not do it. He wanted to, oh how he wanted to. This was lunacy, risking his life, his livelihood, for a stranger's child. But he could not overcome the urgency of her need, stronger in him than his own. He shook his head, backing away from the cellarer's challenging stare, looking for an opening. More people were now craning their necks toward the commotion behind and to the left. Jean dodged around the cellarer, feeling his glare acutely, and plunged into the crowd.

He pushed his way through them, gasping for breath and nearly deafened by the pounding of his own heart. Finally he stopped, exhausted, out of the spray of stones. The people around him ignored him, returning to the easier sport of stoning the bound adulteress.

The little girl's body shook against his chest. Jean held her tightly, his hand cupping the back of her head. Her dark curls brushed his fingers and he could feel the deep shudder of her silent sobs, the high, quick pounding of her heart. Shielding her face, he turned to look at the woman again. She knelt in the dirt, no longer screaming but writhing with pain as the rocks struck her.

It was not the same woman at all. How could he have imagined that she was Sorrow? Even with her head bowed, he could see that this woman's cheeks were broader, her features plain and more filled out than the other. She was clearly at least ten years older, with dull brown hair, not shimmering black, and she was not wearing a black kirtle but only a dark undershift. What had made him imagine it was her? A shudder of relief passed through him.

The child stirred against him. Where was its father? He looked around.

On the other side of the square a man stood at the forefront of the crowd. Those nearby pressed rocks into his hands. His face was twisted in rage and pain, his mouth open, but his voice was swallowed by the crowd's roar of encouragement as he flung stone after stone at the bound woman, hurling them at her with a crazed ferocity, too close to miss. They tore into her flesh, pounding her into the ground, crushing her against the wet red dirt.

Jean closed his eyes. The heat of the crowd was like a fire surrounding him. He held the child tightly, listening to her quick little breaths and her fluttering heart and feeling the dampness on her cheek through his tunic. He had been older than her when he lost his mother, but still too young. He held onto her as nobody had held him.

When he opened his eyes again, the woman was no longer visible. A mound of stones had grown around her, with only a few small hints of what lay hidden beneath them—a bare foot, a red-brown fold of fabric, three outstretched fingers.

Someone tugged on the sleeve of his tunic. He looked down into the face of a boy, ten or eleven years old. Jean stared at him blankly.

"You have my sister," the boy said. He let go of Jean's tunic. Jean saw his hands trembling. His face was very white, his eyes wide and blank. He spoke with no expression at all.

Jean set the girl down. He had been holding her against him so tightly it hurt to loosen his arms, to let her go. She leaned against his leg, blinking. The boy took her hand and turned to lead her away.

Jean's arms hung empty at his sides. "Do not look back," he said.

He watched the backs of the children walking away from the square. The boy held his little sister's hand tightly, keeping her close beside him. That twisted angry man stoning his wife would be no help to either of them.

"Never look back," he called after them.

His voice broke on the words.

# Chapter 8

"Go break your fast in the guesthouse," Celeste told Marie, shaking her awake as soon as dawn broke. She had been up half the night trying to think what to do while her lazy maid slept.

Marie rubbed the sleep from her eyes. "But I eat in the kitchen with the servants."

"Then offer to carry things to the guesthouse. And keep your eyes and ears open while you are there."

Marie looked at her blankly.

"Find out who is staying here, where they are going, when they will leave." Anything that would help her to get away.

When Marie left, she went through her belongings. Nothing but ribbons and hair pins in the silk bag beside her brush and comb. The pins were decorated with colored glass instead of gems. Worth something, perhaps, but where were her sapphire pins? Surely she had not sold those for the abbey. Or the ruby ones that sparkled in her dark hair, and matched her—

—Well, perhaps Lord Bernard had been practical in not sending those with her, she thought, rubbing her thumb against her bare finger. At least she remembered her jewellery. Much good the memory did her now! Still, it was a positive sign. The vestiges of her illness were receding.

She continued searching through her scanty possessions. Nothing of any value. A peasant would have more wealth about her. Perhaps she could sell the cloak?

She lifted it down from the wall hook and shook it out. It jingled. She shook it again. The unmistakable sound repeated. She knelt on the floor and patted it down until she found the money pouch tied inside, under the left shoulder. Her fingers trembled as she opened it.

Thirty deniers. Had Lord Bernard hidden the purse in her cloak to prevent its being stolen, or had she hidden it from him before he brought her here? That would be a useful thing to recall. Either way, she now had money. She could leave the convent.

The tower bell was ringing Mass when Marie finally returned.

"There are eight people staying in the guesthouse, My Lady," Marie said, hurrying to help Celeste into her kirtle. "Three peasants working for their keep and five pilgrims on their way to Cluny to celebrate the Feast of the Assumption." She began to braid Celeste's hair, piling the thick black braids about her head.

"Pilgrims? Describe them to me."

"An older woman escorted by her maid and her husband's manservant. They are accompanied by a Cluniac monk and a young man who is traveling with them, but he does not wear the red cross of a pilgrim."

"Is the woman nobility?"

"No, Lady. They address her as 'Mistress Blanche'."

That was good. A commoner would not question a Lady about her reasons for traveling. "When will they leave?"

"They argued about that while they ate. The young man wanted to leave this morning. He is eager to get to the Assumption Market, but the monk said it will last all week. Imagine, a week-long market…"

The Cluny market! Everyone with something to sell would be there. And the peddler had been travelling north! With her ring in his pouch, no doubt.

"They are leaving this morning?" Oh, pray they had not left already. She leaped up, ready to run to the door.

"No, My Lady, tomorrow morning. The pilgrims insisted on taking a day to rest. The monk said their horses were tired, but I think it is the old woman who needs the rest."

"They are on horseback," Celeste groaned. "How can we travel with them?" Perhaps there was a horse for sale in the abbey stable? She sat down abruptly. "Pin up my hair quickly, Marie. I will recover at Mass today."

"Travel with them? We are going with them?" Marie gasped. "To Cluny?"

"I am going with them." She could not afford two horses; she would have to leave Marie behind. That was inconvenient. A Lady would never travel without her maid. Even the wife of a common landowner or merchant would have a maid. She sighed. "There is no mount for you."

"Why can I not ride Blackie?"

"Blackie?"

"The pony. You remember Blackie, My Lady."

"Of course I do. Where is he?"

"In the stable, right beside Honey."

"You told me Lord Bernard left only one horse in the stable."

"One of *his* horses. Honey and Blackie belong to you. You brought them with you from your father's house." She spoke patiently.

*I am not fooling her,* Celeste thought. *She knows I cannot remember.* She examined Marie's face closely. The girl looked back at her, her eyes wide and earnest in her open face. *She will not tell; she is bound to me.* Why or how remained a mystery, but looking into the girl's face, Celeste was certain of it. Nevertheless, until she knew its source, she dared not trust Marie's loyalty too far.

"I was ill when I came here," she said. "There are things I was not aware of. Pay it no mind. We will go to Cluny with the pilgrims."

Marie clapped her hands and gave a little hop, grinning broadly.

"Stop that," Celeste said, rising from her stool. "We must go to Mass. And then I will speak to the Abbess."

"…It is a miracle. I am fully recovered," Celeste concluded.

"Yes, I witnessed your little miracle," the Abbess said, leaning back in the chair behind her writing table. "Nevertheless, I cannot write you a letter of permission to travel to Cluny."

"It is a holy pilgrimage! To thank the Virgin on her Feast Day for my miraculous recovery when I knelt before her image today during Mass."

"I will send a message to your husband. When he comes, he may take you to Cluny."

"The celebration of the Assumption will be over then."

"Mass will still be said. Holy Mary will still hear your prayers."

*The market would be over.* Celeste clenched her gloved hands below the table where the Abbess could not see. "Did my husband send me here to be a prisoner?"

"He did not send you here at all. He brought you at your own insistence."

"I asked to come?" *Never. It must be false.*

"You were distraught. You would not eat, nor allow your husband's physic to attend you. You said that God would find you here and nowhere else, or you would die."

She paused. Celeste stared at her, speechless.

"'Find you'—A strange choice of words," the Abbess continued. "God does not lose us, though we might lose ourselves. You were near to madness in your grief."

Had she lost herself? Misplaced her self? She touched the cross at her throat. No. Her soul was not lost. She had resisted the demons. But she had changed. Had been changed. That other was gone, was lost. The weak one, the girl full of sweetness and obedience and faith. But she had had some courage, after all; she had run away. What had she been running from?

The Abbess was watching her. She forced herself to smile. "And Holy Mary found me here, and healed me."

"So it would seem."

"Do you not believe me?" She raised her chin, insulted. Even if she were speaking falsely she should be believed; she was a Lady.

"I do not believe in people. They are seldom as they seem. Only God is constant."

"God need not change: He is omnipotent," Celeste said bitterly, before she could prevent herself. Only the powerless must learn to adapt.

The Abbess regarded her silently.

Celeste endured her scrutiny. She obviously guessed at more than Celeste was saying. Still, the woman was her aunt. She must have some feeling for her sister's daughter.

"You must let me go," she said. "You are my aunt."

"I am not that kind of aunt."

Celeste looked down. She was a prisoner, then. Her fingers curled into fists; she forced them to straighten. What would the earlier Celeste do, the one who had been lost?

She would submit to the Abbess' decision. She was a paltry thing. Celeste would not even pretend to be her. She raised her head.

"I am not ready to meet my husband yet."

The Abbess nodded. "The truth at last. But it is a poor reason for holy pilgrimage."

"I have promised Our Lady that I would go. It is not your place to prevent me."

"It is if your reason is a false one."

"Or yours."

The Abbess sat back. After a moment she said calmly, "I am not keeping you here for your husband's sake, child."

"You should be helping me, for my mother's sake."

"I act for God's sake."

Celeste lowered her eyes. She would gain nothing by antagonizing the woman.

"And now there is the problem of your possession."

Celeste froze. "I am not possessed," she whispered when she could breathe again.

"Do not tempt me with stupidity, child. It does not matter whether you are or not. The accusation is enough."

"Not if you deny it."

The Abbess raised an eyebrow. "Your charade this morning before Our Lady's statue helped. If only I could trust you not to follow it with some foolishness like running barefoot through the abbey gates or tearing your mattress apart again."

Celeste flushed. "I will be more circumspect now that I am well."

The Abbess sighed. She tapped her finger on her table.

Celeste held her breath.

"These rumours of demons and possession excite my nuns and novices, disturbing them from their meditations. Their souls are my responsibility, and their souls are not focused on God."

"Perhaps you should send me away for a while? On a holy pilgrimage? For the sake of the abbey and the souls entrusted to your keeping."

The Abbess smiled. "Your absence, I admit, would restore their attention to God, and a pilgrimage may confirm your innocence. If the pilgrims will accept you in their party."

"Their confessor has already agreed. I spoke to him after Mass."

The Abbess' gaze cooled.

"I would not waste your time asking, if it were not possible for me to accompany them."

"Five days. I will let your Lord husband know that you will be back here then, ready to return home to him."

"We are going to Cluny." Celeste waved the Abbess' letter of permission in front of Marie.

"Oh! Think what we will see!" Marie did a pirouette in the middle of the room and laughed out loud. "They say the cathedral is the most beautiful in all of France, and the largest in all the world! And the food at the Feast of the Assumption is better than the King is served in Paris. And the festival market! It is so big you cannot see it all in one day, and there is nothing that you cannot buy there!" She stopped suddenly, blushing.

"It would be best if we could leave today," Celeste said. The stable boy was already on his way to Lord Bernard. She had five days to find her ring and return wearing proof of her husband's vow.

Marie's outstretched hands beckoned her. She and Marie used to hold hands and twirl each other in a circle, Celeste remembered suddenly, when she was Marie's age, and Marie but a child. She would throw her head back and let her hair fly behind her as they twirled, abandoning herself to happiness. She watched Marie twirl. She wanted to join her as she once had, to forget that Marie was a peasant and she was a Lady. But she had lost the ability to reach out, to abandon herself in a shared emotion. To share an emotion. Marie's joy was inexplicable to her, a spice she had lost the ability to taste.

"The Festival of the Assumption," Marie cried, hugging herself.

I know what it is to be happy, Celeste thought, watching Marie. She could not remember how it felt, but she remembered twirling with Marie. She had been happy like Marie, breathlessly happy. How strange the memory felt, a foreign language she no longer spoke.

If she had really sold her sorrow, would she not be happy now? Or was happiness dearer bought than that?

Or easier lost. She could not remember when it had fled her. Never mind: she had been happy once, and she would be again. But first she must reclaim her ring and her station. She would not be destroyed by a crafty peddler.

The ride to Cluny took most of the day.

"We could walk there faster," Celeste muttered under her breath when the young monk signalled their third rest stop to accommodate the old woman. He was as solicitous of her as if she was nobility. He should have paid more attention to Celeste, who was a Lady, than to the old woman, however rich her husband might be. But he did not seem to understand that.

Celeste stood under the shade of a tree beside the road, refusing to admit that she, too, was tired. She had not ridden in months, and would have been content with their pace if she were not constantly aware that the boy would reach her husband tonight. Would Lord Bernard come for her at once?

He would assume she was waiting for him at the abbey. He need not rush to her. If he felt that way about her, he would not have let her go in the first place. But then, why set a spy on her? If something had happened in his castle as she feared, something that involved him, he might come at once.

And when he found her missing? She had assured the Abbess she would return in five days. Lord Bernard would be told that when he arrived. Even if he left his castle as soon as the boy arrived, she would be three days gone when he reached the abbey. He would surely wait two more rather than ride to Cluny and try to find her.

She must confront the peddler alone when she found him. If Lord Bernard learned she had willingly given away her marriage ring, it would not matter that she had later retrieved it.

Celeste put her hand to her forehead, wiping away salty beads of perspiration. Even in the shade, the sun was hot. She untied her flask and tipped it to her lips. The water was warm and stale.

Lord Bernard might not come at all. He might be away from the castle when the boy arrived.

He might, he might, he might! No wonder her stomach was queasy and her head pounded. She spread her cloak on the ground and sat upon it. She was not as badly off as Mistress Blanche, who sagged in her saddle and coughed repeatedly. She sat a few feet away against the tree, her face pale and glistening with sweat and fever spots on her cheeks.

"I am sorry to slow you down," Mistress Blanche called to Celeste while they waited for the manservant to bring their horses. "I am going to the Mass of the Assumption to pray to Holy Mary to cure me." The effort of speaking brought on another fit of coughing.

*At this pace we will arrive too late,* Celeste thought. "Holy Mary will cure you, as She did me," she replied politely, standing up to avoid the old woman's spittle.

The Abbess had warned her this morning that fevers could leap from person to person, like fleas.

"Holy Mary has healed me; she will protect me on this pilgrimage to honor her," Celeste had replied. She knew the language of piety, even if she had lost the rhythm of its meaning.

The young man travelling with them helped Celeste into the saddle, his face twitching with impatience. It was a miracle he had not ridden on and left them.

Their dragging pace did not dampen Marie's enthusiasm. She chattered to Mistress Blanche, keeping a little distance between them as Celeste had ordered and raising her voice to cover it. She hummed little tunes to herself. She speculated on what they might see at the market to everyone in the party, oblivious to their lack of response, and discussed the Festival of the Assumption eagerly with the young monk. She made bracelets and coronets of wildflowers when they stopped to rest, and picked clover and young green shoots for the pony, Blackie.

Celeste wanted to slap the silliness out of her and wanted even more to share such happiness and wondered why the others were so indulgent to a foolish young servant.

The sun dipped in the west. Dusk turned the trees into black silhouettes against an orange sky, reminding Celeste of the midnight garden. She did not want to travel through that silent, silvered darkness. She urged her horse ahead and asked Father Jacques whether they were almost there.

"Soon enough," he replied, which did not answer her question.

At last the tall spires of Cluny's cathedral appeared in the distance. They picked up their pace at the sight, the old woman as eager as any of them to reach their night's lodging.

The guesthouse at Cluny was full when they arrived, and they had missed the evening meal. Celeste was disgusted with her companions and irritated with the young monk for allowing the delays which caused them to arrive so late.

Father Jacques led them to the pilgrim's hostel, but it, too, was full. They wandered in weary circles down the narrow, dark streets. There was no response at the first two inns he brought them to; the third had space for them only in the main hall.

"Mistress Blanche must have a bed," Father Jacques insisted, but all of the private rooms above were taken.

"I will be all right," the old woman assured them, her voice a sickly whisper. "We will stay here."

The monk conceded reluctantly. "Send your manservant if you need me," he said.

"I will make do without a private room, also," Celeste said coolly.

Father Jacques nodded, completely missing her point, and rode off to the monks' dormitory in the monastery.

They left their horses at the stable with Mistress Blanche's manservant and made their way wearily to the inn. The entrance was dimly lit with rush lights. These would be extinguished soon, the innkeeper warned them, as he was on his way to bed, himself.

The inn was smoky and hot, and crowded with the still forms of sleeping guests. They picked their way around the bodies to find space for themselves where they could. The floor rushes smelled of spilled beer, stale food, and urine, and rustled in places suspiciously like the furtive movements of rodents. Too tired to object, Celeste pulled her cloak around her and lay down to sleep.

It was full daybreak when she opened her eyes. She pushed the heavy black cloak off her shoulders and sat up. Most of the guests had already left. She reached for the money pouch tied at her waist; it was still there, reassuringly heavy. She had been wise to pull the cloak tightly around her, despite the heat.

A long table had been set up on the other side of the room, with benches on either side. Celeste rinsed her fingers in a bowl of warm water sitting on the hearth, and tore a hunk of bread from the long, grainy loaf resting on the table. She poured herself a cup of lukewarm ale from the jug beside the bread and sat on the bench. Marie came in, smelling of the stable, to report that Honey and Blackie were well cared for.

If Lord Bernard had left this morning he would reach the abbey tomorrow night. She emptied her cup and stood up. Three days to find the peddler and get back her ring.

They heard the fair before they came to it: the crowing of cocks, the braying of donkeys, the squeal of pigs and clucking of hens, the shouts of merchants and tradesmen hawking their wares and the constant babble of human voices from the large common field at the edge of town. It was the largest fair in France, and people came from all the surrounding towns and villages, as well as distant boroughs. Pilgrims from Brittany, Normandy, Flanders, Germany, England—all the northern realms—had also come to celebrate the Feast of the

Assumption. Every language and accent imaginable added to the clamor and confusion of the crowded market.

Before they reached the commons, Celeste found a narrow alley and ordered Marie to guard the entrance while she walked a little way in. Crouching against the 'stone wall of a building she untied her belt, hitched up her skirts and refastened the belt around the waist of her chemise, letting the deep folds of her kirtle fall over it. She would not be able to get at her money, but neither would a thief, and the market was sure to be full of them.

At the edge of the fairgrounds, they came upon a noisy circle of people. Pushing her way through them, Celeste saw a shallow hole dug into the ground, little bigger than a wagon wheel. Inside this circle two large cocks tore at each other with their sharp beaks and spurred claws. The ground around them was coated with blood and feathers. Excited spectators pressed close to the pit, yelling encouragement to one or the other of the furious birds.

The black cock flew up, sinking his spur into the other's chest, drawing a spurt of blood. As he fluttered down again, the red cock's head darted forward. Its vicious beak tore into the black cock's head, leaving a bloody socket where its eye had been. The black cock hopped back, shaking its head from side to side as it tried to see in both directions. It staggered like a one-eyed drunk, to the hilarity of the crowd.

"Come away, Lady Celeste," Marie cried. Her voice sounded frightened and on the verge of tears. "This is horrible! You never liked cock fights before."

Celeste watched the russet-colored cock finish off the black one, opening its chest with its sharp talons and pecking at its half-blind head, scattering flesh and blood and black feathers over the ground. The black cock fought bravely, but it was finished when it lost its eye.

"I should have put a bet on the red cock," Celeste muttered.

Behind her, Marie began to sniffle.

"It is only a cock!"

"It used to make you weep, to see an animal wounded." Marie was crying herself. "You said it was worse than hurting a person, because animals could not understand."

"I am not as young and foolish, now." Celeste turned away. Weeping over wounded animals? Absurd. Yet she felt a loss, as though some part of her had been removed. How could she be someone she could not remember? Of course she was the same person. When her memory came back it would all be clear, and she would not be a stranger to herself.

The fair was not as big as Marie had predicted, but it was larger than Celeste expected. Marie skipped here and there ogling everything at the merchants' stalls and running back to tell her.

"Stop that," she said. What was the point of looking at goods they could not buy? What did she care about them? Lord Bernard had bought her gowns and jewels and she had run from him into a nunnery. Beautiful things had a price.

Failure also had a price. There would be those glad to see her pay it, no doubt, envying her climb into nobility. She looked about for the peddler, determined to disappoint them.

What would she say when she found him? Would he recognize her? She would have to send Marie on an errand so she could talk to him privately. And if he denied having her ring, or refused to give it back?

He would not dare. He was a peasant and she was a Lady. She need only find him.

"Fortune! Hear your future revealed!" a dark-haired, olive-skinned man cried suddenly beside her. Startled, she looked his way. A gypsy woman stood at the center of a small crowd, telling fortunes.

The gypsy's loose woollen robe was dyed with a bold, striped pattern. Her hair was hidden under a wide-brimmed yellow hat. Several gypsy men in equally bold attire stood around her, their dark faces smiling and animated while their eyes watched the crowd intently. The fortune-teller held her customer's hand in hers, examining it and occasionally touching the lines on the man's palm while she spoke. As she told his fortune, the man exclaimed several times in surprise and delight, interpreting her predictions according to past and present events in his life.

Celeste looked down at her palms. Was her past written there? Was her whole life already mapped out, beginning to end, if she could only read it? She closed her hands. Did she want to?

The gypsy said something which made the man laugh. Celeste looked up. His face glowed with delight.

She pushed her way through the crowd of spectators, ignoring their protests. If other people knew their past, why should she not know her future? Why should the gypsy not make her as happy as she had made that man? Perhaps, at the least, she would tell her where to find the peddler. She reached the front of the crowd as the fortune-teller finished and let the man's hand drop. Celeste held her left hand out, palm up, in front of the gypsy. The woman reached to take it.

One of the gypsy men stepped forward, frowning, holding his cupped hand toward her.

She could not reach her purse. If she left to find somewhere private to retrieve it, the gypsies might move on. She thrust her open palm toward the gypsy woman until their hands touched.

The fortune-teller gasped. "What have you done?" she cried, pulling her hand back and staring at Celeste's palm.

Celeste's fingers curled over her exposed palm. She forced them open again. "I want to hear my future."

The woman looked at her pityingly. "You have no future, unless you can undo what you have done."

# Chapter 9

Celeste yanked her hand back. She turned and ran, dodging through the crowd, humiliated by the stares of those who had heard the gypsy. The faces of strangers stared after her, cold and accusing.

She had been here before, or at a fair very like this, when she was Marie's age, with her parents and her older brother. Her parents had stopped at a merchant's booth to look at cloth, and stood there arguing over how many new kirtles she and her mother would need when Lord Bernard came to visit. The name meant little to her then, a man she had met once; she had not been told why he was coming back.

She had grown bored and wandered away, following some jugglers. Their wit and dexterity held her enthralled until they cast their cloaks on the ground with a flourish. She had no coin to toss and looked up, realizing only then how long she had been following them. Where was the cloth merchant's stall? Where were her parents and her brother?

She tried to retrace her steps but the jugglers had wound their way through the fair and she could not remember which way she had come. She searched the crowd, looking for a familiar face in vain. To her left she spied a stall piled high with cloth. She pushed her way over to it, but when she got near it was not the same merchant. She looked around, trying not to cry.

"Have you seen a cloth merchant?" she asked a passerby.

"There are dozens," the man said. "Which one do you want?"

"He had a—" She stopped. A beard or a moustache? Or both?

"There are two cloth merchants back that way."

She ran off in the direction he had indicated. Neither merchant was the one her parents had been talking to. They directed her down another row of stalls. She was tired now, but she kept going, searching the crowd as she went. Where was her brother? He always found her when they played the hiding game. "Please, find me," she whimpered, struggling through the crowd.

So much time had passed. Her father would be cross, he hated waiting. Would he go home without her? She rubbed her eyes, beginning to weep despite her efforts not to.

Someone seized her from behind. She twisted around with a cry of fear.

"I thought I would never find you," her brother said, grinning down at her.

She threw her arms around him, buried her face in his chest. "I knew you would find me, Pierre."

There was no one to rescue her today as she ran through the fair. She raced past merchants, tradesmen, and entertainers, as frightened as the child in her memory. She was lost in the present, without a past to moor her; only wisps of memory like the edges of a frayed rope torn from its anchor. All around, people shouted and laughed after her as she ran.

She reached a clump of trees and stopped in their shadows, bent over, pulling in great shuddering breaths and wiping her eyes furiously. Marie caught up with her there and stood silently catching her breath.

Celeste glanced sideways at Marie. She had cried out when she heard the fortune-teller's words, and she would not meet Celeste's eyes now.

*Undo what you have done.* Celeste pursed her lips as though she had spoken aloud. Her chest fluttered, panicky, the way it had in her nightmare. Why had she been so frightened inside her husband's castle? Frightened and helpless, like a lost child.

Marie's eyes were closed, her lips moving soundlessly in prayer. Did Marie know what had happened there? Celeste shivered. If Marie knew anything, she did not want to hear it.

*You have no future.* Or was it the loss of her ring? Had the gypsy seen its absence, read the consequences on her hand? What future did she have if Lord Bernard set aside their marriage?

She had not prayed in a long time, she realized, watching Marie. Had she done something so terrible her soul no longer yearned toward God? But she had insisted on being sent to a nunnery. She had hoped God would find her there, the Abbess said. When had that hope withered away? The Abbess' words came back to her: *Imagine what you would become if you could feel no sorrow.*

Was that the deed she must undo, her trade with the peddler?

She straightened. Foolishness! How could the gypsy know anything? It was a trick to entertain her audience at the expense of someone who held out her hand with no coin in it. She was becoming as superstitious as Marie, standing there with her hands clasped and her eyes closed. The child was probably praying for protection from her mad mistress.

Celeste sighed. It would be no use trying to dissuade the girl of her superstitions; she had tried that before. "The gypsy spoke true," she said, instead. She waited until Marie looked up. "There is little future for a woman who has run away from her husband."

"Is that what she meant?" Marie's eyes shifted uneasily.

"What else?"

"Nothing," Marie said, too quickly.

"The gypsy is wrong," Celeste continued. "I have not run away. I am on pilgrimage. Mistress Blanche is on pilgrimage without her husband."

"She had his permission."

"I think that is what the gypsy saw. I did not get my husband's permission to come here."

The fear eased in Marie's face. "Lord Bernard was not there to ask," she said.

Celeste smiled. "That is true."

"But you will go back to him?"

"Of course I will. He is my husband."

"Then you do have a future," Marie said. "You must have, Lady Celeste, because my future is with you."

"Everyone has a future," she said. The child was right about her own: who else would tolerate such an awkward, outspoken little maid?

Marie's face brightened. "Then we can see the rest of the fair?"

How quickly Marie's moods lightened. Like a homing pigeon, she was drawn irresistibly toward happiness, as though it were her nest. It was Celeste who had no home until she regained her ring. "Yes," she said grimly. "We will search the rest of the fair."

Celeste tried to remember what the peddler was selling, but she had seen only his face, leering down at her, and his coin. She pushed through a group of people gathered around a merchant's stall. Not him.

She glanced at the vendor's table, piled high with gray woollen cloaks. Each cloak had a bright red cross sewn on the right shoulder. There was also a stack of broad-brimmed gray hats, with small red crosses on their front and scarves sewn to them. Tall wooden staffs leaned at the side of the table, and leather scrips, made to carry a pilgrim's badges and other small treasures, were tied to pegs around the edges of the table. A steady flow of money poured into the hands of the merchant standing behind the table as people chose the items they needed and others took their place.

"Why are so many people buying pilgrim's garb?" She had not directed her question to Marie, but the girl answered.

"Cluny is the beginning of many pilgrim's routes: one of them goes to the Apostle James's tomb at Santiago de Compostella, and another to Saint-Gilles and Marseilles, where ships leave for the Holy Land. Father Jacques told me while we rode here."

"Mince pies! Hot pies and pasties!" a voice cried from a stall behind them. "Salty and sweet!"

The savory smell of hot meat pies reached Celeste, strong enough to make her mouth water. She was surprised she had not noticed it before and breathed it in hungrily. Mixed in with the rich, meaty aroma was the sweet smell of apple and berry pasties, even more tempting than the pies. Their dinner was paid for at the Inn, but if she had not hidden her money beneath her kirtle she would not be able to resist buying one.

Would there come a time when she could not buy herself a meal? Would she ride back to Lord Bernard a woman in possession of her position and her past, or a hungry, helpless beggar?

She took a deep breath and hurried on, peering left and right at each vendor. He must be here. But when she had walked down every row of stalls, she still had not found him. Had he left already? It was late afternoon now. Or was he selling his spices outside the vendor's area? She looked wearily toward the edge of the fairgrounds. Why would he set up there, so far from the crowds of buyers?

"A jongleur!"

As soon as Marie said the word Celeste remembered hearing a jongleur sing his stories to the accompaniment of his fiddle. Lord Bernard had arranged for one to come to the castle and entertain their guests at Yuletide last. His stories had come to life in the leaping flames of the hearth fire, while his voice rose and fell across the room singing of heroic deeds and battles, of love and loss and redemption.

Had she been happy then? Her memory of the jongleur was rich with the passions in his stories, but she could not recall her own emotions. Had she smiled down the table at her husband, had she laughed at his jests and opened his Yuletide gift with delight? An intense emotion swept over her. She caught her breath—and it was gone. She frowned in concentration, but could not call up even an echo of the sensation, let alone the reason for it. How would she find happiness, when she could not remember where she had left it?

Was the peddler a demon who bought her memories rather than her sorrow? "Holy Mary pray for us," she whispered before she could stop herself. What worse thing might he do to her if she found him and demanded her ring back?

No, he was no demon, just a peddler.

Then how had she lost her memory?

A lance of fire behind her eyes made her gasp. She brushed her hand across her brow. She was exhausted. She would rest a while, and listen to the jongleur.

He was singing the last lines of the Song of Roland as they reached him. A rain of coins fell onto the cloak he had spread on the ground beside him. When he was satisfied, he scooped them up and introduced a new song: the forbidden romance between Tristan and his Lord's wife, Iseult. He sang it sweetly, playing his fiddle in sympathy with the mood of the poem. They listened to the entire piece, lost in the romance and tragedy of the tale.

"I wish I had something to give him," Marie sighed when it was over and others were tossing coins onto his cloak.

Celeste shrugged. The jongleur's cloak held a quarter as many coins as she had in her pouch, and he had been singing all day. He was doing well enough.

She looked around to discover that most of the merchants were packing up. The market was over. She jumped up, scanning those left; the peddler was not among them.

"What are you looking for, My Lady?" Marie asked, hurrying to keep up.

"Father Jacques," Celeste lied quickly. "We will need an escort back to the abbey in two days." So soon! Tomorrow they would attend Mass to celebrate Mary's Assumption to Heaven. Surely the peddler would be there, or at the feast that would follow. She must find him tomorrow!

Over a thousand people crowded into the Cluny cathedral to hear the Mass for the Assumption of Mary. Celeste stood at the front among the nobility, nauseated by the hot, still air. She would have preferred a less conspicuous position, but Father Jacques might have mentioned to the Abbot her miraculous cure at the sight of Holy Mary's image, and her subsequent pilgrimage here to thank the Virgin. She must be seen among her rank this morning.

Her decision was justified when the Bishop began his Latin sermon, for he mentioned her cure among other miracles at this holy time. He did not point her out, but she had been compelled out of courtesy to introduce herself to those around her, who were now glancing sideways at her. They would not forget her, if her husband came asking. At least she had not divulged where she was staying.

Marie squirmed beside her, shifting from foot to foot on the hard stone floor. She straightened when the Bishop began to speak in French, and listened anxiously to the perils of a soul without the intercession of the Holy Church.

When the monks, led by the Bishop, began their procession out, Celeste went to the statue of the Virgin Mary and knelt down. She had claimed to be on pilgrimage to thank the Virgin and must do so. She made the sign of the cross, then pressed her palms together, leaning her forehead against them. It was so hot. "Holy Virgin," she whispered. What next? She had used to pray. "Holy Mary—" There must be a prayer to do with healing.

*Holy Mother Mary, send down your healing. You, who lost your son, spare me the suffering you endured. Heal my Etienne. On the strength of my faith, let him be spared...*

In a rush, the memory returned: thus had she knelt and thus had she begged. And she had been refused. The words she sought now died in her breast. Holy Mary had not healed Etienne and would not heal her. There was no mercy in Saint Mary, then or now. She had pleaded and she had grieved. Now she was only weary: empty of emotion and empty of prayer. She rose slowly to her feet.

They were among the last to leave the cathedral. It was a long walk back to the inn, through the town square. They heard the babble of voices before they reached it.

"Let us walk another way around," Marie suggested, when their street turned into the square and the noisy throng became visible.

Celeste hesitated. "Go learn what is taking place," she said. "I will sit there." She motioned to a stone bench in front of one of the buildings at the corner of the square, where she would see everyone passing by.

While Marie was gone the crowd grew, filling the square with jeers and raucous shouts. So many people. Celeste stood on the bench, searching for the peddler, until she saw Marie returning, and stepped down.

"They are stoning an adulteress," Marie said, her round face scrunched up.

The tragic song of Tristan's love for Iseult, married to another, was still fresh in Celeste's mind. Was this adulteress bewitchingly beautiful, like Iseult? Celeste walked toward the square. Perhaps she herself had had an illicit romance. Perhaps that was the source of her sorrow—that she had dared everything for a great passion and now they were separated? The wife of a Lord would not be stoned like a commoner; she would be sent to an abbey.

"We are not going to watch?" Marie gasped, stumbling after her.

Celeste frowned. "Why should I not?"

"You would never have done so before."

"Do not tell me what I would or would not have done before my illness," Celeste cried. "What does that matter now?"

"Not before your illness," Marie's lower lip trembled. "Before you sold the nail."

Celeste stared at Marie until the crowd roared again, enticing her to push her way forward where she might see the woman's face. Had the woman been happy with her lover? Was that happiness worth the risk she had taken?

The shouts and jeers of the crowd were deafening. Celeste stood on tiptoe, craning her neck to see the woman kneeling on the ground.

When they began throwing stones, the woman bowed her head to avoid them. Her hair fell forward, hiding her face. It was impossible to tell whether she was beautiful or not.

A large stone hit the side of her head. Celeste was close enough to see her shudder with the impact.

She looked away. Life was not like the jongleur's songs. What did it matter now if the woman was beautiful, or whether she had been happy? And what did it matter that she would die for it? The woman was guilty. Even the innocent were not spared; why should the guilty be?

A child ran out of the crowd to her right, crying for her mama. The woman looked up. She was disappointingly plain, and when she started to scream she seemed very ordinary. Celeste had at least admired her silent fortitude.

A man ran into the center of the square. His back was to Celeste as he bent down, lifting the child, who had fallen.

The adulteress pulled against her bindings toward him. Her mouth opened, but Celeste could not hear what she cried out. Her eyes were wide, desperate. Not even the smallest residue of happiness or passion showed on her face as she looked at the man. Was happiness so fleeting, then? Well, what had she expected?

The man turned away from the adulteress, carrying the child, but the crowd would not let him in. He stepped forward, giving her a clear look at his profile—

"You!" she cried, staring at the peddler.

"You know this man?"

"He cheated me!"

"I offered to buy his dinner, and now I learn he is a friend to sinners and a dishonest man. Here." The man pressed several stones into her hand.

Without thinking, she threw one at the peddler. It glanced off his shirt. She imagined his face leering over her, felt the pain as he ripped her ring from her finger. Raising her hand she flung the two remaining stones as hard as she could.

"My Lady, no!" Marie's frantic voice cried behind her.

Her stone hit the child's cheek, drawing blood. The child screamed, and lay still.

She had killed a babe. She killed him!

"No!" she screamed. "No! I never meant to hurt him!"

The peddler looked in Celeste's direction. His face was filled with sorrow, an agony of grief…

A wave of dizziness hit her. Her knees buckled.

# Chapter 10

"Y ou will have to put her aside." Eleanor reached over the table to cut a leg from the guinea fowl with her knife. The juices ran down her chin when she bit into it.

As though Celeste were a morsel of meat to be tossed aside when he had had his fill. Lord Bernard said nothing, not trusting his voice against the anger that burned in his chest. His sister had never shown any fondness for his wife. Not that he had expected a friendship between them. Celeste was the same age as Eleanor's third child—the son who had married off his sisters and evicted his mother from their Anjou castle within a year of his father's death. Neither of the daughters had invited their mother to live with them, forcing her to rely on her brother's charity. Eleanor was no longer favourably disposed toward the young.

"You have no just cause to do so."

Bernard glanced at his cousin: Raimond, always the courtier, honor-bound to defend his Lady Mistress. Celeste had a ready friend in him.

"She is as beautiful and as useless as when you married her," Eleanor said. "And no fit wife for you."

Was that sarcasm in her voice, or bitterness? She was a plain woman, and would not have married at all without her title and handsome dowry; nor would her daughters be married if their father had not settled their dowries before his death, so that their brother could not get at the lands and monies meant for their prospective husbands. Even so, they had not married well. Bitterness, then, Bernard decided.

"Lady Celeste has borne a healthy son," Raimond said gallantly.

"Who has died."

"Not from any neglect on her part."

There was no denying that. Celeste had been a devoted mother. Too much so. It was unnatural, the way she had doted on the child. He caught Eleanor watching him.

She would not speak this way if Celeste were gentry-born. Nevertheless, she only voiced what others were already saying. Three months had passed since Etienne's death.

"She will never give you an heir now. She cannot even manage your household."

"You did not want me to wed her from the beginning," Bernard said, breaking his silence. Immediately he regretted it. Now he had joined this conversation, he could no longer ignore it.

"No, I did not! A Lady would have more steel in her than that little wisp of a girl will ever have. But you would not listen to me, and look what it has led to. You have no wife, no heir, not even a pretty bed-mate."

No steel? Celeste was full of courage. He had known it the first time he saw her, a child of twelve, racing a horse much too big for her across the field toward her father's manor, well ahead of the man who had been sent to fetch her home by her embarrassed parents. He had seen it in her eyes, curious and unafraid, when she knelt with her family to pay him homage. He had wanted her then, had made himself wait two years for her to grow to womanhood. And if he had not known her dauntless spirit already, he knew it when he brought her to his castle, five times the size of her father's manor, and saw her lift her chin and hold her gaze steady, despite the tremble in her leg, pressed against his in the carriage. Eleanor thought her weak because she allowed Eleanor to continue to manage his household. When he asked her about it, she had looked surprised. 'It makes her happy,' she said. 'She is your older sister, I thought you would want me to please her.' He was ashamed to admit that making Eleanor happy had not occurred to him.

"If you set her aside you will ruin her," Raimond said.

"She can enter a nunnery," Eleanor countered coolly. "She already has. Free her to follow the life she chose when she left your castle."

"Enough!" Barnard slammed his fist into the table. "I have not decided to put her aside." Were they so obtuse as to think he wanted this? That he would ever find another woman who stirred in him the feelings Celeste had? If she showed any signs of improving, of forsaking her grief and her anger... He stabbed his knife into the venison, slicing off a chunk, and bit into it, scowling. Eleanor was right: He must have an heir.

He left the table more conflicted than he let them see. Eleanor could manage his household, but she could not give him a son, and he must have one soon if he wished to secure his holdings. Eleanor's son was sufficiently engaged in mismanaging his father's estate, without inheriting Bernard's as well. He could leave his title and lands to his cousin, Raimond, but Raimond had no sons and Eleanor's boy would surely dispute it; that would be all King Louis needed, to step in. Without a direct descendant, the King would confiscate his castle and holdings to pay for the war with Britain's King Henry, which was sure to come sooner or later; that or another crusade. And that would be the end of their family title.

He must set her aside.

Was he behaving as callously as Raimond implied? Had he ruined Celeste's life? What a beautiful child she was, with her dark hair and fair skin, and those huge, dark eyes, so full of candour and trust. When he had returned two years later and seen her as a woman, he had wanted nothing so much as to stare into those wide, deep eyes, to unbraid that rich abundance of hair and run his hands through it, to fan it out across his pillow and bury his face in its softness. He had not been able to resist her; would not be able to now, were she before him.

That was the truth of it, and Eleanor saw it, and scorned him for it. Nor was she alone; how many others laughed behind their hands at his foolishness? Celeste was no fit wife for him; a fault of her birth, not her character. He needed a wife at court with him, to help him advance in Louis' favour, and that Celeste could never do. Perhaps this was his opportunity to make a wiser choice.

He passed the yard where the two boys he was fostering were practicing their swordplay with his men. On seeing him they stopped and bowed. He waved them back to their lesson.

A stable boy appeared before him as soon as he entered the stables. "Saddle my horse," he said, more sharply than necessary. The boy bowed and ran off to obey.

Bernard did not follow him. Alone at last, he leaned against the stable wall. Raimond's words cut into him, as painful as a battle wound. Had he ruined Celeste? Had he asked too much of her? Wed her too young? Failed her in some irreparable way without even realizing he was doing so? That beautiful, tender girl. He groaned under his breath.

The night before she left for the convent, he had come to her room for one last attempt to talk her out of leaving. She lay across her bed, moaning to herself. She was wearing a plain black kirtle that covered her like a shroud and her hair was tangled and dirty despite her child-maid's attempts to clean and comb it. Her eyes were open, so wild and filled with grief he could not bear to look at her; he backed out of the room without speaking.

He sighed. It served no purpose to relive the past. How could he have known she would crumple under adversity? In every other way she seemed so stalwart. A sickly son makes a poor heir; she should have understood that, and consoled herself with thoughts of another child.

And yet, Etienne had not seemed sickly. He had been a robust infant until that fever. Even then he had fought it bravely, had seemed to overcome it. The day his fever broke, ah, their joy that day! That night he had taken Celeste to his bed and loved her with the same sweet tenderness they had shared the first night of their marriage. But she had insisted on returning to her own room, where she had had Etienne's cradle placed while he was ill. And the next morning he was dead.

The clip of horse hooves broke through his thoughts. He raised his head.

"Your horse is ready, My Lord," the boy mumbled.

"Bring him." Bernard strode out of the stable, followed by the boy leading his large hunter.

He swung into the saddle. A good, hard ride would clear his head. He urged his horse into a trot across the stable yard, and then into a gallop when he reached the meadow. The past could not be altered. As for the future—well, Eleanor was right: he must find a wife of his own station. It must be done. In truth, a part of him welcomed it. Not yet, though. Another month or so would make no difference. Meanwhile, he would return to Louis' court; he had been away too long. After his ride, he would order preparations begun for the journey to Paris.

Bernard saw the horse as soon as he rode into the yard. It had been ridden hard and was still damp with sweat. The stable-boy had removed its saddle and was walking it in wide circles in front of the stables to cool it down.

He pulled his stallion to a halt and tossed the reins to a waiting groom. "Where is the messenger?" he demanded, annoyed that one of his animals had been used so ill, and anxious in case it had been necessary. He swung down from the saddle and strode toward the kitchen where the groom pointed.

The boy leaped up from the bench as soon as he saw Bernard.

"My Lord," he choked out, around a mouthful of chicken he was trying desperately to swallow.

"What is your news?"

"Your Lady wife is recovering," the boy said, bowing to cover a coughing fit.

"Recovering?" Bernard glared at the boy. Was she better or not? The boy could not speak for coughing. "Bring ale!" he roared.

"She sits in the garden and attends Mass," the boy gasped after drinking deeply from the proffered cup.

"Is she completely well?" He would overlook the treatment of the horse and reward the boy handsomely. "She is well?" he repeated, grinning despite himself. To hell with a suitable wife!

"I... I do not know, My Lord."

"You do not know? Did you speak with her? Did she give you a message for me?" Had she sent for him to come for her? He would go tonight, by God.

"N... no." The boy looked frightened. "My mother bade me come."

"She sat in the garden and attended Mass? That is all you can tell me?"

The boy nodded miserably.

"You did not see her yourself?"

The boy shook his head. "My Mo—"

Bernard left the kitchen. Curse the boy and curse his mother! He had told the wench to send her boy with a message from his wife when she recovered. Was she so eager for the money he had promised that she had forgotten, or was Celeste unable to write? Or unwilling? Was she well or not?

He would look an anxious fool, riding into the abbey to greet his wife if she were not healed. Worse, if she were well and refused to see him. He cursed out loud. Nevertheless, fool or not, he would go. He was planning to ride to Paris at any rate, and the Abbey of Sainte-Blandine-de-Lugdunum was on the route.

Eleanor met him in the great hall while he was ordering the servants to pack his things.

"What word did the messenger bring?" she asked, aware as always of everything that occurred at the castle.

"Very sparse. He claims My Lady wife is recovering but offers no proof. I will stop in on my way to court, and see for myself."

"And if she has not recovered?"

"Then I will stay in Paris until Yuletide is over." He smiled wryly, knowing he had not answered her question.

"What then, if she has recovered?" A not too subtle prod: he did not need reminding that Celeste could not accompany him to court.

"I will have Raimond and two of my men escort her back here, and follow as soon as King Louis gives me leave."

"Not Raimond."

He sent the servant scurrying with a final command before he turned to her. "Why not Raimond?" He asked. She had objected too quickly, and now she hesitated too long in answering. "My cousin would be disappointed to miss King Louis' court, but he will do as I bid."

Still she did not reply.

"What is it, Eleanor?" He spoke quietly, watching her.

"I know nothing." She spread her hands dismissively.

"What do you suspect?" It would not be nothing. She was as watchful as a hawk over her domain.

She glanced at him, her expression inscrutable. "There is something between Raimond and Celeste."

"Impossible."

"Do not believe me, then. Go your merry way like a fool—"

"What have you *seen*, Eleanor?"

"Nothing. Nothing to put words to. Only the way he looks at her, talks to her. They have a secret."

# Chapter 11

"Lady Celeste! Lady Celeste!"

"…my fault," Celeste moaned, dazed by horror and unable to recall its source.

"No, My Lady," Marie sobbed beside her. "You did not mean to hit the little girl."

"I should not have pressed the stones on her," a man's voice muttered nearby. "I did not know she was a Lady."

Stones? Little girl? What were they talking about? She opened her eyes.

A half dozen faces stared anxiously down at her.

"Pierre." She smiled, recognizing one of the faces. He had found her in the crowded market, as she knew he would. She reached up to embrace him. He looked startled and pulled back.

"It is not Pierre, Lady Celeste," Marie said, her eyes wide. "She thinks you are her brother," she whispered aside.

Celeste flushed. Of course it was not Pierre. Pierre was—

She had had his image so clearly in her mind, and now it slipped away. She looked around, disoriented.

"Where am I?" she asked, blushing at her confusion.

"We are at Cluny, My Lady," the young man who was not Pierre said.

"You fainted," Marie added, wringing her hands.

Celeste propped herself up on her elbows. She was lying on the stone bench where she had sat earlier, at the side of the crowded square. She had... pushed through the crowd, to see... the adulteress. Yes, she remembered the adulteress.

"We should return to the inn. You can rest there, out of the sun, My Lady."

Something else had happened in the square. She had been watching the woman being stoned, and then—

"My Lady—"

"Be quiet, Marie. Let me think."

She closed her eyes. An image came to her: a face, sharp and suspicious, peering down at her.

The peddler! Her eyes flew open.

"Are you well, Lady?" Marie asked.

He was here! Did he still have her ring? She would find him, and order him to return it. Lord Bernard could not deny their marriage then. She would take the nail as well if she must. She sat up, swaying a little as she fought down a surge of dizziness and nausea, and reached out for support.

Marie grasped her arm. "My Lady?" her voice rose anxiously.

*His face leered over hers. "I can end your suffering."*

Oh God, what if it were true? What if he gave them back, the ring *and* the nail, and she fell ill again? A sense of it came back to her, the overwhelming despair, the constant weariness, the grief so deep and sharp within her it hurt to move, the burning eyes of demons beckoning her...

She shrank back against the wall. Not that, she did not want that back. She closed her eyes, replacing the face she remembered with the one she had seen today, confused and frightened, tormented by sorrow, overwhelming sorrow—her sorrow!

"Please, My Lady," Marie insisted.

She must have her ring back. She would not be set aside, forced to live in wretched poverty and silence at the abbey, laughed at by everyone for daring to reach too high. But only the ring.

She stood up shakily, looking around. The woman was no longer screaming. How much time had passed? Was the peddler gone? Had he been stoned? If he was dead, she would never get her ring back. (If he was dead, was her sorrow dead with him?)

"Will she be all right?" a man's voice asked.

She turned to look at the speaker: the man in the crowd, behind her. He had known the peddler. He had given her the stones to throw. A wave of dizziness weakened her.

"Get me... get me away from here," she clutched the man's arm.

"We are staying at the Red Cock Inn," Marie said.

"I know it. I can help you take her there." The man took Celeste's arm. "Can you walk?"

"With your assistance," she murmured, holding his arm.

When they were far enough from the square not to be overheard, Celeste straightened. "That man and his child. In the square. Are they—"

"The child is safe," Marie said.

"That child is no more his than mine," the man said, scowling. "He is a travelling peddler, lodged at the monastery. I cannot think what devil-ridden impulse caused him to interfere with the monks' justice, but he will regret it. You were right to stone them, Lady."

"You know him then?" Celeste frowned at Marie to quell her objection.

"Not I! I only spoke to him briefly before we went to the square."

"Let us not speak of him at all!" Marie cried. She leaned behind Celeste's back to hiss: "Can you not see it distresses her?"

Celeste gritted her teeth until she tasted blood. She would have Marie whipped. She would choose another maid and send Marie away in the night without a penny!

"Do not concern yourself, Lady," the man said. "You will not see him again. He will leave for Lyon at first light, I have no doubt of it."

"Lyon? Are you certain?" She would keep Marie after all; her foolish chatter was useful.

"Sir—" Marie began.

Celeste stumbled, stepping hard against Marie's ankle.

The man tightened his clasp on her arm. "All the peddlers and vendors will go to Lyon for the market next week. I myself am a metal smith; I will be leaving in a few days. But after what he did today, he would be wise to go at once. You will not see him again."

"That is reassuring." She withdrew her arm.

The peddler was not in the town square when they crossed it on the way to the public feast, after their rest. The square was vacant, except for others like themselves, skirting the edges to get to the commons beside the monastery. The bailiff's men had removed the body, leaving only a pile of blood-stained stones. Celeste surveyed the empty square regretfully. What had come over her when her stone hit the child? Regret, of course: she had intended to hurt the peddler. But it had been more than that. Panic. Her heart pounded at the memory. And that crowd of people, breathing all around her, just like her nightmare... She turned and hurried past.

He was not at the commons. Saying she needed some air, she had walked all around the feast grounds, Marie trailing behind, wringing her hands. Admitting defeat at last, she returned to the inn. She would have to go to Lyon.

The next morning Celeste looked for Mistress Blanche. She would know how to reach Father Jacques, who could help her find a group to travel with. Although it was still early, neither the old lady nor her maid were among those sleeping on the inn floor. Celeste walked around the room until she spotted the old woman's manservant. He was deeply asleep and did not waken easily. When at last his eyes focused on her, his expression was instantly wary.

"Where is your mistress?" she demanded.

"Is she not in the room?"

"See for yourself." She gestured around at the rousing guests.

"Not down here. The innkeeper's room. She paid him for it, last night. He and his wife went to sleep in the stable."

"Has your mistress' illness worsened?" She had been paler than usual last night at dinner.

The manservant's eyes moistened; he sniffed loudly, wiping his nose on a dirty sleeve, and pointed upstairs.

Celeste was reluctant to go to a sick room, but she had to speak to Father Jacques. She climbed the stairs as she had in her dream, afraid of what she would find, and stopped before an open door, trembling. Father Jacques' voice came through the doorway, low and calm, reciting the last rites. Celeste crept forward.

She fixed her eyes on Father Jacques, ignoring the bed. A deep, rasping sound came from it, the grate of indrawn breath as jagged as glass. Father Jacques finished his prayers and looked up.

"Have you come to pay your respects?" he asked.

"An escort," she stammered. "I need an escort to Lyon." She barely knew what she was saying. The words fell out of her mouth in a desperate attempt to block the harsh struggle for air coming from the figure on the bed, and the soft, wet rattle that followed each laboured breath. "I have been praying all night about this."

Father Jacques sank wearily onto the stool beside the bed.

"Much of the night," she amended, in case he had seen her sleeping when he came to attend to Mistress Blanche.

"Why do you wish to go to Lyon?"

"To pray at the Basilica de Fourviere."

"Does your husband agree to this second excursion?" He looked directly at her for the first time since she had entered the room.

"My husband has little time for religion," she said, reciting the arguments she had decided upon. "So I must be devout for both of us." It was likely true; Lords were not known for piety, they were too busy with governance and war.

"I cannot encourage a wife to act against her husband's will."

He looked very young to be saying something so foolish, Celeste thought.

"Even for the benefit of his soul? Of both our souls?"

"Why do you need to pray at the Basilica de Fourviere?"

"To give thanks for my recovery, and pray for my husband."

"You gave thanks at the Mass for Mary's Assumption."

"Is it wrong to thank God twice?"

He looked at her quietly without replying, until she looked aside.

"Do you doubt that God heard your prayers here?"

She looked back at him, but he was watching Mistress Blanche again. He spoke softly, as though addressing the sick woman. Celeste looked down at her.

Mistress Blanche lay on the bed still dressed in her green silk kirtle, a thin white sheet drawn up to her waist. Her face was white, as translucent as the beads of moisture on her forehead. The blue lines of her blood pulsed weakly, obscenely visible through the thin veil of her dry skin. Her eyes were closed. She lay without moving except for her fingers, which plucked restlessly at the sheet with small, desperate movements.

*Etienne had lain so still, his face as pale as hers with all the life-color gone from it.*

Father Jacques dipped a cloth into a bowl of water and wiped it across Mistress Blanche's forehead. Celeste held her breath, afraid he would tear the fragile layer of skin that held her together.

*She dabbed cool water on Etienne, just so, watching the tiny rise and fall of his chest until its movement was barely visible. She leant her ear against his lips, seeking the whisper of air between them.*

*"No!" she cried, when Lord Bernard sent for a priest. But when the priest came, her hope wavered. She let him bless the child, as though Etienne's little soul had had time to sin.*

*"You may leave now," she said as soon as the prayers were finished. "My son is not going to die."*

*Lord Bernard escorted the priest out. She heard him excuse her behaviour, and the priest's haughty response as they walked away.*

*"Etienne," she whispered, bending over her son. She lifted him out of his cradle. He was hot and limp in her arms, and as light as the pale moonlight stealing through the window. She rocked him gently in her arms, and sang softly, under her breath:*

*Where has it gone, the smiling sun?*
*Little birds, where have you flown?*
*Close your eyes, my little prince,*
*Here with your head against my heart,*
*Close your eyes and follow them.*

*His eyelashes fluttered against his pale cheeks. Celeste drew a breath that trembled in her throat. Her voice shook as she sang:*

*Under the sea is the smiling sun,*
*Asleep in their nests are the little birds*
*Prince of the drowsy, dying day*
*Lay your head against my heart*
*Close your eyes and follow them.*

"Lady Celeste? Do you believe God did not hear you?"

Celeste looked up, shaken. Father Jacques was watching her, waiting for her answer.

*...Prince of the drowsy, dying day, lay your head against my heart...*

"He did not hear," she said.

"If he did not hear you at the Mass for Mary's Assumption, will he hear you in the Basilica de Fourviere?"

Celeste looked down at Mistress Blanche, dying in a strange bed at the end of her pilgrimage. Father Jacques covered her restless hands and held them still. His hands were slender and soft, accustomed to prayer, not labour. She looked down at her own hands, as soft as Father Jacques'. She had prayed. How she had prayed!

"No," she said.

The room filled with the terrible soft rattle of Mistress Blanche's breathing. Father Jacques dipped the cloth into the water and gently patted her face again. "You might be surprised, where God can hear you," he said.

"Is she very bad, Father?" Marie stood in the doorway, staring wide-eyed at Mistress Blanche.

"She is near the end."

"Is there anything to be done?"

"Send her servant to fetch his master. And pray for her."

"I will, Father," Marie said solemnly.

Despite their prayers, Mistress Blanche died two days later. Her maid informed them of it while they were breaking their morning fast. She wept as though the woman had been her mother, not her mistress.

"Father Jacques must find an escort for us soon," Celeste said to Marie, when the maid left them. "Before all of Cluny's visitors leave."

"Pilgrims stop at Cluny all the time." Marie wiped her eyes on her sleeve. "The innkeeper's wife told me. The Abbot of Cluny wants them to stay at his guesthouse and the townspeople want them to stay at the pilgrim's hostel or the inns."

"We might wait weeks for a group we could join to happen by."

"I will talk to the Abbot about it today," Father Jacques said, behind her.

Celeste turned, blushing. "I did not know you were there, Father," she stammered. He looked exhausted. As soon as he had drunk a mug of ale, he left for the monastery.

Father Jacques returned in the late afternoon. Celeste hurried over to him. "What did the Abbot say?"

He looked at her oddly, without answering.

"They have all gone without me!" Celeste cried. She had feared this would happen; he had waited too long to make his enquiries. If only the old woman had died sooner!

"I have spoken with the Abbot." His voice sounded strange. "I am going to Jerusalem."

"You! What about me?"

"You and Marie may pilgrimage with me."

"To Jerusalem?"

"We will stop at Lyon. You can leave us there."

"Just us three?" How could he protect her from thieves and cut-throats?

"A group of six pilgrims approached the Abbot for a monk to accompany them and hear their confessions. The Abbot has already sent out monks with earlier groups, and now he is sending me. To Jerusalem." He stared at her, as though unable to believe his own news. "We are leaving in ten days, when they have made their preparations."

Ten days? She could not wait ten days. The market at Lyon would be over in four days. "Thank you, Father Jacques," she said, nearly choking on the words.

"Go to the other inns. See if there is a group travelling to Lyon," she ordered Marie as soon as Father Jacques had gone.

"Lady Celeste!" Marie stood at the door of the inn, hopping from foot to foot.

"What is it?" Celeste hurried over. "Have you found a group of travellers we may join?"

"Not here. I must talk to you in private." Marie whispered. "Please, come away!" she added urgently.

"Very well." Celeste followed her out onto the street.

As soon as they were alone, Marie grabbed her arm. "I saw him!"

Celeste froze. The metal smith had been wrong: the peddler was still here!

"What did you say to him? Did he speak to you?" Celeste demanded when she could speak again. Had he told Marie about the ring? She grabbed Marie's shoulders, barely restraining herself from shaking the girl.

"I ran away." Marie was close to tears. "He did not see me."

"Where is he?" Celeste looked around as if she might see the peddler peering down the street at them. "Tell me quickly."

"On the road near the monastery."

"So he is leaving. In which direction was he heading?"

Marie shook her head. "He has just arrived. I saw him riding through the gates of the monastery."

"Riding? On his donkey?" The poor beast had been overburdened already.

"On his stallion." Marie looked at her strangely.

"His stallion?" Celeste straightened. "Who did you see, Marie?"

"Lord Bernard."

# Chapter 12

Jean made his way through the gates of Cluny onto the busy road south. Pilgrims in their broad-brimmed hats and grey tunics walked at a good pace or rode briskly off, looking refreshed and eager to continue their pilgrimage. Peasants in short russet tunics and mended hose walked humbly at the sides of the road, while tradesmen, landowners and merchants in dyed linen drove their wagons down the middle, moving aside only when nobility with their colored silks and cloaks embroidered with gold and silver threads, swept past them in carriages and on horseback.

The constant babble of conversation and the harsh accents of foreigners grated on Jean's ear, and the frequent clatter of hooves and calls to "Make way!" jarred him. His head throbbed. It was two full days' walk to Lyon.

He had had little appetite for the feast and even less for conversation. He had taken a few bites of the roasted pig and returned to his room, which was just as well. After his inexplicable rescue of the child, he was a pariah. Even the loose-tongued metal smith avoided him, not that he cared to talk to that fool.

All night he had tossed restlessly with dreams of the girl at the abbey: Sorrow. The memory of her despair exhausted him at each awakening, and oppressed him even now despite the warmth of the day and the fine weight of his money pouch.

If that were not enough to make his head ache, there was that look the cellarer had given him when he left the monastery this morning: a look which did not bode well for future business. Jean had earned it, interfering in the stoning of a proven adulteress. The monks had all been there—they were behind the verdict even if the bailiff and his men carried out the trial and execution.

Whatever made him rush to the child's rescue? He had never done anything so stupid. He was a careful man, not one to be compelled by a flood of emotion to save a stranger's child. The adulteress and her daughter were none of his business; his business was peddling spices and other goods. His business was making money, and he had never been distracted from that before. Now he had earned the disapproval of the cellarer of Cluny. He could barely digest his morning meal for thinking about the significance of that look.

It was well past mid-day when he remembered that he had not met with the Abbot of Cluny. The realization brought him to a standstill. The donkey, glad of a rest, snatched a weed from the roadside and chewed thoughtfully while Jean stood dumbfounded beside it.

He had not kept his appointment with the Abbot. An appointment he had been granted with reluctance because he promised it would be worth the Abbot's time. He was sick at the thought, so nauseated he would have run to the side of the road if he had been able to move. He leaned against the donkey, which swished its tail at him unsympathetically.

Perhaps the Abbot would not remember? He may not even have noticed that Jean did not come on one of the busiest days of the year at his monastery. Jean clutched at the pathetic hope.

"Is aught amiss?"

He had passed up a certain sale, a lucrative one, after setting it in motion. What could have made him forget so completely? Even his weariness and his headache could not explain such a momentous oversight.

"Is there aught amiss, friend?"

What if the Abbot had seen Jean rescue the child? What if he took Jean's absence as a comment on the stoning? Jean groaned aloud.

"Are you ailing, then?"

He had missed his opportunity to be rid of the nail, wherever it came from, and to be rid of her with it... Because he was ensorcelled! Why had he not seen it, that black hair, those dark eyes like bottomless wells, her pale face filling his dreams...?

No, that was madness! He had not bought her sorrow! It was not even a coffin nail she gave him.

"Good Sir, what ails you?"

Jean gasped as he felt himself roughly shaken.

A tall pilgrim stood directly in front of him, searching his face with concern. His companions clustered about them.

"Nothing ails me!" Jean snapped, shrugging himself free of the man's grasp on his shoulders and glaring round at them.

"You have been muttering to yourself," one of the pilgrims said.

"For a good while, like one caught in a spell," another added.

"I recognize him. He was at the stoning. He—"

The tall pilgrim waved the speaker to silence.

"A spell? I am not spell-bound," Jean cried.

The pilgrims watched him warily. One of them made the sign of the cross, another touched the emblem at his shoulder.

"No one is accusing you of it," the tall one said quietly.

"I-I just remembered something."

The pilgrim nodded. "Walk with us, then, while you collect yourself."

Jean saw the heavy silver cross round the man's neck and then, under the hood of his cloak, the circle of his tonsure. He must be the group's confessor. And Jean had flung his hand aside!

He could do nothing now but agree. A request by a priest to walk with him was not a suggestion. Other travelers on the road would be watching, approving the priest's Christian charity. If Jean refused his company, he would be outcast, ready prey to thieves and ruffians hiding in the thick woods beside the road. Worse, it could be taken as proof that he was bedevilled. He was lucky the priest wanted to walk with him, after he had rudely thrust the man's hand from his shoulders.

He nodded his thanks, putting a good face on it, and fell into step beside the priest. No need to hurry, though. Sooner or later, the pilgrims would tire of his cumbersome pace. He slowed his step a little, sighing as though with weariness.

"What is your name, friend?" the tall priest asked, curbing his stride to match Jean's. The pilgrims traveling with him fell back a little.

"Jean le Peddler, Father."

"And where are you headed?"

"Lyon."

When the silence became noticeable, Jean added, "to sell my goods to the wine merchants."

The priest nodded. Was he waiting for Jean's confession? He would wait a long time.

"What do you sell?"

He was the patient sort, then. Willing to creep up on it. But he would get little from Jean for all his patience. Jean knew enough to keep counsel with himself; he had learned that lesson early.

"Spices," Jean answered. "Hose and shoe leather. And handkerchiefs blessed at Santiago de Compostella." The man would know all that already if he had seen Jean at the market.

"Do you take them to Santiago yourself, to be blessed?"

"I am a peddler, not a pilgrim like you." Jean shrugged self-deprecatingly. "I know a priest who goes on pilgrimage to Santiago every few years. He takes them for me." A married priest, who kept his wife hidden at Zaragoza in order to appear in compliance with the church's new laws; who feigned his pilgrimages to visit her and was willing to swear, for the price of a sou to aid in her upkeep, that the handkerchiefs had been blessed at Santiago.

"Perhaps you are on your way to Santiago?" Jean asked, turning the talk away from himself.

"No, we are headed for Marseilles to board a ship for the Holy Land."

"May God bless you on your blessed journey," Jean said, turning slightly to include them all as he crossed himself. A little ostentatious, but it appeared to reassure them. No one under a spell would be able to make the sign of the cross.

He was annoyed to find that he felt reassured, also. It increased his irritation with the pilgrims. Superstitious fools. The girl had not cast a spell on him. It was his own fault he had missed an opportunity to make a profitable sale at Cluny. He was tempted to turn around and walk straight back to the monastery. But he would be going against the flow of people, and in a few hours he would be alone on the road. It would be dark before he reached Cluny, and he carried a full money pouch. No, he could not go back. And he could not sell the nail at Lyon, it was too close to Sainte-Blandine-de-Lugdunum. What if *she* went to see the nail from Jesus' cross at Lyon, and recognized it?

Well, there were other monasteries and churches on his route, though none as rich as Cluny or the Basilica de Fourviere at Lyon.

"Do you have a family?"

The priest was not satisfied yet, even if the pilgrims with him were.

"I was thinking of them when you came upon me, Father. Missing them." Jean spoke in a low voice, as though it were a confession. If it had been true, it would be one. That was another rule: never think of home when he was away.

The priest's face relaxed slightly. A few details and he would be convinced. Jean gritted his teeth. Trading was trading and home was home; no good would come of mixing them. But he would have to do it, have to share his family with this prying priest. The man would just keep at him otherwise, and perhaps set the others wondering about a man who would not open up to a priest. Best get it over with. He put on a pitiable expression, as a homesick person might show.

"Simon is the oldest. He will be able to come with me in another year." Some would have considered him old enough now, among them Simon himself, but Jean had put it off. Simon would not find it easy to forget home. Simon was soft inside like a woman. Jean would have to take that out of him, and it would not be easy. It had to be done, for the boy's own good—but not for another year.

"Gilles is a jester, but a good boy. And quick." Gilles was as sharp as they came. Gilles would understand the game. He kept his eyes open, that one. There was none of Mathilde in Gilles; he was all Jean's.

"Mathilde lost two after them, but she is a good woman. A pious woman." Maybe too pious. He had had to go to some lengths to convince her that the handkerchiefs were actually being taken to Santiago to be blessed. He would have to hide the truth from Simon, too.

"And a good mother. She taught the boys to cipher well enough for a tradesman. And to pray, as well." He was babbling. Mathilde did her job and he did his. No need to sound idiotic about it. But the priest was smiling now, if a bit condescendingly.

"And the little one?"

A man had no protection against a priest. Jean looked away, but it was too late for that. Once a man started talking about home it was all there, in his face.

"Jeanne. She is two years of age." That was all. He would say nothing more.

"Dark hair, like her mother? Like your Mathilde?"

Jean nodded once. He looked up, met the priest's eyes. He was smiling at Jean with genuine warmth now, but underneath, just a hint of smugness. He thought he had learned something Jean had not meant to tell.

"She calls her mother 'Mama'?"

Jean kept walking. He gave nothing away, not in his face or his breathing or the slightest move of a finger. What was the priest getting at? He appeared to attach some significance to his questions that Jean could not fathom. Was he trying to trap Jean somehow?

"All children call their mothers that," he replied. The pause had been too long, but he said it anyway.

"That is true. But not all men remember it." The priest clapped him on the back. "Well met, friend!"

Jean blinked, confused. The priest's thoughts were too subtle. Nevertheless, he nodded, accepting the tribute. It was as good as a letter of protection. Anyone on the road who had heard the priest say it, or seen him clap Jean's back, would come to his aid now if he was in trouble. Nevertheless, Jean was not pleased. He had paid too much for it.

The priest lengthened his stride. "Safe journey home!" he called over his shoulder as he moved ahead. The pilgrims in his charge hurried to catch up with him, smiling or slapping Jean on his arm or his back as they passed. Jean endured their goodwill. They would most likely tell others ahead to watch out for him. The priest was that type of man—a born shepherd.

The trouble was, Jean did not like being considered a sheep.

Jean walked until it was too dark to see the sides of the road, even with the campfires of weary travelers strung out along it. He did not need to stop at dusk to make a camp as the other travelers did; a spice seller would be welcome at any fire. He kept a small leather container of salt and rosemary and a few local herbs to add to the stew pots that he was invited to share.

He thought again of the scene at the town square and the cellarer's glowering stare. "Huh!" he said, defiantly, as though the monk could hear him. "Huh!" He did not regret it. He did not regret it after all! He could still feel the child's thin arms around his neck, and he was glad she was not lying stone-cut and still beneath a mound of human cruelty, like her mother. What if it hurt his business?

What indeed? Was he as fond-foolish as the priest believed him to be?

Well, what of it? He would not behave so impulsively again, but he was glad he had saved the child, and that was the end of it. Whether he had acted this way before or not, it was done, and he would not regret it. One act did not make him as foolish as his mother. It did not make him anything at all like her.

He was back on the road at dawn. As the morning progressed, however, an uneasy reluctance slowed his pace. Travelers whose campfires he had walked past the evening before now passed him by. The donkey shared his lassitude—or at least was inclined to take advantage of it. The beast required more prodding than Jean had the energy for. Together they trudged down the road, each step slower, more sluggish than the one before.

Toward Sainte Blandine de Lugdunum.

Toward the Abbey of Sainte Blandine.

Toward the girl with dark, unfathomable eyes in a pale face, with hair so black it shimmered. The girl whose ring he had taken.

The girl who had sold him her sorrow.

Every step he took was harder, until he simply stopped, unable to go further.

"Homesick again, friend?" Someone slapped Jean on the back, then threw an arm across his shoulders.

"You did not see us when you passed last night, heh?" The tall priest continued, taking in Jean's bewildered expression and wrapping his easy conversation around it. "I was hearing confessions, or I would have called you to join us. But here you are, walking with us again."

The strong arm across his shoulders pulled Jean forward. One of the pilgrims slapped the donkey's rump sharply, and they were moving again.

The priest did not force Jean to talk. He left him to his silence and chatted with the others in his entourage. He kept his arm over Jean's shoulder, though, and Jean was miserably glad of it. If there were any lingering malevolence waiting here to punish him for taking advantage of the girl, the priest's silver cross would surely protect them both.

As they approached the fork in the road which led to the abbey, Jean watched the road warily, but there was no pile of black cloth lying beside it to trap him today. Not with the priest's arm guarding him.

They were passing the road now.

Now it was behind him. He let out a breath he had not known he was holding.

"Shall we stop at the Abbey of Sainte Blandine for our midday meal?" one of the pilgrims walking behind them asked. "Here is the road that leads to it."

Jean stumbled, his knees buckling. What was he doing walking with these men, here of all places? If he met up with the girl, if she told her story to them, he would be condemned, ruined. What if she were still at the abbey?

The priest's grip tightened around him until he regained his footing. "Not yet, I think," the priest said calmly. "Let us go a little further before we stop."

Jean breathed. He drew the air in slowly, painfully, trying not to gasp for it. Trying to hide the depth of his distress from this priest who prided himself on his perceptiveness. One breath, and then another. She was not on the road.

One footstep, then another, and another.

They were past the road to the abbey now. The main road curved slightly. Now the abbey was well behind them. Jean's tread grew steadier. He had let this foolishness go too far; surely it would all end now, the dreams, the doubts, the ill-considered actions.

Now even the fork in the road was no longer visible. The priest's arm on his shoulders felt heavy, confining, with its implied familiarity. He took a deep breath, straightening.

The priest, sensing it, loosened his hold. As he did, he leaned down and murmured in Jean's ear, "Do not worry yourself so. The girl is all right now."

# Chapter 13

ord Bernard? Lord Bernard is here? At Cluny?"

"That is what I have been telling you," Marie wrung her hands in the way that so irritated Celeste.

"Are you sure?" She grabbed Marie by the shoulders and shook her. "Are you sure it was Lord Bernard?"

"Yes!" Marie cried, stumbling backwards. "He was a road's width from me. I hid behind a bush and watched him ride across to the cathedral with his men. Do not strike me, Lady!" She raised her hands to cover her cheeks.

"How many men?" She should slap Marie for her impertinence, but then she would have to wait even longer to get anything out of her.

"Three henchmen. One of them held his horse when he went into the cathedral. And Raimond."

*A tall, dark man, younger than Bernard, closer to her age. His ...cousin.* The memory wavered, carrying a mixture of warmth and threat. She shook her head.

Lord Bernard was here. The Abbess must have told him she had gone to Cluny.

Why had he pursued her here? Like a sparrow fleeing a hawk she turned and twisted, and still he came after her. She could not meet up with him now. Not when she was so close to reclaiming her ring. Was it not enough that she had to worry about finding the peddler—

The peddler! What if he was still here, at Cluny? If he had not left yet? Oh God! If they should meet, and Lord Bernard find his ring in the peddler's possession—

"We must leave at once," she cried.

"Leave?" Marie's face paled. "You must go to him, Lady. He is your Lord husband, and he has come for you."

"You forget yourself!"

"Because I love you! I want you to have a future!"

Celeste drew back sharply, looking around. No one was near enough to hear. She would have to dismiss the girl when this was over.

"Calm yourself," she said, breathing deeply herself. "Lord Bernard does not know that you have seen him. He will not know I left knowing he was here."

"What if he sees us leaving?"

Celeste hesitated. Lord Bernard might well see them leaving if he was staying at Cluny. They could leave by the town gate, but that would mean circling back to reach the road to Lyon. It would take time, and time increased their likelihood of being intercepted.

"We must disguise ourselves."

"As for a masquerade?" Marie asked doubtfully.

Celeste choked back a laugh. She took a breath to calm herself, and thought a moment. It must be something subtle that would hide them without drawing attention. Peasant's garb? The thought of wearing coarse russet was distasteful. At any rate, they would be riding horses, not walking like peasants.

Pilgrim's cloaks! There would be hundreds of pilgrims leaving Cluny, all wearing the cloaks they had bought at the fair. And why not wear such cloaks? They were pilgrims, also. She gave Marie her purse and sent her on the run to buy two cloaks, and two of the wide-brimmed hats as well.

"Be careful not to let anyone at the Inn see them when you return," she cautioned. "Carry them under your cloak and pack them into our baggage before you come to dinner."

Returning to the inn yard, Celeste sought out the stable boy and instructed him to saddle her horse and the pony. "Have them ready for me and my maid to ride after dinner," she told him. "They must have some exercise." She felt foolish as soon as she said it. A Lady would not explain her actions to a stable boy. But he only nodded and went to find her tack.

She entered the inn and sat at the table. The innkeeper's wife handed her an earthen bowl filled with hot stew. Although she had no appetite, she forced herself to eat. Who knew when they would eat again?

Marie returned and stood at the door, looking in. Celeste discretely motioned her toward the corner of the room where she had piled their belongings. Marie went over and knelt with her back to the dinner table. Celeste dared not watch her, and was relieved when at last she came to the table and sat beside her with a single tiny nod.

While they ate, Celeste kept her eye on the door. Her hands shook as she lifted the bowl to drink the thick broth. Lord Bernard must know by now that she was not at the monastery guesthouse. The Abbot would remember her from the Bishop's sermon and send for Father Jacques to tell her husband where she was staying. He might already be on his way to the Red Cock Inn. She rose, biting her lip to keep from hurrying, paid the innkeeper's wife for their meal and went to retrieve her belongings. Her basket, when she lifted it, was reassuringly heavy. She walked casually across the inn to the door, although every muscle in her body ached to run.

Their mounts were waiting outside. The stable boy tied their baskets behind the saddles after they were mounted, his hands slow and clumsy, as if they had all day. At last they clattered out of the courtyard.

Their horses' hooves rang against the cobblestones, loud in the quiet streets now empty of the crowds of pilgrims. Celeste cringed at the noise, hoping it would not draw attention.

She turned onto a narrow street a short distance from the inn, where they could not be seen, and stopped. Taking the pilgrim's cloak out of her basket, she wrapped it around her despite the warmth of the day, and tied one of the hats onto her head, ordering Marie to do the same.

Celeste's hands trembled on the reins as they trotted through the town toward the road south. At every corner she expected to see Lord Bernard and his men riding toward her. If he caught her fleeing, how would she explain?

On a cobbled street running into the town square, she heard hoof beats and turned to look.

She recognized him at once. She would know that strong, unguarded face anywhere: the dark, wavy hair, calm brown eyes, soft upper lip and generous bottom lip curving into the thick black beard that covered his cheeks. The lined, handsome face of her husband. She stared at him, unable to breathe.

"Lord Bernard!" Marie gasped beside her.

"Pull your cloak around you," Celeste whispered. He was talking to one of his men riding beside him, and had not noticed them. The way he sat his horse, a little back in the saddle and very straight, forcing the huge beast to change its center to him, the way he held his head and gazed around the square, radiating confidence and mastery… She could not look away.

She pulled the brim of her hat lower, shielding her face, until she could no longer see him, but only feel him across the square, like a lodestone, drawing her. She bit her lip until she tasted blood, the taste of her nightmares, of fear and violence. Her horse shied beneath her.

The horses! Even if he did not recognize them in their pilgrim's garb, the horses would give them away: a dun gelding and a black pony together. They should have taken separate routes and arranged to meet at the gate.

"Stay behind. We must not ride together," she hissed, urging her gelding ahead. She wished she dared go faster. Every step her horse took seemed interminable as she crossed the side road at the bottom of the square. Would he look her way, would he recognize her, before she reached the corner and passed out of sight of the square? She sat rigidly on her horse, willing herself not to turn, not to raise her head beneath the brim of her hat to see him again, not to show in any way her terrible awareness of him as his horse trotted through the square toward her.

What was this fearful attraction he held over her? She was drawn to him as a moth to a candle. And he would destroy her, as the flame consumes the moth. As he had nearly destroyed her in his castle. What had she learned in that castle that had separated them, that had nearly driven her mad and sent her fleeing to the abbey? The familiar pain began in her temples. She urged her gelding across the cobbled street until at last a row of merchant shops obscured the square, and she was finally safe.

Marie's pony cantered up beside her. The girl was pale and breathing heavily. Her hat was askew, tilted to hide her face. "He did not see us," she gasped, leaning her head back to peer up at Celeste from under the wide brim.

Celeste turned and kicked her horse into a canter.

They were the only pilgrims passing through the gate this late in the day. Celeste rode with her head down, hiding her face. She should have left right after Assumption. There had been hundreds of pilgrims leaving then. She felt the gatekeeper's eyes on her and Marie as they passed through the gate and onto the road to Lyon. Her back tingled with the strain. She was certain a cry would go up behind them at any moment.

When the road dipped, taking them out of sight of Cluny, she urged her horse into a gallop and raced along the road until she and the horse were both drenched in sweat.

She had escaped. She pulled the horse to a stop, laughing out loud, and dismounted, stretching her legs after the hard ride. She had never traveled without a male escort before, and that, too, was exhilarating. While she waited for Marie to catch up she took off her cloak and tied it behind her saddle.

Marie arrived and pulled the pony to a stop, still panting from the run. She looked around apprehensively, and did not dismount or take off her pilgrim's cloak.

Her nervousness irritated Celeste; no one would attack them in the daytime so close to Cluny, where their screams might be heard. Nevertheless, she swung back up into the saddle. There would be others on the road ahead, who had started out earlier. They would have to catch them up before dusk. But for now her independence pleased her.

"Where are we going?" Marie asked.

Celeste kicked her horse into a gentle canter. "To Lyon," she called over her shoulder. She would get her ring back after all. And when her memory returned, she would know what to do. She was no longer too sweet or too pious or too obedient to take care of herself. If the fever, or sorrow, or the sale of a crooked nail had taken that out of her, it was best gone.

And yet, she remembered her husband's face, and felt something fierce flutter in her breast, and stop her breath, and ignite an ache that spread through her.

They rode without stopping all afternoon and into the evening, passing only a few peasants on foot. Celeste kept them at a brisk pace despite her weariness. She had expected to find more travelers along this road. There was an inn at Sainte Blandine de Lugdunum, but it was too close to the abbey where she had been so ill and unhappy. She had nearly died of unhappiness there. Happiness was not a place that one could go to, it was not as easy as that, but there were places that one could avoid.

Dusk was falling when they saw a campfire beside the road up ahead. Celeste slowed her horse. They could not afford to be too fastidious about the company they kept this evening or they would have none at all, but she must not be foolish with her trust, either.

A half-dozen figures sat around a fire, too far to make out clearly. She advanced warily, shielding her eyes against the setting sun. A man got up to tend the fire. His brown robe and hood revealed him to be a Franciscan friar. She kicked the gelding into a trot.

"Wait, Lady Celeste," Marie called in a carrying whisper. "Stop a moment."

"Well?" Celeste demanded, when she had halted the gelding and still Marie did not speak. "What is it?"

"They…they are holy men."

"Yes. We will be safe with them."

"Will…would they know if someone is going to hell?"

Celeste sat very still. "Why do you ask?" she said, in a low voice.

"I must say something." Marie did not look at her, but at the distant fire.

"Consider carefully before you do."

Marie muttered something under her breath.

"I cannot hear you." Celeste glanced at the monks by their fire. She and Marie must look suspicious, conferring here.

"I said, I told a lie," Marie repeated, avoiding her eyes. "I know it is a sin and I will go to hell."

"Who did you lie to?" Marie's afterlife was not her concern; the lie, however, might be.

"I was so afraid when I saw Lord Bernard!"

"Who did you lie to?"

"The innkeeper."

"The innkeeper? You lied to the innkeeper? What did you tell him?"

"I told him we had decided to go to Paris. I told him not to tell anyone. Will I go to hell, Lady Celeste?"

Celeste laughed. She kicked her horse forward. She did not know whether Marie would go to hell, but she was fairly certain Lord Bernard would be going to Paris.

"Will I?" Marie called behind her.

She laughed again. "Not before we reach Lyon."

The Franciscan friars discussed their request for several minutes before the friar they had spoken to came over to them again.

Where are you going?" he asked.

"To Lyon," Celeste said.

"Your husband is in Lyon?"

"My Lady's brother lives there," Marie said, when Celeste did not answer.

Pierre lived in Lyon? She concentrated on his image as she had remembered it when the stranger leaned over her in the town square. It evoked brief scenes from her childhood: the two of them riding in the woods on their ponies, inventing games together.

"To visit my brother," she agreed.

The friar went to speak with the others. He returned to tell them they could share the friars' camp, but they must sleep on the opposite side of the fire from the Franciscans.

They reached Lyon in the early evening. Pierre's estate lay east of Lyon, his manor perched on the crest of a gentle hill. The track leading to it was wide enough for their horses to trot abreast between the deep ruts made by wagon wheels. On either side of them, rows of grapevines stretched across the hill facing the sun, spaced so that each row would not cast a shadow onto the higher one behind or the lower one in front.

As Marie pointed out the direction, Celeste remembered visiting her brother here, and her childless uncle. Pierre must have been fostered by their uncle, and inherited the estate from him. She remembered laughing here, and hiding in the vineyard for Pierre to find her, and sitting beside him on the wagon when he and Uncle took the barrels of wine into Lyon. The memories came to her easily, with no accompanying headache. She was smiling by the time she reached the manor and swung off her horse, tossing the reins to a servant.

"Tell Pierre de Lyon his sister has come to visit," she said. The servant went to do so, leaving the stable boy to hold her horse.

"Celeste," Pierre cried, appearing at the door of the manor and hurrying toward her. "How did you come here? You look well?" It came out as a question.

"I am well," she said.

A wide smile lit up his face. He was not much taller than she was, dark-haired and dark-eyed as she had remembered him, with a small-boned, wiry body. His complexion was sun-darkened, like their father—the land did that to men—but his features were hers. He stopped before her, holding his arms out. Celeste stepped into them, closing her eyes. The way he smiled, the feel of his arms around her, the grape and sunlight scent of him, everything was familiar.

"What brings you to Lyon, sister?"

"You," she murmured, holding on to him.

He laughed and kissed her on each cheek. "Take their belongings inside, and see to their horses." He leaned back to look at her. "We have been worried for you."

She smiled. She remembered him completely; no secret misgivings or headaches plagued her here.

"But where is Lord Bernard?"

"Oh, he is too busy to come visiting."

"Surely you did not travel alone?"

"No, of course not," Celeste stammered. She should have anticipated his questions; naturally he would be surprised to see her. "The rest of my party stopped at Lyon."

"We could have put Lord Bernard's men up," Pierre protested. "He will take it as an insult."

"I was not accompanied by his men, but by a group of Franciscans."

Pierre looked shocked. Before he could ask more questions, she said, "It has been a lengthy journey, Pierre."

"Of course. You must be tired and thirsty." He tucked her hand in the crook of his elbow and drew her toward the manor. "You have chosen a good time to come. We have just bought fresh spices from a peddler and the cook is eager to try new recipes. Isavel has ordered the kitchen maid to prepare a meal for you."

"Thank you," Celeste said, covering the rumble in her stomach with her hand. They had left the friars at their prayers, and had not eaten since yesterday's dinner at the Red Cock Inn, but she would not tell Pierre that. Her unexpected arrival appeared suspicious enough.

Inside the main hall, a table in front of the hearth was already set with three cups of wine. A servant placed a trencher piled high with cold meat and fruit beside one of the wine cups and motioned for Marie to follow her back to the kitchen.

A blond young woman who appeared to be Celeste's age came toward them. "Welcome, Lady Celeste," she said, reaching to clasp Celeste's hands. Beneath her sleeves, her wrists were brown from the sun, her hands as dark as a peasant's. If this was Isavel, Pierre had certainly married beneath himself.

The woman leaned forward and kissed both of Celeste's cheeks, while Pierre beamed down at her. Celeste returned her greeting, murmuring, "Thank you, Isavel," as though she remembered the woman. She slipped her hands out of Isavel's coarse grasp as soon as she was able.

The kitchen servant reappeared with a bowl of water and a small towel. Celeste removed her right glove and dipped her hand into the water to rinse away the dust of travel, drying it on the towel. Holding the right glove in her gloved left hand, she speared the meat and fruit pieces with her delicate Lady's knife and ate hungrily.

Pierre and Isavel sat across from her sipping their wine, having already eaten, while Celeste devoured the food on the trencher. They stared occasionally at her gloved hand, but refrained from commenting. Celeste pretended not to notice their curiosity.

Pierre smiled approvingly when she had finished. "Your appetite has returned." He motioned to the servant to take away the trencher to be given to beggars later.

"We had not heard of your recovery," Isavel said.

"It was quite sudden. Marie took me to mass, and when I knelt before the statue of Holy Mary, I was healed."

"All at once?" Isavel's eyebrows rose.

I see you are not as pious as I used to be, Celeste thought. "I was very tired at first, and suffered from headaches. And I was weak from having eaten little during my illness. But I am completely recovered now. It was a miracle." She finished with an air of finality meant to discourage further questions.

"I am surprised Lord Bernard agreed to part with you so soon after your recovery," Isavel persisted. "Perhaps he will join you here?"

"I am afraid he cannot," Celeste replied. "He has gone to Paris." She smiled sweetly at Isavel. "The meal was excellent. Pierre told me a spice peddler visited you."

Isavel flushed. "Yes," she said, sliding her rough hands beneath the table into her lap.

"I must send a message for him to stop in at Lord Bernard's castle. Do you know where he is staying?"

"I do not."

"Ahh. Then perhaps he mentioned where he is from?"

Isavel rose. "Lady Celeste, I am not nobility, but I am the wife of a wealthy wine merchant. I do not have personal conversations with peddlers."

"Isavel." Pierre shot Celeste an apologetic look.

"Of course not. Forgive me," Celeste said smoothly. "I will have Marie give him my message at the market tomorrow."

"I would be happy to help you choose some cloth for a new dress at the market. I expect you will want one now that you are no longer staying at an abbey."

"How thoughtful of you." Celeste rose and bid them good night. She crossed the hall as grandly as she could in her horrid black kirtle, calling to Isavel over her shoulder to send her maid up to her. Let Isavel remember that Celeste was a Lady while she was only the wife of a wealthy merchant.

A proud and unpleasant woman, Celeste thought as Marie unpinned her hair. One who instinctively sought another's weakness. An image of the one-eyed cock came to her mind. She pushed it away.

No wonder Pierre was surprised by her visit, married to such a hostess. If Isavel learned of her loss of memory, she would delight in telling everyone. She shuddered, imagining the mocking laughter as she floundered from error to error with no vision of the past to guide her.

Her stomach ached, upset from the long ride and heavy meal. Sleep would settle it. She climbed into bed, telling Marie to snuff out the candle.

Darkness rushed over the room, thick and black as smoke.

Just so had her illness, her fever (her bargain with the peddler?) snuffed out her past, leaving her no memories to illuminate the present. She lay on the soft feather mattress, utterly blind.

*The deep breathing of sleepers surrounds her as she crosses the great hall. The stairs are dark and narrow—she must hold the wall for support. At last she stands swaying at the threshold of her bedchamber.*

*The door opens slowly, the quiet scrape of its movement ominous in the darkness. Her feet are frozen to the cold stone floor; she cannot even raise her hand to cover her face, although she cannot bear to see inside the room. The door is fully open now; she cannot breathe, her terror is so great.*

*How small it is, so small it makes her ache. It only covers half the bench it rests on.*

*She steps through the doorway, stretching her hand toward the little wooden casket—*

Celeste woke drenched in sweat. She lay still, panting, as it dried, leaving a salty tightness on her skin. She breathed the cool night air in deeply, remembering the silence she had felt at the abbey when she first awoke from her illness. She had blamed a passing fever. So it was: a fever of grief, an illness of despair.

She sat up. No, a malady of weakness. How had she been undone by something as common as the death of an infant? Every woman endured that. The Abbess had called her bold, but she was not. She remembered the little wooden coffin clearly now, and the upstairs room. She closed her eyes, concentrating.

A rush of fear swept over her. Something else had happened in that room. She opened her eyes, gasping. She must not go back to the place where it had happened, nor walk through the halls that might recall it. It would overwhelm her if she did, as it had before. She pressed the palms of her hands tightly against her forehead.

Slowly, the pounding eased, and with it her fear. Of course she would go back. She had nothing to fear now. The girl in her dream, the girl that she had been, was a helpless, frightened, superstitious thing. Lord Bernard had owned that girl, as he owned his hunting dogs, his hawks, his horses; and she had acquiesced to being owned. The peddler had taken advantage of that girl, the Abbess had bullied her, her own father had used her to buy a noble bloodline.

But she was no longer that girl. She had sold her along with her past for one denier. She had made a good bargain after all.

# Chapter 14

It was a trap. The priest knew all about the girl, knew what Jean had taken from her. He was being tested. If Jean did not confess, and quickly—

He opened his mouth, but no words came out.

He had made confession on countless Sabbaths. He went with a prepared script of harmless venal sins: impatience with his wife, envying his neighbour, coveting another man's possession. The sort of things they expected to hear from him.

This was a real confession.

*Never confess, his father's voice insisted.*

This was a dangerous confession.

*Do not give them the proof they need, he warned Jean's mother.*

This would be a public confession.

*Keep quiet.*

He closed his mouth. They had abandoned him as a child, left him to fend for himself, scavenging and stealing to stay alive. But he had learned one lesson from his parents' deaths: never trust anyone. They had kept him alive, by teaching him that.

The priest patted Jean's arm. "Never mind. The words will come when you are ready. Meanwhile, rest assured, the girl is safe with her brother and her father."

"Her father?"

The priest looked uncomfortable. "We must pray that he will learn forgiveness. He is a good man, I am sure, in other circumstances."

*The girl's father?* He was talking about the little girl at Cluny! He must still think Jean linked that child to his own little Jeanne. To him, that explained this strangeness that had come over Jean, a strangeness that was more than a distraction.

But not a spell. The priest had made that clear. A priest would know the difference.

What if it were as simple as a child who looked and spoke like Jeanne?

As simple and as complex as that. Because home was home and family was family, and everywhere and everyone else was not. If that was no longer true, then Jean was no longer Jean. And if not Jean, then who was he?

No! The priest was wrong. It was not the child who haunted him, nor lingering thoughts of his family, as he had claimed earlier. It was the mysterious black-eyed young woman, with her ring and her nail. The nail that he had not been able to throw away, that he had forgotten to sell when he had the chance. The nail that he still carried, because it was bound to the ruby and to him by his ill-omened trade. He closed his eyes, but they danced in his mind, the shiny nail as black as sin and the brilliant, gold-clawed ruby as red as the sorrow of God and the blood of His martyrs.

"It is a spell, Father." He could barely form the words.

"No, it is not." The priest spoke firmly, loud enough to reach any in his company who had overheard Jean's admission. "Good does not come of spells. Children are not saved because of a spell. 'Suffer the little children to come onto me,' our Lord said. He does not work through spells. Therefore you are not under a spell."

Jean was embarrassed at the extent of his relief. He glanced sideways. Everyone nearby was watching. What a spectacle he had made of himself.

"Well then," he said. He gave the donkey's halter a perfunctory yank. "Then that is settled. For me, anyway." He glared accusingly around at those watching.

The priest patted his shoulder again. They resumed walking.

It was a great relief to reach Lyon just after sunset and part company with the pilgrims. Jean walked briskly through the narrow, twisting streets. The late summer breeze was rich with familiar scents: horse dung and wood smoke, sewage tossed from windows and floor rushes swept into the streets, freshly-baked bread, carrot and onion stews, fish and fowl roasting over hearth fires. People called from open windows to one another and children in the streets laughed and squabbled at their games. Jean smiled and nodded as he passed townspeople, slyly assessing the quality of their clothes and the weight of their purses.

The merchant's house where he hoped to find a welcome was not as large as most, but Jean had stayed there before. He would be well-fed and allowed to sleep in the loft for a reasonable barter of spices. Despite its distance from the hearth and consequent lowly status, Jean preferred sleeping there rather than in the large hall, as it allowed some measure of protection against theft. Even if other guests shared the loft, and there usually were others, it would be impossible for anyone to make off with his goods without being seen carrying them down the ladder. He found the building he was looking for and knocked on the heavy wooden door.

"Jean the spice peddler," he said when the door opened. The steward closed the door without a word. Jean remembered him: an unpleasant fellow, resentful of having to serve a man less well-born than himself. It was one of the things Jean liked about staying here.

In a few minutes a stable boy arrived. Jean followed him through a gate in the tall wooden fence, into the inner courtyard. The surly steward was waiting at the door. Jean let the boy take his donkey to the stables, giving him a coin to unharness the weary animal and guard his things, and followed the servant up the narrow stairs to the floor above the undercroft. They entered a small, dark anteroom, separated from the great hall by screens. The steward led him into the hall.

It was an older house, without a separate kitchen. Three female servants stood around the hearth fire in the center of the room. A well-dressed middle-aged woman with a clutch of keys hanging at her waist stood behind them issuing orders as they fussed over a haunch of pork sizzling on a spit above the flames. A large, black stew pot hung beside it. The long table had been set in the middle of the room and benches placed on either side, ready for dinner.

Smoke burned Jean's eyes, despite the hole high above the hearth and the open shutters on the narrow windows around the hall. The woman spoke sharply to one of the servants, but her voice was drowned by the crackle of fat falling into the fire and the rushes scratching on the stone floor under Jean's feet as he followed the steward across the room toward her.

To his left, steep stairs set into the stone side of the wall led to the upstairs rooms. Several screen partitions created extra rooms along that side of the hall. The other walls were hung with tapestries depicting hunting scenes, battles and feasts. A ladder at the far end of the hall led up to the loft, where Jean expected to lodge.

The woman greeted him, asking in the same breath to see his wares. He bowed, hiding his smile. She wanted to make her choices before he visited her neighbours.

"Your steward bade me leave them and come in to you, Mistress Marguerite," he answered.

The steward received a look that cheered Jean thoroughly, but Marguerite only said, "Get them and bring them here." When the steward left, she returned to supervising the cooking of their meal until his goods arrived.

She bought a blue silk handkerchief blessed in Jerusalem, the scarlet ribbon, and a pair of green hose for her husband as well as nearly a sou's worth of spices, measured on his scales, which he asked the steward to retrieve from one of the panniers. Jean was scrupulous in his weighing, tipping the balance slightly in her favour. The merchant's wife would have everything weighed again on her own scales after he had gone to sleep. If she was satisfied, her neighbours would hear of it. Finally, Jean offered her two squares of leather in return for his meals and lodging.

"We have shoes," she said proudly, looking at the bag of cinnamon sticks which she had touched longingly but not opened. He offered her two sticks, though they were more than double the price of the leather. She accepted them with delight. It was worth it when she instructed the steward to carry Jean's barrels and panniers up to the loft where he was to sleep, and to be sure to bring them down again the next morning for him.

The next two days made up for Jean's difficult journey to Lyon. The sullen steward delivered his barrels and wadmal bags to the stable every morning, and carried them back to the loft each evening. One of his barrels had been empty since Cluny, but he had the steward hoist it up and down along with the other, for the pleasure of seeing his expression as he did so. It was less amusing this year than it had been last year, however, and when he saw the servant rubbing his back the evening of the second day, and noticed gray hairs at the corner of his cap, he left the empty barrel in the loft and carried the other one up himself, cursing his foolishness as he did so.

The wine merchants were eager to buy his spices—what was wine without a well-seasoned meal to go with it? The pottery merchants asked what the wine merchants had bought and would not be outdone by them. Jean feared he would have no spices left for the market, a satisfying concern indeed.

At the end of the second day, he climbed contentedly into the loft. The mistress of the house, still pleased with her cinnamon sticks, had given him a tallow candle only half burned, to take up with him. He set it carefully on the planked wooden floor of the loft, a little distance from the thick straw pallet made up for him.

He was alone in the loft. The two boys who had shared it with him—nephews of the silk merchant—had left that day to return to their home. It was a rare treat to have a place to sleep all to himself. He removed his boots and wriggled his feet in his hose, stretching his legs out before him. He looked at the barrels, one empty and the other nearly so, and sighed with satisfaction. The money pouch was a heavy weight at his side. Why not look at it? No one was here to see.

He untied the pouch from his waist and loosened the strings. Slowly he tipped it up, letting the precious coins fall into a heap on the floor beside the candle. The thin, yellow line of light above them turned the brown coins into gold. He looked at them a long moment, imagining that he could do anything he wanted with them. Then he began to count.

First, the money to feed them all winter and buy next year's spices. He counted out the coins he would need, setting them on the floor aside from the first pile. He made it a generous pile, more than he had spent this year, for he could have sold more of the rare spices today if he had them. When he was through, he still had nearly a third of the coins in the original pile. He smiled down at them.

He must keep some extra for his side goods. He would not buy hose again, but the shoe leather had sold well; he had only four pieces left. He would decide what else to offer next year when he saw what came in on the ships. Two years ago he had bought some fine sewing needles made in Constantinople, and sold all but one which he had intended to give to Mathilde at Yuletide. Then one of his barrels turned out to have a leak and he had found most of the spices in it dampened when he unsealed it. He had to sell them for half what he had bought them for, and could not afford to keep the needle for Mathilde.

Carefully he counted out a smaller number of coins and added it to the pile for next year's wares.

There was still more left. And there, at the bottom, lay the ring. He frowned. What if one of the merchants had seen it when he was making change today? They would wonder where it had come from. One of them might have recognized it. How careless he was being, how foolish. He scooped it out of the pile and pried the lid off the empty barrel, tucking the ring into one of the large wadmal bags lying at the bottom of the barrel. He thought for a moment, then rifled through one of the panniers until he found the nail and the pilgrim's badge, and tossed them into the wadmal bag as well before refitting the lid tightly onto the barrel.

He sat down again in front of his two piles of coins. There had been years when he had had only a few coins left over from those needed for another year's trading, or none at all, to get them through the winter. He remembered one other year when he had had this much extra. Jeanne was born that year. Mathilde's labor was difficult; mother and babe had nearly been lost. He had had to send for a doctor.

He shook his head to clear it. Home was home and trading was trading.

Jean looked down at the smaller pile of coins. He hesitated. But he was alone in the croft—who would notice?

"Never look back," he muttered under his breath. It was a rule. He looked again at the little pile of coins, seeing faces on them, Mathilde and the boys, little Jeanne.

No one could see him here.

Quickly he counted out three deniers. Gilles was growing; he would need a new tunic. Jean added a fourth for hose. He needed a new tunic himself; he added two deniers to the third pile, feeling better. This was about trading; a trader must look prosperous.

There were still a surprising number left. Jeanne would be nearly three when he got home. Time to start thinking of her dowry. It was up to him to see she married well. Six deniers: half a sou. That would make a very good start. He smiled to himself.

Mathilde had not had a new kirtle in… He shrugged. Too long to remember. She had not asked for one. He looked at the dwindling pile of his profits. He had promised himself for years that he would set aside something for bad times. But there was still the ring, and the nail and the badge. He could sell them in Avignon, or at Narbonne. He might give the ring to the priest to sell in Spain when he visited his wife. Even if the fellow kept a portion of the sale, he would do well—and who would question a priest? He grinned and counted four deniers into the third pile, and one more for a new white veil as well, to cover Mathilde's thick, brown hair.

There were—he counted them out—eight deniers left. But there was still Simon to consider. Simon would be coming with him next year. It was time. Jean had been on his own, scrounging for food, when he was much younger than Simon. Perhaps that was why he kept putting the boy off. But Simon would not be alone or afraid; his father would be there to protect him.

He scooped up the eight deniers. A trader could not look poor—people would wonder about the quality of his wares. Simon would need a new tunic, new hose, new shoes. Jean decided to set aside two of the pieces of leather, one for him and one for Simon. And a warm cape with a hood. And a pouch; Simon would need his own money pouch.

Jean counted out the coins. It would take most of the remaining deniers, but he could already see Simon in his new outfit. He pictured his son turning around to show off his cape, the pride on Mathilde's face, mixed with a little worry, perhaps, and the envy on Gilles' face. He laughed under his breath. Gilles' turn would come. Then he imagined Simon's face, earnest and young, trying hard to smile.

Jean was not home very much of the year, but he knew more than Simon thought he knew.

Simon did not want to come with him, even though he had protested again this year when Jean declared he was not yet old enough. Simon wanted to be apprenticed to a blacksmith. He loved animals, and he was good with them, and good also at working with his hands, at shaping things. He did not hate fire the way Jean did; he was drawn to it, despite Jean's warnings.

"It changes things," Simon said. Jean agreed with that, although Simon saw how it made iron and metal malleable, while Jean saw how it devoured wood and flesh, how it could eat up a boy's childhood and spit the ashes at his feet.

Simon did not see that. Simon would rather be a blacksmith's apprentice with holes in his hose, a threadbare tunic, and worn out shoes, than be dressed like a merchant's son and barter for sales at distant markets. Gilles should come with him. Gilles would like the traveling and the fairs and festivals and all the people he would meet. Gilles would like haggling over a price until he struck a profitable deal.

Simon had never asked to be apprenticed. He knew they had no money to buy an apprenticeship. It made more sense for Simon and Gilles to work with him, to build up his trading route. Why was he even considering the boy's whim?

But if he got a good price for the ring, and sold the nail and the pilgrim's badge to the monastery at Narbonne...

No, it was not possible. There would be nothing left to set aside. There would be no new kirtle for Matilde, or tunic for Gilles, and what would he do about a dowry for Jeanne?

Jeanne was a baby. It was too early to think about her dowry.

He knew that was not true. He was not likely to get many windfalls like this. There were worse things that were far more likely to happen. He should set something aside.

But even so...

Jean put his hand over the little pile of coins for Simon. He pushed them toward the pile intended to clothe them all.

He was not being sensible.

Even so...

He pushed the mound of coins for Simon across to join the small original pile, the pile that would not include some set-aside money, after all.

Yes. Even so.

The candle sputtered. The tallow had burned almost completely away. Jean scooped up the piles of coins and poured them into his pouch, being careful not to miss any. He wound the string tightly around it. The candle sputtered again and went out. Jean tied the pouch to his belt. The rush lights in the great hall were still burning, throwing enough light into the loft for him to undress by.

A murmur of male voices drifted up from the hall below. The women had gone to their beds long ago. The loft was too warm for the fur covering they had given him, so he lay down on top of it. It made the pallet as soft as a feather bed. He slept like a lord, and dreamed that his sons were squires at court in Paris.

Jean awoke to see a dull, overcast sky through the windows. He had slept deeply, as he sometimes did after coming to a decision, and had no time to eat more than a few quick spoonsful of the porridge set out for him. He had traded for his keep and it bothered him to waste what he had paid for. He should not have counted out his money that way last night. He had made his decision and he was content with it, but he should not have made it here. A trader needed to think like a trader. He needed to keep his wits, not his family, about him on the road. The broken rule was a bad omen.

The market was bustling with shoppers when Jean arrived. He found a space near the end of a row of farm carts and unloaded his donkey quickly, keenly aware of the sound of buying and selling all around him, and the clink of coins passing into other men's hands.

He glanced up at the sky. Heavy, dark clouds had rolled in on a stiff wind. He did not dare open the lid of the barrel with the last of his spices to let their aromas entice customers over, in case the clouds burst before he could get it shut again. Still, he took his weigh scales from the pannier and set them on top with an open pot of salt which could be covered quickly and a small selection of the less expensive herbs.

He placed the linen handkerchiefs and some ribbons on top of the empty barrel, where they could be admired, and draped two pair of hose over the sides.

He sold the last of his salt to an innkeeper, save the bit he kept for himself on his journey home, an extravagance he felt he had earned; but he did not sell any of his remaining spices. A few people stopped to admire the ribbons and handkerchiefs. He had nearly a dozen people around him at one point, listening eagerly as he explained how the linen handkerchiefs had been carried on pilgrimage by a holy priest and blessed on the tomb of the Apostle James at Santiago. He told how such blessings had brought miracles to those who owned them, and held the group spellbound with stories of lost things found and fortunes won and sudden, wondrous cures. He told it well, as he always did, dispelling the overcast gloom with his compelling rhetoric and extravagant gestures.

On a sunny day he would have sold every handkerchief on display, but not one was bought this morning, though people had gazed at and touched them longingly. There was no one with any money here today. People with money had sent their servants to buy what the household needed—they themselves could wait for a pleasanter day to browse and socialize at the market.

Tomorrow he would do better, if it did not rain. Already, his trip had been profitable. Simon's surprise and delight would warm them all better than new clothes would. And when he sold the ring, there might be new clothes as well. He whistled to himself, a little tune he had known since childhood and whistled to his children. He stopped at once.

Three women approached his area. He recognized them; they had been here before, at the edge of the earlier group, and had not bought anything. He continued packing up.

"Do not ask. He will only cheat you out of what little money you have."

"He would not."

Jean turned.

An old woman stood in front of his barrels. She smiled at him, showing a dimple in her left cheek. "You would not cheat me, would you?"

"Pardon, Madame?" he stammered, to hide his confusion. She was the image of his mother, as she would have looked at this age. He leaned forward a little. No, it was only the slant of her eyebrows and her smile, gentle and a little sad.

"I am a poor woman, but my son is sick. I need one of your blessed linens."

Jean stared at her. The timbre of her voice, the cadence of its rise and fall, all so like his mother's.

*"He cheated you," his father shouted as he and Jean's mother walked into their little hut, before Jean could even ask what they had got at market.*

*"No," his mother replied. "He asked for what he needed and I chose to give it to him." She put her basket on the table and beckoned to Jean, still talking to her husband over her shoulder. Jean stayed where he was, crouched on the dirt floor near his sleeping mat. He concentrated on the big black beetle he had brought inside on a twig, pretending not to hear them.*

*"You saw him, Simon. How poor he is. And he has a family, four little ones to feed, and no home, poor soul."*

*"You believed him?"*

*"The last part I believed, at least. He looked like the weather had knocked him about, had broken him. Think of it, no roof to protect him from rain or wind or hail, no hearth-fire on a cold winter night."*

*"Well, think on this," his father said. "We have a son to feed! You take the food out of your own son's mouth when you throw away our money like that! What if our son becomes sick? What if you or I do? How will your charity help us then?"*

*Jean eyed them sideways from his corner of the room. His father was shaking his head, defeated by his mother's gentle stubbornness. "You do not understand how hard it is to get and keep what little we have, how easy it would be to lose it all," he said.*

*Jean shivered. His stomach ached. It often hurt a little, with hunger, but now it was worse, all knotted up. If only they would not argue. He stared down at the beetle. It had been climbing up and down the little twig all afternoon, prompted by Jean's nudges. It sat still now.*

*"God will provide," his mother replied.*

*"I will provide, you mean! I provide, and you do not appreciate it. We deserve to be poor, the way you squander what little we have."*

*Jean jumped up and raced out of the hut. He ran hard, until the sound of his bare feet slapping against the hard, dry earth and his ragged breath drowned out the empty feeling in his chest, in his gut, drowned out his mother's foolish smile and left only his father's anger.*

*An anger that came to him even now, when everything else had faded; an anger that was more careful of him than his mother's kindness had ever been.*

He tried to summon that anger as he looked at the woman before him, but her smile—his mother's smile, even to the dimple—disarmed him. In the presence of that smile, he no longer wanted vengeance against the poverty of his childhood. He no longer wanted to cheat others, to get back at them for cheating his mother and back at her, for letting them.

He heard himself say, "Two deniers."

He opened his mouth immediately to take it back, but the old woman was already reaching for a square of linen with a hand that trembled. She dropped two deniers into his hand, which had opened reflexively at the appearance of her coins.

"God bless you, Peddler." Her words hit Jean like a slap, shaking away the memory of his mother. He stared at the two deniers, shocked. What had come over him? Pity? Compassion? A peddler could not afford compassion! It was a luxury for the rich, and they rarely indulged it.

Then, by God, he heard a chorus of feminine voices crying "God bless you, Peddler," as other hands reached for the handkerchiefs, until he had a handful of dirty deniers and half of his remaining linen handkerchiefs were gone. He grabbed up those that were left and shoved them into his sack before anyone else came running over.

He could not remain here. Word would spread. Tomorrow he would be besieged by women wanting the last of his goods at unthinkable prices. He had set those expectations in motion, the fault was his. He saw the trap he had made for himself with his foolish weakness; he had to escape before it sprung on him.

The women, bright-eyed with their unexpected fortune, were still blessing him as he dropped their deniers into his money pouch, spilling two onto the ground in his haste, stooping to scoop them up quickly. He packed his remaining merchandise into the open barrel and pounded the lid on quickly with a stone. He strapped both barrels over the donkey's back, trying not to appear in too much of a hurry.

When people's expectations were not met, they became angry, suspicious. Two deniers for a shrine-blessed linen handkerchief would make anyone suspicious. He could not risk staying here in the hope that it would blow over; that no one come from Cluny would remember he had charged four deniers for the same handkerchiefs there, a reasonable price if they were truly blessed.

He saw again his mother's smile on the old woman's face, and felt the child's arms around his neck at Cluny as he carried her to safety. A terrible fear came over him. He was becoming as careless as his mother. No, never! He must leave at once!

It was galling to leave this way, in defeat and, yes, fear. But he had seen peddlers accused of dishonesty and he had no wish to lose a hand as well as his purse. In a man's home town, someone might speak up for him. But here in Lyon he was friendless and alone. He felt once again the anger, the hot, tight heaviness of it in his throat and gut, which had deserted him earlier when he looked into the old woman's face.

He shook his head bitterly and reached for the donkey's lead rope. The donkey laid its ears back and switched its tail.

Compassion, like flies, is attracted to asses, Jean thought.

# Chapter 15

Celeste walked slowly down the last row of stalls. Where could he be? She had walked past every vendor at the Lyon market with Pierre and Isavel, under the pretence of searching for the right color of cloth for her new kirtle. All the while her gaze darted ahead, trying to find the peddler before he noticed her, her mind busy forming excuses to speak to him alone. She stopped, frustrated.

"Well, you have seen them all," Isavel said. "Is there not one bolt of fabric that would suit you?"

"I am sure there are several. But I always enjoy a market, do you not also, Pierre?" Celeste said with a smile she did not feel.

"Yes, we do," Pierre answered, before Isavel could give her opinion.

Celeste turned to look back at the bustling common grounds. She should have insisted on coming yesterday, rain or no rain. But Isavel had been so horrified at the thought of her catching a chill and it bringing on another illness, and Pierre had agreed with her. Instead they had stayed inside, doing needlework. She had been so frustrated, bending over the tapestry, that she pricked her finger hard enough to draw blood, despite the blunt end of the tapestry needle. What a fuss Isavel had made over a few drops of blood on her tapestry!

*He must be here.* She began retracing her steps, examining every stall, despite Isavel's protests.

"Rest in the shade," Celeste suggested. "Pierre will wait with you." Pierre, of course, gallantly refused to leave her. Isavel followed them, her expression grim.

"You may borrow one of my kirtles till you have your own, if you wish."

"I am afraid the color would not suit me. Your complexion is more robust than mine."

She noted with satisfaction, the rush of blood to Isavel's cheeks. Isavel opened her mouth to respond but Pierre put a hand on her arm. She closed her mouth with a snap.

Celeste bit her lower lip. What made her say such things? *She meant to insult your black kirtle,* a voice inside her said. Where did that come from? She had not used to think such things of others.

He was not here. She had seen every stall, walking the grounds twice until her feet ached. Wearily, she stopped at the table of a cloth merchant she had passed twice. She ran her hands over the bolts of cloth without seeing their colors. "Marie, go inquire after the peddler who sold Mistress Isavel her fine spices," she said, holding up a blue silk, as though her words were of little import. "I want him to stop in at our castle near Le Puy. See if you can find where he might be."

The merchant was wrapping her selection when Marie returned. While Pierre paid for the cloth, Celeste pulled Marie aside.

"There was a spice peddler here yesterday, My Lady, but he left when the market closed. No one knows where he has gone. Are we going back to the castle now? What is it, My Lady?"

Celeste stumbled and leaned against the merchant's table.

"Are you ill, My Lady?" Marie grasped her arm.

"No, I am only weary." Celeste straightened as Isavel and Pierre hurried over.

"No wonder," Isavel muttered half under her breath.

"There is the White Lion Inn." Pierre handed the folded and tied silk to his servant and clasped Celeste's arm. "Let us rest and eat a pie before riding home."

She should not have choked down the fish pie. Its rank taste stuck in her throat, threatening humiliation with every bounce of the carriage until finally she had to cry, "Halt!" and rush out to the side of the road. The nauseous stink hung about her, as foul as her mood, all the way back to Pierre's manor.

"My Lady…" Marie, washing her face gently with a cloth dipped in the bowl of rose water she had brought to their room, paused.

"What is it?" Should she return to her husband without the ring? There was little chance she would find it now; not without making her interest in the spice peddler apparent.

"I… I have your cloths, My Lady, if you need them?"

"My cloths?" He had been here yesterday. She should have gone despite the rain. Well, she had not. But she had noticed a few jewel smiths, perhaps she could have a ring made to imitate hers. She did not have enough coins for a real ruby, but—

"Your *cloths*." Marie blushed furiously.

Celeste stared at her. Cloth? Oh, for her courses. What did that matter right now?

"Perhaps you do not need them?" Marie asked. She put down the wash cloth and reached for a towel. "You fainted at Cluny, My Lady. And now you have thrown up twice."

What was Marie fussing about? She drew back from the towel Marie was patting her face with. Were her courses due?

Was she late? Did Marie think— She gripped the bench, feeling a rush of vertigo. "How long was I at the abbey, Marie?"

"Eight Sabbaths, including the one that healed you."

"Eight?"

Marie nodded.

"And before that?"

"Twelve Sabbaths have passed since… since the funeral."

And I have not—?"

Marie shook her head. "It is fourteen Sabbaths since you last bled."

"You would know?" Could it be possible?

"I wash them, My Lady. And I can count. You taught me."

"I have been ill. Sometimes a woman… when she is ill…" It was not possible!

"Yes, I know, My Lady. The herbalist at the abbey told me women often stop having their courses when they are ill, especially if they are thin." She looked at Celeste speculatively. "You are not thin now, My Lady."

"You spoke of me to the herbalist?"

"I did not mention you!" Marie cried hastily. "I knew you would not like it. We spoke about the fever in the village."

It could not be true. "No…" she whispered. Her voice caught on the word. *No, it could not be. She could not bear to think it!*

"If you are with child, it does not matter about the ring," Marie crowed. "Lord Bernard will not be angry, if you are carrying his child."

"I am not!" She wanted to scream and beat at her stomach, the little round stomach she had noticed several days ago. "Get out. Take the water and leave me. Now!"

Marie gave a little "Oh" of surprise, looked at Celeste's face, and scuttled out.

Celeste closed the shutters. She paced around the room. Why had she not had her courses? Was she still ill, her body too weak to follow a natural feminine rhythm? That must be it. Surely she would know if she were with child. She would feel its presence within her, frail and determined, fluttering toward existence. She would sense its tiny will creeping over hers, subverting to itself her cares and her interests, her hopes and dreams. She would be consumed by its tenuous hold on life, would feel as defenceless as it to every puff of misfortune that might brush its fragile light into darkness. She stood in the little room, hugging her stomach, swallowing the bile that rose to her throat.

*They put him into her arms, swaddled in a square of linen. He was as light as a sparrow. He lay still at first, resting after his struggle into life, only his little lips moving, pursing and sucking at the air. They were pink and soft and perfectly formed, a tiny rosebud of a mouth, opening and closing soundlessly. His head began to move from side to side, searching for her. His eyelids opened a crack, shut again, and fluttered opened once more, the long, dark lashes trembling against his pale skin. She watched him, blinking herself, as though they were both seeing for the first time, starting life together. His deep black eyes, her eyes, stared up at her.*

*He could hurt her. He could wound her more deeply than anything else in the world. She was completely vulnerable because of him. If anything should happen to him…*

She could not be pregnant! She could not ever be so vulnerable again. She fell to her knees, pressing her forehead against the bed. "I am not with child," she moaned, clenching her teeth to avoid screaming the words.

"Something is wrong. You know it is." Isavel's voice reached Celeste as she descended the stairs after her rest. Pierre murmured a response too low for her to hear.

"Then how do you explain the pilgrim's cloak I found in her pack?" Celeste paused, listening.

"Send a message! I doubt he even knows she's here."

Celeste trod heavily on the stone step, calling for Marie. The voices below fell silent. When she reached the bottom of the stairs, Isavel had left the room. Pierre smiled and invited her for a walk in the vineyard.

"Fetch a jug of water and take it up to my room," she ordered Marie. Pierre had a worried expression on his face. Whatever he had to say she would rather hear alone.

"Marie," she said sharply. The girl was simpering at Pierre and gave no indication of having heard her.

"Do as you are told," she cried, striking Marie on the cheek.

Marie shrank back, holding her cheek, her eyes brimming with tears.

"Fetch a jug of water for my room," Celeste repeated. "And open the shutters to air it." Marie was besotted with Pierre, blushing and stammering whenever he spoke to her. Celeste itched to reprimand her again when she ran to the kitchen without a word or a curtsey. She turned to see Pierre staring at her.

"Sister, I have never seen you be unkind to Marie," he said.

"I do not mistreat her," she protested.

Pierre did not argue, but his expression disagreed.

"How have I harmed her? I only box her ears when she is impertinent or lazy. Your wife does no different with her servants."

"But you grew up with Marie."

"Yes, I believe that is the problem." She smiled at Pierre. "But I am doing my best to correct it."

He looked at her strangely. "You have changed," he said.

He was her brother, her friend since childhood; he knew her better than she knew herself. How could she pretend to be the same girl he remembered? "People change," she said.

"You defend her because she bats her eyes at you," she added, smiling indulgently. She tucked her hand in the crook of his elbow, walking outside with him. "Have you seduced her?"

"Never!"

"She is a peasant," Celeste shrugged, wondering at the force of his denial.

"Enough." Pierre straightened his arm, dislodging her hand. "I caught her father beating her and whipped him for it. He bears the scar across his cheek to this day." He nodded in satisfaction, then frowned, "although he did not learn his lesson. Marie was only five, but she has remembered. I think I am the only man she does not fear. It is not amusing to suggest I would betray that trust, whether she is a peasant or not."

"Do not be angry, Pierre. I did not know."

"You knew her father beat her. You knew his beatings killed her sister, Lise. When I think that you watched your childhood playmate beaten to death! If I had been there then, instead of here with our Uncle, reading of it in your letter—" His hands clenched into fists at his side.

Celeste stepped back, appalled at his intensity. "But they were servants' children," she said.

Pierre's face showed surprise, followed by a hard, unreadable expression which frightened her more than his earlier outburst had. "Our great grandfather was a servant." His voice was cool, each word spoken precisely. "He worked hard, and was rewarded, and married well, and he saw that his sons did the same, and their sons as well. We may be wealthy, but our blood is common, sister. Do not forget that, now you are a Lady."

She flushed, drawing back. Descended from a servant? Could it be true? She looked down, hiding her face from him. Did her servants know? Did Lord Bernard? Surely he would not have married her if he did. Or did he send her away because he found out? All of France would be mocking her—the peasant who thought she was a Lady.

Pierre grasped her hands. "I know you have not forgotten, Celeste," he said. "I am sorry for suggesting you had. I know why you took Marie as your maid when you could have chosen any of Father's servants to go with you. You did a better job of rescuing her than I."

She looked up, shocked. Was he right? Could she have formed such ties with servants' children? She opened her mouth to deny it, but Pierre was smiling fondly at her once more. She forced herself to smile and let him think what he would.

"I do not like to talk of the past," she said, her voice shaking. She turned toward the vineyard.

"Then we will not. But out of love, I must know something." He put a hand on her arm.

She kept walking, not looking at him, certain her anxiety must show on her face. How would she satisfy him if he asked her a question she could not answer? He would not accept her memory lapses without comment, as Marie did.

"It is not like Lord Bernard, to send you off without his own men to protect you."

"He is in Paris."

Pierre pulled her to a stop. He took her shoulders and turned her to look at him.

"Does he know you are well?" His face looked strained, as though he feared to hear her answer.

If she lied to him now, it would stand between them forever. What a relief it would be to tell him everything: her loss of memory, her nightmares, the fear that kept her away from her husband. Would he laugh at it, reassure her that she was worried for no reason?

Would he be right? Even if his intentions were good, how could he know what had happened in Lord Bernard's castle? That was the problem, right there. For if he did not know, her alarm would appear foolish. And if he learned that she had given away her marriage ring, he would think her wits were still addled and feel compelled to escort her back to Lord Bernard for her own good. She had no doubt he cared for her, but how far dared she trust him?

"Of course he does." It was not entirely a lie, after all. The Abbess must have told her Lord husband when she sent him on to Cluny after her. "When he is summoned to Court, he must go. His wife's health does not matter to King Louis." That also was true. Pierre and Isavel were free to draw any meaning they wished from it.

Pierre released her shoulders. He reached for her left hand, and raised it between them. "You do not wear your husband's ring."

Celeste snatched her hand away. She had gotten used to the lightness of her finger without the ring, and had forgotten to keep it hidden. Even through the glove it was obvious her finger was bare.

"What is wrong, Celeste?" Pierre asked gently.

She could not meet his eyes, gazing at her with such concern.

"You are safe here. Stay with us as long as you wish. Isavel could use your help. She works too hard, but I would never have such a fine vineyard without her working by my side."

"Nothing is wrong," she said sharply. Isavel would enjoy giving orders to Lady Celeste.

There it was, the first real lie between them. It had not been so hard to lie to Marie or the Abbess or Father Jacques. She had not cared about them, or what they would think of her later, when they found out. She drew back, beyond his touch, and imagined it was Isavel she was speaking to, for Isavel would surely hear her answer.

She had sold her jewellery to pay for an orphanage, Marie said. She could say she had given the ring to the abbey in gratitude when she recovered. But Marie knew she had not, and Marie would never be able to lie to Pierre.

"I lost my ring while I was ill," she said. "Lord Bernard is having a new one made for me in Paris." She forced herself to look at him, to smile lightly, and was taken aback by the relief and joy on his face. His arms reached to enclose her. She shut her eyes and bent her head to his chest and felt the closeness between them as though it were not already lost forever.

"I will not see you tomorrow, sister," Pierre told her after their supper. "I will be gone at first light and not be back for several days."

"I shall miss you."

Pierre smiled. "I must sell my wine as well as make it. Sleep well." He kissed her lightly.

*She is in the castle. Even while she lies tangled in its ephemeral reality, she recognizes her dream. She struggles to awaken, tries to scream to her dream figure, "No! Turn back!" but the nightmare continues, and she is trapped inside it.*

*Slowly she climbs the stairs toward her bedchamber.*

*(Stop! Turn and flee while you can!)*

*The door opens. There sits the small wooden casket on the bench, and there, in the bed, she sees the ghostly image of herself. She cannot breathe, her terror is so great.*

*She watches as her dream-self kneels beside the bed—*

*No, she will not look!*

*Her ghostly self stares at the bed, her face filled with horror.*

*She will not look, she will not!*

*"If Lord Bernard finds out, he will set you aside." A man's voice—whose? Standing in her bedchamber, alone with her—Raimond!*

*She looks up, startled.*

*Raimond stands beside her bed, smiling down at the ghostly figure of herself.*

*A scream fills her throat…*

Celeste sat bolt upright, her strangled cry loud in her own ears.

"Mistress?" Marie appeared beside her bed, her eyes wide and frightened.

"Go back to your pallet." Her voice sounded gruff, still panicky. "It was only a dream." When Marie hesitated, she repeated more firmly, "Go back to sleep."

How could a dream follow her from place to place, progressing with each repetition? What sin had she committed to have such a burden haunt her? She closed her eyes, trying to block it out, but it only came back to her more clearly.

*"He will send you away, if you tell him. He will set you aside and no one will take pity on you. You will be utterly ruined if you ever tell anyone."* Raimond's voice, cold and threatening, filled the room.

"I will not tell," she whispered.

Not tell what? What was Raimond doing in her dream? She remembered him, now that she had dreamed him: her Lord's cousin, only a few years older than she. She recalled clearly his kindness, his courtly demeanour, his concern for her. He had confided in her, and she in him.

There had been nothing of that courtly friendship in her dream. Why was he alone with her in her bedchamber at night? What was the secret he insisted she keep?

She closed her eyes. Surely not. Surely not that. She ran her fingers over her belly. Lying like this, on her back, it was almost flat. Had she imagined the bulge? Under her hands she felt only the pleasing roundness of a woman. But she had not had her courses. If she was with child—she was *not* with child—but if she was—whose child might it be?

A wave of nausea overcame her. She leaped from the bed and grabbed the chamber pot, gagging into it until her stomach ached and her throat burned. When she was done, Marie helped her back into bed and took it away without a word.

The days passed slowly. With Pierre away, Isavel was busy overseeing the winery as well as the maintenance of the household. Celeste offered half-heartedly to assist, but Isavel politely declined, urging her to enjoy her leisure. Celeste bit back a sharp retort and left Isavel to her martyrdom.

A seamstress came to measure her for the new kirtle in the morning. In the afternoons she walked alone in the vineyard. Without Pierre's company it was a desolate place. A cloud covered the sun, and the wind worried at her hair; the round bellies of the ripening grapes mocked her and the chattering birds brought on another headache.

If only she could remember enough to know whether she might be with child, and if so… Dear Lord, it must be her husband's child. How could she go back to Lord Bernard until she knew?

Tomorrow she would go to the Basilica de Fourviere and pray to Holy Mary. She would find the words this time. She would pray without stopping, until she was faint, until the Virgin heard her. She must not have a child. She could not bear to fail another child.

Marie was not in her bedchamber when she went up after supper, but she did not wish to call down for her. She would come running upstairs soon enough. She plumped her pillows and sat back against them.

She caught herself dozing and looked up. The room was noticeably darker. Where was Marie? Celeste rose and opened her chamber door. Marie should have her ears boxed for making her mistress come to find her.

The stone stairwell carried the sound of a harsh whisper up to her. She crept to the corner and peered around it. Isavel stood near the bottom of the stairs clutching Marie's arm, forcing the girl close to her. She shook her arm roughly several times as she spoke.

Celeste could not make out her whispered words, but it was clear from her expression that she was forcing some confession out of Marie. Marie glanced over her shoulder up the stairs. Celeste stepped quickly out of sight.

Whatever Isavel was asking Marie, it was certain to be something Celeste would rather she not know. Celeste retreated to her room and

called, "Marie, is that you on the stairs? I have been waiting for you."
She heard Marie's footsteps hurrying up to her.

"Forgive me, My Lady," Marie said, rushing into the room.

"What have you done to need forgiveness?"

Marie blinked. "I—I have kept you waiting," she stammered.

"You have. And who delayed you?"

"Who—?"

"Yes, who. Were you talking with someone? Mistress Isavel, perhaps?"

"I—"

"Consider well before you speak, Marie."

"She made me tell her." Marie hung her head. She began to wring her hands, reached to cover her ears, stopped herself and wrung her hands in earnest.

Celeste decided not to box Marie's ears. Isavel was formidable. "What did you tell her?"

"She asked about your courses," Marie whispered, white-faced.

*How dare she?* Celeste almost spoke the words aloud. She did not need to ask what Marie had told her—the girl's expression was confession enough. She turned away in a cold fury. "Undress me."

Marie obeyed silently. Her hands shook as she lifted the kirtle over Celeste's head.

Celeste climbed into bed without another word, and lay in the dark fuming. How Isavel would revel in Marie's admission. She would, of course, assume the same conclusion as Marie.

She touched her stomach, as though she might feel the truth there, but she could detect nothing, no spark of life other than her own. There must be some other reason for her missed courses. Her breathing steadied as she became calm. The immediate problem was Isavel. She would insist that Celeste was with child, whether it was true or not: she must be silenced. Celeste closed her eyes, exhausted.

175

Celeste woke before sunrise. She lay in bed listening for the noise that had wakened her. There it was again, the soft whinny of a horse.

The horse whinnied again. Her room faced the courtyard and the stables; noise floated up to her window, including the sound of voices. They spoke too quietly for her to make out their words. Deliberately so, she realized, and she began to listen more carefully. One of the voices was Isavel's. Celeste got out of bed and crossed to the window.

Isavel stood near the stable doors talking to one of Pierre's men. He stood close to her, holding the reins of a horse which was saddled and bridled for a journey. Isavel's posture was stiff. There was something furtive in the way she leaned forward so that she need not raise her voice. The man nodded and turned to mount the horse. Isavel looked around quickly.

Celeste ducked beneath the window. When she raised her head again, the man was mounted. Isavel handed him a folded piece of paper with the red seal of Pierre's winery across its fold. The rider bent to take it, then kicked his horse and galloped off.

This time, when Isavel looked around Celeste did not hide, but stood at the window looking down at her. Isavel looked startled, but held her gaze without flinching before she turned away.

Celeste returned to bed. It was too early to rise; even the servants were still abed. She lay staring at nothing in the pre-dawn darkness until her eyelids drooped. Marie's breathing was the only sound in the room: the soft snore of sleep. A lulling sound...

*Prince of the drowsy, dying day...*

She remembered Etienne: his rosebud mouth, his tiny, half-moon fingernails and bright, dark eyes, his black hair sticking straight up at all angles from his soft, pink scalp, his milky smile...

Etienne had not died of his fever. She knew it suddenly with a clarity that made her gasp. Something in that dark castle had killed him.

Her head began to ache. She covered her mouth with her hand, fighting the urge to vomit.

How had he died?

"I did not keep him safe," she whispered in the darkness. She covered her face with her hands. "I did not protect him."

She closed her eyes against the terrible pain in her head, and the worse one in her chest. She had not protected Etienne. She groaned softly and rolled onto her side, hugging her knees tightly to her under the nightgown.

Across the room, Marie shifted and murmured in her sleep.

They believed she was pregnant, Marie and Isavel. What if there *was* another infant, hiding deep within her? Relying on her to keep him safe. To keep him hidden.

There was no child.

But what if there was one, hiding beneath her heart?

She could not fail another child. She could not bear it again.

But if she did? If she allowed this one to die as well, failed a second time?

The pain in her chest was excruciating. She could not breathe for it. Surely she was dying. *There must not be a child, there must not be, there must not...*

She lay gasping for breath, sweating, hot salty tears on her face. *There must not be, not be a child...* the words tumbled through her mind, easing the pain, relieving the pressure. She could breathe again, she could move. *There must not be a child!*

Celeste rose and tiptoed across the room. Tied to her belt was the delicate Lady's knife she used for eating. She brought it back to bed with her. The metal gleamed silver in the moonlight. She shivered. Surely there was no child.

But if there was? She ran her thumb along the blade, testing its sharpness, then held it still in front of her. What if her hand slipped? What if she cut a vital cord and bled to death?

And what if there was another infant, like Etienne, hiding deep inside her? She took a deep breath to calm herself.

Pulling up her nightdress she cut deeply into the pale skin of her inner thigh, as high as she dared below the tendon. A hot stream of blood rushed out. She gritted her teeth and cut into the other thigh. She hoped these were Isavel's best sheets.

"Marie," she said. Her voice wavered. She closed her eyes. She thought of Isavel, eager to tell Lord Bernard the secret she had learned. "Marie," she called again, sharply.

The child sat up with a snort. "My Lady?" she rubbed her eyes open.

"I need my cloths, Marie."

"I am sorry, My Lady, that you are not with child," Marie murmured as she bundled up the sheets and helped Celeste dress.

"It was never in doubt."

"Lord Bernard will forgive you and you will bear him another heir soon."

"Hold your foolish tongue." She sat stiff and silent while Marie braided her hair, then she swept out of the room leaving the girl to make what she would of her mistress' tight-lipped anger.

She found Isavel in the kitchen, hearing the cook's suggestions for the day's meals.

"I would speak with you, sister-in-law," Celeste said evenly, aware of the many ears in a kitchen. Isavel returned Celeste's look with one of proud resolve. After delivering the rest of her instructions, she preceded Celeste outside and across the yard. A stable boy hurried toward them.

"Leave us," Isavel ordered. Her voice trembled, barely discernable. Only she had noticed, Celeste decided.

"What have you done?" She asked Isavel.

"Nothing that would not please a dutiful wife."

Celeste subdued her irritation. "What errand did you send your man on this morning?"

Isavel hesitated. "I have invited Lord Bernard to visit us," she said, lifting her chin defiantly.

"He is not at his castle to receive your message."

"My messenger is on his way to Paris."

Celeste's hands curled into themselves with the effort to control her anger. The impertinent, interfering—

"You are his wife," Isavel said primly. "You must do your duty."

Celeste leaned forward, her eyes narrowed. "Do not presume to teach me my duty. I am not his horse. I am not his hound. I do not wait for his call, or quiver for his attention." She was shivering. It was only the pain in her thighs and the loss of blood. She leaned against a stall door.

Isavel's face had turned white. She glared at Celeste.

"Was there anything else in your message?"

"What else would I tell him?"

"Nothing," Celeste said. "I am afraid I have spoiled a pair of your sheets. My maid will wash them when she washes my cloths, but the stain rarely comes out."

Isavel turned a shade whiter.

"Why does Pierre love you?" Celeste demanded, clenching her teeth on the words.

"Because he knows I love him. Because I would never betray or abandon him, as long as I draw breath."

Celeste drew back. Betray and abandon? Was that what the woman thought of her? She turned away. So be it.

"If you have little care for your husband, think of your brother!"

"This has nothing to do with him."

"Nothing to do with him? How can you pretend to have no idea what Lord Bernard's patronage means to Pierre?" Isavel cried. "There are many wine merchants in Lyon; not many as wealthy as Pierre, for no others have a sister married to nobility."

"My marriage is convenient for you."

"It is not inconvenient for you, either. But that is not my concern. Pierre is my concern."

"Pierre? You pretend you did this for Pierre?" Celeste did not hide the scorn from her voice.

"You are so selfish you cannot see anything else in others." Isavel glared at Celeste. "Any other woman would be pleased to know her marriage benefited her family. Any other woman in your situation would understand how much her relatives' prosperity depended upon her Lord husband's goodwill. She would not carelessly jeopardize that goodwill, as you are doing. Perhaps you do care for your brother, but you are so blinded by yourself that you will destroy him. And because of Pierre's love for you, he will allow you to." She straightened, breathing deeply. "But I will not allow it."

"What will you do, Isavel?"

"Why did you marry him? Lord Bernard asked you if you were willing. He would not marry you otherwise."

"You are lying. Just as you would have lied about sending a message to him if I had not caught you doing so."

"Pierre told me, when he asked me the same question."

Pierre said so? Had Lord Bernard asked if she was willing? She pictured him as she had seen him in Cluny, sitting tall and confident on his stallion, exuding power as the sun exudes light. Yet he had asked her permission. Her heart skipped. Could it be true?

She turned without a word and left Isavel standing in her stable.

The sun beat down on the grapevines as she walked between them, following the path she and Pierre had often walked. She had not considered what reprisal Lord Bernard might take against Pierre. Was he the kind of man who would destroy a brother-in-law for sheltering his sister without her husband's knowledge? That did not sound like a man who would not marry without his bride's consent. Which was true and which was the lie?

Sunlight and moonlight, she thought, remembering the garden at the abbey. Isavel called her selfish for not considering Pierre's welfare. But Isavel's fortunes were tied to Pierre's, and she was not concerned about Celeste's well-being. So which of them could call the other selfish?

Sunlight and moonlight. Was there a way to see people as they were, without one's own concerns casting light or darkness over them? Isavel thought well of Lord Bernard; Marie feared him. Even if Celeste remembered how she had felt about her husband, even if she still felt it, too, much had happened between them. They were in moonlight now and everything was changed.

What did it matter, after all? Whether it was Lord Bernard's castle which filled her nightmares, or Lord Bernard himself whom she was fleeing, the result was the same. She would have to be gone before he came here, if she did not want to go back with him. There was no sanctuary for her here, or for the unfortunate babe, if there was one, trusting in her frail resourcefulness.

She went to the stable and ordered her horse saddled up.

# Chapter 16

The rain began as soon as he left the market grounds, and continued into the evening. Even under his cloak, huddled against a tree trunk between the donkey and the barrels, Jean was wet and shivering. Yet he dared not go further into the woods. Having left the market a day early, he was alone on the road. At least here, at the edge of the woods, he would be able to see anyone approaching.

Curse the old woman, and curse his foolishness! A moment of pity and here he was: wet, cold and alone by the side of the road.

*Death with his sharpened sickle waited only for a momentary slip...*

No! He was nothing like his mother and would not suffer her fate. He knew the worth of the coins that fed his family, the value of his life. He did not deserve to lose them.

It was the fault of that black-eyed girl. He had had no pity for her and now he was besieged by the useless sentiment. He knew there was something about her eyes as soon as he looked into them. She had done something to him, despite what the priest said. He crossed himself in the dark.

The motion calmed him. He had escaped. No one would remember the price of his handkerchiefs a year from now. Perhaps the old woman's son would even recover.

*Never look back.* He was alone, but not without resources. He pulled his knife from his belt and held it in his left hand. In his right he gripped his strong walking staff. He had fought thieves off before. He would rather take his chances on the road than face a mob of angry townspeople convinced he had been cheating them, or a bailiff who would take his entire purse in exchange for his life and still order his left hand chopped off. He settled back against the tree, glaring into the darkness around him.

Halfway through the night, the rain stopped. Jean drifted into a cold, uncomfortable sleep.

The donkey woke him, braying and surging to its feet. Jean was up almost as quickly, straining to see in the darkness.

Several murky shadows crept between the trees, slightly darker than the surrounding gloom. He swung his staff up as the first one came at him, and heard a satisfying CRACK!

"Get the animal," another one cried, rushing forward. The donkey brayed and kicked, struggling against the rope that tied it to the tree.

Jean raised his knife, swinging his staff toward a movement at the corner of his eye. A grunt, a curse, and then the staff was wrenched from his grip; they were upon him.

"Take the beast away!" someone shouted.

The donkey! His livelihood! Jean gave a strangled cry. He looked around wildly, saw its hindquarters disappearing into the woods and lunged in that direction, slashing at his captors with his knife. He felt it sink into soft flesh, began to pull it back out—

A flash of metal and his gut was on fire. He gripped his belly, feeling hot, sticky liquid between his fingers. He pitched forward.

It was far too bright. Why was the night so full of light? Jean opened his eyes a slit. The sun hovered directly overhead, as brilliant as the face of God staring down at him. Blinded by its radiance, he turned his head. Waves of pain and dizziness swept over him.

When they subsided he opened his eyes again. He was lying on his back on a grey pilgrim's cloak tied between two long walking staffs. Four men in pilgrim's tunics surrounded him, one holding the end of each staff. He swayed a little with the slow rhythm of their movement as they carried him forward.

It was too much. That he, Jean le Peddler, was being carried to heaven by four pilgrims. He closed his eyes, overwhelmed.

*"Papa! Papa!" Jeanne's thin little voice cries out to him, muffled by the thick fog. He runs toward it, his arms reaching, disappearing at the elbows into the clinging grey dampness.*

*"Papa!" Her voice is fainter now, coming from his left. He turns and stumbles blindly toward it.*

*"Papa, m'aidez!"*

*No, from the right. Why is he so disoriented? Her voice is only a whisper of terror in the distance, begging him to find her. "Jeanne!" he screams, charging into the fog.*

*"Papa..." Her sweet little voice pleads from the other direction.*

*"Jeanne! Jeanne!" He turns and runs to the left again, swinging his arms in front of him. "Jeanne! Where are you?"*

*Silence.*

*He falls to his knees, weeping as the fog closes in, blinding him completely.*

*A heavy weight settles into his arms. He looks down, squinting through the fog—*

*"Jeanne." He bends over her. She is so still. Her face and arms are bruised and cut, crusted with blood. She has been hit, over and over...*

*"Jeanne," he whispers. Why is she so cold? He hugs her against him. So cold and still, in the fog that curls around her. Not even a*

*breath of movement. He shakes her gently. A stone falls out of her tangled hair. She begins to disappear, evaporating like smoke. He grasps for her, clutching wisps of air in his aching arms.*

*He should never have loved her so much. He should never have let himself love her...*

Jean opened his eyes slowly, squinting in the bright daylight. A priest stood over him, his lips moving in quiet prayer.

"Ee-av-ees-ahh," Jean mumbled. His head pounded, his entire body throbbed with pain.

"Confiteor deo omnipotent," the priest said gently. His voice came from far away, although he was standing quite close. There was something familiar about him. Jean squinted up at him, and was immediately dizzy. He drew a breath. A bolt of pain lanced through his side.

"Beatae Mariae semper Virgini..."

The priest was saying the prayer of confession. What did he want Jean to confess? Had the bailiff from Lyon caught him? Was he receiving the last rites before his execution?

"I am not a thief." He tried to speak clearly. The priest bent down as though he could not make out Jean's words. He waited, bent over, for Jean to confess.

*I am not a thief,* Jean thought, willing the priest to understand. He closed his eyes.

"Quid quid deliquiste," the priest murmured.

Jean felt the priest's fingers touching his eyes, his ears, his nostrils...

"Libera nos, equisetums, Domine,"

...was comforted by the lingering coolness of the oil where the priest had touched him...

"Ab omnibus malis, praeteritis, presentibus, et futuris..."

The familiar words of the rite of extreme unction flowed over Jean.

"…perducat te ad vitam aeternam."
*I am dying,* he thought.

*The air is full of smoke, suffocating him. Waves of heat pour over him, radiating from his gut, burning his side, his eyes, his forehead.*

*The forest is on fire! The flames snap and roar all around him, like a wild beast. He opens his eyes, panting. A man in a pilgrim's tunic stands over him, the beads on his rosary clacking together, his eyes closed in prayer. Behind him, Jean sees a wall of flames.*

*Fire! He has no breath to put behind the word. He tries to raise his head. A shower of burning embers flies toward him. "Mama!" he screams.*

Someone has been wounded. The bitter smell of herbe au charpentier was very strong in the night. Jean heard heavy breathing nearby and tried to call out. A woman leaned out of the darkness, her mouth curving into a smile above him. He could not see if she was young or old. She reached behind her and brought a cup to his lips. The heady scent of poppies filled his nostrils. He gulped the hot tea down, desperately thirsty despite the vile taste, and fell asleep again.

Jean drifted awake to the sound of a bird singing nearby. It must be morning already, he thought wearily. He had slept past dawn beside the road, a foolish thing to do. For a while he did not think any further than that. He was too worn out to worry over his foolishness; and anyway, it was morning now. The night, and the dangers in it, were over. He lay with his eyes closed, listening to the bird, drifting in and out of sleep.

The birdsong stopped. Jean strained after it, letting his breath out with a sigh when it resumed.

Something was wrong. The smells were not right. Where was the clean scent of pine and walnut trees, and sweet wild lavender growing along the edge of the woods? He should have the dusty grit of the summer road in his nostrils and feel the early morning air moving over his face. He should hear the donkey pulling against its rope to graze a little further from the tree, swishing insects away with its tail. He should not feel so weary, as though he had come through a long ordeal, and his chest and side should not ache like this nor his head feel heavy and tight with the residue of pain.

The bird stopped singing.

Jean opened his eyes warily. He was not beside the road but lying in a narrow bed in a small room by himself. Daylight poured into the room through a window recessed into the wall adjacent to his bed. A small, brown sparrow perched on the stone ledge of the window.

The wooden door across the room creaked open. The sparrow shook out its wings and fell into the sunlit sky.

A serving woman entered with a bowl of gruel. Jean tried to sit up and gasped at the pain. A thick poultice covered his left side and half of his stomach. It was partially soaked with blood, but the blood was drying and cracked at the edges of the poultice.

"Where am I?" He wanted to ask how long he had been here, also, but it was hard enough to force out the first question.

"You are safe." The woman tapped her finger lightly against his mouth. "Do not try to talk. Eat and rest."

She reached behind his shoulders and raised him gently. The pain made him groan aloud. She let him rest before holding the bowl to his mouth. He gulped at the warm, thin gruel, suddenly famished. It needed salt to give it flavour, or the smallest pinch of cinnamon to hide the greasy aftertaste, but even without these it was delicious. He licked the edges of the bowl like a starving mongrel.

Later, when she left, his stomach ached as though he had gorged himself. The movement had caused his side and head to throb again. He closed his eyes and tried to sleep.

The tolling of church bells wakened him. They must be ringing vespers, judging by the fading light coming through the window. Other bells tolled in the distance, one from very far away. What towns were they ringing for, he wondered, and then, more urgently, where was he?

Several people had carried him for what seemed a long time. Was that real, or was it a dream? His memories were muddled, laced with pain and nightmare. He had thought he was being carried to heaven; he had imagined he was being robbed; he had seen Jeanne dead. But she was safe at home with Mathilde. Was anything he remembered true?

He looked around the room for his belongings. A single barrel stood in the corner, near the window. Perhaps the other barrel was in the stable, with his donkey. *His donkey, braying as it was led away in the night...*

A jolt of panic brought him upright in his bed. He was immediately dizzy and nearly blinded by the pain in his gut and side. He eased himself down again.

When the pain subsided, the panic was still there.

"Help!" he cried out. His voice was too weak to carry. No one could have heard him. He fell back against the thin mattress. Perhaps he had nothing to fear. Perhaps it was only nightmare or illness, playing with his mind.

Jean pushed the bedcovers down. He untied the poultice slowly, panting with the effort. A jagged cut began just above his belly button and ran down around his left side at the waist. The skin on either side had been roughly sewn together. The stitches were crusted with blood, but there were no black lines under the skin above or below the cut, so the poultice had done its job and drawn the poison out. The pain that left him breathless came from his side, above the wound. He probably had a broken rib or two.

Jean pushed the sheet down further. His legs were bruised and swollen, but did not appear to be broken. He wriggled his toes. It hurt all the way down his legs to do so, but he was satisfied with the response. He retied the poultice and pulled the sheet up again. The effort exhausted him. He lay back and closed his eyes.

Heavy, measured footsteps approaching his door wakened him just before it swung open. The tall priest he had met on the road entered his room. Jean closed his eyes quickly to hide his surprise.

How had the fellow got here? They had parted company in Lyon many days ago, or so it seemed. Was he dreaming again? Was he back in Lyon? He listened intently with his eyes shut.

The priest's footsteps crossed the room and stopped beside his bed. "Are you awake?" he said.

Jean opened his eyes cautiously.

"You are recovering."

He sounded relieved. He had not been told, then, about the handkerchiefs that were not really blessed. He would not be so friendly if he knew.

"We feared you would die, but God has chosen to spare you."

It was the same voice that had said the last rites over him. So that had not been a dream.

"Would you like a drink of water?"

"Yes—" Jean's voice came out thin and high, like a boy's.

The priest did not seem as surprised by it as Jean was. He poured some water into a cup from a pitcher on the table beside Jean's bed. The water was warm and slightly silty, and Jean had never drunk anything so good. He stole glances at the priest while he drank.

Someone in pilgrim's robes had sat beside him, reading aloud from a Book of Hours. There had been only one person in the room, but the faces and voices had changed, sometimes a man, sometimes a woman.

He had dreamed he was in heaven with them; that somehow, in the pilgrims' company, he had bypassed purgatory, and he feared he would be caught out and sent back. He remembered trying to talk to them, to explain everything—the handkerchiefs, the woman who sold him her nail and her ring—but they ignored him, insisting on reading aloud the lives of the saints which so engrossed them. What might he have revealed to them in his fevered babblings and earnest confessions?

"Where am I, Father?" he asked carefully, when the cup was empty and the priest had lowered him back against the bed-pillows. "What has happened to me?" His voice still sounded strange. Had he been screaming, also, in his delirium?

"Do you not remember?" The priest's voice was gentle. He looked down at Jean with pity.

Jean turned his face away. He did not want his question answered after all. "I am tired," he said, trying to keep the panic from his voice.

"We found you three days ago, beside the road. You had been set upon by thieves."

Jean groaned. His donkey. His donkey had been taken into the woods.

"Two of them lay dead on the road near you. The others had fled, leaving you there. We thought you were dead also, and were astounded to find you still alive. We carried you here to Prevote Venissieux, where we have been tending you with the help of the innkeeper's wife. She knew what to put on the poultice and what herbs were needed in your drink to ease the pain."

"Where is my—" Jean could not finish.

"All we found of your belongings was that barrel..." The priest's voice trailed off.

Jean closed his eyes. "All is gone? Everything?" His donkey and his purse?

"Not everything," the priest said.

Jean glanced at the barrel standing beside his bed. He remembered it now, the empty one. Even thieves could not be bothered carrying off an empty barrel. "Everything," he said dully.

There would be no new kirtle for Mathilde, no tunic for Gilles, no dowry for Jeanne.

There would never be an apprenticeship for Simon.

"You have your life," the priest rebuked him gently.

He had no money to buy next year's spices. He was ruined; they all were. He had seen his mother's smile and let her carelessness slip over him.

"Yes, my life," he said, pronouncing it as though it were a curse. How could he go home like this? How could he face Mathilde with nothing to offer but an empty barrel?

The tall man shifted on the wooden stool. Jean remembered he was talking to a priest. "I owe you thanks," he said.

"We did what any Christian would have done." The priest made a dismissive gesture with his hand.

Jean looked at him. Surely he knew that was far from true.

"For which I cannot even repay you," Jean said. The words were bitter in his mouth, tasting of charity. It was not a spice he cared for.

"We will be repaid."

Jean would have told him how charity was repaid, but it was not right to say such things to a priest. The priest took his silence for weariness and left him. Soon after, however, one of the pilgrims came in.

"Father suggested I might read to you," he said, holding up his Book of Hours.

Jean shrugged. They were paying for his keep.

The pilgrim sat down quickly and began flipping through the pages of his book, looking for a passage to read. Something uplifting, he had probably been told, to raise Jean's spirits and fortify his faith. He found the page he wanted and looked up with a determined smile.

Where had he seen that expression before? Jean looked at the pilgrim more closely and recognized him from his dream of being in heaven. The pilgrim began to read slowly, emphasizing the fortifying parts.

He had not skipped purgatory after all.

One or another of the pilgrims was nearly always at his bedside. They tried to pray with him, but he gave them no encouragement. They sat by his bed reading aloud from the lives of the saints while Jean lay trying to think of a way he could feed his family and wondering how they would make it through the winter. Perhaps Mathilde had not spent everything he had given her last year. Perhaps she had had a good yield from the little garden she kept. They could sell the eggs from her hens and make do with porridge, and in spring they could sell the hens to buy some spices for next year's trip...

And how would he carry the spices to Cluny and Lyon without a donkey?

Jean went round and round the problem, like a rat in a wooden box, but it always came back to that. He could no longer sell spices. He must return to them with nothing. Mathilde and the boys did not need his help with the garden or the hens. He would just be another empty belly to feed through the winter.

It would be better for them if he never returned at all.

Jean became aware of the silence in the room. He looked up. The pilgrim was gone. The priest stood just inside the door, half in shadow, watching Jean. Was he real or a dream? His face had the same expression now as when he had caught Jean daydreaming on the road and bade him walk with them.

"Is it possible to take on another's sorrow, Father?" Jean asked.

The priest walked over to his bed. "Is that not what our Lord did for us?"

"I thought he took on our sin."

"What is the root of all sorrow?"

"Sin," Jean said obediently. He knew his catechism. It had nothing to do with this seeming transference of grief that he had unwittingly embarked upon.

When the silence stretched out, Jean looked up. The priest gazed back at him calmly, giving no indication of what he sought. Revealing nothing, as unreadable as fog.

The fog from his dream of Jeanne wrapped itself around Jean.

"Loss," he said, his voice flat and certain. "Loss is the root of sorrow."

The priest nodded gently. "It is what we lose that shapes us, not what we have or what we gain. *'My God, why hast Thou forsaken me?'* So spoke our Lord on his cross. And in that moment we knew him for who he was, because of what he had lost. For our sakes. Yes, it is possible to take on another's sorrow. But very rare."

"I never wanted her sorrow," Jean murmured when the priest had left. "It was only a superstition." He said it again, louder, defying the twilight shadows creeping across his room. "It is only foolish women's lore. I did not buy her sorrow." He felt better then, and slept.

In the morning the sunlight falling through his window bleached away his fears, leaving only the clarity of his misfortune. When the priest appeared at his door Jean stared at him without interest.

"It is the Sabbath," the priest said. "I have come to pray with you, since you cannot go to Mass."

"I cannot pray," Jean said.

"Then I will pray for you. You need only bend your head."

Bend his head. Bend to God's will. Was it God's will that he be destroyed? Was it God's will that his family go hungry, that Gilles would not sell spices with him and little Jeanne would have no dowry and Simon would never be a blacksmith?

Whether he bent his head or not, these things had already happened. Only they did not know it yet, Mathilde and Gilles and Simon and Jeanne. They would not know it until he went home and told them.

The priest stood by the door, watching him.

"Why do you keep after me?" he cried.

The priest came to his bedside and knelt down beside him.

"Because you are a soul in change," he said. "And a soul in change might find its way to God."

"Or not," Jean said.

"Yes," the priest replied. "Or not." He bowed his head and began to pray.

# Chapter 17

Celeste entered the pilgrim's hostel at Lyon. She had ridden off impulsively after her argument with Isavel. Now she stood at the door of the hostel, feeling like a fool. A Lady would have her husband's men-at-arms escort her wherever she cared to go. Even a widow would send her man or have her priest arrange an escort, not come herself. She hesitated on the threshold.

"Lady Celeste."

She turned, startled. "Father Jacques." She swallowed, forcing the surprise out of her voice. "I am glad to find you here." She looked past him: a group of pilgrims sat at the table he had left to come to her. Several were watching their exchange. His pilgrimage to Jerusalem! He had had to wait—what?—ten days? Had she been with Pierre that long?

"I was told you went to Paris."

Celeste blushed. "I have been visiting my brother, Pierre. He lives just outside of Lyon."

"Pierre. Paris. Perhaps the innkeeper mistook the message."

Celeste blushed again.

"Have you come looking for me?"

"Yes," she said quickly. "I—my maid and I—would like to join your pilgrimage."

He looked startled. "But your journey was to the Basilica de Fourviere, here in Lyon."

"I mean to go to Jerusalem," she said, surprising herself as she said it. Jerusalem? Why would she go to Jerusalem? But she found herself smiling. Jerusalem. It sounded far away. It sounded safe and free and golden: the Holy City. No one would dare to laugh at a woman who had pilgrimaged to Jerusalem.

"I have a letter of permission from the Abbess." She drew the Abbess' letter out of her scrip and handed it to him. It was the permission that she had been given to journey to Cluny, but Father Jacques might think that she had stopped off at the abbey on the way to Lyon and requested a second permission for a longer pilgrimage.

He would discover her deceit at once if he could read. Celeste drew in a silent breath. There was no avoiding this moment. She had never met a monk who could not read, but she remembered Mistress Blanche asking Father Jacques to read from her Book of Hours during a rest stop on their journey to Cluny. He had sat beside the woman with the book in his hands, and never once looked down at it. He must have memorized every story in it, Celeste had thought at the time, and only later had it occurred to her why he would do so.

He took the letter but did not look at it. "Have you considered this?"

She met his gaze without comment.

"A pilgrimage is a serious undertaking, Lady Celeste."

"It is."

Father Jacques sighed. After a moment he said gently, "We sometimes travel long distances to speak to those who are far from us. Do you think that God is distant?"

Celeste's lips tightened. This was the way priests talked: in riddles, meant to trick you. How should she know where God was? She had thanked him for her cure at Cluny, but he had not answered her. Instead, Lord Bernard had shown up, and the peddler had disappeared with her ring. She had begged Holy Mary to give her an empty womb. She had received no answer from her, either.

"Do you have your husband's approval this time?" Father Jacques asked, when it was clear she was not going to answer his riddle.

"My husband placed me in the Abbess' care, and she has approved my pilgrimage."

"I see." He glanced briefly at the letter before handing it back to her.

Celeste looked down, hiding the relief she was sure must be evident in her face as she returned the permission to her scrip.

"This is a much longer pilgrimage. There will be hardships and danger, sometimes more than one can bear. It is possible that your... problem... can be resolved in some other manner. God does not always require a pilgrimage."

She took a deep breath. What problem was he referring to?

"Sometimes we require it of ourselves," Father Jacques continued, "to make atonement for our sins, or fortify our faith, or free our souls from the weariness of despair."

*Her feet are frozen to the cold stone floor; she cannot bear to see inside the room. Something happened there, something to drive all hope away forever—*

She willed her mind clear. Father Jacques was watching her. Could he, like the gypsy, see some hideous flaw in her, some unrepented sin? She swayed and would have stumbled, had Father Jacques not caught her shoulder.

"Those who go on pilgrimage are blessed," she said, clutching his arm.

"Such blessings come at great cost."

What cost did he mean? Oh, what did it matter? There was a cost to everything, including staying here now that Isavel had sent a message to her husband. No, she must get away! She needed time to sort out what had happened in her husband's castle, time to decide what to do. Time to learn whether there was another infant to consider, and a sin to account for. A pilgrimage would give her that time. She let go of his arm and straightened, raising her chin to look at him levelly. Whatever evil thing she had done in her past, whatever failures had been tallied up against her, she would be cleansed of them in Jerusalem. If this priest would not take her, she would find another way.

"Do you need to go?" The quiet intensity in his voice surprised her. Her eyes brimmed with tears, the answer so tight in her throat she could not say it.

He nodded. "That is the way one should feel about Jerusalem."

"What does Lord Bernard say about this pilgrimage?"

Although Isavel had asked the question, Celeste addressed Pierre when she answered. "He does not know about it. But you may tell him if he comes here looking for me." He must know the truth, in case Isavel was right about Lord Bernard. "I am sorry I did not tell you sooner. I have only today learned that we are leaving tomorrow morning."

"Your escort stayed in Lyon all this time?" Pierre asked.

"One of our party was ill. He is recovered now. They are at the pilgrim's hostel." It was only a small lie, of no importance.

"Do you have the Holy Church's permission?" Isavel demanded.

"I have a note from the Abbess of Sainte Blandine." She spoke sharply, looking at Pierre, not his presumptuous wife. Surely the woman would not dare ask to see it.

"Why did you not mention this while you have been with us, Celeste?" Pierre asked.

"I am sorry."

"How many are in your party?" A worried frown creased his brow.

"Eight." She hoped she had remembered correctly. "And a priest, our confessor. We are enough to protect ourselves, dear brother."

"This is not right!" Isavel cried. "She must return to her husband."

"I will, when my pilgrimage is finished." Again she spoke for Pierre's sake, and she gave him the truth. Where else should she go?

Marriage to Lord Bernard had been the final step in raising her above her grandfather; she would not descend again.

Celeste pulled her horse to a stop to bid Pierre farewell before joining the group of pilgrims waiting for her. Pierre patted Marie's shoulder, making her blush furiously, before sending her off.

"Be gentle with Marie," he said to Celeste, 'She is devoted to you." He kissed Celeste on both cheeks. "And be gentle with yourself, sister."

She returned his embrace.

"If you see my husband, tell him that I am well, and safe." She looked toward the group of pilgrims. "And that I look forward to being reunited with him after my pilgrimage to Santiago de Compostella." She could not look at him as she mouthed the lie.

"I will pass on your words to him."

*He knows.* She looked aside, ashamed. "God be with you, Pierre," she said with difficulty.

"God go with you, Celeste." He waited till she looked at him, and smiled at her. "Go with my blessing, sister."

There were six pilgrims waiting with Father Jacques: a middle-aged Lady wrapped in her pilgrim's cloak against the dampness of the morning; her maid, a saucy brown-haired girl who had pushed her cloak aside, revealing her red linen kirtle; the Lady's son, a tall, skinny boy who appeared to be about fourteen; two men-at-arms who took their orders from the Lady; and an older, sour-faced man introduced as the Lady's cousin. The boy and the men-at-arms did not wear pilgrim's cloaks, but one was tied behind the boy's saddle. The sour-faced cousin clenched his cape around his chest, scowling from time to time at the dishevelled bundle behind the boy's saddle.

"We have a lengthy journey, which will afford us numerous opportunities to come to know each other," the Lady's cousin said, as soon as the initial greetings were over. His voice was high for a man, and he spoke through his nose. "I suggest we commence at once."

Behind his back, the boy looked across at his mother's maid and pulled a face which perfectly imitated the officious cousin's. The maid coughed into her handkerchief.

Celeste looked at the group of pilgrims, wondering why Father Jacques had questioned her motives.

The men-at-arms spurred their horses into an easy canter and the group set out.

While they rode, the others told stories of their homes and families, or speculated on what they would see and do in the Holy Land. Celeste remained quiet. She did not notice the things they pointed out: a small red fox peeking at them from behind a bush, a sweet thrill of birdsong, the suggestive shape of a cloud and what it signified.

Lady Yvolde rode up beside her. "Are you in mourning?" she asked gently, looking at Celeste's black kirtle.

"I—"

*I lost my son.* If she said it, Lady Yvolde would be full of sympathy, and she would have to pretend a sorrow she did not feel. She barely remembered the child, and though she had tried, she could not recall his death. No. She was done with grief.

"I stayed at an abbey before I came on pilgrimage. I have been ill, but I am well now."

Lady Yvolde nodded. They rode together in a pleasant silence.

The days ran into one another. No new memories occurred to Celeste as she rode. Had she remembered as much as she was going to? Yet still nightmares pursued her, fragments catching her unaware in the shadow under a bush or the stray comment of a companion. Finally, she took Marie aside at a rest stop and asked her outright what had happened just before she became ill.

Marie looked startled. "Etienne died," she mumbled when Celeste repeated her question.

"I know that," Celeste said, annoyed. "Do you remember anything else, something I might have forgotten?"

"Is this a game?" Marie asked. "Because I need more hints."

"I am weary of games," Celeste said.

Late in the afternoon, Marie urged her pony up beside Celeste's gelding. She did not speak, but rode beside her silently, until Celeste glanced down at her.

"Lord Raimond would not let me stay with you."

Her voice was so low Celeste had to bend to hear her. "Lord Raimond?"

"That is what he made us call him. But I know he is only Lord Bernard's cousin."

"He sent you away?" What was the child trying to tell her?

The bent head trembled. Was she weeping? "The night Etienne died. He said I snored, and I would wake you, that you and the babe needed sleep. He sent me to sleep in the hall." She looked up, hiccupping, her face wet with tears. "I do not snore, Lady Celeste."

Raimond had sent her maid out of her bedchamber? To be alone with her? She shivered.

"I should have been there," Marie cried, weeping openly.

Celeste recalled the adulteress at Cluny. Surely not. A sudden, vicious pain lanced her temples.

"You may box my ears if you wish," Marie sobbed.

"I do not wish," Celeste said, gritting her teeth against the pounding in her head. "What else do you know?'

"Nothing," Marie sobbed. "I was not there."

Celeste looked at her sharply, but there was no accusation in Marie's face, nothing ugly or insinuating, only regret. Regret and fear? What was Marie afraid of?

"Stop crying." Celeste glanced around. If the other pilgrims were aware of the fuss, they were pretending to ignore it. "Dry your eyes, Marie. It was not your fault."

"Do you forgive me?"

"Yes, of course." Her head pounded fiercely.

"Thank you, Lady Celeste! You are the kindest, best of mistresses—"

"Be quiet," she said, cutting off the stream of praise. Up ahead, Brother Jacques had stopped under a copse of trees, signalling a rest break. "Compose yourself," she whispered before they reached the others.

At sunset they drew near the road which led west toward Le Puy, where Lord Bernard's castle lay. Celeste slowed her horse, letting the others pass her. Marie trotted up and rode beside her.

Should she turn onto it and return to Lord Bernard? It was not far to his castle from here. Perhaps he was there now, waiting for her?

She imagined him greeting her as she rode up, looking at her the way he did, as though he would devour her. The memory surprised her, so clear, so intense. She felt a deep ache for him in her gut, in her groin and her thighs, tight against the warmth of her horse. She caught her breath. She must go to him. He drew her…

How? Why did the thought of him draw her when she could remember nothing else? How could she trust an emotion so detached from all reason? Like a loose thread, torn from the garment that made it useful. How could she trust a fallen thread of memory?

They were almost at the road now. Celeste looked down it, conscious of Marie watching her. That same road continued beyond Le Puy, west to Santiago. If he went to Lyon, Pierre and Isavel would tell him she was headed there. Would he go all the way to Santiago, searching for her? What would he think when his enquiries turned up no sign that she had passed that way? After this second misdirection, her intent would be clear. No lie she might conceive would hide the fact that she had run from him. She stared down the narrow road.

*The first time she had taken this road, she was a bride of fifteen, riding to her new home. The castle, as they drew near it, was magnificent, backlit by the sun, the flags on its turrets snapping in the wind. They rode across its mighty drawbridge, the clatter of their horses' hooves and carriage wheels against the solid timbers echoing over the moat. She saw her husband's emblem etched in stone in the arch above and rode beneath it proudly, feeling the thick, cool walls enclose her. Inside, she had gazed in delight at walls hung with rich tapestries, beautifully carved furniture adorned with cushions embroidered with gold and silver thread, silver dishes and candlesticks on the table.*

She smiled, remembering. If she turned down this road, she would return to a life of privilege and wealth.

She reined her horse in.

If she turned down the road to Le Puy right now, everything she had done could be explained—a desire to thank God for her recovery at Cluny, an impulsive visit to her brother on her way home, a tiny lie that she was going to Santiago in order that she might surprise him, knowing he would stop at his castle before continuing to Santiago, and find her waiting—

"My Lady, we must go back," Marie whispered beside her.

Celeste looked down at her. The girl was sweating in the hot sun, the freckles standing out in her white face, her pale lips trembling.

If she did not go back now, she might never be allowed back. Even Marie understood that.

*Peasants had lined the road to see Lord Bernard and his new bride riding toward the sunlit castle. She waved back at them timidly, until she saw that Lord Bernard ignored them, sitting tall and proud beside her. She straightened then, and lowered her arm, but she could not stop smiling, the day was so bright, the castle she rode towards so beautiful, the man beside her so handsome she could barely credit that he was her husband now. And then she had seen the castle, and trembled at its splendour.*

She pulled the reins sideways, turning her horse toward Le Puy. Whatever had happened later, this was a true memory, as real as her hands on the reins, as the breeze on her face, as the beating of her heart. She had been frightened by dreams and the misgivings of her child maid. Lord Bernard would not set her aside because of a ring. She would not allow it. She would ride back now with her head held high and dare anyone to mock her.

Marie pulled her pony around. "Father Jacques," she called. Celeste raised a hand...

Something moved deep inside her, stopping her breath. She felt it again, a fluttering in her womb, a tiny, invisible ripple across her belly: the astonishing, unmistakable quickening of life.

"My Lady?" Marie asked.

She was with child.

She groaned, bending forward, holding herself. She was with child. But whose?

"Lady Celeste?" Father Jacques had turned at Marie's call. He waited on the road to Jerusalem, looking back at them.

The infant within shivered against her heart, butterfly-frail, trusting her to protect him.

To care for him, as she had cared for Etienne, sleeping beside his cradle. And Etienne's fever had broken. Oh, she remembered the cool feel of his forehead, the even sigh of his breathing, the joy so tight and painful in her breast!

Her head pounded fiercely. Etienne had not died of a fever.

The infant moved inside her, as though in fear.

She squinted under the brim of her hat and thought she could see Lord Bernard's castle, a tiny black speck far down the road. Etienne had died in that castle. How had he died? In what way had she failed? The sun shone brightly overhead, but the distant castle hunched beside the road like a spider, dark and silent.

She turned her horse and urged it ahead to join Father Jacques and the other pilgrims on the route to Jerusalem.

# Chapter 18

"I t is time you walked."

Jean woke, hearing the words a beat behind their articulation. One of the dour pilgrims stood in his room, his glance cool and scornful.

Jean looked away. What did he care what this pilgrim thought of him?

"You have been slothful in your recovery. The priest will not say it, but I do."

The thought of the priest's pity was worse than the pilgrim's scorn. He had never been a beggar.

Jean turned onto his side and pushed himself up, trying to use the muscles in his stomach and side as little as possible. He swung his legs slowly over the side of the bed and stifled a groan. The pilgrim reached out to help him but drew his arms back when Jean glared at him.

The wooden plank floor was cold against his bare feet under the sparse rushes. He pushed himself upright. His feet were so swollen they did not feel flat against the floor but rounded, as though he were walking on sausages. He wobbled and threw his arms out.

The pilgrim caught him, held him steady until the agony in his side eased. He did not look so scornful now.

Jean tottered around the bed, leaning heavily on the pilgrim. With every step his pain increased and his legs grew weaker. He held his side tightly with his free hand and gripped the pilgrim's shoulder with the other, until he could go no further, and had to let the pilgrim carry him back to bed.

The man came every day. Jean hated the sight of him, but gradually his strength increased until he could hobble down the stairs alone, to sit in the courtyard between the inn and the stables. He watched the comings and goings of others without interest, but the sun was warm and no one in the stable yard spoke of saints.

The pealing of Matins woke Jean: four separate bells, tolling in their church towers. The clearest, ringing out a full, even tone, must be from the church here in Prevote Venissieux. Then there were two higher notes, a beat behind each other, from smaller bells in nearby villages, and finally a faint, solemn toll coming from a much greater distance, chiming out in counterpoint to the others.

This morning the medley included a fifth stroke, rhythmic but dull. Pause-and-beat-and-pause-and-beat: as though someone were beating out the time for the bells. Jean frowned, listening intently. The sound reminded him of something unpleasant, although he could not place it outside its current cadence as part of the chorus of Matins. He pushed the bed sheet aside and sat up slowly, holding his side. When the pain eased, he hobbled across the room, stopping now and then to breathe, until he reached the window. He leaned against it a moment before opening the wooden shutters, latched across the window against the night air.

The window faced directly onto the town square. Two men stood in the middle of the square, their broad, bare chests and muscular arms glistening with sweat although the early morning sun had barely begun to warm the day. They stood on a wooden platform, pounding a tall post deep into the hard, dry ground in the center of the public square, with huge wooden mallets. They had worked their alternating strokes into a steady rhythm: Lift-and-pound-and-straighten (pound—the other mallet struck the pole) and-lift—

A small group of children stood a short distance from them, watching. One little boy had found a stick and was copying the movements of the men in perfect time, raising a little puff of dust each time he hit his stick against the ground.

Jean stumbled back from the window and slapped the shutters closed, fumbling with the latch to secure them.

The bells had stopped tolling. The incessant pound-and-pause-and-pound of the men driving stakes into the ground echoed across the square, loud and harsh without the music of the church bells to soften it. Jean lifted a heavy wool blanket from the bottom of the bed, dragged it over to the window and draped it across the shutters. It made the room dark but it dulled the noise outside. He lay down on the bed. The muffled pounding sounded now like a heartbeat, deep inside him. Groaning, he rose and limped across to the door, holding his side. Slowly he hobbled down the stairs to sit on the stone bench against the inn in the courtyard. The square was behind him now, on the other side of the inn.

"They are going to burn a heretic," the tall priest said, sitting down on the bench beside him.

Jean closed his eyes. He leaned back against the cold stone wall. Fire was a terrible thing. He never went to watch a burning, even when his absence would be noticed. He did not care about the heretics—they brought their fate upon themselves—but he hated fire.

"I must leave," he said in a tight voice. "I must go home."

"I am glad to hear you say it at last," the priest said. "The inn is full of guests come to watch the burning tomorrow. Some of them will be traveling in the same direction as you."

"No, today. I must leave now." He struggled to his feet.

"That is not possible. It would be better if you not mention it again."

Jean sat down. What had made him say that aloud? He must regain control.

"I may be trusted," the priest said with a small smile.

"I am eager to see my wife and sons," Jean said stiffly.

"I understand."

A kitchen maid came out the inn door. She called a greeting as she crossed to the stable. The priest responded with a smile. "She has been very helpful to me."

Jean nodded. What did one say when a priest admitted in private that a girl was helpful?

"One of our pilgrims is ill," the priest said, as though aware of Jean's thought. "He will not finish his pilgrimage." He looked down at his hands, clasped tightly in his lap.

"He was ill when we began our journey. We have stopped at many holy shrines since then. He will be blessed for what he has done as well as what he attempted to do."

Are we blessed for our attempts? Jean wondered. He did not think it was enough to try. His mother had squandered their safety in every way, while he had done all he could to guard his family, save once, once only, because of an old woman's smile; and still the result was the same. There were no blessings dispensed for trying.

In the night he woke, screaming, from a dream of fire, feeling the searing of his own flesh engulfed in the sizzle and crackle of the flames as he struggled out of sleep. He lay sweating in the hot, still air. An old nightmare. He had not dreamed it since he married Mathilde. *L'eau p'tite,* he called her–a little water–because, lying beside him, she drove away the fiery nightmares of his childhood.

*"L'eau p'tite,"* he whispered in the darkened room, letting the cool sound of the words chase away the lingering heat of his dream.

He limped to the window, pulled the blanket down, and opened the shutters. A refreshing breeze blew in. He left the window open and returned to bed.

He woke again at mid-morning, groggy with having over-slept. Through his window came the shuffle and jostle of people gathering in the square, calling greetings to one another.

"Mama, will she have horns? And a tail? Will her eyes be red, Mama?" a little girl demanded incessantly beneath his window.

"Heretic!" a man's voice cried.

The wound in Jean's side throbbed.

"Heretic, heretic!" the crowd roared in rhythm with his pain.

A cleric's voice rang out across the square, harsh and self-righteous, exhorting the heretic even now to save her eternal soul through confession.

"If I have sinned, I will meet you in hell, for you will surely go there after this day's deed!" a woman's voice cried. A horrified silence followed her words.

In his bed, Jean smiled.

"Light the fire," the cleric said.

"Burn her!" "Burn the heretic!" voices called.

The wind blew smoke in through his window. The woman began to scream.

He closed his eyes, cupping his hand over his exposed ear. By God, he hated fire! He lay rigid and angry on his bed, berating himself. He had heard women scream before. The suffering of strangers was not his business.

The sound and smell and heat of fire filled the air, suffocating him. He gritted his teeth. It was her own fault: she knew the cost of heresy.

The smell of burning flesh came through his open window, sickening him.

Would she never stop screaming? Why was the fire so slow? It should have silenced her by now. He leaped from his bed, ignoring the stabbing pain in his side, and hobbled to the window.

The woman writhed and groaned against the stake, her face twisted in a hideous anguish as fire encompassed her legs, reaching hungrily upwards.

"More faggots!" Jean screamed. His voice, still weak, could not be heard over the noise of the crowd and the snapping of the fire and the agonized screams of the woman. "Throw more faggots on the fire, for the love of God!"

Were they made of stone? Did they have the hearts of demons? He would go down himself and feed the fire, and end her suffering!

A man directly below looked up and caught his eye: the pilgrim's priest.

Jean stared at him, unable to look away, mesmerized by the intensity of his expression. The woman screamed again.

The priest turned back. He raised his hand and moved it slowly, heavily, in the hot air, drawing the four points of the cross, resting it against his breast. A calming movement, strangely soothing.

Others in the crowd had crossed themselves, a quick sign to ward off evil. The priest had not drawn a ward. He stood with his head bent, as though he had drawn the heretic's suffering into himself, and Jean's as well, and held their pain in the hand cupped over his heart.

Jean backed away from the window and slammed the wooden shutters closed. A man could not take on another's suffering.

He stumbled across the room with his hands clasped over his ears and fell onto the bed.

The priest was wrong. Trying was not enough.

*The crash of the door being flung open jolts him out of a deep sleep. He huddles under the thin blanket on his pallet, squeezing himself*

*against the wall, too terrified to call out for his parents. Moonlight filters through the open door. In its eerie light four armed men march across the room to the curtain around his parents' bed. An arm reaches up and tears it away.*

*Mama is kneeling on the bed, holding the blanket tightly around her. Only her face shows above it. Her eyes are wide, terrified. Papa leaps to the floor between her and the men.*

*"Heretics!" the man who tore down the curtain yells. Jean can see the spray of his saliva in the moonlight. "Filthy Jews!" His voice fills the little hut, thick with a fury Jean has never heard before, not even in Papa's worst tempers.*

*"Seize them!" Two of his men lunge toward Mama and Papa. He gestures sharply to the third. "Find their blasphemous writings."*

*Jean knows what they are looking for. It is hidden under the mattress on his parents' bed. Mama read from it before he went to bed. Before Papa came in, because Papa could not read and even if he could, he would never approve of the things that Mama read. It is their secret, the very important secret Jean keeps with Mama. He tries not to look at the mattress. He wants to close his eyes, but he is too afraid. He presses back against the wall, into the shadows.*

*Papa leaps at the man giving the orders, grabs him round the throat. "Run!" he screams.*

*Mama shrieks with terror. It is too late for her to run; one of the guards already has hold of her. The other two leap on Papa, trying to pull him off their captain, but Papa is too strong for them.*

*"Run, Jean!" Papa screams.*

*Jean jumps up and races for the door. He has never heard Papa scream like that.*

*"Run!"*

*Jean races out the doorway.*

*"Run, Jean, run far away, and never look back!" Papa screams behind him.*

Jean sat bolt upright, gasping in the darkness. He could still hear his father's voice reverberating in the small, dark room. The acrid scent of burnt flesh and wood smoke wafted in through the window. He swung his feet over the side of the bed, his heart pounding with the need to move, to run for his life, but there was nowhere to run.

"She did not treasure her life," he said. His voice in the night sounded faint and frightened, less real than the voices in his nightmare or the memory of the heretic's screams. He saw his mother, kneeling on her bed, crying, and the face of the woman screaming as she burned. He said again, more loudly, "She did not treasure her life. She did not deserve…"

…*to keep it.* He sat alone in the night, unable to finish his sentence.

His face was damp. He did not cry; not ever. He shut his eyes, but still the tears seeped onto his cheeks, foolish and futile. He had not even known the woman who died today. The tears burned him, as though they had boiled up inside him a long time before spilling out. He tried to hold them back but they burned his throat and scorched the skin of his face as dry as a parchment and then they poured out, and futile or not, he could not stop them.

He tried to weep silently but there was not enough air in the room; the fire had sucked all the air out of it. Only the suffocating stench of death was left. His chest ached and his lungs burned and he doubled over on his narrow bed, holding himself, holding himself, and still the pain poured out of him. He heard a wailing, low and guttural, the sound of an animal in mortal agony, and he realized it came from him.

He fell sideways and curled up into himself, tightly, his forehead resting against his knees. He rocked on the bed with his legs against his chest and felt a great, searing sorrow fill him.

"…*to lose it,*" he whispered.

# Chapter 19

She was alive! Lord Bernard crumpled the letter in his fist. He had imagined her lying in the woods somewhere between Cluny and Paris, having been set upon by outlaws. He had suffered nightmares envisioning the cruel indignities forced upon her before her murder, and wakened tossing and clenching his fists in his bed. He had been able to think of nothing else, while his men scoured Paris, and then the towns between, asking after her; and all this time she was safe and well with her brother. By God, he would murder her himself for what she had put him through!

Raimond stepped forward, his face pale.

"She is in Lyon with Pierre. Unharmed and untroubled." He glared, as if it were Raimond's fault that she was so carefree while he had been so tortured.

Once again they would smile behind their hands, the courtiers of King Louis' court. They would don expressions of sympathy, hungry for gossip, and ask whether he had found his wife, their lips twitching with the effort not to laugh. Not his Lady wife—he might wed her, but he could not make her a Lady—not in their eyes, and not while she continued to behave so… infuriatingly common! Running around the countryside unescorted! Her death would have been tragic, but this— this made them both high comedy.

"I will let your men know."

Bernard groaned. They were still out searching for her. "Do it," he said, waving Raimond away.

He had not expected Celeste to help him advance his position—the Queen would never make her a Lady-in-waiting. But he had expected her to run his estate quietly and produce heirs, not ruin him. His wife's madness had made his counsel suspect, and now there would be questions as to whether a man who could not control his own wife could lead men.

Eleanor was right: he would have to set her aside. Despite her beauty and his feelings for her, even if it meant returning her sizeable dowry.

A knock on the door interrupted his thoughts. "Enter," he called without looking up.

"A message for Lord Bernard."

Bernard straightened.

"You are invited to joust in the tournament in three days' time, to celebrate the King's daughter, Marguerite's, visit." The messenger rolled up his scroll, waiting expectantly.

King Louis favoured tournaments, as did his Queen, Adéle de Blois. Even so, Lord Bernard might have been able to decline—the invitation was no doubt being issued to every nobleman presently at court—had it not been arranged to honor Marguerite. He had seen the girl, a pretty thirteen-year-old just beginning to show a woman's figure, ride into her father's court this morning. She had looked nervous and he had pitied her, joining the court of a father she would not remember and a step-mother she had never met. She was wed at two-and-a-half to Henry Fits Empress' son, and had grown up in the English court. And now the Prince, fifteen-year-old Hal, had been crowned the future King of England by the Archbishop of York, but Marguerite had not been crowned with him. Louis had invited her to visit him in a cold fury, thinly disguised as paternal affection. With Louis Capet's list of grievances against King Henry increasing, this was no time for one of his Lords to slight Marguerite by refusing to joust in a tournament arranged to celebrate her visit to the French court.

"Tell my liege Lord that I am honored."

The messenger bowed and left.

Bernard cursed vehemently and at length. The best he could hope for from this tournament was to sustain no injuries and avoid being 'captured' by young knights hoping to demand a ransom for his freedom. He might need Celeste's dowry after all.

She was alive and well. He carefully flattened the note from Lyon against the table in his chamber and read it again. Why was it from Pierre's wife, and not from Celeste herself? And why had she told the innkeeper she was going to Paris? A flight of fancy which good sense had corrected? Or a deliberate attempt to send him in the wrong direction? *Would* she wait for him in Lyon?

Of course she would. He would send a message directing her to do so. Unless she chose to return to his castle? Yes, she was well and should return home. He would send his cousin and two of his men to escort her, with orders to make certain she stayed there. It was a generous thing to do in the circumstances, when he could use his men around him for the tournament.

He could decide what further steps to take after the tournament. He strode across the room and opened the door.

"Find Raimond de Le Puy and tell him I wish to see him," he ordered a passing page boy, who ran off to obey.

# Chapter 20

Jean rose before dawn, unable to sleep. He pulled on his hose and his worn shoes—if they had not been so worn, the thieves would have taken them, too—and limped down into the courtyard behind the inn. He sat on the narrow stone bench against the wall of the inn, facing the stable. The air was crisp and damp, only slightly tinged with smoke. He closed his eyes and let the earthy animal smells of horses, donkeys and cows waft over him, along with the pungent odour of manure, the sweet smell of hay and the rich scent of the butter churn beside the barn door. He breathed them all in, the smells of the living. He should have slept here, in the stable yard.

He heard movement and opened his eyes. A stable boy stood at the barn door, yawning and stretching in the grey half-light. He bent down to pick up a bucket and headed toward the well. A man came out of the inn and called something to the boy.

"I am hurrying," the boy called back in a thin, nasal whine.

The scent of porridge and ale and cooking sausages drifted through the open inn door. Jean's stomach rumbled, but he did not want to leave the courtyard. The man went back in and shut the door. Jean leaned against the cool stone wall of the inn and closed his eyes.

He felt strange, the way he once felt after he passed a stone. Something small and hard inside him was gone.

When he was little, someone told him he had his mother's smile. The hard lessons he had learned from her death were still true, but he could remember her smile now, could feel it on his own face and not despise her for it. She had not deserved her death; but she had died just the same. His family had not deserved this, but it had happened. He had never been a coward—it was time to face them, and do what he could for them.

The inn door creaked. Jean opened his eyes.

Three men came out. They walked across to the barn, calling for the boy to saddle their horses, and had he watered them yet? Had he overslept, the lazy fool? They had left orders that they would leave at dawn.

At last they clattered off, leaving Jean to his rest, but by then the stable yard was no longer quiet. A cock had begun crowing its salute to the rosy light stealing across the sky and two mangy dogs chased each other across the yard, yapping. A kitchen girl came out to milk the cow; Jean could hear her complaining to the animal, and the boy laughing as he passed her, leading another horse out of the stable.

"Hitch him to the wagon."

Jean opened his eyes. The man who had spoken was standing beside a small wagon, little bigger than a cart, with low wooden sides and a single raised seat at the front. The back of the wagon was open. A plank of wood leaned against it, ready to be hoisted into place across the back when the wagon was loaded. The man was shorter than Jean and somewhat plump, but the softness was only in his belly. He hefted a barrel into the back of the wagon and leaped up to roll it against a burlap-covered pile, all the while issuing orders to the stable boy and watching to make sure the horse was hitched correctly. His tunic was of good, heavy russet, and his hose looked new, though both were dusty from the road.

"Where are you headed?" Jean called.

The man looked up. His expression was careful but not startled. He had not missed Jean's scrutiny.

"Why do you ask?"

"I need a ride."

The man snapped his fingers at the boy, who lifted the wooden plank up to him. He slid it into place and lashed the ends with rope.

"I heard about you. The fellow set upon by thieves." He stepped over the plank and jumped down. "I am a merchant, not a pilgrim."

Jean nodded. This was a language he understood. "I have a barrel upstairs, in good condition. A merchant can always use another barrel."

"So you are a merchant?"

"A peddler. Spices and other goods."

The man walked around the horse, checking that the harness was firmly strapped the way he wanted it. "There are two others inside headed for Avignon, and I cannot take three," he said from behind the horse.

Jean nodded, as though accepting that. Let the man wait a while. If he had liked the look of the two, he would have already offered them a ride. The merchant came back around his wagon and looked at Jean.

"They will eat twice as much of your provisions, and give you nothing in return," Jean observed.

"Except protection."

Jean pursed his lips. "I killed two of the thieves. With another man by my side they would never have harmed me." An exaggeration, but the first part was true.

"That was before your injury."

"I heal quickly."

"But still you cannot walk."

"I cannot run," Jean corrected. "If we are set upon, you can be sure I will not run away. I will be fighting for my life, as well as for your merchandise."

The merchant examined the harness without answering. A careful man. Jean liked him.

"The barrel is sound and well-made."

The man slapped the horse's rump and approached. He stood before Jean squarely, hands on his hips, looking him over, as though he had not already.

"I do not cook for others."

"I can cook," Jean said. He smiled affably. "If you provide the food."

The man grunted.

"Where are you headed?"

"Marseilles. No side trips."

"Take me as far as Saint-Gilles."

"Show me the barrel."

Jean rose. He entered the inn and climbed the stairs to his room, gritting his teeth against the pain and forcing himself not to limp. The merchant, following behind, would be watching for that.

There were two empty wadmal bags in the bottom of the barrel. "I keep the bags," Jean said. "They were not part of our bargain." He lifted them out and tossed them on the bed.

The merchant examined the barrel carefully and then straightened. "I can give you half an hour to get ready. Then I leave, with or without you." He hoisted the barrel across his shoulders and left the room.

Jean picked up one of the wadmal bags. There was nothing else to take; even his staff had been stolen. He held the bag by a corner and shook it flat. Something flew out of the open end and skidded across the floor. He frowned and walked around the bed. There was nothing on the floor that he could see; it must have rolled under the bed. He would have to bend down and reach under and then get up again and it would all hurt his side. He thought of just leaving it, but what if it was a denier, tossed into the bag at market when he was too busy to open his purse? He shook his head. No use dreaming. Nevertheless, he lowered himself to his knees and peered under the bed. It was too dark to see anything.

He bent further down, ignoring the pain, and swept his arm across the floor. He felt something hard, and closed his hand around it. He had to kneel beside the bed a moment, panting, waiting for the spasms to subside. He knew already it was not a coin. It was the wrong shape. He opened his hand and stared down in disgust. A nail.

He drew his breath in sharply.

Bent a little at the end. The hair on his neck prickled against his skin. He dropped the nail onto the bed and stared at it. He had tried to throw it away, tried to sell it at Cluny, believed it had been stolen with the rest of his goods. And still it stayed with him.

*"Sorrow!" her voice cried, hollow and unholy. A cry devoid of hope; a cry from hell.*

Stayed with him, even when he had lost all else.

Everything else? He scrambled to his feet, wincing at the pain, and grabbed both bags, holding them upside down over the bed. The ruby ring and the pilgrim's badge fell onto the sheet.

"Aghh!" he gave a strangled cry. He stared down at them, wanting to laugh with relief and at the same time frightened. He reached out, then pulled his hand back, afraid to touch them. The ring lay blood-red against the silver emblem from Jerusalem. Surely nothing evil could touch a holy relic? Slowly he picked them up. They were solid and cool in his hand, real.

He was not ruined. What did it matter how they had remained with him? He could sell them for enough to buy a donkey, and some spices. Not as many as usual, but enough for a start. They would be hungry this winter, but they would make it through, and then he could start again. He sat down heavily, wiping roughly at his eyes.

Outside, a horse neighed.

He took a steadying breath and hurried down to the innkeeper's wife to borrow a needle and thread. "To mend my hose," he told her.

Back in his room, he picked open the hem to his tunic and carefully sewed the nail and the ring and the badge at intervals inside it. He examined the outside hem carefully to make sure they did not show.

The merchant was waiting. Jean hesitated on the stairs, then turned down the hall.

221

He found the priest saying the last rites over the dying pilgrim, and waited awkwardly at the door.

"I have a ride home, Father," he said when the priest finished the prayers.

The priest nodded without looking up.

What does he care? Jean thought. I am not one of his pilgrims. He was surprised to find it bothered him.

"I am sorry—" Jean gestured toward the bed where the dying pilgrim lay, letting his words trail off. "I thank you for your help."

"I am not the one to thank." The priest rested his hand on the dying man's arm. "He paid for your care and lodgings with the money he had saved for his pilgrimage."

"Well then," Jean shifted awkwardly. "I will... pray for his soul." He was embarrassed as soon as he said it. The priest would know it for a lie; he knew Jean did not pray.

"Yes," the priest said, looking directly at him now. "Pray for him. That is how you can repay your debt."

Jean flushed. But he was the one who had offered the bargain. He nodded reluctantly. "I will, then. Farewell, Father."

The priest rose and clasped his shoulders. He regarded Jean with the same intense expression Jean had seen on his face in the town square. "You carry sorrow with you," he said.

Jean started, tried to pull away.

"Do not be ashamed. Your sorrow is a holy emotion. Our Lord's sorrow saved us all."

He let Jean go. Jean stumbled backward, toward the door.

"Wait," the priest said. He crossed the room to where the pilgrim's belongings lay, and brought his staff over to Jean. "He does not need this where he is going, and you, I think, will."

The merchant was seated on the wagon with the reins in his hand when Jean hurried into the stable yard.

"You are late," he said. "I hope you are a good cook."

"I am," Jean said. The merchant's lips twitched briefly.

Jean used the wagon wheel to clamber up into the back of the wagon, leaning on his new staff and gritting his teeth against the spasm in his side. He lowered himself onto the burlap-covered mound, which turned out to be agreeably soft.

He was on his way home. He would not have to tell Mathilde that they were destitute. But all his misfortunes had begun with the nail and the ring, and he feared they were not finished with him yet. He was acutely aware of them bound into his tunic. Bound to him, and he to them.

They were all he had to save his family.

# Chapter 21

The little band of pilgrims continued south, away from Le Puy. Celeste rode with them, leaving behind the castle with its dark and brooding secrets, taking with her precious little money, an incompetent maid, and an unwanted infant.

Everything conspired against her happiness. And now this.

She felt a tiny movement deep within her. It held her hostage, trapped by its vulnerability, and hers. If she could only be sure it was her husband's. But Etienne had been his, and Etienne had not been safe within his father's castle.

She touched her hand to her belly. She would not let this child come to grief. Or bring her grief; the two were intertwined. If she could save it, could keep it safe, she might remember her past then, and escape it. Be free of it at last: a life for a life.

She rode slowly behind the others, away from Le Puy, toward Saint-Gilles where they would take a boat to Jerusalem.

Jerusalem. The Holy City. The dream of heaven, where God had stepped down onto the dusty soil to talk to ordinary men and women, to eat their food and drink their wine and sweat under the hot sun beside them; to lie down weary after a long day, and suffer pain and thirst, and wonder, in the end, if he had been forsaken here.

Jerusalem. The city where God had pitied man. Where he had healed the blind, the lame, the sick. This infant would be safe in Jerusalem. She could leave him there, with the priests. It would not matter whose child he was to them. And no one else need know of him. Then she could return to Lord Bernard. With or without her ring, he would find he had little support in setting aside a wife so pious she had trod in Our Lord's footsteps in the Holy City.

First, she must get to Jerusalem. How much longer would it be before she showed, even under her loose kirtle? She jerked her hand away from her belly, looking around quickly. No one had noticed.

Father Jacques would not let her travel with them if he learned of her condition. She should not be riding now. She had stopped riding as soon as she guessed she was carrying Etienne, even before she felt him quicken inside her, but this time she had no choice. Travelling to Jerusalem was safer than being cloistered with her maids in Lord Bernard's dark castle, bearing a babe who might destroy them both.

The infant moved again, a tiny flutter beneath her heart, bringing moisture to her eyes; she turned her face to let the breeze blow it away. She *must* remember how Etienne had died so that this one could live, however painful that knowledge might be.

They stopped at an inn in Prevote Venissieux the second night. The innkeeper's wife chattered as she served their meal. They had just missed the burning of a heretic. She described it in such detail that the Lady's pretty maid was put off her meat pie and could eat only the bread and cheese and salted fish and fruit.

"You are wise to sleep here the night," the woman said, bringing in wine and a fresh loaf of bread. "There is a desperate band of thieves in the woods outside our town. They attacked a man who camped by the roadside and nearly killed him. A group of pilgrims carried him here, where he lay upstairs between life and death for weeks."

Celeste let the woman's voice fade into the background. She was weary and hungry after two days of riding and not interested in the highlights of life in Prevote Venissieux.

"...a peddler. A big man with a sharp face," the innkeeper's wife said in answer to a question from the boy. "And he had such nightmares about it! He kept calling out, asking about his donkey and a ring, which those vile cutthroats must have stolen also."

Celeste choked. She set down her mug of wine so quickly it sloshed over the brim, spilling onto the table. Marie patted her back as she coughed, but the others were all engrossed in the woman's tale.

"At first we thought he would die. He kept mumbling on about heaven, as though he were halfway there and could see it." She crossed herself solemnly and left them with that thought while she went to the kitchen to fetch another jug of wine.

"They stole everything except an empty barrel," she said, returning with the wine and an apple pasty to end their supper.

"Is he still here?" Celeste asked. Her voice cracked on the last word.

"Oh, no. He left yesterday. A merchant from Marseilles gave him a lift on his wagon."

Marseilles. The peddler was travelling south, just ahead of them. But he had lost her ring to thieves. She would never get it back now.

How could he have suddenly appeared in this insignificant little village? It was too strange to be chance. What perverse, inexplicable force drew her after him without her will or knowledge? He had lost everything, the woman said, but no one would consider a bent nail as anything much. Did he still have it? Was the nail pulling her toward him? Was that what the gypsy had warned her of? *Undo what you have done.*

She could never take back her ring and the nail now. The sorrow she had seen in the peddler's face would never become her own again. She was free. So why did she feel a weight of dread settling over her? Why did she still feel the presence of demons around her?

Celeste wrapped her cloak tightly about her despite the warmth of the evening, and lay down on the rushes. She heard Father Jacques murmuring his prayers across the room, a comforting sound. She listened to the low, steadfast rhythm of his Latin, not trying to hear the words, just letting them surround her in the darkness, lingering in the air like a blessing.

A shaft of moonlight from the window sliced through the air above her. Celeste closed her eyes. The light and the prayer were not for her; she was cut off from his blessing.

The men-at-arms were vigilant on the road next morning. The Lady's nervous cousin cried out alarms three times, which turned out to be nothing more than the wind in the trees, a deer, and another traveler on the road who had stepped into the bushes to relieve himself and was startled to face the raised swords of the two henchmen when he emerged.

The boy cantered from one side of the road to the other between the men, looking into the forest on either side with his hand on his sword, occasionally stealing glances at his mother's maid to see whether she noticed.

"My husband's men-at-arms are excellent swordsmen," the Lady said, riding up beside Celeste. She had introduced herself yesterday as Lady Yvolde de Bourges, and had not seemed put out by Celeste's lack of conversation, but cantered beside her in a companionable silence.

"I am not concerned," Celeste replied. If robbers attacked them, no doubt she would be frightened, but she could not rouse herself to fear them in advance. She had too much else upon her mind.

"You have great faith."

"We are on pilgrimage; we all have faith."

"Do we? I have sometimes thought it is doubt that makes us go on pilgrimage."

Was Lady Yvolde questioning her motives? "I did not take you for a doubter," Celeste said coolly.

"Doubt is the prerequisite of any journey."

What was she supposed to say to that? Admit it? Deny it? "Why doubt?" she asked, intrigued despite herself.

"The soul journeys toward faith, the mind toward understanding, the body toward courage. Yet none of these pilgrimages is undertaken without the seed of doubt. We doubt our faith, our knowledge, our courage, and seek to prove them."

"You make doubt a virtue."

"A necessary flaw. Have you not met men who are utterly certain of themselves?"

Celeste smiled. "I concede; doubt is indeed a virtue. Have you discussed your theory with Father Jacques?"

"Only the part on strengthening my faith," Lady Yvolde replied.

Celeste laughed.

"And what is it that journeys toward happiness?" she asked, smiling still, as though the answer was of little import.

"Ah, the most difficult journey of all. The journey of the heart."

"Why should it be so difficult?"

"Because that journey requires all three: faith, understanding and courage."

"Sheathe your sword, you foolish boy," the portly cousin cried.

The boy came galloping toward them, brandishing his sword at the shrubbery beside the road.

"I must see to my son," Lady Yvolde said with a sigh.

They joined another group of travellers that night, camping together beside the road. The men-at-arms kept watch by turns. Celeste lay awake, considering Lady Yvolde's comments. Marie whimpered beside her. "Go to sleep," she whispered crossly when the whimpering continued.

"I am afraid," Marie mumbled.

"You have a knife," Celeste hissed. "If anyone comes near you, use it."

"But it is not very sharp. It does not even cut bread well."

Celeste rolled over, trying to find a comfortable spot on the hard ground. Marie whimpered again, the noise muffled against her arm. But Celeste was conscious of it now, waiting for it; even muffled it would prevent her sleeping. Again the miserable little sound came. She had been beaten by her father, Pierre said. She might keep this up all night.

"There are no bandits!" Celeste hissed. "The innkeeper told us that so we would pay to sleep at his inn."

"What about the man they nearly killed?"

"Nearly," Celeste whispered scornfully. "I could make up a better tale than that."

Marie was silent, comparing it, perhaps, to the stories Celeste had made up when they were young. At least she was quiet. Celeste reached for her own knife, in its sheath at her belt. Could she use it? If someone came at her, would she? She tried to imagine it, to picture a figure lunging at her in the dark. She thought of her nightmares, her helpless terror. She had not been a girl who could fight back.

Somewhere in the woods on the other side of the fire a twig snapped. She gripped the knife fiercely. Oh yes, she would use it.

In the morning it began to rain, a cold, steady drizzle which persisted for two days. Their clothes were wet, their capes clammy and uncomfortable even after they hung them on branches by the campfire. The saddles rubbed against their damp clothes and chaffed their skin into painful rashes. The cuts on Celeste's thighs opened again and bled, she had to wrap them in cloths while pretending to relieve herself.

When the sun came out at last, it burned their faces and necks because they had stopped wearing their heavy, sodden hats. The Lady's cousin developed a toothache and moaned about it to anyone who would listen. Her maid complained of headaches and begged them stop so she could rest in the shade. The boy whined incessantly; he was hungry, bored or tired in turns. He sulked when his mother's maid would not ride with him and teased Marie until she was in tears. Celeste wanted to take a switch to them both. Only her brother's admonition to be kind to Marie restrained her. If Pierre could fault her for it, so might her travelling companions.

Lady Yvolde commiserated, cajoled, and encouraged them all. Celeste admired her calm persistence in keeping them moving. She, herself, was stoically silent. What had they to complain about, compared to her? Father Jacques, who had so indulged Mistress Blanche on the trip to Cluny, followed Lady Yvolde's lead and maintained a steady pace. Apparently he had decided none of them would die of their complaints.

On the fourth evening, as they were preparing to bed down beside the road, Marie approached her. "You must make confession, My Lady," she said in a low voice.

She had suggested this to Celeste before, and Celeste waved it aside as she had done then. This time, however, Marie persisted.

"You must! We are on a pilgrimage and Father Jacques is our confessor."

"Mind your place," Celeste snapped.

"Please, Lady Celeste," Marie cried, wringing her hands.

Celeste closed her eyes briefly, striving for patience. "Why should I make confession?"

"The others—they are talking about it. About you not making confession. They say God will not bless a pilgrimage if the pilgrims are not—"

"Not what?" Celeste demanded, narrowing her eyes. How dare they criticize her, while they whined and fretted about nothing!

"'Pure in their intent.' It is not me, Lady Celeste! It is the others who say it!"

"Who? Not Lady Yvolde?"

"No! She would never. It is Monsieur Robert. But the others listen to him."

The sour-faced cousin. He complained more than the boy and slowed them down more than the silly maid. "Why should I care what he says?" Celeste said, disgusted.

"What will become of us, Lady?" Marie cried, wringing her silly hands. "Lord Bernard will not take you back now, and if Father Jacques asks us to leave—" The rest was drowned in weeping.

"What has Father Jacques said?" Celeste demanded.

Marie stopped crying with a hiccup. "They have not spoken to him yet. But they will. Do not wait for them to speak to him, Lady Celeste."

Father Jacques would not leave a Lady stranded in some town along their route because she did not make confession. But he had warned her to take this pilgrimage seriously, as a holy undertaking.

"What have I to confess?" she wondered, regretting her words at once. She had a good deal worth confessing, and Marie knew it. "Never mind!"

"I confessed to sloth," Marie said, her distress subsiding into hiccups. "Sometimes when the cock crows (hiccup), I wish he would not, quite yet. And to envy (hiccup)."

"Envy?"

"Agnes has a ribbon," Marie mumbled. "A beautiful (hiccup) red ribbon. She weaves it into her hair—"

"Who is Agnes?"

Marie looked at her wide-eyed, as though she could not believe Celeste did not know. She forgot to hiccup.

Celeste flushed. Agnes would be the maid who had the boy and the sour-faced man acting equally foolishly.

She looked across the campfire where Agnes stood. A bright red ribbon was braided through her thick, brown hair. Her linen kirtle was a darker red, and was cut nearly as full as her mistress's. She noticed them watching her and turned, flouncing the skirts of her kirtle.

Celeste became aware of her own dull black kirtle. She had had to leave Lyon before her new one was finished. She glanced at Marie's, so short it no longer covered her ankles, although Marie had let it down until there was no hem at all. She must have grown while they were at the abbey.

She looked up from examining Marie's kirtle. Marie's cheeks were scarlet. A tear stood on her lashes. Across the campfire, Agnes laughed.

Celeste raised her chin haughtily and stared at Agnes until the girl remembered her station and bowed her head. Her eyes made a mockery of the subservient gesture.

"Come with me," Celeste ordered. She walked over to the bundle of her belongings and opened the basket, reaching for the cloth bag which held her hair things. After a moment of searching through it, she held up a long silk ribbon.

"It is blue, not red," she said to Marie. "It will match your eyes and look nicer in your yellow hair than a red one would."

Marie stared with her mouth open, not daring to take the proffered ribbon. Growing impatient, Celeste let it go. Marie caught it before it touched the ground.

"Now you have your own ribbon," Celeste said. "Did your confession accomplish as much?"

Marie did not answer. She stood gawking at the shiny blue ribbon in her hands.

Celeste closed her basket. Unfortunately, however, Marie was right. She should at least appear to be a pilgrim, and pilgrims made confession. She walked resolutely across to the priest.

"Father, will you hear my confession?" she said, before she could change her mind. Lady Yvolde's thin-lipped cousin was sitting beside the monk. Celeste saw the surprise on his face before a false smile covered it.

The young priest led her a little distance from the others, and stopped just out of hearing, where the men-at-arms could still see them. Celeste knelt in front of him and folded her hands.

"Confiteor deo omnipotent," he began.

When it was her turn, Celeste said, "Mea culpa," and stopped. She could not remember anything before she had met the peddler, and she was not going to reveal their bargain. Nor had she any intention of disclosing the trail of lies and half-truths that had brought her here, including those she had told him.

"Mea culpa…" Everyone was guilty. Only babes were innocent.

*He lay in her arms, his pale little face still. Prince of the drowsy, dying day—*

Her head began to pound.

"I have been impatient with my maid," she said quickly. She had slapped Marie. No, that was not a sin, it was a necessity. Everyone punished their servants; how else would they learn?

"I have not gone to confession for—" Three? No, it was more than three weeks now since she had seen the peddler, and who knew how long before that? "—two months." The pounding in her temples distracted her. "I was ill," she said.

Was that enough for one confession? She looked up. He stood before her quietly, his hands clasped above her head, waiting.

She closed her eyes. What else could she confess to? Not a lie, but not—

"Have you been an obedient wife to your husband?"

His words shocked her. No priest had ever said such a thing to her. She wanted to slap him for his daring. Instead she found herself saying, "I do not know, Father."

She felt his hand on her bent head, heard him forgive her everything. "…In nomine Patris, et Filii, et Spiritus Sancti. Amen."

She was angry and at the same time strangely comforted as she rose to her feet.

"Go in peace, child," he said, "and leave your sorrow with God."

Celeste stumbled. "I have already left my sorrow behind."

"Have you?" Father Jacques asked. He waited until she looked up.

Her heart pounded. "Has Marie—?"

"I am bound to silence when I hear confession."

"Marie is prey to many superstitions." She was sorry she had confessed her impatience with Marie. She could not box her ears right after doing so. "I do not believe in the superstitions of peasants, Father." She began to walk away quickly, before he saw the tremble in her legs.

"Lady Celeste."

She turned back to him.

"Do not take these peasants' tales lightly. There is great power in symbols."

*Deep, slow breathing surrounds her in the darkness. She feels her way carefully across the great hall. If she does not touch them, stumble against one of them, they must continue sleeping.*

*Wake up! She tells herself. But she is trapped inside the dream. The weight of the darkness, the roughness of the wall against her hand, the death-like cold of the stairs under her bare feet are all infused with the intense reality of nightmare, more vivid and substantial than anything she has experienced awake.*

*Slowly, the door of her bedchamber opens. She gasps, desperate to cry for help, but dares not disturb the false slumber of those below. They would rush up the stairs, not to help her, but to accuse her.*

*The wooden box on the bench is so small its size mocks her. It should fill the length of the bench. It should be long enough for her to lie down in, to draw death over her as well.*

*She is kneeling beside the bed, her knife in her hand. She stares at it, horrified. A scream rises in her throat. Her fingers open, dropping the knife…*

*A hand reaches out of the dark and wraps around her left hand, swallowing her small white fist within it. Blood oozes between her fingers, dripping onto the floor…*

Celeste awoke screaming. She shook her left hand and wiped it fiercely against her cloak, uttering short, piercing shrieks. There was nothing in it. She peered at it but the night was too dark for her to see whether there was any mark. She raised it to her nose. It smelled of sweat, not blood.

"What?" "Who's there?" "Where are they?" Her companions stumbled up from sleep, clutching their staffs and knives and staring around them.

"Help! Thief! Help!" Monsieur Robert shouted, huddled under his blanket.

The men-at-arms ran to Celeste and positioned themselves between her and the forest, holding their swords ready. "Where?" one of them asked curtly.

Celeste blinked, pulling herself out of the nightmare. A cool night breeze blew across her fevered brow and dried the beads of sweat. The moon was hidden in cloud, too dark for her to see clearly.

"Where?" he repeated, a sharp edge to his voice.

"There." She scrambled unsteadily to her feet and pointed vaguely toward the woods. "I think he ran away."

"How many?"

"One. I only saw one," she stammered, trying to tamp down the situation without raising their suspicions. She could not tell her companions, standing with their weapons ready, that she had had a bad dream.

A dream or a memory? Bile rose in her throat. She clapped her hand over her mouth.

"He was trying to steal our horses," the boy cried, brandishing his short sword.

The men-at-arms sheathed their swords. A single horse thief now run off was no threat.

Celeste swallowed. Only a nightmare. She breathed the cool air in deeply.

Father Jacques knelt in prayer, giving thanks now instead of requesting aid. Monsieur Robert came out from under his blanket and tried to comfort Agnes, who pouted prettily. The boy sheathed his sword, his mouth forming a moue of disappointment.

Lady Yvolde approached Celeste. "What is troubling you so?" she asked quietly.

She had not looked toward the forest, Celeste realized. She looked into Lady Yvolde's face, at its mixture of compassion and peace, and wanted, very badly, to tell her everything.

Marie ran over. "Are we safe now?" she cried, looking at Lady Yvolde.

"Perfectly safe," Lady Yvolde told her gravely. She looked back at Celeste.

"I am not troubled," Celeste said.

The deep breathing of sleeping people surrounded her. For a moment, at the edge of waking, her nightmare returned. Then she heard the soft whinny of a horse nearby and the low, drawn-out hoot of an owl in the woods, and a quiet grunt as one of the watchmen shifted position to keep himself awake. She opened her eyes. A sheen of moonlight diffused the sky with silver.

She felt a flutter of movement deep inside her. "Do not fear," she whispered to him, this stranger in her womb for whom she had no feelings, whom she would never hold and never grieve over. "I will take you to Jerusalem." Then she would stop dreaming. She could resume her life when she had safely disposed of him. She thought of the nail she had felt in her hand, the one she had sold to the peddler. Her stomach clenched. It was not sorrow she had wanted him to take from her. Her dreams were not about sorrow.

She stood up quickly and shook out her cloak. Lady Yvolde's man looked over at her, then returned to watching the forest. Had she seen scorn in his eyes? Had he guessed that there was no thief in the night?

She went a little way into the bushes to perform her toilet. When she returned, the harsh moonlight had brightened into dawn.

Father Jacques was awake and kneeling in prayer. It must become a habit, waking in the darkness to pray. She wondered what it felt like, subduing oneself to constant obedience.

Like being a woman, she thought. Only he chose his obedience. Unless he was a younger son, as trapped into his submissiveness as any woman.

The others began to stir. They did not relight the fire, but ate dry bread and drank from their flasks warm water that tasted faintly of leather while they packed their things and prepared for another long day of travel.

# Chapter 22

**J**ean limped through Saint-Gilles, glad of the pilgrim's staff. No one would note his infirmity here: many strangers limped, crawled or were carried into this town to pray at the tomb of Saint-Gilles, the patron saint of cripples.

It was a long, slow walk to the small wooden hut with its straw-thatched roof at the edge of town. A strong Mistral wind pulled at his tunic and threatened to topple him. He shivered. His cloak was keeping some thief warm now. He hoped they had fought over his goods and killed one another.

It would be warm in his hut. He had filled the chinks in the walls with mud to make it snug in winter. Jean had slept in manors and castles and monasteries, but the thought of that little hut and the straw mattress he shared with Matilde quickened his pace as no other dwelling could.

"'Way, beggar!"

Jean stumbled sideways as the carriage swept past him. He stood catching his breath, looking down at his patched hose, his worn shoes…

They would be frightened to see him limping home, without the donkey. They would believe themselves ruined, Mathilde and the boys, and try to hide their despair, telling themselves to be glad he had made it home. He could not show them the ring—better they never saw it— so how would he reassure them?

The merchant's section was straight ahead. If he sold the ring now— *Never trade at home.* That was the rule that kept him and his family safe. A rule to abide by.

Besides, he was dirty and ragged. The metal smith would see his need at once and take advantage of it. Better to have Mathilde wash and mend his clothes and trim his hair and feed him a good chicken dinner as she always did to celebrate his homecoming.

He smiled to himself. She would boil the chicken in her big black pot over the fire until the meat was white and tender, swimming in its own juices. Then she would throw in onion and parsnip and herbs from her garden. The little hut would fill with the smell of their fine feast. He licked his lips and turned from the metal smith's doorway. When he was stronger, he would take the ring to Marseilles, sell it to a merchant who did not know him and would ask no questions.

The rows of joined houses grew lower and narrower as he walked further from the town center, until they ended altogether. He was on the outskirts of Saint-Gilles, where people like him built their mud-and-wattle huts, with a little land for a garden and if they were lucky, a hen coop. Someday, with Simon and Gilles helping him, they might move into a town house and live like proper merchants, and Mathilde would buy their food at the market. The dream was farther away now than it had been in Lyon, but it might still be possible.

When he saw his hut, he paused. How quiet it was; as quiet as a graveyard. He shook away the thought. Mathilde must have sent the boys on some errand to keep the hut quiet while Jeanne was napping. Even the chickens obliged her, for there were none in sight, nor any clucking coming from the henhouse.

He pushed the door open and stepped inside. "Mathilde—" his voice broke off.

She was kneeling on the dirt floor beside one of the children's pallets. She raised her head to look at him. Her eyes were bruised and hollow. "Thank God you are home," she whispered.

He stood at the door, unable to move or speak. "Who?" he said, forcing the word out.

He knew already. He had dreamed it. Jeanne—the name lodged in his throat.

Mathilde looked down at Jeanne, lying so still on her little pallet.

"She is not—?"

"No," Mathilde said in a voice that stopped his heart. *Not yet.*

Jean limped across the room.

"You are hurt," she cried, rising to help him.

"It is nothing. It will mend." He waved her arm aside and lowered himself to the floor.

A bowl of water sat beside Jeanne's pallet. Jean wrung out the cloth in the water and wiped her forehead. Her cheeks were as scarlet as glowing embers against her pale face. He dropped the cloth into the water and lifted her, cradling her to him. She was hot against his chest, like a little candle burning itself out.

"Where are her brothers? Send them for a doctor."

"I have." Mathilde's voice was dull. "He has come three times, and bled her. We sold the chickens to pay him. There is nothing more he can do. I have sent Gilles and Simon for the priest."

"No!" Jean stumbled to his feet, holding Jeanne. "She will not die."

Jeanne's eyes opened. "Papa..." she whispered.

"Yes, Jeanne!" he cried. "Yes, it is Papa. I am here, Jeanne."

She closed her eyes again.

"You see? She is clear-headed, she knows me."

The door burst open. Simon and Gilles rushed in, with the priest behind them. "Papa! Papa!" they cried, running to him.

"You are not needed here," Jean told the priest. "She spoke to me. She is not dying."

The priest stopped in the doorway.

"Jean," Mathilde said, coming close to him. "Jean, we must."

"Consider her soul," the priest said.

"She will recover. They said the last rites over me, and here I stand." Beside him he heard Mathilde's sharp intake of breath.

"They said the last rites over you?" Simon's voice broke at the end, deflecting the shrill boy's cry into a man's deeper tone.

"I must do for Jeanne what was done for you, and pray that it be God's will for her to recover, as well."

"Please, Jean," Mathilde whispered, touching his arm.

Jeanne murmured something, turning her head fretfully. Jean listened, but she did not repeat it. He heard only her breathing, ragged and shallow, against his heart.

The priest approached and held his palm over Jeanne's burning forehead. "In nominus Deis…"

She was so light; a little sparrow in his arms. Jean held her tightly, his eyes blurring until he could barely see her. It is the fog, he thought. I dreamed it, and it is happening. His blood pounded in his ears, drowning out the sacred rites. He felt Jeanne burning against his chest and Mathilde weeping at his side and the boys clinging to him, and just below Gilles' hand, the leaden weight in the hem of his tunic.

I have brought this upon us, he thought.

The fog closed in. He stood alone, holding sorrow in his arms. It was as light as a lie, as heavy as the sin in a man's soul.

When the priest left, Jean laid his daughter on her pallet. She appeared to be breathing a little easier.

"Where is our donkey?" Gilles asked.

"Stolen by thieves."

Mathilde put her hand to her throat. "How badly are you hurt?" She reached toward him.

"I will heal." His voice was bitter. He did not look away from Jeanne.

"Sit down," Mathilde said. "Simon, watch your sister and wipe her forehead with the cloth." She bustled about, setting bread and ale on the table before him. "It is all we have. Eat," she commanded when he did not take them. "I cannot lose you both."

He took a bite of bread. Gilles stood at the table watching him, his eyes wide in his pale face, full of questions.

Mathilde sat across from him in the other chair. How weary she looked.

"I have some money. Set aside. With someone," he mumbled around the thick, dark bread.

Mathilde nodded, forcing herself to smile.

Jeanne's fever waned the next morning but it returned by mid-afternoon. Mathilde boiled willow bark and yarrow, and they took turns sitting Jeanne up and forcing her to sip the hot, bitter tea. Jean sat beside his daughter, listening for the thin sigh of her breathing, while Mathilde prayed.

She was still breathing. Each time he bent his ear to her little mouth, she was still breathing.

"Papa, tell me about the thieves. Did you kill them?" Gilles asked, coming to sit cross-legged beside him.

"Two of them."

Gilles grinned. "And the others all ran away?"

Jean shook his head. "They beat me and left me for dead."

"But you did not die," Simon said quickly. Gilles shot him a scornful glance.

If he had died, would Jeanne be well? If he had not brought the woman's sorrow home with him? What if he threw the nail away? But he would have to throw away the ring as well, it was part of the bargain.

And what if Jeanne died anyway, and the boys and Mathilde went hungry because he had thrown away the only valuable thing they had left?

"Papa?"

"A priest found me," he said. "A priest with a band of pilgrims. They carried me to an inn and cared for me."

"Like the Good Samaritan," Simon cried, clapping his hands.

Jeanne started and gave a weak cry. Simon looked chagrined.

"Go outside and tend the garden," Mathilde said, bending to wipe Jeanne's forehead.

"I will watch her," Jean said when the boys had gone. "Get some sleep." He sat beside his daughter and watched her breathe, the rise and fall of her chest barely discernable. He waited for her to open her eyes again, to say his name again.

When Mathilde shook him awake in the morning, he leaped up in a terror. He had slept little all night, dozing and waking to listen for Jeanne's breathing. "Jeanne—?" he gasped.

"No," she said. "She is a little better this morning. I want you to watch her while I get more willow bark."

He rose and sat by Jeanne. Her breathing was better, as Matilde had said. He leaned forward and kissed her. She was still hot with fever. "Be well, Jeanne," he whispered. "Please, be well."

He went to the table where Mathilde had set out some porridge for him, and dropped heavily onto a wooden stool. Something sharp dug into his thigh. He lifted the hem of his tunic and tore the threads loose. Pulling the ring and the nail out, he dropped them onto the table. They rolled against each other.

He stared at the long, gleaming nail. Had it come from a child's coffin, after all? Behind him, Jeanne whimpered on her pallet. He held his breath until her breathing was even again.

The wadmal bag he had carried home lay on the floor beside his stool. He lifted it up and tossed the cold, bent nail inside, out of sight. Jeanne was better today. The nail was only a nail, after all.

The hut was very quiet. Jean ate his porridge slowly. The brilliant ruby winked up at him. Without thinking, he picked up the ring and tried it on. It was too small for his ring finger, but fit snugly onto his little finger, turning his rough hand into a Lord's hand.

He did not hear Mathilde come in until she gasped beside him. He tried to pull the ring off but she had already seen it.

"Jean," she cried, her voice frightened. "What have you done?"

He twisted the ring, trying to get it off. "I have done nothing. I received this in trade."

She sat down slowly, laying the willow bark and a small posy of white yarrow flowers on the table. "Who would barter something so valuable?"

"Someone who wanted my spices!" Why had he not thought up some plausible lie to tell her in case she saw it?

"Jean, I am not simple. That ring is worth more than a barrel of spices."

The cursed thing would not pass over his knuckle. He felt his face reddening. What right had she to question him? "Hold your tongue, wife. You mind your house and I will mind my trade!"

"Take it off!"

"I am trying to!" They were both on edge, worn out by sleeplessness and worry. He should walk away now, give them both time to calm down. He knew it and he did not care. He gritted his teeth and yanked on the ring, scraping his knuckle, and threw it on the table.

"Is this why there is no money for next year's spices? Is this why we have no donkey to carry your wares? So you can wear a rich man's trinket on your hand?" Her cheeks were flushed; tears of anger stood in her eyes.

"The donkey was stolen by thieves!"

"They stole the donkey and left that ring?" The scorn in her voice infuriated him.

"They did not find the ring! It was in that wadmal bag. They thought the bag was empty." He had never seen her so unreasonable. She was frightened for Jeanne and exhausted, but so was he. She should know that, and not push him too far.

"What else are you hiding from me?" She bent and grabbed the bag from the floor and shook it over the table.

The nail fell out. It clattered loudly against the wood, rolling sideways until the ring stopped it. Mathilde drew her breath in sharply. In the silence that followed, they both stared at the nail.

Mathilde lifted her hands to cover her face. Her shoulders began to shake.

"Mathilde—" Jean reached toward her.

Her face was still buried in her hands but she sensed his gesture and flinched away.

"Mathilde," he said again, pleading.

"You bought someone's sorrow. You brought it home to us." Her voice, behind her hands, was unfamiliar to him. He wished she would shout again.

"It is only a superstition," he said, hearing the tremor of doubt in his own voice.

She dropped her hands. "Is Jeanne's illness a superstition? Look at her. And the thieves, were they a superstition?"

He looked away from her, wanting to deny it but unable to. He had been warned. He had dreamed of Jeanne's death, and he had ignored it, convinced himself it was but a fever-dream.

"I did not mean to buy it." He had laughed at the woman, had started to pass her by—

"She gave you her ring so you would take the nail."

She knew him that well? He flushed and could not answer her. The nail and the ring lay on the table side by side, condemning him. He should have given them back. He should have searched and searched however long it took until he found the woman and made her take them, held her finger and forced the ring back onto it if he had to. Mathilde must know he would never harm Jeanne, never! "Mathilde—"

She looked at him as though he were a stranger. "You sold Jeanne's life for a gold ring."

"No!" He leaped up and slapped her, hard.

The minute his hand touched her cheek he regretted it.

"Mathilde—" His faltering apology was drowned out by a strangled cry behind him. Simon and Gilles stood in the doorway.

Gilles looked from his father to the ring.

Simon stood with his mouth half-open, staring from Jean to Mathilde. He cried out again, a frightened, choking sound, and turned and ran away.

# Chapter 23

They clattered into Saint-Gilles down a stone road so wide four horses could ride abreast. "A good Roman road," Lady Yvolde said, cantering her horse alongside Celeste's.

"Will it take us to the sea?" She had heard that the Mediterranean stretched out to the horizon like the blue sky fallen down to Earth; that when the wind blew, a million stars shone in its waves, leading Christians to the Holy Land as the Star of Bethlehem led the wise men to his birth.

"Saint-Gilles is not on the Mediterranean," Lady Yvolde replied. "It was built a few miles inland on the Petite Rhone, to shelter its harbour from storms."

"Will we not board our ship here, then?"

"Oh yes. The river is wide and deep enough for the great sea-faring vessels. Ships from all parts of the Mediterranean have been visiting Saint-Gilles since it was built."

The streets were as crowded as Cluny during its festival, with many people dressed in pilgrim's garb. Was she really here, about to board a ship for Jerusalem? Celeste saw the same excitement in the faces of the pilgrims around her that lifted her own heart. Was it the pull of the Holy Land? Did it draw Christian souls to it, like a lodestone? She wanted to kick her horse into a gallop and race toward the quay, but the streets were busy and Father Jacques kept them to a courteous trot.

The buildings on either side were dark and narrow, with Roman arches and tall wooden doors reinforced with iron frames and bars. Occasionally, through open doors, she caught sight of inner courtyards. A few were light and airy, open to the sun; others were protected by massive, arched stone ceilings. Narrow, cobbled side roads between the rows of houses meandered off the wide main streets.

A Roman settlement: heavy and dark and pagan. The further into its center she rode, the more it closed in on her, dispelling her earlier excitement. How many hopeful pilgrims passed through this dark city to die in the jaws of the sea? She felt an urgent desire to board the boat at once, before she lost her courage. She pulled her cloak around her. A pilgrim's cloak. A pilgrim bound for the Holy Land. Had not Christianity dispelled the darkness of the pagan Roman Empire? She need not fear the darkness of this town, for she was travelling toward the light.

*"Until you undo what you have done, you have no future."*

This was what the Gypsy meant! The hot light of Jerusalem would bleach away her dark past. She would leave the infant there, in the cradle of Christianity, to be raised in the light of the Holy Land. She sat taller on her horse and smiled as Father Jacques led them to the pilgrim's hostel, where they would rest and take refreshment while he secured their passage.

Celeste watched him walk off with the two henchmen, wishing she could go with them. They waited. The boy wanted to ride closer to the ships, explore the town, walk along the quay, go to find Father Jacques and bring them a report. Lady Yvolde bade him stay where he was a dozen times, each one as patient as the last.

She had rested until she was exhausted by the time Father Jacques returned. A ship leaving tomorrow for Jerusalem was already full, but another was expected within a week.

A week, she thought. And then it must unload its wares and passengers, and be readied again for voyage. "Can they not be bribed?"

"They have already been, beyond capacity," Father Jacques replied. "Have patience, Lady Celeste. Jerusalem will still be there when we arrive."

Celeste flushed. Patience! Anything could happen in a week. Thieves could steal their passage money, a storm could blow in, delaying or damaging the second ship. The peddler had headed south and Lord Bernard had come looking for her—unlikely as it may be, she lived in fear of either of them suddenly appearing. Or someone might discover she was pregnant. Father Jacques would not take her with him if he knew she was with child. She wanted to scream when she heard patient Lady Yvolde ask the hostel keeper about rooms. He told them many of the pilgrims would be sleeping on the boat to Jerusalem, to secure their place. There would be two rooms available shortly, one for the women and the other for the men.

Celeste sat on a bench by the open door gazing in the direction of the port and inwardly seething. Monsieur Robert left to find a barber to pull his sore tooth, taking Father Jacques for spiritual support. Marie asked if she might walk about the town with Agnes. Lady Yvolde's son, Geoffroy, had offered to accompany them.

"You do not like Agnes," Celeste said. "And Geoffroy made you cry."

"Agnes is much nicer today."

"You are too forgiving. She does not want to be alone with Geoffroy, that is why she is being pleasant now."

Marie giggled. "I would not either."

"Go, then, if you wish."

Left on her own, Celeste watched the fortunate pilgrims leaving the hostel. If only they had travelled faster, they would be among this group. She stood up. Who would notice one more person boarding the crowded ship?

She would be on her own among them, with no one to protect her.

But they were Christian pilgrims, after all. She hurried across the room to her bundle of things, lying where the servant had dropped it.

The port was farther than Celeste had thought. Her feet hurt and she was beginning to wonder if she was making a mistake when the road curved over a slight rise and the port lay in front of her. She stopped and stared down at it.

She had thought the streets crowded. The open port was a mass of people of various skin shades and all styles of clothing. A steady babble of French, Latin, German, Arabic and other foreign tongues she did not know rose from the harbour in an unintelligible cacophony. Beyond the milling crowd, ships of all sizes were moored along the wide river as far as she could see. Many had their sails furled, while others bobbed on the sparkling water, their white sails snapping in the sun.

She searched the docks eagerly. Which was the blessed ship that would take her away from France, away from her moonlit past, into the sunlight of Jerusalem? There! That one, with the crowd of pilgrims in front of it. So many—would there be room for all of them? She rushed down the street, pushing her way through the press of people toward the docks. She was glad she had once again hidden her purse underneath her kirtle. Crowds like this were thick with thieves and scoundrels.

It had not been difficult to find the ship to Jerusalem, but getting close to it was another matter. Lady or not, no one made way for her. The closer she got, the thicker the crowd became, until she was jammed among them so tightly she could not take a step without everyone around her moving also. Her ears were assaulted by voices calling, shouting, crying, laughing, singing and chattering in every language on Earth. She could see nothing beyond the bodies pressing against hers, holding her upright, moving her forward with them through no volition of her own.

The sun shone down on the quay, its heat searing, its brightness hurting her eyes despite the wide brim of her hat. No breeze could reach through the crowd to cool her. Her legs shook with exhaustion, her feet ached, her head pounded, she sweated in the tight embrace of bodies. The crowd began to spin. She blinked and shook her head, but the spinning continued, faster and faster. She was going to throw up. She swallowed, spinning, spinning in the heat, falling into darkness...

She came to groggily, still upright in the press of people. The man beside her was slapping her face gently, calling for those around them to give her air, as if there was any leeway for them to move aside. He blew vigorously into her face—she did not know whether the movement of air or his foul breath had revived her. She raised her head, pulling away. Her legs felt unsteady under her, but she had not thrown up.

"We are almost there," he said encouragingly. "The gangplank is only three or four paces ahead."

Celeste looked where he was pointing. The ship was indeed close, rising over the heads of the crowd. She smiled, raised her hand to wipe her damp brow...

Her pack! It was gone. She must have dropped it when she fainted. She searched the ground. "My things! I have lost my pack, a bundle tied in a black cloak. It is gone!"

Over her head the man called for those behind them to look for a black bundle, fallen to the ground. An anxious minute later someone yelled, "Here!" Her pack was hoisted aloft and passed, head over head, up to her. She clutched it with a cry of relief and a half-dozen heartfelt "Merci"s.

The crowd thinned as they inched forward. At last the gangplank was in sight. Two swarthy bare-chested men stood in front of it, wearing the wide-legged pants of Saracen. Celeste gasped. A Saracen ship! She was placing her life in the hands of infidels. And she was travelling alone, with no companions to look out for her. The man who had helped her earlier was already climbing the gangplank, having dropped his pouch of coins into the chest at the Saracens' feet.

"Your money," one of the Saracen sailors said, holding out his hand.

"It is... it is under my kirtle."

Those close enough to hear laughed. Celeste blushed.

"No money, no passage." The sailor frowned, looking over her head to those waiting with their money ready.

Scarlet with embarrassment, Celeste bent down and cautiously raised her kirtle, exposing her thin summer undershift. The men near enough to see whistled and laughed. The Saracen grinned broadly, enjoying her discomfort.

She fumbled to untie her money pouch without exposing her swollen stomach, her haste causing more laughter before she was able to drop her skirts and hand over the pouch.

The sailor, still grinning, opened it. His grin faded. "What is this?" he demanded, stirring the coins with his finger. "You sought to cheat us?"

"No!" Celeste drew back. "There are over twenty deniers there. Surely that is enough for a single passage?"

The sailor dropped her pouch into the chest. "You are short a sou. That is for our trouble. Be gone!"

"What do you mean? I am going to Jerusalem. Let me board!"

The Saracen growled something in his language and took a step toward her. Celeste backed up, frightened, stumbling against those behind her.

"Give me back my money! I will find another ship," she cried fighting to keep her voice steady.

Behind her, calls of "Give her her money!" were drowned out by others advising the sailors to "Get on with it! We want to board!"

The Saracen, his face ugly with anger, raised his staff. Celeste threw up her arms, shielding her face.

"Halt!" Two armed men pushed their way fiercely toward her, followed by a priest.

"On danger of your immortal soul, do not lay a hand on her, a Christian Lady on pilgrimage!" Father Jacques shouted over the grumbling of the crowd. He drew the sign of the cross in the air above Celeste.

Two more sailors appeared at the top of the gangway, but the crowd rallied, calling "Shame!" and "Infidel!" to the sailors. With a grimace of rage the Saracen reached into his chest and threw Celeste's money pouch toward her. Lady Yvolde's henchmen, swords raised in one hand, each grabbed one of Celeste's arms in the other and quick-marched her away.

Lady Yvolde was waiting at the door of the hostel when they rode up. Without a word she helped Celeste up the stairs to the room that had been prepared for them. Celeste could not stop shaking.

"There, there. You are safe now," Lady Yvolde said, steering Celeste into a chair. Marie ran in with a bowl of water, her mouth open.

"Leave it and go, child," Lady Yvolde said gently, cutting off Marie's questions. She picked up the cloth and washed Celeste's face and neck. Celeste closed her eyes. How could she have taken such a risk? Had she taken risks with Etienne? Was that why he died? She began to weep.

Lady Yvolde unpinned Celeste's hair and began to brush it, long, slow strokes. "Have you a clean kirtle in your pack?" she asked. Celeste nodded squeezing back the last of her tears. Lady Yvolde handed Celeste the basin and a towel, and went to get the kirtle.

"I have some yellow lace," Lady Yvolde offered, looking into her pack. "It would look pretty at the neck of your kirtle."

She opened her mouth to refuse, but Lady Yvolde had draped the lace around the neck of the clean black kirtle. It did look pretty.

"Thank you," she said, her voice quivering. She dipped her hands into the water and rinsed her face, drying it on the towel, then pulled her sleeves back to wash her arms as well.

"Your husband is indulgent, to let you travel without him," Lady Yvolde said, sewing the yellow lace at the neck of Celeste's kirtle.

Celeste looked up. "As is yours," she replied. She patted her skin dry with the cloth. Her clothes were stiff with sweat and dust and she did not feel any cleaner than before she had washed.

"My husband died two years ago. We were happy together. I am blessed in my grief."

Celeste looked away, clenching her hands inside the cloth she had dried them on. "Grief is not a blessing."

"The ability to grieve is a blessing. And having loved someone: that is a blessing. The way grief keeps his memory alive: that, too, is a blessing. Grief keeps our hearts tender."

"The heart's journey is toward happiness, not grief. So you said."

"Yes, I did." Lady Yvolde smiled. "Sorrow is a stop along the way. It gives us time to notice other people, to understand and help them if we can."

"We cannot help anyone." Celeste replaced the towel on the table. Her hands were still shaking. "We cannot help even ourselves."

"Do you not find it comforting to have someone understand what you are feeling?"

For a moment Celeste longed once again to unburden herself to this woman. She opened her mouth—

And closed it again. She was responsible for a child's life, whether she wanted the burden of it or not. She had been weak and tender-hearted once, and that child was dead. "No," she said.

Marie came into the room and dropped into a shaky curtsy. "Supper is ready, Ladies. Do you want Agnes and me to bring it up to you?" She looked at Celeste. Her eyes teared over.

"I will come down," Celeste said, calmly.

Lady Yvolde knotted and bit off her thread. She offered the kirtle with its yellow lace to Marie, to help her mistress change into it.

"Oh, how pretty the lace is," Marie exclaimed.

"Go tell the hostel keeper to set aside space for us at the table," Celeste commanded, taking the kirtle from Marie.

When Marie was gone, Celeste turned to Lady Yvolde. "You need not wait for me." She could not remove her kirtle and shift in front of Lady Yvolde. Her swollen womb was becoming apparent; only the generous folds of her kirtle protected her from detection.

"It is no inconvenience," Lady Yvolde replied. "It would be unseemly to rush ahead of you to supper." She rose and went to her bag to replace her needle and thread.

Celeste quickly pulled off her sweaty, travel-stained kirtle and shift, keeping her back to Lady Yvolde. She groped behind her for the clean shift she had laid on the bed, found it and slipped it over her head. She was not used to putting on her own kirtle and struggled with the folds of cloth until she found the sleeve openings. She pulled it quickly down over her shift and turned to find Lady Yvolde watching her.

"You will not be able to hide your condition much longer," she said.

# Chapter 24

e must do it," Gilles said.

Simon frowned. Gilles had begun speaking that way when Jeanne got sick and their mother was too distracted to worry about them. He had always insisted on his way, but before he had been stubborn. Now he sounded like he thought he was in charge. Simon was the oldest; it was not up to Gilles to make decisions for them.

"Papa will never allow it," he said.

Gilles looked at him as though he were a half-wit.

He flushed scarlet. Of course Gilles did not intend to ask Papa. "He will be furious when he finds out," he amended, feeling as foolish as he sounded.

"And after he yells at us, he will be relieved. You know Papa. He did not buy the ring because he wanted it—he bought it because someone else did not, and was willing to sell it cheap. Mama knows that. But she is too upset about Jeanne to listen to him, and he is too proud to tell her again." He spoke slowly, as though explaining something to a child.

"It would be stealing."

"They will keep fighting as long as Papa has the ring."

Simon winced. Gilles knew exactly what arguments to use on him.

"He is going to hit her again." Just saying it out loud made him feel sick, although all men hit their wives. It was a man's duty, and Simon knew that. Papa did it less often than most, only when Mama was truly obstinate.

Gilles hesitated. "No." He looked puzzled. "Something happened. Papa has changed." The stubborn expression returned. "But they will keep arguing. Do you think their shouting will help Jeanne get better?"

Simon was tempted to accuse Gilles of not caring about Jeanne, of using her illness to win an argument. But Gilles loved their little sister as much as he did. It was just that he also wanted to win the argument, and right now, mentioning Jeanne would do that.

"The metal smith will cheat us. We do not know how much the ring is worth."

"I do."

"How could you?"

"I know how much everything is worth."

Simon paused. Gilles never bragged. He cared too little about other people's opinions to bother. "How do you know?"

"I pay attention."

Gilles was using his patient voice again. It irritated Simon, but Gilles was right. Simon could never remember how much anything cost. Mama sent them to the market together when she could not go herself, but she gave Gilles the money. Simon was there because of his height; the merchants thought he was older than his nine years, and showed him some respect. They thought he was letting his little brother hold the coins to make Gilles feel important. Gilles played into that, closing his fist and pouting and refusing to give up the coins until they offered Simon a good price. Gilles never minded what they thought of him as long as he was satisfied with the final bargain.

"Market is one thing; jewellery is another."

"I pay attention to their faces."

"Where would we say we got it?" he asked, ignoring Gilles' tone.

Gilles smiled.

He ignored that, too.

"We sell it to someone who will not ask," Gilles said.

Getting the ring was harder than they thought. The wadmal bag lay in plain view in the corner of the hut. In plain view of everyone, including Mama and Papa, who never left Jeanne alone. They had to wait till the middle of the night, when Papa was snoring behind the curtain and Mama finally nodded off, sitting against the wall beside Jeanne's pallet.

Simon held his breath as he watched Gilles crawl across to the wadmal bag. He was glad his pallet was not the one closer to it, and ashamed of being glad. It was dark in the hut, with only the moonlight through a small window lightening the gloom, but he saw Gilles reach into the bag and feel around. Then, with a little snort, Mama shook herself awake. Simon gasped before he could stop himself. Gilles yanked his hand out of the bag. He stood up, stumbling a little, as though he were still half-asleep and going outside to pee.

Mama bent over Jeanne, wiping her face with the dampened cloth. Gilles returned, giving him a tiny nod and a smile before lying down again.

He closed his eyes and tried to sleep. He had thought he would feel relieved if Gilles got the ring without being caught, but now that they had it, he was more afraid than ever.

"I want to get this done quickly," Simon said as soon as they left home the next morning.

Gilles stopped walking and faced him squarely. "Papa will forgive us for taking the ring," he said. "But he will never forgive us for getting a bad price for it." He started walking again, faster.

"All right, all right." Simon ran to catch up. "But the fewer people who see us with it, the better."

"Why, brother, do you think Papa stole the ring?"

"No! Yes." He hung his head. "Mama thinks so."

"Mama does not. She wants Papa to think more about the family. She knows he is no thief." Gilles' lips twitched.

"Mama is right," Simon said, ignoring Gilles' secret smile. Papa did not steal it, he thought. He grinned at Gilles.

Gilles shook his head. "Papa thinks about the family," he said. "It is all he thinks about. Mostly he is thinking how not to think about us."

Before he could respond, Gilles turned toward a doorway. "Here we are. Put the ring on your finger." Gilles thrust it into his hand. "And keep your wits about you, Simon. Do not agree to anything until you see me nod."

The ring was heavier than he expected. He closed his hand around it. What if it fell off his finger? His hands were damp and slippery. Would the metal smith see his hands sweating and be suspicious? He rubbed his empty hand on his tunic and transferred the ring to it, rubbing the other one dry as he followed Gilles into the metal smith's.

The shop was one of two built into the undercroft of a building, with a wooden wall dividing them. There was a low, arched window at the front, beside the door, and a row of rush lights along the far stone wall which cast a thin yellow line of light unevenly across the room. A long wooden table near the window displayed samples of the metal smith's jewellery: a silver necklace, bracelets and rings, two brooches, and a half-dozen buttons and buckles. They looked lumpy and poorly-formed compared to Papa's ring.

At first he thought the shop was unattended. The fire was cold and a spider web stretched from the water wheel to the anvil. Simon was startled when a figure emerged from the shadows at the back and came toward them. The metal smith was a short, swarthy man with dark eyes and black, curly hair. His tunic and hose were so dark he looked like a shade himself, and he rattled slightly as he walked.

Simon bit his tongue to keep his teeth from chattering.

Gilles shut the door behind them and walked toward the man, but Simon stayed where he was, just inside the door.

The man stopped a few feet away and studied them, particularly Simon.

He stared back. Several silver chains hung about the smith's neck; the source of the rattling noise he had heard. The metal smith gestured Simon over.

Behind his back, Simon slipped the ring onto his finger. It slid on easily, but when he pulled it, his knuckle held it as though it were made to fit his finger. He splayed his hand across his stomach, hooking his thumb in his belt as he had seen Papa do. The ruby caught the light from the window and shone as bright as fire.

The metal smith glanced at it, then quickly up at Simon again, his haughty expression replaced by one of interest. He motioned Simon to a small table in the middle of the room.

"How can I help you, young sir?" he asked.

So this was why Gilles told him to wear the ring into the store instead of carrying it as he had wanted to.

"I wish to sell my ring." He took it off and set it on the table in front of the metal smith.

"May I?" the metal smith asked. At Simon's nod he lifted it and examined it closely, twisting it in the light to observe the cut of the stone and even biting the band delicately as though he knew the taste of gold.

"It is gold," Simon said stiffly, as Gilles had coached him on the way here. "The stone is a ruby."

The metal smith replaced the ring on the table between them. Even Simon could see that he wanted it. He sat down on a stool beside the table, motioning Simon to sit down also. Gilles pulled a stool over beside Simon's and made a show of climbing onto it. Simon was embarrassed for Gilles, who looked like a six-year-old even though he was eight, until he realized that Gilles was doing it intentionally. It was all a game to Gilles, he thought: a stupid, dangerous game.

Simon tried not to fidget while the metal smith took his time examining the ring. Why did he not suggest a price? What if he thought it was stolen and called the bailiff? How would they prove it was not? He looked over his shoulder at the door. What if someone came in and saw them? Gilles kicked him underneath the table.

"There are other metal smiths, if you do not like it," Simon said, as casually as he could, to make up for glancing at the door. Gilles had told him to say that, too. But he was supposed to wait until the metal smith named a price. Did he sound foolish, saying it ahead of time?

"I will have to break it down," the metal smith said. He looked at Simon sharply.

He knew it was stolen. But Gilles had said it was not. Simon opened his mouth to say it was not stolen. No, that would make him even more suspicious. "Suit yourself," he said with a shrug. He wanted badly to check the door again.

Gilles turned to Simon. "Why should it be broken? They make good rings in Lyon."

Simon had no idea what Gilles was talking about, but the metal smith asked, "It comes from Lyon?"

Simon nodded.

The jeweller smiled. "Two sous," he said.

Simon bit his tongue to keep from gasping. They were being offered a fortune!

Before he could answer, Gilles' hand shot out and grabbed the ring. "I do not want to sell it! You said I could have it when I was old enough to wear it," Gilles cried in his little-boy voice.

Simon looked at the metal smith and grimaced, the way Gilles had taught him to do at the market.

"Two sous, six deniers." The metal smith turned from Simon to Gilles, "For two sous you can buy anything you want, boy."

"I am six," Gilles said, dropping two years from his age. "Six is not very much. Ten is better."

"Are you going to let him lose you a sale?" the metal smith demanded of Simon.

Simon swallowed. He did not think he had the nerve to start again with another metal smith. But Gilles would not care. Gilles would have them bargain for a week before he was satisfied. Simon nearly groaned at the thought.

Gilles glared at him. "You promised me."

He hesitated. Gilles could do nothing about it if he agreed.

Under the table, Gilles kicked him again.

But Gilles was right about Papa. He would never forgive them for letting someone cheat them.

He sighed. "He is my brother."

"Two sous, eight deniers. Not a denier more."

"Gilles," Simon said, bending down as though talking to a child. "Think about it. I could buy a smaller ring that would fit you now." Please, let us get this over with.

The shop door opened. A Lady entered, followed by her maid carrying a horse's bridle.

"Can you repair the hoop on my horse's bridle?" the Lady asked the metal smith as she walked toward them. "It is worn near breaking." She motioned to her maid to carry the bridle around the table to the metal smith, paying no attention to him or Gilles.

"Next door," the metal smith said, waving toward the adjoining wall between the shops as though he were swishing away a fly. "This is a jewellery shop. Saddles and bridles next door." He dropped the ring onto the table, pushing it toward them. Simon's eyes widened. The smith was as nervous as he was.

The Lady glanced at the table in passing. Her eyes widened. Her face, already pale-complexioned, turned paler. At once she looked away, first toward the door she had come in through, then at her maid, then the metal smith.

Simon held his breath. It was not stolen. Papa and Gilles both said so.

Gilles reached for the ring.

Had he seen the Lady look at it? Get it away quickly, Simon thought. But Gilles did not appear to be in any hurry.

"My Lady's ring!" the maid cried.

Gilles' fingers wrapped around it. "I would rather keep this one," he said in his child's voice.

What was he talking about?

Gilles' foot nudged him under the table, very gently

"You promised." Gilles' voice sounded now as though he were about to cry.

Simon had always admired that skill, but this time he was numb with fear. "Papa bought it for me, to do with as I wish." He mumbled the words, taking his cue from Gilles but convinced that they were fooling no one. Gilles had *said* it was not stolen.

"You have My Lady's ring," the maid repeated.

"It is not," the Lady said. She backed away from the table.

"Show it," the maid insisted, grabbing Gilles' wrist. The bridle dangled from her other hand. "Open your hand." She shook Gilles' wrist.

"It is my brother's ring." Gilles' fist tightened around the ring.

Simon received another kick under the table. "Papa bought it for me in Lyon," he said dully. They would be arrested. They would have their left hands cut off. He blinked rapidly, trying not to cry.

"Lyon? That is near where it was lost," the maid said triumphantly. "How did you come by it?" she demanded of the metal smith.

"Me? It is not mine! I have nothing to do with it," he cried. "They brought it here, with their lies—"

"It is not my ring," the Lady interrupted. "Let the boy go, Marie. You are mistaken." She backed halfway to the door.

Simon stared at her. Everyone but Gilles was staring at her.

She turned her back to them. "Come, Marie." She reached the door and yanked it open.

"But—"

"Now!" She swept through the door without looking back. The maid glared at Gilles. She dropped his wrist and scrambled after her mistress.

"Get out!" the metal smith roared at them, as soon as the door shut behind the women. "And by God, learn your lesson from this."

Simon leaped up ready to dash for the door, but Gilles remained sitting on his stool.

"My Papa bought this ring," he said, staring at the metal smith. "He can prove it."

The metal smith snorted.

"Call the bailiff," Gilles said.

Was he mad? Had he completely lost his wits? Simon trembled on his toes, ready to run.

The metal smith looked from Gilles to Simon.

Gilles was mad! This whole escapade was doomed; he had argued against it from the start, and if he were not mad as well, he would be out the door and half-way home by now. Let Gilles get his hand cut off for his stubbornness.

Gilles was his little brother.

Simon took a deep breath and drew himself up as tall as he could. "Call the bailiff if you doubt us."

They walked across town without speaking. Simon shook with anger and relief and was afraid of what he might say if he opened his mouth. He had grown too big to fight with Gilles; it would be unfair. But if he said half of what he was thinking, Gilles would tackle him and he would fight back, fair or not. He clenched his hands into fists at his side.

The walk calmed him, especially as Gilles had to trot to keep up, and tried to conceal it. When they were almost home, he stopped walking. Gilles stopped beside him.

"It was her ring," he said. He looked straight at Gilles, daring him to refute it.

"Yes," Gilles said. "I wonder why she denied it?"

Simon shrugged. He had just wanted Gilles to know he knew.

No, he had wanted to be sure.

He started walking.

No. He had wanted Gilles to deny it.

Their parents' raised voices could be heard through the window before they opened the door.

"What have you done with it?"

"Nothing!"

"You have hidden it, so I could not insist that you take it back, along with the nail."

"I cannot take them back. I told you that. I have no way of finding her."

"You brought her sorrow on us. You must take it back to her!"

"That is foolish talk! You sound like—"

Gilles pushed the door open noisily. The voices stopped.

Simon hesitated outside, but Gilles reached back and grabbed his arm and dragged him in. "Tell them," he ordered.

Mama and Papa looked at him.

"We—" his voice cracked. He licked his lips and swallowed and looked at Gilles. It was Gilles, he wanted to say. It *was*. But he had gone along, and he was older. A year and a half was older.

Gilles raised his hand and dropped the ring onto the table. "We tried to sell it."

Mama stared at the ring.

"Tried?" Papa said. His voice caught, as though he was afraid.

Papa was never afraid.

From her bed, Jeanne whimpered, a weak, sickly sound, nothing like the way she could carry on when she was well. Mama rushed over to her.

"The metal smith would not take it," Gilles explained.

Papa looked at Gilles and back at the ring.

His eyes were wide, as the Lady's had been. His face was pale and grim.

Papa *was* afraid.

# Chapter 25

I t is your ring. I know it!"

"How could it be my ring? I lost it in Sainte-Blandine. There are many rings with rubies in them." Celeste walked quickly down the road to the pilgrim's hostel. Marie, with her shorter legs, had to run to keep up.

"If you had seen it, you would know."

Celeste turned sharply, raising her hand. "I saw it. It is not mine. If you say so again I will box your ears."

Marie skidded to a stop. She covered her ears with her hands, the horse's bridle straddling her head. "You are not yourself, My Lady," she protested.

"If you speak of this again, I will send you back to your father."

Marie turned white, but she held her tongue.

Celeste resumed walking.

How had her ring come here? How was it possible? She dared not acknowledge it was hers, even to Marie; people would talk, ask questions, and sooner or later the whole story would come out. Lord Bernard would be made a laughingstock—his wife giving away his marriage ring over a peasant's superstition. What titillating gossip that would give the gentry. *Blood will out,* they would say. *You can marry a peasant's granddaughter to a Lord, but she is still a peasant.* He would set her aside, ring or no ring.

Those boys must belong to the band of thieves that had robbed the peddler. Well, the metal smith had it now. She dared not claim it and she could not afford to buy it from him. Cluny, Lyon, Prevote Venissieuv, Saint-Gilles: at every step of her journey the ring mocked her, always just beyond her reach. She saw it again, sitting on the smith's table, close enough to touch, and yet she could not.

Just so, her mind mocked her with memories of her past—never clear and close enough to claim, never distant enough to forget.

Behind her, the bridle slapped against the stone road as Marie ran to keep up.

She forced herself to slow down, to appear unconcerned. When she was bound for Jerusalem, she would leave all this behind. If only the ship would come soon. She would be safe on this one, travelling with a group.

The ship arrived the next day at mid-morning. Geoffroy saw it come in and came running for Father Jacques, who rushed down to the quay to secure them a passage. By dinner hour, he had still not returned.

The afternoon dragged on. If even half the crowd she had seen at the quay wanted to go to Jerusalem, they would not fit onto one boat. Father Jacques was too patient, he would not push his way to the front. He had failed; the vessel was already full, as the previous one had been.

"If there is no room on this ship, we must go to Marseilles," she said to Lady Yvolde as they sat down to their supper. "There will be more ships there."

"Our pilgrimage is in God's hands," Lady Yvolde said. "We will wait to hear what Father Jacques tells us when he returns."

Celeste pushed aside her trencher of chicken and boiled onions, unable to eat.

Monsieur Robert, having finished his, reached across the table for it.

"I am still hungry," Geoffroy complained.

Monsieur Robert made a sour face. Nevertheless, he scraped a small piece of meat and most of the onions onto Geoffrey's empty trencher. "If you are still hungry, eat the trencher," he muttered.

Geoffroy flushed.

"Robert," Lady Yvolde said.

"It was but a jest," Monsieur Robert said, lifting a large piece of chicken to his mouth.

Celeste had risen to leave when Father Jacques walked in. He was not smiling. She watched him walk across the room to them, her mouth too dry to speak.

"I have booked our passage."

"On the ship?" She had been so certain he had failed, she could not grasp his words. Behind her, Monsieur Robert snorted and Geoffroy laughed, breaking off abruptly when his mother looked his way.

Father Jacques smiled. "Yes, on the ship to Jerusalem. I, too, find it difficult to believe." He laughed. "We are going to the Holy Land."

"But you were not smiling—" Their passage was secured. They were leaving France, at last.

"It is more expensive than I was told. We will have to pay two sous each."

"Two sous? They are robbing us!" Monsieur Robert exclaimed.

"They are infidels!" Agnes cried.

"For you, as well?" Lady Yvolde asked.

"Do not concern yourself about me," Father Jacques said. "There is a Cluniac cell here, they will pay my way."

"Well then," Lady Yvolde said. "It is more than we thought to pay, but not more than we are able to. Take your supper, Father."

"You may have my place," Celeste said, moving aside.

She walked to the stairs. Two sous each. Even if she left Marie behind, she would not have enough. She entered the room and closed the door behind her. Her hands trembled as she untied her purse and poured the coins inside it onto the bed.

Nineteen deniers. Where would she get the rest? And another two sous for Marie, as well as money for food and lodging when they reached Jerusalem? And how would she pay for their passage home? She put a hand to her forehead, trying to think. Perhaps the ship's captain would accept a note? She was a Lady, after all, and Lord Bernard would pay him when she returned. But she had neither her husband nor his seal to assure her debt.

She walked to the window. The sun was setting. Streaks of orange and gold curdled the sky. The first star had come out, as hopeful and as frail in the vast, fiery sky as a child's twig boat on an ocean. In the distance, the tall mast of a ship speared the sky.

She must get on that ship. She touched her abdomen, but when the child moved under her palm, she yanked it away. She would not hold this child.

A light knock came at the door. Celeste scooped the coins into her purse. "Enter," she called. Lady Yvolde opened the door.

"Are you feeling unwell?" Lady Yvolde asked, glancing at her belly.

"I have a headache."

"Another?"

"It will pass." What did the woman know of her headaches?

"Four sous is a lot of money." Lady Yvolde waited until Celeste turned to face her. "I am quite wealthy," she said. "I can pay your passage and your maid's." She hesitated, looked at Celeste's stomach. "Unless you have decided not to risk such a journey right now."

Celeste looked back steadily. "Every choice before me carries a risk," she said. "I do not need your money." *Or your sympathy or your understanding.* Lady Yvolde did not understand her. How could she, when Celeste did not understand herself? But she was leaving all that behind, her troubled past, her nightmares. Lady Yvolde would not buy it with her sympathy and carry it with them to Jerusalem.

"It is not shameful to accept the help of a friend."

Celeste turned away. The door opened and closed behind her.

Celeste picked up her money pouch. The peddler's coin was inside, indistinguishable from the rest. It had not bought her happiness, but when she used it to secure passage to the Holy Land, it would buy her peace. She left, taking the back stairs to the stable yard.

The stable was full of shadows when she entered, but the sound of rustling straw and horses neighing as the stable boy went from stall to stall feeding them reassured her.

"I would speak to your master," she said.

She was standing by the stall that held her gelding, surveying the horse over the half-door, when the innkeeper arrived. She heard him approach and saw, at the edge of her vision, how he paused also to examine the horse. He had guessed why she wanted to talk with him.

"I intend to sell my horse and pony," she said. "I will not need them when we sail for Jerusalem."

He looked into the stall, pursing his lips as though he did not particularly like what he saw.

"The horse is sound," she said. "And the pony as well. My husband will meet me with fresh mounts when I return, or buy these back. There is no need to leave them idle in their stalls." She shrugged as though she did not need the money, as though the sale was of no importance at all.

"And the saddles and harnesses?"

She let her breath out slowly, frowning slightly as if considering his request. "That depends on your price. Of course, if you do not want them, I can go elsewhere." *Please do not make me go from inn to inn like a common horse trader.*

"A sou for the two of them, and their tack."

"One sou?" she laughed. Was he bluffing, or was that all they were worth? She had never bought a horse, but Lord Bernard had paid much more for his warhorse. He had boasted to her of the price—four sous. So surely these two were worth more than one sou. "If you are not more interested than that, I will sell them elsewhere." She thought quickly.

"A ship has just come in, full of pilgrims returning home. They will need mounts."

"Two sous, with their tack."

"Three sous."

Now he laughed. "No one will give you that." He leaned against the stall door. "Two sous. That is a fair offer, Lady."

It was still too little. She must have enough for her passage back, as well. What if she were stranded in Jerusalem? Even in the Holy City, she could not eat air, she could not drink sunshine.

She felt him watching her.

"You have a maid, have you not? Is she going with you?"

"No," she said dully. She could not even consider taking Marie.

"I need a kitchen maid." He hesitated. "Is the girl pretty?" He said it so casually at first she did not understand.

"Two sous, eight, with the girl," he said, in a low, husky voice that made Celeste shiver.

She shook her head. "No."

"Two sous, ten."

She opened her mouth to refuse, and shut it again. She must get on that ship. And why should she not sell the girl? Marie was useless as a maid.

*Be gentle with Marie,* Pierre's voice whispered in her head. *She is devoted to you.*

She frowned. It was the old Celeste Marie loved. They all loved that weak and pious girl, but what help had they been? She had had to save herself, and she would do so now. Of course she would sell Marie. If she had thought of it earlier, she might have been able to keep her horse.

"Is she the pretty one?" he asked again.

No, she started to say, but then she saw his expression. He thought Agnes was her maid. "Yes," she said.

He leaned toward her, leering. "We are agreed, then?" he said. There was a cruel eagerness in his voice.

The shadows in the barn had lengthened, concealing her face from him. *No,* she wanted to say. What would he do to Marie, when he found he had been tricked? But then the tiny movement, the bubble of life, fluttered within her. She *must* get to Jerusalem. She could not afford to be weak and sentimental.

"We are agreed."

She returned by the back stairs, climbing them slowly. The room was empty. She threw her bag onto the table and went to the window.

The vibrant streaks of sunset that she had seen earlier were gone, replaced by the darker shades of dusk. She could still see the mast of the ship, its sails bound tightly against the evening wind. Was it the one that would take her away from here?

She turned at a noise behind her and saw Marie looking at her, her eyes full of questions.

Celeste looked away. "I have sold the horses."

"The horses? Blackie and Honey?"

Celeste straightened and met Marie's gaze coolly. "I did what I had to do."

"Lady Yvolde would have given you the money. I heard her!"

Celeste looked at Marie.

"I was not listening! I just... I just heard!"

"It is done." All this fuss about a pony. If Marie knew the whole of it... Well, she would tell her at the last moment, and leave quickly. She did not look forward to that moment. The thought of it made her voice sharp: "I am a Lady, not a beggar. It is for me to do what I will with what is mine."

"You are not even sorry. You loved Honey, once. Now you are not even sad to part with her." Marie turned and ran from the room.

The girl's bad matters would not be her concern soon enough. And she was not sad: Marie was right. Perhaps the peddler's coin had bought something, after all.

The breeze, cool from the river, blew in through the window. She turned, shivering. She should close the shutters, light a candle. Yet she stood looking out, straining to see the tall mast of the ship that would take her away. She could no longer make it out against the dark sky. Instead, when the clouds parted the moon appeared, low and swollen and blood red, a malformed thing, like a child born too early. She gave a low cry and pulled the shutters closed.

Celeste kept the gelding to a trot on the town streets. This morning, when Marie asked whether they might go for a last ride she had almost refused, but now she was glad she had changed her mind. The early morning air was crisp. She pulled her cape around her and lifted the hood over her head. The horse was warm against her legs, its gait even and brisk.

"Lady Celeste," Marie said, riding up beside her. "I saw the boy." She lowered her voice: "The one with your—the ring. I think he is following us."

Celeste looked around.

"He has turned down another street."

"Then he is not following us, if it was he. You are imagining things."

Marie opened her mouth to speak

"I told you it is not my ring," Celeste said sharply.

Marie closed her mouth.

Horses' hooves clattered against the cobblestones of an intersecting road. Celeste reined in her gelding and looked toward the noise as they came into view.

A large black war horse emerged a hundred yards ahead from a street on the right, followed by three other stallions, powerful beasts but smaller than the warhorse.

Beside her, Marie gasped.

She shaded her eyes and stared at the riders cantering toward her. The sun was behind them, blinding her, turning them into shadow figures, dark and menacing. She could not make out their faces, but she would know that horse anywhere. She sliced the reins sideways, wrenching her horse's head to the left, and dug her heels into its flanks. The gelding plunged down the side street. Her hood fell back from her head.

Peasants scattered right and left in front of her as she galloped down the narrow street. A resounding clamour of horse's hooves followed her. She bent low over her horse's neck. She had almost escaped. He must not stop her now. Where could she run? Where could she hide from him? At the end of the street she pulled her horse sharply sideways into another street.

Directly in their path was a handcart, piled high with fruit and vegetables. The vendor, hearing them almost upon him, dropped the hand pull and scrambled aside. Celeste pulled hard on the reins.

The ring on the left of the bridle snapped, flinging the rein loose. The right rein, still attached, yanked the horse's head sideways. It lunged blindly, slamming sideways into the cart, throwing Celeste forward and tearing the second rein from her grasp as she fell.

The gelding screamed and reared, hooves flailing the air directly above her. She tried to roll away. The movement sent unbearable pain searing down her back.

A thin shadow leaned over her. Someone grabbed the dangling rein and pulled the gelding's head hard to the left.

"Calme-toi, calme-toi," a boy's voice said.

The horse's hooves pounded down, barely missing her. It reared again, but it was no longer directly above her, and its hooves did not thrash the air so wildly.

"Ça va, mon grand, ça va," the voice said soothingly, pulling the horse's head further sideways, forcing it down well away from her. "Eh, bien," the boy said quietly. The horse snorted and shook its head, but did not rear again.

She closed her eyes and lay still. The pain in her back was excruciating.

"Lady Celeste?" Raimond's voice brought her back. "Are you hurt?" he demanded. "Are you hurt, Celeste?" He grasped her arms.

She stared at his hand, the tanned, strong hand she had dreamed of.

She felt something warm and sticky between her legs. A sharp cramp twisted across her abdomen. "Oh!" she cried.

"Where are you hurt?"

Blood, hot and wet between her thighs. She screamed.

Raimond scooped her into his arms and stood looking around—

She could not feel his arms, she could not feel anything, only the blood. She screamed, long, piercing shrieks, over and over, clutching her abdomen, holding him, holding him in—

"Where are you staying?"

"At the inn," Marie cried.

"Take me there."

She could barely hear them. She was so cold. She felt herself falling into darkness, fighting it. Someone was screaming.

Her shift was damp against her legs. Who was that screaming, her cries ragged and shrill?

She was so cold, so cold. All she could hear was the screaming, deep inside her now, screaming and dying, inside her—

# Chapter 26

**S**he is on to her knees beside the bed, staring down at her bloodied fingers. Raimond's strong hand reaches out of the darkness, grasping her hand. "You have not told, have you?" he whispers fiercely.

She pulls away, but he holds onto her. "No," she gasps.

"Good." The larger hand releases hers, leaving behind a gift that burns her hand.

It lies, long and thin and hard, scorching her palm. She closes her fingers, blocking it from sight, holding it so tightly her fingernails dig into the flesh of her palm. Blood oozes between her fingers and drips onto the floor. The sight fascinates and horrifies her. She wipes her fist across her nightgown, leaving a scarlet smear on the white fabric. She stumbles up and races from the room, down the stairs, his soft laughter behind her.

They are all awake, waiting for her. Their eyes stare at her out of the darkness, condemning her as she stands petrified at the bottom of the stairs. Murderer! Murderer! Their low, insidious chant echoes in the castle's great hall...

"I have killed him! Murdered him!" Celeste bolted up.

"You are dreaming, Lady. You have never hurt anyone."

Celeste opened her eyes. She could still see the nightmare figures staring at her from the corners of the room, their eyes accusing her where she sat in the bed. She cringed against the mattress, choking out a sob.

"What is it, My Lady?" Marie dabbed gently at Celeste's forehead with a damp cloth.

Celeste brushed it away and tried to get up. A fierce jolt of pain in her arm made her cry out. She fell back onto her pillow.

"Please, lie still, Lady. You have broken your arm."

Celeste closed her eyes, nauseous with the residue of pain. Under the sheet, she felt her abdomen. It was still rounded, but it felt smaller now, empty. Between her legs she felt her women's cloths. She groaned, and turned her head away.

The infant was gone, his tiny, butterfly movements stilled forever.

Her stomach heaved. She turned her head to the side of the bed, but there was nothing inside her; only a burning trickle of bile, which dribbled from her lips. Marie wiped it with the cloth.

"I will get Lady Yvolde. She will know what to do." Marie jumped up and ran to the door. She hesitated, looking back. "Do not move, Lady Celeste."

Her body felt heavy, weighted down. She could not even lift her head. The infant was dead. She had failed. She waited for the crush of sorrow; instead she felt only indifference. She was relieved, then frightened. Why did she not grieve?

Her babe was dead and she could not care at all. She had no memory of violence done her; only this coldness that had been growing inside her, held back by the stirring of life, by a single good intention which had failed. Even about that, she did not truly care. Why could she not care? She wanted to. Her child had died; she wanted to grieve for it. She did not want to be this cold, unfeeling woman. The silence she had so welcomed into her mind and heart at the abbey was suffocating her!

She had thought she was stronger now, but she was only indifferent, utterly detached from everyone around her, even her own infant. What had she become?

The door opened. Lady Yvolde entered. "How are you feeling, child?" She sat on the chair beside the bed and reached for Celeste's hand.

Celeste pulled her hand away. "I did not protect my child." Why should this woman care for her, when she could not care for her own child?

"You must not say such things." Lady Yvolde's voice was firm. She took Celeste's hand again. "It was an accident. You are not to blame."

"I did not care for him." Celeste turned away, wishing she had not said it aloud, wishing it were not true. She should be grieving; instead, she felt relieved. Nothing was required of her now, no one depended on her.

Lady Yvolde hesitated.

She is remembering that I rode my horse, Celeste thought. She is thinking that I went on pilgrimage knowing I was pregnant, that I did not withdraw with my maids and my embroidery to wait out the days carefully. She thinks I am grieved that I did not *take* care.

It was all true: she should have taken more care. She should not have gone riding this morning, she should have sold Marie and the horses sooner and bought her way onto the earlier ship, not dawdled as though she and the babe had all the time they needed. But that was not the worst of it, that she had not been careful.

"I did not love him," she said clearly. That was the worst. It could have been anyone's child, for all she cared.

Lady Yvolde held her hand. "You will," she said, looking down at Celeste pityingly. "However you came by him, when he is born, you will love him."

Celeste blinked. She had not thought of that. Was the infant conceived against her will, as Lady Yvolde assumed? Had Raimond forced her? That would explain her lack of feeling, her inappropriate sense of relief, the fear in her dreams. But it did not fit her memory of Raimond, however fragmented: his courtly manners, his smile, his concern for her.

She blinked again. When he *is* born? "The babe... he is... he is not...?"

"Oh, my dear!" Lady Yvolde pressed her hand. "You did not know? Your babe is safe. You have not lost him."

"He is alive?" She pressed her hand to her belly.

Lady Yvolde nodded. "I believe so. You have several cuts on your thighs. The blood, I believe, is from them."

She had not killed him. She closed her eyes, feeling weak.

But what did it matter? She could not protect him now. They would not let her board the ship knowing she was pregnant. She had still failed. This infant would die, as Etienne had, now or in Lord Bernard's castle. And she would not care. She shuddered, revolted.

"Your husband is on his way. He will be here tomorrow, or the day after," Lady Yvolde said, breaking the silence.

*He will set you aside.* Raimond's warning echoed in her head.

It was over. She could do no more. She had not saved the babe, or herself. She turned her head to the wall.

"Your husband's cousin wishes to see you."

"No."

"Lady Celeste..."

She did not turn back. There was nothing anyone had to say that interested her.

"No one here knows about the infant."

She looked at Lady Yvolde.

"It is your secret. You must decide whether to tell it or not. Your maid and I have taken charge—" she took a breath, "—of everything. No one knows but we three."

Celeste stared up at her, unable to think what to say.

"Your husband's cousin sent for the barber to bind up your arm. He says it is a clean break and will heal straight, but your husband may want a physic to see you when he arrives."

*Lord Bernard will set you aside if you tell him,* Raimond had said, as he pressed the nail into her hand.

"I will go to the abbey," she said dully, looking away again. It did not matter whether she told or not. Secrets had a way of coming out. Lord Bernard would set her aside. She should never have married him. She should have known her station.

She closed her eyes. Even now she did not care. She could not grieve for herself any more than she grieved for her babes. It was wrong. It was sinful. It was a relief.

"Wake up, Lady Celeste, wake up!"

Celeste opened her eyes to see Marie's anxious face above her.

"I cannot delay him any longer. He insists on seeing you."

"Help me up." She gasped with pain as Marie raised her to a sitting position.

The door burst open. Raimond stood in the doorframe. She stared at him.

Then he smiled, the full, beautiful smile she remembered. Her fear had been groundless; he had ever been her friend. Had he not extracted the nail for her, given it to her to make her well? He must have found her request foolish—she was embarrassed to remember it—but he had indulged her, as a good friend would. And warned her that her husband was not so indulgent.

"Are you well, Celeste?" His voice and expression conveyed such concern she could not help smiling back.

"Leave us," she said to Marie.

"I am recovering from your bad judgement." She spoke jestingly. He had acted badly, racing after her, even if she had provoked his pursuit by running away.

To her surprise, his face drained of color. "My judgement is better than yours, as you well know," he said.

She flushed. She had been foolish to want the nail, but how dare he throw that in her face now? "It was you who did it, not I," she said. Her dreams had shown her that much.

He took a step toward the bed, his face twisted so that she hardly recognized him. "Whatever you think you know, you had best forget it." His voice was low, menacing.

She stared at him, shocked. Why was he so angry? He was her friend, her ally. What had got into him? She straightened in her bed to cover the pounding of her heart. "Call Marie back. It is not seemly that we are alone together."

"It is too late for that. Have you told anyone?" He leaned over her, his face dark and tense.

"Marie knows. She saw it."

"What did Marie see?"

"The nail." She blushed, saying it aloud.

"The nail?" He looked surprised, then turned his face from her. When he looked back, he appeared amused. "So Marie knows about the nail." He chuckled. "Well, she will not tell our secret."

He smiled down at her, that warm, open smile she remembered. Above his dazzling smile, his eyes were cool, calculating. Why had she never noticed that before? She blinked and it was gone.

The door opened a crack. "Lord Bernard has come," Marie cried breathlessly through it. They heard boots pounding up the stairs.

"Do not talk to him about all that," Raimond whispered. "Else he will believe you are still mad." Again, that flicker of expression in his eyes, gone before she could identify it.

"My Lord," she heard him greet her husband in the hall. She took several deep breaths.

Lord Bernard entered and stood looking at her, his face so tight with emotion she could not read it. She stared back defiantly. He had come to set her aside. He would be surprised to find she no longer cared.

"Let me see your arm," he said, breaking the silence.

"Why?"

"I know something about broken limbs."

"I am not one of your horses."

"Then I will not need to have you held down while I examine you." He came to the bed and touched her shoulder, squeezing it gently. His fingers were warm and strong. She sat still as his hand moved down her arm, wincing only when he reached her bound forearm. He let go at once.

"It will heal," he said gruffly.

"Then you have wasted a trip."

"Apparently not. I have arrived in time to prevent you taking a voyage likely to end in worse than a broken forearm." When she remained stubbornly silent, he burst out, "Are you mad, racing off like that with only a girl to guard you?"

"I am not mad."

"Then you will be content to give up this foolhardy pilgrimage. We will go home as soon as you are well enough to ride."

His puckered eyebrows made him look bewildered rather than angry. How could she have forgotten that expression, and the way his mouth moved when he spoke, full and sensuous, even when he was angry? She looked aside. "I cannot go back with you," she said.

"Because of the pilgrimage?" He hesitated. "Or because of Etienne?"

"It does not matter. I do not care about either now."

He paused again. I have surprised him, she thought. The girl who once cared about everything.

"It is better not to care too much," he said.

He did not know about the second pregnancy, but even so, how could he accept what she had said? "Do you think I want to be the kind of woman who does not care about my child?" she demanded.

"I think it is time you acted like a woman, not a child."

He scowled at her, but his anger strangely calmed her. "I am not a child," she said, turning her face from him. Whatever else she might be, she had not been a child since Etienne died.

*You have no future,* the gypsy's voice taunted her. She had tried to be stronger, more resourceful, but she had failed. She was done with trying. She held up her bare ring finger for him to see.

"I will not go back with you."

# Chapter 27

How pale she was, lying in her bed. He had come as soon as the tournament was over, having received Raimond's message of her accident.

How dared she go racing off across the country as though she were invincible, with her small, bound arm a testament that she was not? She sat up in her bed glaring at him, and he was weak with relief to see those huge dark eyes no longer blinded by madness and grief. He stood watching her, the intense stubbornness on her lovely face as she struggled to sit up, biting her tender lip to stifle the pain. He could not set her aside now that she was well, not even if the whole of Louis' court scorned him for it.

He had been allowed to touch her only in order to check her arm. His hand still burned from the feel of her shoulder, soft and warm beneath her nightdress. He could barely breathe while he examined her arm.

And then she said, "I will not go back with you."

"You are coming home with me if I have to carry you bound across my saddle," he roared.

"How was Paris?" she shouted.

He stood with his mouth open, staring at her. She had deliberately misdirected him to Paris, then to Santiago. He had suspected, but not wanted to believe it. If Raimond had not made enquiries at the pilgrim's hostel in Lyon— And here she was, flagrantly taunting him with her deceit! How was Paris, indeed!

Despite himself, he laughed.

His response startled her. She smiled ruefully.

"Let us start again," he said, feeling generous because, whether she wished it or not, she would be coming home with him. He pulled the stool over to the bed and sat beside her. He could feel the heat between them, as urgent and sweet as it had ever been. He was sure it was not just him, wanting her. He could see it in her eyes, in the tension in her body, in the warmth radiating from her skin. Why was she fighting it, trying to antagonize him? She had changed. Not in her attraction to him, or his to her, but in some deeper way, something essential.

"I sold my sorrow," she said. There was a challenge in her eyes that he had not seen before. "With your ring." She held up her bare finger once again.

"I have noted that the ring is gone. And you believe that has made you well?" Surely she could not think so, unless she was still deluded, unable to reason clearly. Someone had taken advantage of her fragile state. He would find the scoundrel and make him pay for it.

"You are not angry?"

Oh he was angry, but not at her. And it would do no good to let her see it. "You are worth more to me than a ring. A ring cannot order my household, or warm my nights and give me sons. It is more important that you are well again."

She turned her face away, frowning. There was something else, something she was not telling him. He waited for her to speak.

"I sold my sorrow, and with it, my past."

What was she talking about, 'sold her past'? Were her wits still addled? No, he would not think it, nor upset her by suggesting it. "Then you must reclaim it."

"I cannot."

"There is always a way," he said, trying to sound reasonable despite the absurdity of the conversation. Would he have to set her aside after all? "Do you know where the ring is?"

"No," she said, too quickly.

How young she was, barely seventeen. She did not trust him; he saw it in her quick glance and inexperienced lie. What was she hiding from him? He looked down at her profile, the set line of her jaw. She had changed. There was a new strength in her, a resolve; she was a woman now. But not the woman he had hoped she would become. Her attitude of detached indifference puzzled and irritated him. He waited until she looked up again.

"Is it my ring or your wedding vow that you do not want to reclaim?"

# Chapter 28

She stood outside the pilgrim's hostel, watching the door from a corner of the street where she would not be seen. The infant, wrapped in a thin blanket, whimpered in her arms.

"Shh, shh," she whispered, holding the hot little body close to her and rocking it soothingly. "Are you certain it is her?" she asked the boy standing beside her. He nodded.

"And this is where they brought her?"

"Yes."

"She is a Lady? On pilgrimage?" she frowned, rocking the restless babe.

"The stable boy said so, Mama. I only know what he told me."

The baby cried, a weak little mew of misery.

"What if she does not come out? Let me go inside and bring her to you, Mama."

"No! She has already seen you twice. I will not risk my son to save my daughter."

"Papa did not steal the ring."

His face was set and stubborn, but looking into his eyes, she saw that he was afraid she would tell him he was wrong about his Papa.

He *was* wrong. Jean should never have taken advantage of a mother's grief. But Jean knew that now. Every time he looked at Jeanne, she could see he knew, though he would not admit it.

"He said he did not," the boy repeated. He was so young it hurt her.

"Then he did not," she said. "But it is still hers, and all that comes with it, and she must reclaim it so Jeanne will live."

"Let me wait here with you."

She shook her head, about to say no. He was not looking at her, but at his sister, his expression a mixture of dread and resignation that was not young at all.

"When I speak with her, you must keep out of sight," she said, instead.

They waited a long time before the Lady appeared. Her left arm was tied in a sling. She was very pale and walked carefully, hiding some pain. The woman's heart went out to her, until she saw her face, as cool and unconcerned as stone. Jeanne whimpered again. She looked down into the pinched little face.

They passed their sorrow onto others, the nobility. They shed suffering as a snake sheds its skin. Whatever Jean had done, this woman had done worse. He had taken the ring to help his family, not believing he would harm them; she had given the ring to help herself, not caring who she harmed.

A man had come out of the Inn to join the Lady. He was tall and dark-haired, and he moved with the easy confidence of nobility.

Mathilde clutched Simon's arm and ducked behind the corner of the building, her heart pounding. Should she still approach the Lady? She had hoped to meet her alone. Jeanne stirred within the blanket, a tiny, fretful movement, and then lay still.

She bent over the blanket, listening. Jeanne breathed raggedly through blistered, parted lips, but she was still breathing.

Mathilde motioned Simon to stay back. She straightened and stepped out from the corner.

# Chapter 29

"I do not wish to take a walk." She wanted to be left alone, the one thing Lord Bernard refused to do.

"The physic, whom you refused to allow to examine you, said going outside would improve your humors. If you do not need a physic, there is no reason you should not walk." He held the hostel door open.

He was impatient to get her moving so they could leave. He must be eager to return to Louis' court. She had said she would go to the abbey, but he had curtly refused.

She had been wrong about the tie between them; that was apparent in his calm aloofness ever since she would not answer his questions. Why should she? He had made it clear her opinion did not matter: he had already told Father Jacques she would not be continuing the pilgrimage.

The growing infant wearied her so, and the weight of the things she did not know, and the things she knew and could not talk about. She was entombed in silence, the same silence that had entered her at the abbey, but now it was a burden, not a relief. *Do you think I want to be the kind of woman who does not care about my child?* she had asked him. Yes, she thought. That is exactly what I wanted. What I still want, may God forgive me.

A peasant woman stepped out into the street, directly in their path. She held something in her arms, wrapped in a blanket.

Celeste shivered and pulled her cloak around her. She did not like the look of the woman. A peasant should step aside for nobility.

The woman came closer. "Look." She held a bundled child directly in front of Celeste. "My little one, my Jeanne. Look at her."

Celeste stopped, shocked. The woman thrust the babe closer.

Beads of sweat stood out on the pale little face framed by the blanket. Tiny eyelashes fluttered against her fevered cheeks; her little rosebud mouth opened, panting for air. Celeste shrank back.

"Move aside!" Lord Bernard said. He encircled Celeste with his arm, drawing her away from the fevered child.

The woman stood her ground. "I have something of yours, My Lady," she said. Shifting the child to one arm, she held out her closed fist to Celeste.

"No!" Celeste's voice quivered. She forced herself to be calm, to sound scornful. "Take your begging somewhere else."

"Perhaps you know what I have? Perhaps you would rather speak to me alone?"

"She will not," Lord Bernard said.

A boy ran out from the corner of a building. "Please! Listen to her," he cried.

"Go back, Simon," the woman said.

Celeste opened her mouth but could not make a sound. *No*, she thought, staring at the boy, *oh no*.

"What do you want here, boy?" Lord Bernard demanded.

Simon ran to his mother's side.

"No," Celeste whispered, looking from him to the woman.

"What have you to do with my wife? Tell me, boy!"

"I... I held the horse when it reared..."

The woman stepped in front of her son and opened her hand.

A large ruby winked up at them, a spark of fire against the peasant's rough palm.

"No!" Celeste cried, stumbling backward. She felt Lord Bernard glance at her, but she could not look away from the ring.

"That is a rich bauble," Lord Bernard said. "How did you come by it?"

How casual he sounded, as though he did not know his own ring.

The boy stepped up beside his mother. He looked at Celeste.

She opened her mouth to deny the ring, but the boy's expression stilled her voice. They were all watching her, the woman and the boy and Lord Bernard. What did they want of her, the woman's expression so accusing, the boy's so earnest and trusting? She had done nothing wrong, not to them.

"Take it back," the woman said, her face calm and unafraid. "We do not want it."

They had planned this, the woman and her son, had set a trap for her so she would have to take the ring back. They were not innocent. Perhaps the peddler had even put them up to it, told them to demand money. She saw again his greedy face leering over her. What trick was he playing now? She flushed, and drew herself up proudly. She was no longer vulnerable, as she had been then. She could condemn them all, could claim they stole the ring. Lord Bernard would believe her, and have them punished. Her lips parted, but she could not give words to the lie.

The babe cried, a pitiful, fevered sound. Her small hand rose and fell back weakly into the folds of the blanket. The mother parted the blanket and kissed the child's pale forehead. Wisps of fair hair framed her thin little face and lay in damp curls against her cheek.

"She is innocent," the woman said. Her voice trembled. "She is my child, my baby, and she is innocent."

"What has that to do with me?" Celeste cried. "I have not failed that child." She flushed, realizing what she had said.

"You know what you have done," the woman said. She held out the ring. "Take it back."

"I cannot!" She would be consumed by grief again. And when this second babe died—

"Enough!" Lord Bernard took the ring from the woman's outstretched hand and turned to Celeste. Her hand lay helpless in the cloth sling. He slipped the ring onto her finger. "Reclaim your past," he said quietly.

She stared down at the ruby, winking slyly on her finger. Nothing: she felt nothing. No tide of memories washing over her, no madness of grief, no despair. She let her breath out slowly. The ring was a pretty jewel, nothing more. She flushed, furious with herself. How foolish she had been, letting her head be filled with nonsense.

The woman reached into the pocket of her sleeve and withdrew a shiny black nail.

Impossible! Celeste shrank back. It could not be the same nail. How had they journeyed here together? A ring would be guarded. A ring might change hands any number of times and not be lost. But a nail, a common nail, along with it? Yet it was her nail—she could see it lying in her bloody hand as she had dreamed it, remembered the feel of it, cold and cruel, when she held it out to the peddler, and the relief when he accepted it. The hairs on her neck prickled. It was an evil thing, she would not take it back!

The woman moved closer, holding the child so Celeste could not help but look at her. "You will never know peace if she dies." Her voice was low and fierce. "How could you ever be happy, carrying such guilt?"

"You go too far," Lord Bernard warned, stepping between the woman and Celeste.

*I have done nothing to her.* She opened her mouth, but the words caught in her throat. This woman was the peddler's wife! She had sold him her sorrow, and now his child suffered as Etienne had.

No, Father Jacques said it was not possible, the Abbess, also—

The Abbess said it was a sin. Was that why God had not heard her prayer? Because of her sin?

"Take your sorrow back," the woman said. She held her head up, looking directly at Celeste, not peasant to nobility but woman to woman, mother to mother. She believed Celeste could save her child.

The infant whimpered. Celeste looked down at the pale little face in the blanket.

What if her babe was a girl, the one she could not care about, the one she had tried to abandon in Jerusalem?

*It could be anyone's child,* she had told herself. She looked at the child struggling to breathe, her cheeks flushed with fever: Anyone's child.

The child turned her head, and lay still. *As still as Etienne, feverish and weak in her arms.*

Could she save this one?

The little girl opened her eyes. They were startlingly blue, as blue as the sky, as blue as the sea to Jerusalem…

She fumbled to untie the money pouch on her belt, one-handed and awkward in her haste. "Take it," she said, thrusting the pouch toward the woman. "I do not know which coin is his. Take them all."

The woman accepted the pouch. She pressed the nail into Celeste's left hand, lying in the cloth sling. It touched her palm, cold and hard, its black point falling across the gold band on her finger…

*Something has wakened her, although it is not yet dawn. Etienne is lying beneath her arm. Why is he so still? She touches his face, shivers at the coolness of his skin. A terrible foreboding fills her. She holds her hand to his nose and mouth, feeling no movement of air. But his fever had broken! She shakes him gently, then with increasing urgency, crying "Etienne! Etienne!" He does not wake, not even when she begins to scream.*

*"Quiet!" Raimond's voice breaks through her terror. "Lord Bernard will set you aside if you tell him. You have killed his son."*

"No!" she screamed, remembering, remembering everything. "I cannot undo what I have done!"

The nail dropped from her hand.

"Help me, boy," Lord Bernard cried, catching her as she fell.

# Chapter 30

Celeste opened her eyes. She was in the guest room of the hostel.

Lady Yvolde, on a chair beside her bed, looked up at her movement. "Is there any way you can avoid excitement?"

Celeste touched her belly.

"He has survived. But it would be best if you could stop falling."

Celeste struggled into a sitting position. Her arm, in its sling, lay across her waist, the ruby gleaming on her finger. She winced and looked away.

"Would you like a drink?" Lady Yvolde gestured toward a jug of small ale on the table.

Celeste stared at it. A nail, bent at the end, lay beside the jug. "That nail was from my bed," she said. *Raimond's hands on hers.* He had found her digging into the wood with her little knife, her fingernails broken and bleeding, and had used his larger knife to dig out a nail from the bed where Etienne had died. She remembered everything clearly now, neither consumed by grief nor oblivious to it.

"I was not honest with you," she said. "I am in mourning, as you thought. My son died."

"You need not talk of it if you do not wish to."

"I must tell someone." She looked down at the ruby. "He was very ill. My husband sent for the priest to secure his soul to heaven." She paused, feeling again her grief as she cradled his limp body and listened to the priest.

"Afterward, I could not bear to lay him in his cradle, which I had ordered brought into my bedchamber. I took him to my bed, and lay him beside me, so weak, so hot, struggling for every breath. I watched him all the night. I drew a breath with every breath he took, and blew my own breath into his mouth when he faltered." She paused. "And in the morning, his fever broke. He drank a little milk, and smiled at me." She smiled, remembering her joy.

"That evening, I went to my husband's bed, and we were happy together." She stopped. She had been with her husband. It was possible the infant she carried was Lord Bernard's! She touched her belly, smiling sadly. If so, she had been trying to protect him from the wrong parent.

"In the night I woke, thinking of Etienne, and was afraid for him, and went back to my room. He was asleep in his cradle. I carried him to my bed." She frowned. She did not remember doing that. Why, when all else had returned, did she not remember taking him into her bed again? But she must have done so. What else did she not remember about that night? Could it be worse than what she did remember? Her throat tightened, unable to say the rest.

"Do not berate yourself for falling asleep," Lady Yvolde murmured, taking her hand. "Even the saints succumbed to exhaustion."

She began to weep. The tears burned her cheeks and fell onto the sheet and onto Lady Yvolde's hand, covering hers. She had not wept when Etienne died. What right do the faithless have to weep? She turned her head so she would not see Lady Yvolde's face, and forced herself to continue. "It is not that I fell asleep," she said, "but in my sleep, I rolled over."

He might have lived. God had spared him, for his innocence, for the sake of her prayers. His fever had broken. It was not God who failed him; it was his mother.

She wept bitterly, uselessly. Tears would not bring him back. She could weep down Noah's flood, and still he would be dead and gone from her forever.

It was guilt, not sorrow, that had pursued her, that she had tried so desperately to escape. But guilt cannot be cast off. It had seeped into her bones and blood with every breath she took until it permeated her very being. She would never be free of it, no matter how far she ran or how much she forgot or how little she cared about anything.

"He is with God now," Lady Yvolde said gently.

"He missed so much."

"You missed so much. And I am truly sorry for all the joy you could have taken in him. But what did he miss? He was born, he lived and he died. That is all any man has. He was loved and cared for and mourned. That is more than many men receive. He was baptized and sealed to heaven. That is as much as any man can hope for."

Celeste leaned back against the pillows, closing her eyes. And what of the other? He had not yet lived at all. He was neither loved nor wanted, not even by his mother. She would love him now, if she could.

Lady Yvolde released her hand and brought a damp cloth from the washbasin. "You have suffered enough," she said, wiping Celeste's face gently. "It is time to forgive yourself. Lord Bernard does not blame you; he is distracted with concern for you."

"I have never told my husband. Raimond found me in the morning." *Lying on top of Etienne.* She could not say it. "He put Etienne back into his cradle, and told everyone that he had died there."

Why had he come into her bedchamber? Twice he had done so. "Another secret," she murmured.

"Perhaps you should tell this one," Lady Yvolde said.

"Shall I help you dress, My Lady?" Marie asked, poking her head through the doorway soon after Lady Yvolde had left.

Marie! Oh, dear heaven, Marie! She had sold this child, with little more hesitation than she had sold Blackie and Honey. And she had done so knowing Marie would be treated less gently than the horses. She looked away, ashamed.

"May I help you?" Marie asked again, hurrying in.

"You have been a good and loyal maid to me while I was ill," Celeste said, nearly choking on the words. "I will… I will buy your pony back." She prayed the girl would never learn her mistress had sold her, too.

Marie dropped into a deep curtsey. "Oh! I love you, Lady Celeste!"

"I have not deserved your affection."

"You have," Marie insisted. "You have, My Lady."

Celeste smiled down at her. She patted Marie's round cheek. "Well, I will do so from now on," she promised. "And now you may help me dress."

"Oh, I had forgot," Marie said, when Celeste was dressed. "Raimond sent me to tell you he wishes to talk with you."

"I am going to the stable to make sure Honey and Blackie have not been sold. Tell him he will find me there."

"This is a strange meeting place, Lady Celeste," Raimond said, approaching her in front of her horse's stall.

She flushed. "I wanted to talk to you alone. About the night Etienne died."

His charming smile disappeared. "You know as well as I."

"Raimond—" She turned toward the stall, too embarrassed to look at him. "I do not know. I cannot remember taking him to my bed."

He watched her a moment, then smiled chidingly. "It is not necessary to deny it to me. I will not tell your secret."

"Is that our secret?"

"What else?" There it was again, that tension she had felt in him the other day. As though he were threatening her, beneath his mild tone.

"Marie told me you were there that night. She says you made her leave, that we were alone together."

He arched one eyebrow. "What are you thinking, Lady Celeste?"

She blushed a second time. Had she never noticed the mockery behind his jests? She drew herself up straight. "What happened that night?"

"Ahh. You believe we had a tryst." An expression of cool amusement crossed his face. "My Lady, you are the wife of my Lord Cousin. I would not dare presume you bear me more than the kindest friendship. Perhaps you have been confused by dreams during your illness." He bowed ironically. "If so, I am honored."

His smile was mocking, but in his eyes she saw... anger? She had seen that anger before. Yes, soon after she arrived at her Lord's castle. Raimond had approached her alone, he had—touched her. She had moved away at once, shocked; and he had looked then as he did now.

But he had never given a sign of it again. They had forgotten it, had become friends...

"Why were you in my room when I woke up?" she demanded. This smirking, arrogant man had never been her friend. A terrible thought occurred to her. "How did Etienne die, Raimond?" she asked, even while she thought, *No, it cannot be.*

"You took him to your bed and in your sleep, rolled onto him," he said in a low, tight voice. "You smothered him."

All this time she had believed it. But he did not; she saw that in his eyes watching her, judging whether she had taken the bait this time.

"That is a lie." Her mind reeled. She had not killed Etienne.

"Who are you, to accuse me?" In two quick strides he was beside her, his arm raised to strike her.

"Do not dare," she gasped.

He laughed. "Oh, I dare. You would be surprised how much I dare."

She opened her mouth to scream, but he clasped his hand over her mouth and nose. She kicked him, struggling to breathe.

"And now," he whispered into her ear, "I will have to kill you, also."

She bit his hand, sinking her teeth into the flesh until she tasted blood. With a cry he released her. She screamed.

He struck the side of her head, sending her reeling into the wood slats of a stall. She gripped the wood to keep from falling. She would die. She would die here.

She pushed herself from the stall and ran toward the stable door. He grabbed her skirt and pulled her back, throwing her to the ground. She struggled against him, desperate, grabbed a fistful of straw and threw it into his face. He swore, loosening his hold to brush at his eyes. She twisted sideways, reaching for her knife, but he grabbed her again, pinning her down with his body.

"You thought yourself too good for me! An untitled girl, too good for me?" His hands circled her throat, squeezing.

Her lungs were on fire, desperate for air. Pinpoints of light exploded before her eyes. She fumbled at her side, found her knife in its small sheath, plunged it into his arm—

Air! She gasped, sucking it deep into her, coughing and gulping it in frantically.

He cursed and slapped her, knocking her head sideways.

Suddenly his weight was gone. She rolled onto her side, gasping and coughing, her ears ringing from his slap.

"Do not die! Do not die Lady Celeste!" Marie cried beside her, patting her back.

"Take him away before I kill him with my bare hands!" Lord Bernard roared.

Celeste struggled up, still coughing. Two men held Raimond. His face was red with fury.

"He killed Etienne," she gasped. "He smothered our son."

"She is not in her right mind," Raimond said coldly. "Her wits are addled. She took him to her bed and rolled onto him. She killed him, not me."

Lord Bernard bent over her. "Has he hurt you, Celeste?"

"Ask Marie." Her voice came out a ragged croak. He must believe her, she must make him. "Ask Marie about that night."

"He sent me away," Marie sobbed. "Lady Celeste was asleep, and so was Etienne. He was asleep in his crib."

"They are both lying," Raimond cried.

"Quiet!" Lord Bernard said. "Your own actions betray you." He nodded to his men: "Take him to the bailiff."

Lord Bernard helped her into the inn and over to a bench near the hearth. He ordered wine and bade her drink it as soon as the kitchen servant brought it.

"What will happen to him?" Her hands shook as she lifted the wine to her mouth.

"He is nobility. King Louis will decide his fate."

"I thought he was my friend." She shuddered, feeling sick.

"You will never see him again. He will be stripped of his titles and rights, and banished from France. Louis has an ambitious cousin; he will make an example of Raimond." Lord Bernard slumped against the wall. "I should have watched him more closely. Eleanor tried to warn me."

"But she dislikes everyone close to you." Celeste finished his thought. "You could not have known. He deceived us all."

"I knew you blamed yourself. I tried to tell you not to."

"I shall listen to you more."

"You will listen to me less. You have a mind of your own, now."

"Yes. Does it trouble you?"

He sighed. "I expect it will give me great deal of trouble."

She remembered that crinkle around his eyes and the little rise at the edges of his mouth when he was amused. She had loved that face, loved it still. She rose and went to him, slipping her arm around his waist. "Would it be best if I warned you, when there is going to be trouble?"

He laughed, and pulled her close. "Yes, that would be best."

Marie was unpinning Celeste's hair after supper when Father Jacques came in. "We have come to say farewell," he said. "The ship for Jerusalem leaves in the morning. We will board tonight."

Lady Yvolde and her family came in with him. "I will visit you in Le Puy after we return," she said, embracing Celeste.

Her son bowed to Celeste and Lord Bernard gravely, and stole a kiss from Marie before running out. Marie blushed furiously, trying to frown. They heard the pompous cousin scolding the boy all the way down the stairs.

"We will also leave tomorrow," Lord Bernard said when they were alone. "Will you be pleased to go home, Celeste?"

"I do not know," she said gently, because she could see it worried him. She was no longer afraid of the castle. There would be no more demons watching her from the shadows, she knew that now. But there were other memories waiting for her return.

"I shall miss Etienne when I am there."

"Then he will draw your soul to heaven after him, and mine with yours." He ran his finger lightly over her cheek, making her shiver. "But not before we have other sons and watch them grow to manhood, and daughters as beautiful as you, to take our place here."

She would tell him there was one on the way already, when they were back in his castle. He would only make a fuss about her riding if she told him now. She smiled at him sweetly.

He bent and kissed her. His lips sent a shock through her, stopping her breath. She kissed him back eagerly, felt him hesitate and then respond, his lips pressing hard against hers, his tongue teasing her mouth open.

When he released her she laughed, low and breathless. "Let us go home," she whispered. "Quickly."

# Chapter 31

"ome is home and away is away," he told them. "We are not peddlers at home."

"Why did you bring the ring here, then?" Gilles asked.

"I am telling you the rules, not answering insolent questions," Jean roared.

Simon hunched down on the bench; Gilles looked interested.

"Now a metal smith thinks you may be a thief. And a Lord, as well." He glared at them. "Here, in your home town. This is where you must be above suspicion. This is where we must all be safe."

"I am sorry, Papa." Simon's eyes were miserable with guilt.

Gilles shrugged.

He did not know. How could he? They had protected him too well.

"Mathilde."

She turned from the black iron pot suspended above the fire, in which their dinner was simmering. She had not spoken to him since she had returned to the hut with Jeanne. Simon had had to tell him of their meeting with the Lord and Lady.

"I have something to tell you. To tell you all."

Mathilde came and sat on the bench beside the boys, across from him.

He sat down. "My parents…"

He stood up. Sat down again.

"My mother read heretical writings. She brought one into our home." He looked at his hands, lying empty on the table. "When I was Gilles' age." He took a breath, waiting until he could continue.

Mathilde reached across the table and placed her hand on his.

"You think you are safe here, where people know you," he said, looking at Mathilde's small hand on top of his. "But safety must be guarded. Must be treasured."

"What happened?" Simon asked. "To your mother?"

"She thought she was safe." He looked at his sons. "She had lived in that town all her life, and her parents, and their parents. She took her safety for granted. That is what happened." He clenched his hands into fists under Mathilde's, and looked aside.

He saw again his mother's face, mirrored in the table, her smile gentle and a little sad. That smile, with its deep and brooding love, had filled his childhood. He had imagined Mother Mary wearing that expression as she bent over the world. It was where he lived as a child, safe in the curve of that smile. Then, one night, his mother and her smile and his childhood were all taken from him.

"But they were not safe," Gilles said. His voice was quiet, but something was gone from his face. There was a bitterness in his eyes that Jean had not seen there before.

He had put it there, that expression. He had had to. "They were not," he said, in the same quiet tone as Gilles. They all knew the punishment for heresy.

Mathilde squeezed his hands. "I am sorry," she said gently.

He nodded. Taking a deep breath, he forced his hands open. They lay helpless on the table, under Mathilde's.

He was supposed to shelter her.

"It was not my intention to bring the ring and the nail here. I was wrong to do it." He looked at each of them. "I endangered you all."

"Yes," Mathilde agreed. She looked across the room at Jeanne, sleeping peacefully on her mat, the fever gone. "But it is over and done."

"No," he said, glancing at Gilles and Simon. They had assured him the metal smith accepted their story, but what would the Lord do? His wife had her ring back, but she had fainted, Simon told him. Lords were hard to predict. When he got over his concern for her, he would be angry. Better to diffuse that anger than wait for it to strike.

And if he was not angry?

He withdrew his hands from Mathilde's. "It is not over yet," he said thoughtfully.

He arrived at the guesthouse with Simon and Gilles just as the Lord and Lady emerged. The other pilgrims had gone to the ship; they were alone as he had intended to find them. He stopped at the sight of her.

She was wearing a long, black cape which made her look larger than the slight figure he remembered. Her hair was properly braided up, the shining black coils dimmed by her veil. She was not the frail, desperate creature who had haunted his soul, forcing ridiculous acts of kindness from him which he should still be regretting but somehow could not. She was a Lady now; it showed in her carriage, in the way she held her head, in the confidence of her step. Her large, black eyes were beautiful and sad, but no longer the wells of despair he had carried with him since their meeting. Had their transaction healed her?

Gilles and Simon looked at him as he hesitated.

"Do not appear afraid," he said to Simon. Fear was a confession of guilt. And to Gilles, "Do not be too bold."

He took a deep breath, quietly so the boys would not notice, and strode forward, intercepting them.

"My Lord and Lady," he said, bowing low. He pressed the boys into a bow beside him with a hand on each of their shoulders.

The Lady drew in her breath sharply at the sight of him. Her Lord husband grasped her elbow to steady her. He scrutinized Jean through narrowed eyes.

"I am pleased to see you looking so much better, My Lady," Jean said.

"I am pleased she has my ring back," the Lord said coldly.

"And I," said Jean. "It caused me no end of trouble." He glanced at the Lady.

Her lips twitched in what appeared to be humour. "Dreams?"

He was surprised, but covered it quickly. "Among other things." He looked at her Lord. Yes, he was right about him. "But I have come on a more substantial matter. To plead for your forgiveness, Lord. If there was fault it was mine, not theirs. Visit your wrath on me, but spare my sons." He pushed them forward a step.

The Lord looked surprised a moment. Then he regarded his Lady wife. She was looking at Jean's boys.

Simon fidgeted nervously, but his eyes were steady and his face as calm as he could hold it. Good boy.

Gilles looked back at the Lady with a sweet smile. Do not overdo it, boy.

"I will work for you in return for the harm I have done."

"It was my wife you wronged."

"Is the baby well?" the Lady asked. Her voice trembled.

"She is completely recovered." He wiped his eyes, a nice touch. And then he felt his throat tighten, and could not speak.

"You saved her, My Lady," Simon burst out, his eyes shining. "You undid the curse."

Jean froze. His boy had just accused a Lady of meddling in curses! He glanced at the Lord, who appeared as shocked as he. "An angel," he stammered, "An angel of mercy!"

She was staring intently at Simon. Her eyes glistened with tears. Ahh, that was good, that look in her eyes. Simon's comment had pleased her. He was almost as stunned by that, as by the comment.

"We could use a boy," the Lady said, "to train to our service."

The Lord opened his mouth, frowning, but his wife's small hand settled on his forearm. There was much power in such small hands.

Gilles stepped forward at once.

"Not that one, I think," the Lord drawled.

Jean pulled Gilles back. "Let me work for you instead, my Lord," he said. "I am stronger, a better worker."

"You are good with horses," the Lady said, smiling at Simon. "I would have been trampled had you not been there."

Simon ducked his head. "It was an honor, My Lady," he said.

"My sons are not for sale," Jean said, noting the blush on Simon's face at her praise, and its effect on the Lady. She squeezed her husband's arm lightly.

"Would you like to work in my stables, boy?" the Lord asked, reluctantly.

Simon grinned.

"He would not," Jean said. "He must learn a trade."

"He could be apprenticed to our blacksmith," the Lady offered.

Simon's mouth opened in a gasp of delight.

"And earn his keep working in our stable," her husband added.

Jean drew Simon to him.

"He will be treated well," the Lady said. She turned to her husband. "He saved my life."

Simon broke from Jean's light grasp and fell to his knees. "I will obey and serve you with all my heart," he cried. "May I be so fortunate as to save your life a thousand times!"

"Once will be enough, I hope," the Lord said. "A thousand would impoverish me." He looked at Jean. "Can he be ready to leave with us in the morning?"

"I am ready now," Simon cried, still on his knees in the dirt.

Jean gave them time to look at Simon.

The Lady squeezed her husband's arm once more.

The Lord reached for his purse, sighing. "Get him some decent clothing," he said, handing Jean a handful of deniers.

"If you insist, my Lord," Jean said, his eyes downcast, speaking slowly as though agreeing against his will.

Simon ran home ahead of them to tell his mother.

"That was well done, for Simon," Gilles said as they walked together.

"It worked out well enough."

Gilles laughed. "I nearly missed your intent, and I know you. You meant Simon to go with them all along."

He stopped walking and looked directly at the boy. "Only a fool admits to all he knows."

Gilles nodded, his expression serious again. "Never change your story."

"But don't push it too far," Jean said. The boy was quick, but he was cocky, too. One day he would make a mistake. Pray God, Jean would be there to repair it.

"Never look back," Gilles finished, grinning.

Jean looked down the road toward their little hut, where Mathilde and Jeanne were waiting for them. He thought of his mother's smile, which had always been waiting for him.

"No," he said. "Look back. Because you carry it home. Everything you say, everything you do, you carry it home."

"That will make trading much harder," Gilles observed.

"Maybe," he rested his hand on Gilles' shoulder. "Maybe not."

# About the Author

Jane Ann McLachlan was born in Toronto, Canada, and currently lives with her husband, author Ian Darling, in Waterloo, Ontario. They spend most days sitting in their separate dens writing on their laptops, each working on their next book. When they get away it's usually to do research.

Between books, Jane Ann enjoys gardening, quilting, travel, spending time with family, and escaping the cold Canadian winters. She is addicted to story, and reads just about any kind of book, but she writes mostly historical fiction set in the Middle Ages and young adult science fiction and fantasy.

You can learn more about her novels on her author website: www.janeannmclachlan.com

Find resources for creative writing on her website for writers: www.downriverwriting.com

# Acknowledgements

I am exceedingly grateful to all the people whose knowledge, time, interest, and enthusiasm have contributed to the writing and publishing of this book.

My family, for their enduring love and encouragement (especially my sons-in-law with their patient and good-natured technical support): Ian, Amanda and Jeff, Tamara and Steve, Caroline and Karl.

My early readers who improved this book with their suggestions: Amanda Darling, Lori Christy, Linda Barron, Sue Skrinda, Lorna Morrow, and Barbara Strang.

Thank you all for forcing me to write better, encouraging me to keep on, and believing in this story.

I also want to thank all the tour guides, gardeners, and historians who answered my numerous questions during my two trips to the south of France while writing this book, helping me to get the period and setting as accurate as possible.

Other books by Jane Ann McLachlan

**Historical Fiction:**
The Sorrow Stone
The Lode Stone

The Girl Who Would Be Queen
The Girl Who Tempted Fortune

**Memoir:**
IMPACT: A Memoir of PTSD

**Creative Writing:**
Downriver Writing: The Five-Step Process for Outlining Your Novel

Books by J. A. McLachlan

**Science Fiction:**
Walls of Wind
The Occasional Diamond Thief
The Salarian Desert Game

**SF Boxed Set:**
Walls of Wind and The Occasional Diamond Thief

Made in the USA
Monee, IL
03 June 2021

70137314R00173